Children of the Lamp

THE BLUE DJINN OF BABYLON

As John's feet touched the gravel path he saw something race toward him; something larger than a dog, but moving too fast to see exactly what it was. Its head was massive but recognisably half human, with broad, rounded ears and outsized teeth. These dripped with saliva as, laughing horribly, the croucher lunged. John screamed, certain his last minute on earth had come…

Also by P.B. Kerr:

Children of the Lamp
The Akhenaten Adventure
The Cobra King of Kathmandu

THE BLUE DJINN
OF BABYLON

P.B. KERR

■SCHOLASTIC

*This book is dedicated to Natalie,
Clemmie and Freddie Clough.*

Scholastic Children's Books
Euston House, 24 Eversholt Street
London, NW1 1DB, UK
a division of Scholastic Ltd
London ~ New York ~ Toronto ~ Sydney ~ Auckland
Mexico City ~ New Delhi ~ Hong Kong

First published in the UK by Scholastic Ltd, 2005
This edition published in the UK by Scholastic Ltd, 2006

Copyright © P.B. Kerr, 2005
Cover Illustration © David Wyatt, 2006

10 digit ISBN 0 439 95585 8
13 digit ISBN 9 780 439 95585 0

Printed by Nørhaven Paperback A/S, Denmark

10 9 8 7 6 5 4 3 2

Papers used by Scholastic Children's Books are made from wood grown in
sustainable forests.

CONTENTS

CHAPTER 1

THE DJINN WHO CAME IN FROM THE COLD

"I want to be a witch," said Philippa. "With lots of warts."

"And I want to be a vampire," said John. "With real blood on my teeth."

"Both of you know that's quite out of the question," their mother said briskly.

"We have this argument every year," sighed John. "I don't see what you've got against it, Mom. Halloween's just some harmless fun."

John and Philippa Gaunt, who lived at number 77, East 77th Street, in New York, were twins who liked the same things as any other kids. Things like trick or treat. But they also happened to be djinn, with extraordinary powers to do things, like granting three wishes. Or at least they did when the weather was warmer. Djinn, being made of fire, don't much like the cold, and young, inexperienced djinn, like John and Philippa, are almost powerless in cooler climates. This is why, more often, djinn are found in hot desert countries. Now, while New York is very hot in summer, the winters are very cold and, even by the end of October, it was starting to get a little chilly. But this year Halloween was unseasonably warm and, partly as a way of making it up to her children after forbidding them from going out trick-or-treating with their friends, Mrs Gaunt, who was also a djinn, had a suggestion for them.

"Look here," she said. "Why don't we take advantage of these temperatures and go into Central Park, where you can both take on the shape of an animal – just to keep yourselves in practice. After all, this might be the last occasion on which you will able to use your powers before the winter sets in."

"But I don't want to be an animal," said Philippa. "I want to be a witch. With lots of warts."

"And I want to be Dracula," persisted John. "With blood on my teeth."

"And I say no," insisted Mrs Gaunt. Now, many years ago, not long after she had met Mr Gaunt, she herself had forsworn the use of her own djinn powers, although for reasons that were still a little unclear to the twins. John thought it might have had something to do with the fact that their father, Edward, was a human being and, nervous about having two children who had the power – at least during the summer months – to turn him into an animal. Perhaps for this reason alone, Mrs Gaunt had made an earlier agreement with John and Philippa, that they should only use their djinn powers after clearing it with her. Just in case they did something in haste that they later might regret, for the power of a djinn, even a young djinn, is very great. But she was also aware that young djinn need, occasionally, to exercise their powers, if only for the sake of their good health and general well-being.

But the twins were not yet persuaded that becoming an animal was at all preferable to trick or treating.

"I don't get it," persisted John. "Why don't we celebrate Halloween? You've never actually said what you've got against it."

"Haven't I?"

"No," chorused the twins.

Mrs Gaunt shook her head. "Perhaps you're right, at that," she admitted.

"So let's hear it," said John. If he sounded sceptical it was because he thought his mother was taking Halloween too seriously.

"Well, it's really very simple, dear," she said. "Halloween makes light of a subject most humans know nothing about, and it's a very difficult time of year for tribes of good djinn, like ours. You see, many centuries ago, wicked tribes of djinn such as the Ghul, the Shaitan, and the Ifrit, persuaded gullible humans to use this particular time of year to worship them, in return for not being harmed. People dressed up in costumes that were once supposed to represent those evil djinn they worshipped. And they laid out treats of food and wine for them in order that they would not be tricked. This is why our tribe, the Marid, have always refused to have anything to do with it. Now do you understand? Really, I'm quite surprised that you can take any of this quite so lightly, after all you went through this summer with Nimrod."

The twins were silent for a moment as they considered Mrs Gaunt's explanation. It had never occurred to them that their own djinnkind might be the true origin of all that was wicked about Halloween. And unlike most children, they knew only too well that an evil djinn could bind and enslave a human, or even another djinn, to its will. In their first summer as djinn, they'd seen evil close up in the shape of Akhenaten's ghost, and in the person of Iblis, the leader of the Ifrit, which was the wickedest tribe of djinn. At first hand they had witnessed what real evil was capable of doing. The Ifrit had actually murdered a man in Cairo called Hussein Hussaout. Mrs Gaunt was quite correct. There was real evil abroad in the world, all right.

Philippa shrugged. "Now that you've explained, it makes a lot of sense, I guess."

"I'm glad you think so, dear," said Mrs Gaunt.

"Sure," said John. "You're just looking out for us, right?"

Mrs Gaunt nodded. "I'm a mother," she said. "That's my job."

They started in the Central Park Zoo. But having decided that it really didn't look like much fun being an animal in a cage – the polar bear looked especially miserable – they quickly left the zoo and set out to find some animals in the park that were running around free, whose bodies they might borrow for an hour or two.

After a while Philippa had decided to take on the shape of a squirrel and had a great deal of enjoyment racing up and down trees, and even chased some tourists who weren't quick enough at handing over their nuts. She hadn't bargained on having fleas, however, or on a chipmunk with an attitude whose tree she made the mistake of climbing. And, when a cat began stalking her, she was quite glad to return to being a girl again.

John found it a little harder to select an animal he wanted to become. In his eyes, chipmunks and squirrels seemed a bit too cute and girly, and he had just about reconciled himself to returning to the zoo, and becoming a polar bear after all, or perhaps one of the sea lions, when he saw something that was much more appealing to him. Near the ice rink, a man was showing some children a display of falconry. No sooner had John seen the beautiful blue-and-beige peregrine falcon on the man's gloved hand, than he had consulted his mother, uttered his focus word (which was ABECEDARIAN), and assumed the shape of the falcon, whose name was Malty. (Focus words are the secret words the djinn use to help them focus their djinn power, in the same way a magnifying glass will focus the power of the sun onto a very small spot in the centre of a sheet of paper so that it burns.)

Peregrine falcons are the world's swiftest birds, and John had a marvellous time flying higher than the trees and dive-bombing a couple of dumb pigeons, and a guy doing tai chi, before swooping down to the prey offered by Malty's handler – and all at speeds of more than 200 miles per hour.

John's experience of being a falcon was not without its unpleasant side, however. For several hours afterward, John still found himself retching when he recalled the disgusting taste of the dead mouse given to him as a reward by the falconer.

In spite of this, John decided that what he wanted most for Christmas was a peregrine falcon. And after thoroughly researching them on the Internet, he broached the subject with his father.

Edward Gaunt was a human and therefore, what the twins' uncle Nimrod (himself a great and powerful djinn) referred to as "mundane," which is to say that, like all

5

human beings, he was not made of fire but of earth, and therefore quite ordinary. This did not mean, however, that Mr Gaunt did not exercise considerable authority over his fantastically gifted children. Especially in winter, when he knew they were more or less powerless. Then he was much more inclined to treat them like ordinary children and to forbid them from doing or having things of which he did not approve. Such as having a peregrine falcon, for example.

"I could understand it if you wanted a canary," Mr Gaunt said from behind his newspaper when John had mentioned the idea to him over breakfast one morning. "Even a parrot. But a falcon? A falcon is a very different kettle of fish, John. Falcons are predators. Suppose it attacked someone's dog in the park? Suppose it attacked an old person? I could find myself in court being sued for millions of dollars. And then where would we be?"

"Dad," said John, "this is a falcon we're talking about here, not a pterodactyl."

But Mr Gaunt was not persuaded.

"If you want a pet, then why don't you get a gerbil or a hamster like –" He was about to say "like any normal boy" when suddenly he checked himself, remembering that his son was hardly that, no more than his daughter was like any normal girl. Sometimes it was easy for Edward Gaunt to look at the twins and forget what they were. After all, they looked like normal kids. They weren't even identical twins. John was tall and dark, while Philippa was shorter, with red hair and glasses. But he knew only too well that when the summer came and New York's temperatures rose into the nineties, he would once again have to be a lot more careful how he spoke to them both. Just in case one of them decided to turn him into a dog. It wouldn't have been the first time that something like that had happened. His own wife had turned Mr Gaunt's two brothers, Alan and Neil, into Rottweilers (now the Gaunt family pets) after they had attempted to murder him for his not inconsiderable fortune.

Of course, neither John nor Philippa were the kind of djinn who would ever have contemplated turning their father into a dog. No matter how annoying he might have seemed to them. They were Marid after all, which is to say they belonged to one of the three tribes of good djinn that tried to increase the amount of good luck in the world, and who were opposed to the three tribes of bad djinn that tried to make more bad luck for humankind in general. Even so, John was pretty cross when his father refused to even consider getting him a peregrine falcon for Christmas. This was on top of a couple of other problems he was having.

It was a cold December morning in New York. The schools were closed for the holidays, and the first snow of winter had just started to fall. From his bedroom window, on the seventh floor of their house, John watched the snow with Philippa, and shivered. Each flake reminded them of how long it might be before they could use their powers again. Feeling the cold much more than any human, John pulled on another sweater and wrapped his arms around himself, a little horrified by what he was seeing. He and his sister were only twelve years old, but both of them were old enough to recall New York winters that had lasted long into April.

"It's just our luck," he groaned. "Just our luck to be djinn in a city where the winters can last four months."

"It seems like forever since I was really warm," said Philippa. Coming away from the window she sat down on the polished wooden floor and leaned against an enormous radiator. "I don't feel like I've really been warm since that afternoon in the park. When I was a squirrel and you were a falcon."

"Don't talk to me about falcons," muttered John, sitting down beside her. He was already feeling depressed, but the arrival of snow that cold December morning only served to lower his spirits even further.

Just before lunchtime, however, the snow stopped and their mother came to see if the twins wanted to go out with her to do some Christmas shopping. John and Philippa jumped up from their spot beside the radiator and ran to their closets for, unlike human children, young djinn always like to go shopping.

They put on their biggest boots and several of their warmest coats and set off down Madison Avenue with their mother who was wearing her thickest sable coat, an elegant fur hat, a pair of rabbit-lined Tommy Trinder boots, and Blue Max ski glasses. Even dressed for the snow, she managed to look more glamorous than any actress at the Academy Awards ceremony.

For a while things went well. The twins bought a book for their father and, for their uncle Nimrod, a handsome red Campbell&Bummer tie that they felt sure he would like, since red was the only colour of tie he ever wore. But standing on Rockefeller Plaza watching the ice skaters and listening to some Christmas carollers singing "We

Wish You a Merry Christmas," the twins began to feel strange. At first the feeling wasn't much more than a general nervousness, but after a few minutes the twins started to breathe rapidly, to sweat, and even to feel nauseous, as if they might actually throw up, or perhaps, faint. Straightaway, Mrs Gaunt guessed what was happening to them.

"There's too much wishing going on around here, that's what's happening," she explained, and quickly hailed a cab to take them home again. "Humans wishing for this, wishing for that, wishing each other a merry Christmas, not to mention all the best wishes and the good wishes. Christmas is just one big wish. That's OK if you're mundane. But if you're a young djinn in a cold climate there's nothing you can do about any of these wishes, even if you wanted to. And it's affecting you both for the worse."

"I do feel a little strange," admitted John, when they were sitting in the taxi. "Sort of dazed and confused."

"So what's new?" Philippa said weakly, but John felt too tired to respond in kind.

"I should have realized that this might happen," said Mrs Gaunt, scolding herself. "TMW is very common at this time of year. I used to get it myself when I was a child in London."

"TMW?" whispered Philippa. "What's that?"

"Too Many Wishes," said her mother.

Philippa nodded. She'd heard of Subliminal Wish Fulfillment, which was when a djinn granted a wish to a mundane without realizing it. Like the time she'd unconsciously arranged for their housekeeper, Mrs Trump, to win the New York State lottery. But TMW

9

was something quite new to her.

"You'll be all right in a minute," said Mrs Gaunt. "As soon as we get you warm again. But this has made me think that perhaps you two ought to see a djinn doctor. Just to help you through your winter torpor."

"Winter what?" groaned John.

"A stagnation of normal djinn faculties," said his mother.

A few minutes later the cab pulled up outside their home, and Mrs Gaunt hurried her children through the curved ebony door and straight into the living room where a fire was burning quietly in the grate.

"Sit down by the fire, children," she said. "We'll soon have you warm again."

Finding the log basket empty and only a couple of pieces of coal left in the scuttle, Mrs Gaunt called for Mrs Trump's help. Despite winning the lottery, Mrs Trump had continued working for the Gaunts because she was fond of them, especially the children, although she had no idea that they were djinn, nor that it was thanks to Philippa granting her wish that Mrs Trump had won her $33-million fortune.

Mrs Trump appeared in the doorway, smiling pleasantly to show off her expensive new dental work. Underneath her smock she wore a Christian Ribbentrop dress, and a five-strand pearl necklace. With her hair cut and coloured by Pierre Petomane of Fifth Avenue, she was looking better than ever.

"Mrs Trump, the twins have caught a chill," said Mrs Gaunt. "We need to build up the fire and get them warm again. If you could fetch some more coal, I'll get some logs."

"Yes, Mrs Gaunt."

While the two women fetched wood and coal, the twins huddled by the fire. A moment or two later, two huge dogs came into the room. Having seen what the problem was, they disappeared briefly, and then returned, each carrying a good-sized log in his huge, powerful jaws. The dogs dropped the wood onto the coals and then took up a position on either side of the fireplace, as if standing guard over the children.

John smiled through teeth that were chattering with cold, like castanets. He found it easier to believe that Alan and Neil had once been human than the fact that they had once tried to murder his father. For as long as the twins had been alive the dogs had looked after them, and if one thing was certain it was that their loyalty knew no bounds. John and Philippa had asked their mother if, after such a long period of loyal service, it might not be right for her to turn Alan and Neil back into people. But Mrs Gaunt had said she was very sorry she couldn't do that since the animal transmutation had been for life. Besides, she had taken an oath never again to use djinn power.

So John had asked if *he* might return Alan and Neil to human form, at least in the summer when the temperatures rose and his own djinn power kicked in again. Mrs Gaunt had replied that unfortunately this was not possible either because an animal transmutation could only be undone by the djinn who had made it. All of which had prompted Philippa to ask her mother if there was any circumstance in which she might ever again use her own power.

"Just one," she had told them. "If your lives or your father's life were ever threatened."

Mrs Trump returned to the living room and put some coal onto the fire. She was followed closely by Mrs Gaunt with more logs, and soon the fire was blazing fiercely. The twins yawned contentedly like two cats, as the heat of the flames penetrated their bones and encouraged the subtler kind of fire that burns inside all djinn, young or old.

Mrs Gaunt picked up the telephone and began to dial a number.

"Who are you calling?" asked Philippa.

"A djinn doctor."

"There's really no need," said John, who hated doctors almost as much as he hated dentists.

But Mrs Gaunt was already speaking to the person on the other end of the telephone.

"That's lucky," she said, when she had finished her call. "It so happens that Jenny Sachertorte is here in New York with her son, Dybbuk."

"Who is Jenny Sachertorte?" asked John.

"Dr Sachertorte is a djinn doctor. She runs a holistic health spa in Palm Springs that's used by people in Hollywood, although most of the treatments she offers were invented for djinn. It turns out she's opening a new clinic here in New York. That's why she and her son are here now. That, and because Mrs Sachertorte doesn't live with Dybbuk's father anymore, and Dybbuk has to spend some time with him over the holidays. So be nice to him when you see him. I think he's a little upset by all that has happened. Anyway, they'll be here any minute now."

Even as she spoke, the doorbell rang.

"That was quick," said John.

"Dr Sachertorte doesn't believe in using mundane forms of transportation," explained Mrs Gaunt. "She still travels in the traditional djinn way."

"Which is what, exactly?" said Philippa, but Mrs Gaunt, who had already gone into the hall to answer the door, didn't hear her.

"A magic carpet, I suppose," said John as, feeling a little warmer now, he shrugged off his last coat.

Through the living room door came two strangers followed by Mrs Gaunt who was already explaining how, in addition to winter torpor, the twins were obliged to cope with their having promised not to use djinn powers without her permission. Dr Sachertorte nodded gravely while her son, Dybbuk, tried and failed to hide a snigger.

"Children, this is Dr Sachertorte, the djinn doctor I was telling you about. Jenny, this is John and Philippa."

Dr Sachertorte snatched off a pair of large black sunglasses and smiled warmly at the twins. Her long wavy hair was black and shiny as if made from the same plastic as her sunglasses. She wore a blue trouser suit, covered with blue rhinestones, and a pair of blue, high-heeled shoes. Her glamor was of a more obvious kind than that possessed by Layla Gaunt: Jenny Sachertorte, MDj looked like she'd just stepped off a stage in Las Vegas.

"Pleased to meet you," said Dr Sachertorte. "This is my son, Dybbuk. He's the same age as you so don't let him

13

try to persuade you he's older. Dybbuk, say hello to John and Philippa."

Dybbuk made a noise like a bassoon and rolled his eyes up to the top of his long-haired head. He wore a rock shirt, jeans, a leather jacket, and a pair of motorcycle boots that looked like they'd been around the Daytona International Speedway by themselves. Philippa thought he looked older than twelve. Not that she had much time to think about this. Dr Sachertorte had already taken hold of her wrist and was holding a small pendulum over her pulse. She did the same thing to John, paying close attention to the direction in which the pendulum was spinning, and then nodded.

"Djinn are a little like lizards," she said quietly. "They need exposure to heat. I'll prepare you a food supplement to fix this problem. That's a long-term remedy. Right now we need to draw as much heat as we can into your bodies. I've brought a few things with me that will do this. Dybbuk, get my bag, will you?"

Dybbuk rolled his eyes again and retrieved a navy blue leather Gladstone bag from the floor. From its capacious interior, Dr Sachertorte produced three earthenware bottles.

"I call this my djinn and tonic," she said. "It's a levitator. Volcanic water from the hot spring at Nobody's Perfect, my health spa in Palm Springs." She handed a bottle to John and one to Philippa, and then one to Mrs Gaunt herself. "You too, Layla," she said sternly. "I expect you could use a levitator." She winked at the twins. "That's just a fancy djinn doctor word for a pick-me-up."

"It feels hot," said Philippa. "And kind of lively. Like there's something moving in here." She pressed her hands

14

hard to the earthenware bottle. "Or something that's boiling. Like the water in a kettle."

"Now drink it all up before it gets cold," said Dr Sachertorte.

Seeing their mother drink her own levitator without any hesitation, the twins did the same and discovered they enjoyed the taste; but what was even better it left them feeling better immediately. Dr Sachertorte hadn't finished with them, however. She reached into her Gladstone bag and took out two smooth flat rocks the size and shape of saucers, and then handed one each to the twins.

"Wow," exclaimed John. "This is hot, too."

"That's a salamander stone," said Dr Sachertorte. "It comes from the centre of the earth and won't ever lose its heat. Not for sixty or seventy years, anyway. You can keep it in your pocket when you're walking around the city, and in your bed at night. Like a hot-water bottle. It will help to keep you both energized and stop you from feeling torpid."

"Thank you, Jenny," said Mrs Gaunt, and hugged the other woman fondly.

"Don't mention it, Layla. I'm glad to have been of service."

Mrs Gaunt looked at the twins. "Children," she said. "Dr Sachertorte and I have a lot of news to catch up on. Why don't you take Dybbuk into the kitchen and have Mrs Trump fix you all some sandwiches?"

But, looking at Philippa, Dr Sachertorte added, "Tell Mrs Trump to make sure Dybbuk doesn't have any salt, will you, dear? Salt makes him disruptive. Doesn't it, Dybbuk?"

Dybbuk rolled his eyes once more and then followed the twins along to the kitchen.

They found Mrs Trump in a bad mood. Lately she was often grumpy, and the twins knew why. After winning the New York State lottery, Mrs Trump had spent some of her fortune on an apartment in the famous Dakota building, on 72nd Street. There she employed a cleaning woman named Miss Pickings, who did very little work for quite a lot of money. With Mrs Trump out all day, working at the Gaunts' house, Miss Pickings just sat around watching TV and drinking coffee. Mrs Trump would have dismissed her except for the fact that Miss Pickings had successfully sued her previous employers for unfair dismissal. Poor Mrs Trump was terrified that if she fired her, she would find herself in court.

Miss Pickings was just one of the two problems John was going to work out the very minute he found his powers restored by some warmer weather. His other problem was that he was being bullied at school by a boy named Gordon Warthoff. John had thought a lot about what he was going to do to Gordon Warthoff. His last name seemed to cry out for him to be turned into a warthog but, somehow, John didn't see his mother agreeing to that. There were times when he felt it was inconvenient to have been born into a tribe of good djinn. If he'd been one of the Ifrit, who were the most evil tribe of djinn by far, Warthoff would already have been eating termites and living in some muddy pit in the African savanna, like the warty swine he was.

CHAPTER 2

IMAGINE

After lunch, John and Philippa took Dybbuk upstairs and showed him their rooms. He was the first djinn of their own age they had met and the twins thought him more interesting than he seemed to find them. Indeed, it was soon clear that Dybbuk viewed them with contempt.

"Is your mother for real?" he said. "You guys have djinn power but don't use it on account of some stupid promise you made her?"

John bristled. "I don't know that I'd describe it like that exactly."

"But we did make her a promise," added Philippa.

Dybbuk laughed out loud. "You guys are unbelievable."

"But even if we wanted to use our power, we couldn't do it," said John. "Take a look outside. It's too cold."

"Sucker," said Dybbuk. "That's what they want you to think. Like everything in life there's a way around these things, if you know how." He threw himself into John's armchair.

"You mean you can use your own djinn power?" said Philippa. "Even though it's cold?"

"Not exactly," said Dybbuk. "My mother's put a binding on me. To stop me from using my power until she

17

figures I'm in what she calls 'a responsible frame of mind'."

"Why did she do that, Dybbuk?" asked John.

Dybbuk winced. "Buck," he said. "Just Buck, OK? I hate my name. One of the guys at school was giving me a hard time about it. Said I was evil and stuff. So I turned him into a cockroach. Just for a while. But my mom was really mad about it. That and something I did to my math teacher."

"Wow," said John, whose admiration of Dybbuk was now complete. He'd dreamed of doing something horrible to his own math teacher. "What did you do?"

Dybbuk grinned, basking in the other boy's hero worship. "This teacher, Mr Strickneen, was always on my case. Because I didn't get quadratic equations, 'n' stuff like that. So I figured I'd let him know exactly what it felt like. To be lousy at math. For two whole days the idiot couldn't even add two plus two, let alone solve a quadratic equation. He thought he'd really lost it. "

"Awesome," said John.

"But then my mom asked why I wasn't getting any more math homework and I told her. Which was stupid, because she fixed it so that I can't use my power for a while. With a binding."

"How does that work, exactly?" Philippa asked him. "The binding?"

"She made me forget my focus word."

"Couldn't you just think of another one?" suggested John.

Dybbuk shook his head and pushed his hair out of his eyes. "It's not that simple, wet-wipe," he said. "A focus word is like a password on a computer. You have to remember the old one in order to change it to a new one."

"How long is your mother going to keep you out of action?" said Philippa.

"Until we get back home. You see, I'm supposed to be spending time with my dad while I'm here, and Mom doesn't want me doing something to his new wife. Nadia, my stepmother, is not a djinn. She's an interior decorator."

"And would you do something to her?" asked Philippa. "If you could?"

Dybbuk grinned. "Sure. Wouldn't you, if your dad moved out and got himself a new wife?"

Philippa thought about this for a moment and then said, "I'd probably turn her into a bat. I can't think of anything worse than that. I hate bats."

Dybbuk shrugged. "Yeah. Maybe. But you know, if it was someone I really disliked, I'd probably unleash an elemental on them. That's much more horrible than some stupid bat."

Philippa looked at John, who shook his head.

"Don't say you guys don't know about elementals?" snorted Dybbuk. "What have they been teaching you two wet-wipes? Apart from nothing? Elementals are mini demons that live inside the eight elements. You know, earth, air, fire, and water; and the noble elements, spirit, space, time, and luck? Fact is, Nadia is busy decorating their new apartment, so I'd probably set a water elemental on her. Flood the place. Just for kicks." He laid a hand on their shoulders. "Maybe you guys could help me out here. I mean, you could put an elemental in motion for me."

"I don't see how," said John. "Like I said, it's too cold for us to use djinn powers."

"And like I said, that's just what they want you to think. To keep you out of trouble. You know, I could probably show you how to get some power back. If you promised to unleash an elemental on my stepmother."

Philippa shook her head firmly. "I'm afraid we couldn't do something like that," she said. "And besides, we wouldn't know how even if we wanted to. Would we, John?"

"No," said John, with less certainty than his sister. He wasn't thinking about Dybbuk's stepmother, Nadia, so much as the bully Gordon Warthoff, and what he might be able to do to him with his djinn power restored. Not to mention what he might do to Mrs Trump's idle housekeeper, Miss Pickings. He could take care of them both. "No, we couldn't do anything like that."

"Hey, it's no big deal." Dybbuk got up from the armchair and looked down at the street. It had started to snow again and this time it was drifting on the sidewalk. "You know, I can see your problem. I'd forgotten how cold it can get in New York. Where we live in California, it's desert. And that makes things easier. As a djinn, I mean. I guess that's why I'm way ahead of you, in terms of sheer power and djinntuition."

"I expect so," said John, thinking how much more attractive Palm Springs sounded than New York City.

"Look," said Dybbuk. "I like you guys. So I'm going to tell you, anyway. The way to fix things for yourselves to have some djinn power while you're stuck in this icebox you call a climate. Do either of you belong to a sports club? And, if so, does that sports club have a steam room or a sauna?"

"There's a sauna downstairs," said John.

Dybbuk grinned. "Then your problems are solved. All you've got to do is sit in there and cook yourselves on full heat. For a while afterward you'll be able to behave like any other djinn." He laughed scornfully. "I can't believe you hadn't figured that out for yourselves."

"We never go in there," said Philippa. "That's why. It makes us feel claustrophobic."

"Then take a charcoal pill before you go in the sauna and you're fixed. Duh. Simple as that."

Djinn take charcoal pills to combat the feelings of claustrophobia they encounter when they are in any enclosed space, but most especially in a djinn lamp or a bottle.

"It's obvious now that you've mentioned it, Buck," said John. "In winter, the sauna even switches itself on automatically in the afternoon so that Dad can go in there the minute he gets home."

"You mean that it's on now?" said Dybbuk.

John glanced at his watch. "I guess so," he said.

"Then what are we waiting for?" said Dybbuk. "Lend me a swimsuit and we'll go and try it out."

So they put on swimsuits, took some charcoal pills, and then went down to the basement.

Mr Gaunt's sauna was like a small log cabin. Inside were several benches built around a stove, the top of which was covered with hot rocks. According to the thermometer on the wall, the temperature was almost one hundred degrees centigrade – twice as hot as any desert the twins had ever been in. And within minutes of entering the sauna and starting to sweat, the twins felt their power returning. John noticed it first as a warm sensation deep inside himself and then found his head clearing, like someone recovering from a bad cold. Philippa felt as if her body was waking up, refreshed, after a very long and satisfying sleep.

Back in Egypt, where he had started to train the twins in the ways of the djinn, their uncle Nimrod had talked about mind over matter. The twins were a little out of practice, but it wasn't long before John had managed to use his recovered power to create a couple of CDs he'd been looking for, and Philippa had made herself a thick terry-cloth robe in which she intended to wrap herself as soon as they were out of the sauna. Neither item seemed an important enough use of power to bother consulting their mother about.

"We should give Buck something for showing us how to do this," John told Philippa.

"There's a new computer game I wouldn't mind having," Dybbuk admitted. "If you're sure." When he told them what the game was called, only John had ever heard of it but, on his own, he didn't have enough power to make it. "Tell you what," said Dybbuk. "We'll hold hands and I'll use your power to focus on the game I want."

"Good idea," said Philippa. "We did this before, John, remember? With Mr Rakshasas. When we made that pink Ferrari in Cairo."

"How could I forget?"

John took his sister's hand and then Dybbuk's.

The first time they tried to create Dybbuk's game

nothing happened; or at least nothing appeared to happen, which Philippa found a little strange given her strong sensation that a certain amount of power had left her body. But the second time they tried, the game materialized right on cue, and Dybbuk looked so grateful that she quite forgot that there had ever been a first attempt.

Soon afterward, Dr Sachertorte took Dybbuk home. And alone in his room, John continued to experiment with his power. He discovered that he could effect a transubstantiation – which is what the djinn call it when they appear out of or disappear into a lamp or a bottle – for up to three hours after sitting in his father's sauna. This gave him an idea as to how he and Philippa might help Mrs Trump. But having listened to her brother's plan, Philippa still needed some convincing.

"I don't know," she said. "I'm really not sure that we should do this, John."

"It's only transubstantiation," insisted John. "It's not like we're going to turn Miss Pickings into a cockroach."

"I'm just not sure that Mother would approve."

"Mrs Trump needs our help, doesn't she?"

"Yes," she said, still a little uncertain.

"Look, it's me who'll do the actual transubstantiation. So this'll be my responsibility not yours." John waited for Philippa to say something and when she didn't, added, "Can you think of a better plan?"

Philippa had to admit that she couldn't.

The next day, while John warmed himself in the sauna, Philippa waited until Mrs Trump's limousine had brought her to work, and then "borrowed" the keys to her apartment in the Dakota from her handbag. When she went to get John from the sauna, he transubstantiated himself into an empty silver hip flask that they had borrowed from their father's desk drawer. Then she dropped the keys and the hip flask into her backpack, put on her thickest, warmest winter coat, and slipped out the front door.

With the snow inches deep, there were only a few cabs, and Philippa had to walk across Central Park to reach West 72nd Street and the exclusive apartment building where Mrs Trump now lived. With its portcullis, dry moat, and sentry box, Philippa thought the Dakota looked like a creepy German castle, which did little to calm her nerves as the doorman nodded her through, and she made her way up to the seventh floor.

The twins had been to Mrs Trump's apartment on several occasions. It was next door to one that had been owned by the Beatle John Lennon who had been shot dead outside the Dakota in 1980. Knowing this, and the fact that Mrs Trump had bought herself a white grand piano, had given Philippa's brother his idea. He was going to pretend to be John Lennon. Or at least John Lennon's ghost.

Entering the apartment, Philippa went straight to the piano, placed the hip flask on top of the adjacent radiator, and then unscrewed the cap. There was no time to linger: Miss Pickings would be arriving very soon.

"You're on your own, bro," she said into the neck of the hip flask. "I'll see you later, I hope. Be careful."

"Just don't forget to come back and get me," John shouted back at her.

Philippa took the elevator back down to the lobby. She was thinking about one of her best friends, Isabel Getty, who sometimes lived in the Dakota, and sometimes in Hong Kong, when the elevator door opened to reveal a tall, thin woman with short, dirty-blond hair and a mouth full of yellow teeth. It was Miss Pickings, on her way to Mrs Trump's apartment. Philippa had met Miss Pickings just once before, a day or two after Mrs Trump had employed her, when Miss Pickings was still being nice and actually bothering to clean the apartment. But meeting her now, Philippa found Miss Pickings was anything but nice; the woman narrowed her eyes and then took hold of Philippa's coat lapel.

"What are you doing here?" snarled Miss Pickings.

"I'm visiting a friend of mine, " said Philippa.

"What's the name of this friend?" demanded Miss Pickings.

"Isabel Getty. Now let me go. I want to leave."

Miss Pickings stood back. With her blue eyes, high cheekbones, and long neck she looked like a Burmese cat, and a nasty one at that. "You're a rude, horrible little girl. And I've never liked you. Do you know that?"

Philippa pushed past Miss Pickings and walked quickly to the door. Any lingering doubts about the wisdom of what John was planning to do to Miss Pickings were now removed.

Inside the hip flask on top of the radiator in Mrs Trump's apartment, John felt as warm as if he was still in the sauna. He waited at least fifteen minutes after the time

Miss Pickings was supposed to show up for work, before transubstantiating himself out of the hip flask and into Mrs Trump's living room. He was well away from the kitchen where Miss Pickings was already sitting in an armchair, drinking coffee, watching television, reading the paper, and using the telephone to make a long-distance call.

John crouched by the piano for a moment and then tiptoed toward the kitchen door, to take a closer look at his victim. Miss Pickings looked like she was settled in for the day and, after a moment or two, she put down her coffee cup, closed her eyes and started to snore loudly. This was bad news for Mrs Trump, but good news for John. He went back into the living room and sat down at the piano.

"Imagine" was John Lennon's most popular and enduring solo song, and it was one of the few things John Gaunt could play on the piano. Young John had a nice voice and managed to sing the whole of the first verse before he heard the sound of footsteps approaching from the kitchen. Quickly, he uttered the word he used to focus his djinn power – "ABECEDARIAN!" And a split second later he took on the shape of an ornament on top of the piano – a kitsch porcelain figure of a boy wearing eighteenth-century costume and playing a harpsichord.

It felt curious being made of porcelain and not having any muscles to move, but the position gave him a grandstand view as a nervous-looking Miss Pickings approached the piano.

"Is there anyone here?" she said, and fingered a couple of notes on the piano fearfully.

If porcelain figures had been capable of laughter, John would have fallen off his little porcelain stool; and it was probably just as well he was, for the moment at least, solid.

After a while Miss Pickings went back into the kitchen, which was John's cue to assume his mundane shape again and play another few bars of Lennon's song before effecting a reverse transubstantiation, and returning to the ovenlike conditions that now existed inside the silver hip flask on top of the radiator. Having decided not to risk playing any more of Lennon's song on that particular morning, in case Miss Pickings discovered him, John settled down to await Philippa's return. It would be at least another ten hours before she could return to the Dakota apartment with Mrs Trump.

Fortunately for John, he would not have long to wait, in the sense that this ten hours wouldn't feel like ten hours. Having entered the flask in a counterclockwise fashion, against the normal northern hemispheric rotation, time inside the flask, which existed outside three-dimensional space, went much more quickly. And to John it seemed as if no more than an hour had passed before he was back home and in his room, telling Philippa what had happened.

"Mrs Trump is right, you know," he said. "Pickings is an awful woman. She was asleep in an armchair when I started to play the piano. She's so lazy."

"Not just lazy," said Philippa. "Mrs Trump thinks she may be a thief as well. Some of her jewellery is missing."

The next day Philippa took the hip flask containing her brother's de-transubstantiated shape back to the

27

Dakota and left him there once again. This time John was feeling more confident in the use of his djinn power. After re-transubstantiating himself, he hid in the linen closet where, temporarily, he abandoned his body altogether and, quite invisible to the human eye, sat down at the piano and played the whole of "Imagine", singing in what he imagined was a good imitation of John Lennon's Liverpool accent. It wasn't. But he didn't know that and, more important, neither did Miss Pickings, who ran screaming from the living room, and locked herself in the bathroom. There, she telephoned Mrs Trump. A few minutes later, she fled the apartment, flinging the door keys and the diamond earrings she had stolen from Mrs Trump's bedside drawer on the floor behind her.

John whooped with triumph, which served to persuade Miss Pickings to take the stairs instead of waiting for the elevator.

Recovering his body from the closet, John telephoned Philippa on her cell phone and learned that Miss Pickings had told Mrs Trump that her apartment at the Dakota was haunted and that she wouldn't ever be coming back to work. Philippa added that Mrs Trump was now looking happier than she'd seen her in a long time – apart from a concern that she might have a ghost, and Philippa had felt obliged to persuade Mrs Trump that there were no such things as ghosts.

"Want me to come and get you?" she asked her brother.

"No need for secrecy now. She's gone, so I can make my own way home." John glanced out of the window. "Besides, it's starting to snow again."

He hung up the phone and prepared to leave the apartment. He was still congratulating himself on a job well done when he almost jumped out of his skin, for he realized he was no longer alone. Standing in the corner of the room was a man with a big red beard and an eagle's beak of a nose. He wore a blue pin-striped suit and, on his finger, a large ring with a moonstone that was the size and colour of an alligator's eyeball and which, held up in front of the man's face, seemed to compel John to stand still. Wearing an angry expression, the red-haired man walked toward John.

"What do you mean, pulling a horrible trick like that on a defenseless female mundane?" said the man. "Explain yourself."

John tried to explain but every time he opened his mouth, something horrible now fell out of it: first a mouthful of pea soup, followed by a piece of broccoli, some lettuce leaves, several artichoke hearts, a piece of turnip, and, finally, almost a pint of creamed spinach. John detested the taste of most vegetables and the sudden taste of so many was too much for him. For the first time in his young djinn life, he fainted.

CHAPTER 3

BROUGHT TO BOOK

When John recovered consciousness he found himself in a different apartment. He knew he must still be in the Dakota because, lying by the window on a chaise longue, the view was the same. The apartment itself was very different, however. Unlike Mrs Trump's furniture, which was new and from a department store, everything in this apartment was old. There was even a large Egyptian desk and some sculptures that reminded John of Uncle Nimrod's house in London. No sound penetrated the thick walls of this other apartment and, as its forbidding owner began to speak, even the grandfather clock seemed to grow silent.

"I'm sorry I scared you like that," said the man, pulling up a chair and sitting down beside John. "Let me introduce myself. My name is Frank Vodyannoy and I am a djinn, like you. I've lived in this building for almost fifty years and, as well as a djinn, I'm also a business agent for a lot of the mundanes who live here. As a matter of fact I've helped almost everyone who lives here with their careers in one way or another. But for my help, I don't know how some of them would have prospered. For fifty years I've been the only djinn in the building. So yesterday, when I detected djinn power in the Dakota, I was a little concerned to see who was using it. But when I came looking for you yesterday, I couldn't find you.

"Then today, when I felt your presence again, I got a little angry. I didn't realize you were such a young djinn. And I was a little rough with you, for which I'm sorry. But like I say, these people rely on me. We can't afford to have a bad djinn in the Dakota."

"I'm not a bad djinn," said John. "I'm a good djinn."

"It's no business of mine what you choose to do with your time, but I won't tolerate idle mischief. Not in the Dakota."

"Honestly," insisted John. "It wasn't idle mischief at all."

Frank Vodyannoy smiled patiently at John. "It didn't look like it," he said. "It looked to me as if you were trying to scare someone. I hate it when djinn do that to people."

"You misunderstand, sir. I was trying to help someone. A mundane woman named Mrs Trump."

"Then you won't mind telling me how," said Mr Vodyannoy.

Feeling a little better now, John sat up and told him what had happened. And when he'd finished, Mr Vodyannoy laughed out loud.

"I like your style, kid," he said. "I used to know John Lennon. Liked him a lot. I think he might have approved of what you did. He had a good sense of humor."

John rubbed his head and swung his legs off the chaise longue. "What happened to me, anyway?"

"You were under the restraint of a djinn binding," explained Mr Vodyannoy. "A quaesitor. It's designed to find out the things you find unpleasant and then make

31

them appear in your mouth. Lucky for you it's just vegetables you really hate because I've seen all sorts of horrible things coming out of people's mouths: snakes, tarantulas, even a rat. You must really hate vegetables."

"I can't stand them, sir."

"Anyway, don't worry," said Mr Vodyannoy. "I cleaned up the mess. The vegetables, I mean. Off your friend Mrs Trump's rugs." He shook his head. "You know, John, I thought I knew all the djinn in New York. Why haven't I met you? What tribe are you? Who are your family? And do stop calling me 'sir.' Call me Frank. Or Mr Vodyannoy."

"My name is John Gaunt, sir. I mean Mr Vodyannoy. My father is a human – I mean a mundane. My mother is Layla Gaunt."

"That explains it. Layla has never introduced her children to djinn society. And the word outside the lamp is that she's abandoned her powers."

"She has."

"Then you must be Nimrod's nephew. Yes, I've heard all about you and your sister. And how you defeated that detestable creature, Iblis. Nasty piece of work, like all the Ifrit. Yes, young man, that was a job very well done. If ever there was a djinn that needed bottling up, it was Iblis."

"Thank you," said John.

"Of course, you'll have to watch out for his sons. They have bad tempers. All those hurricanes we had in Florida, for example. Rudyard Teer, Iblis's youngest boy, was the moving force behind at least two of them."

John frowned. To his certain knowledge Nimrod hadn't said anything to him or Philippa about looking out for the relations of Iblis. It was always possible he'd said something to their mother, but what good was that if his mother had given up using her own powers?

"I'm from the Jann tribe," said Mr Vodyannoy. "Some of us are righteous and some of us are not, but the Jann tribe, like the Marid, is on the side of good luck. We're not as powerful or influential as you Marid, perhaps. But we do all right."

"I'm sure you do." John was thinking that Frank Vodyannoy was just being modest. The quaesitor binding had seemed quite powerful to him.

"I feel bad about inflicting a quaesitor on you like that, John." For a moment he brandished the ring on his finger. "This moonstone made it seem more powerful. And a little hard to control. That's the trouble with moonstones. They're a little unruly. And very Gothic, of course."

"Don't mention it, Mr Vodyannoy. I'm fine. I didn't mean to disturb you."

"That's very decent of you. Very decent and very polite. I like good manners in a djinn of your age. So many djuniors lack all respect for the older djinneration these days. Even those from good tribes."

John thought of Dybbuk Sachertorte for a moment and understood what Mr Vodyannoy was probably driving at. It was hard to imagine Dybbuk speaking to Mr Vodyannoy with anything like respect.

"I tell you what I'm going to do," said Mr Vodyannoy. "For one thing I'd like to make you a gift. Know what a discrimen is, John?"

"No, sir."

Mr Vodyannoy laughed. "It's just a funny word we have for an emergency wish, that's all. My father gave me one when I was about your age. Very useful for when you're in a tight spot sometime. That happens when your powers are still developing. To use a discrimen all you do is utter a code word. It's the same as a focus word but one that a djinn attaches to another djinn as a sort of gift. Or to compensate another djinn. As in your case. For the injury caused."

"There's no need," said John. "To compensate me, I mean."

"But I insist," insisted Mr Vodyannoy. "Now the word I'm going to give you is a German word. German words are very good for discrimens. Especially the long ones because they're impossible to utter by accident. Unless you're German, of course. There's no language quite like German for long words. You're not going to Germany, are you?"

John shook his head.

"That's all right, then. The word I'm going to give you is this one," he said. "DONAUDAMPFSCHI-FAHRTSGESELLSCHAFTKAPITAEN."

"I'll never remember that," objected John.

"Of course you will," said Mr Vodyannoy. "Because you don't have to. A discrimen remembers itself, for you. Whenever a situation crops up in which a discrimen might be of use, a genuine emergency that is, you'll find that word on the tip of your tongue."

John couldn't understand how such a thing was possible. "Perhaps if I knew what it meant," he said.

"There's no need," objected Mr Vodyannoy. "But since you ask, it's a word referring to the captain of the Danube Steamship Company. And believe me, you couldn't get something simpler than the captain of the Danube Steamship Company. I know. I've met one."

"All right," said John. "I'm ready."

"For what?"

"For you to attach the discrimen."

"It's done."

"Oh. Well, thanks, sir. Mr Vodyannoy. I mean, Frank."

"Don't mention it." Mr Vodyannoy glanced out of the window. "The other thing I'm going to do is get you home. Where do you live?"

"Right across the park," said John. "At number 7, East 77th Street. But really, there's no need. I'll walk or take a cab."

"No, you won't." Frank Vodyannoy laughed. "Take another look outside that window. About six inches of snow have fallen while you've been lying on that couch."

John looked down at the park. It was true. He could hardly see the trees, so heavy was the snow now falling out of the sky. Why hadn't he noticed it before? The traffic had ground to a halt, and the park appeared to have been covered in a thick layer of cotton.

"That's the thing about quaesitors," said Mr Vodyannoy, sensing John's surprise. "It takes a while to recover from one completely. That's why I'm going to send you home in the only way that's really weatherproof. By whirlwind."

"No, wait."

"Don't worry. On a day like today, nobody will really notice anything. Believe me."

John had raised his voice to protest that he had been hoping to arrive home quietly, so his mother wouldn't notice, and that he hardly thought this would be possible if he returned by whirlwind. That would certainly require some sort of explanation and he didn't think it very likely that his mother would believe that this was nothing more than an unusual feature of New York's winter weather. But before he could stop Mr Vodyannoy, the air beneath him had started to spin at a tremendous speed, until a small but perfectly formed twister had lifted him gently up off the rug. Trying to keep his balance, John flailed his arms backward and forward like a clown on a high wire.

"Don't try to stand on it, boy," yelled Mr Vodyannoy, opening his seventh-floor window. "Sit down before you fall over. Goodness me, anyone would think you'd never ridden a whirlwind before."

"I haven't," shouted John, sitting down abruptly. But it was too late. The whirlwind, which was no bigger than an armchair and just as comfortable, was already carrying him out of the Dakota apartment building and across the park. John closed his eyes and, endeavoring to put the probable consequences of this mode of travel out of his mind for a few moments, tried to enjoy his trip.

A couple of minutes after leaving the window of Mr Vodyannoy's Dakota apartment, the whirlwind descended toward his front gate just as Mrs Trump opened it to throw some rock salt on the steps to stop the snow from drifting there. She screamed aloud but didn't see John as, carrying a certain amount of snow by then, the whirlwind swept into the hallway like a mini-tornado, spinning Mrs Trump off her feet before careering up six flights of stairs to John's bedroom, and depositing him gently on to his leather chair.

At any other time this would have been very convenient for John, but it so happened that Mrs Gaunt was waiting there. She had just received a furious phone call from Dr Sachertorte accusing the twins of having unleashed a water elemental on Mr Sachertorte's new wife, Nadia, at Dybbuk's request. And Mrs Gaunt was certainly less than pleased to see her son arriving home in a manner that only seemed to confirm that he had been using djinn power without having cleared it with her.

"I hope Mrs Trump didn't see you riding a whirlwind, John," Mrs Gaunt said crisply.

"Er, no," said John. "At least I don't think so. The whirlwind knocked her over and kind of blinded her with snow as I came in just now."

"That's something, I suppose."

A sheepish-looking Philippa appeared in the doorway.

"Now that you're both here," said their mother, "perhaps you wouldn't mind telling me what's been going on? I thought we had an agreement – an agreement that you volunteered – that neither of you would use your powers without speaking to me first. Now I find John riding a whirlwind minutes after coming off the phone with a very cross Dr Sachertorte. It seems that someone set a water elemental on her ex-husband's new wife, Nadia. For the last twelve hours it has been raining inside their new apartment. Yes, raining. Torrentially. Dr Sachertorte thinks that Dybbuk put you up to it."

"That's not true," said John. "We had nothing to do with it."

"It wasn't Dybbuk, of that she's sure. Until she lifts the binding she put on him he can't use his djinn power to tie

37

his shoelaces. Assuming he ever bothers to tie them up anyway. I don't care for that boy. Either way, I'm beginning to believe that I should have asked Nimrod to put a binding on the pair of you."

"We had nothing to do with it. Honestly," insisted John.

"You ask me to believe that, John, and yet here you are, riding a whirlwind through our own front door."

John then confessed to his mother about Mrs Trump's apartment at the Dakota and how she had been frightened of Miss Pickings, and how he had "persuaded" her to leave, and how he had met Mr Vodyannoy, who had been very nice and sent him home on a whirlwind before he could decline. "So you see, I wasn't using djinn power for myself," he said, by way of justification. "But to help someone else."

"That doesn't explain the monsoon in Nadia Tarantino's new apartment," Mrs Gaunt said stiffly.

While John had been explaining to his mother about Miss Pickings, Philippa had been thinking about Dybbuk Sachertorte and the incident in the sauna. "I think that *I* might have an idea what happened." She took off her glasses the way she always did when she wanted her mother to look her straight in the eye and make her believe she was telling the truth, even when she wasn't. "Dybbuk showed us how to get around not having any power in wintertime by sitting in the sauna. We decided to give him something as a thank-you present. Something we made with djinn power. It was a computer game. Only we couldn't quite visualize the computer game he wanted. So we all held hands, and he used our power to focus on the game he really wanted."

"That's right," said John. "Only the first time it didn't work. Yes, I'd forgotten about that."

"But I felt some power still go out of us." Philippa shook her head. "It's true he had asked us to set a water elemental on his stepmother, but we refused. So I think he must have tricked us and did it anyway, without us realizing."

"Didn't Nimrod teach you anything last summer?" sighed Mrs Gaunt. "Never hold hands with another djinn in case they try to harness your power to theirs. It's called djinncantation, and it's where those human spiritualists get their silly notions about holding hands with each other during a séance. Because they imagine it gives them the power of the group. If you must shake hands with someone, then make sure you bend your middle finger back into the palm of your hand, so as to prevent your lifeline coming into contact with another's lifeline." She demonstrated the proper way for a djinn to shake hands. "But since you didn't know about the handshake, I can hardly blame you, I suppose. Only please be more careful next time, children."

"And you're not angry about what I did to Miss Pickings?" asked John.

"I can easily understand you wanting to help Mrs Trump," said his mother. "But mark my words. This matter may yet have consequences you did not foresee. All use of djinn power in the mundane world has a random and unpredictable effect. That was something else I thought Nimrod had made clear to you." Then she smiled. "But no, I'm not angry. Which is perhaps just as well for you. It would have given me no pleasure in forbidding you both from attending Mr Rakshasas's book launch."

"What's a book launch?" asked John.

"A party to celebrate the publication of a book, dummy," said Philippa.

"Old Rakshasas has written a book?" said John, ignoring his sister.

"Yes," said Mrs Gaunt. "Rakshasas's *Shorter Baghdad Rules*."

"It sure doesn't sound like an Oprah choice," said John.

"When's the party?" asked Philippa. "And where?"

"Tonight. Here in New York, at The Sealed Book, on West 57th Street."

"Tonight?" said John. "But why didn't you tell us earlier? Will Uncle Nimrod be there?"

"Of course he will. And that's why I didn't tell you before. He wanted it to be a nice surprise."

The Sealed Book was well-named, for this particular New York bookstore had no door. Except for a window the size and shape of a porthole in a ship and, on the brickwork next to it, the shop's name and address handsomely engraved on a brass plate, no one would ever have suspected there was a store there at all.

"Are you sure this is the right place?" Philippa asked John.

"That's what it says on the invitation," he said, showing her the card with the title of the book and a small map of 57th Street between Broadway and the Avenue of the Americas.

"There's probably a secret way in," said Philippa, and began to read what was written on an illuminated piece of card that was the only exhibit in the shop's round window.

"I'd say we were expected all right," observed John. "And by a very powerful djinn."

"Why do you think that?" asked Philippa.

"Simple. This is the only street in New York with no snow."

"You're right," she said. "There's snow at both ends of the street, but not here."

"Of course I'm right," said John. "And feel the air? It's actually warm. As a matter of fact it's maybe twenty or thirty degrees warmer than the next street. Like a microclimate, you know? That takes real power. Someone – Nimrod, maybe, or Mr Rakshasas – has tried to make the street more comfortable for a lot of heat-loving djinn."

But Philippa was hardly listening. "It's a riddle," she declared finally, pointing to the card in the strange little round window. "I think that if we answer the riddle we can get in. Listen. 'The beginning of eternity. The end of time and space. The beginning of every end. And the end of everyplace'."

John shrugged. "I don't get it."

"No, but I do," Philippa said triumphantly. "The answer is the letter *e*. *E* is the beginning of eternity, the end of time and space, the beginning of every end, and the end of everyplace."

"Where does that get us?"

"Inside," said Philippa, and pressed the letter *e* in the

41

word WEST that was engraved on the shop's brass address plate.

Immediately, a section of the brick wall, including the window, revealed itself as a door on a hidden hinge that swung back to expose not some dark and dismal place, but a light and spacious vault and, inside the vault, a spiral staircase that led up onto another floor from where the sound of a party in progress could clearly be heard.

"Nice going, sis." John stepped quickly into the vault. "Come on. Before the door shuts again."

Philippa followed her brother into the vault and up the spiral staircase as the secret door rumbled shut behind them. At the top of the staircase they found themselves in a large room with a spectacular view, not of 57th street, which was the view they might have expected to see out of a 57th Street window, but of what looked more like the sea in a warmer country. Then, from a crowd of people, a large man wearing a bright red suit advanced toward them with his arms spread as wide as his smile. It was their uncle Nimrod.

"Here they are," he said, hugging the twins fondly. "We were beginning to wonder where you got to."

"We had a little bit of a problem with the riddle at the door," said Philippa.

"Really? You surprise me. It's nothing complicated. Just a little bagatelle by the great English writer Jonathan Swift. To keep the riffraff out."

Nimrod was followed closely by an old man with a white beard, a white turban, and a white suit. He hugged the children happily. "To be sure, a party is only a party if there are some who're not invited," said Mr Rakshasas. He looked like an Indian maharajah; but the old djinn spoke his English like an Irishman, which was the result of having spent many years trapped inside a bottle in Ireland and learning all of his English from Irish television.

"Congratulations on your book," the twins told Mr Rakshasas.

"Congratulations, indeed," said Nimrod. "This is probably the most important book since King Solomon's Grimoire."

Mr Rakshasas smiled vaguely. "Kind of you to say so," he said. "But in truth, my book is no more than the buckle on a very old shoe."

"What's a grimoire?" asked John.

"A sorcerer's manual for binding djinn," said Nimrod. "Of which the earliest and most important example is the *Testament of Solomon*. That's why I made the comparison with Mr Rakshasas's book – *The Shorter Baghdad Rules*."

"Away with ye," Mr Rakshasas said modestly. "Soft words butter no parsnips."

"But they won't harden the heart of the cabbage, either," declared Nimrod. "Mr Rakshasas has spent his whole life writing this book," he told the twins. "You see, over the years, *The Baghdad Rules* have grown very large and unwieldy, with lots of contradictions and inconsistencies. As well as being an important one-volume edition of the rules – rules which, thanks to Mr Rakshasas's book, you may discover with ease and rely upon with certainty – everything of interest about the djinn has now been brought to book, so to speak. In short, Mr Rakshasas has, like a sailor crossing an ocean, completed a work of which we had once despaired."

"I can't wait to read it," said John.

"And you shall read it, John," said Nimrod. "But first let me introduce you both to some of New York's djinn society."

CHAPTER 4

THE DJUNIOR CHAMPION

Nimrod had described the djinn at Mr Rakshasas's party as some of New York's djinn society but, in truth, the djinn to whom the twins were introduced were from all over the world. There was Morgan Mbulu from South Africa, Maud Merrow from Ireland, Oonagh Ponaturi from New Zealand, Toshiro Tengu from Japan, and Stan Bunyip from Australia. One or two were also quite famous in the mundane world: Peri Bannu was a well-known movie actress, Janet Jann was President of a Hollywood film studio, Virdjinnia Nisse was a celebrated sculptor from Norway, and David Kabikaj was a Nobel-prize winning entomologist from Canada.

"I believe you've already met Frank Vodyannoy," Nimrod said to John, ushering the twins toward a group of four djinn standing by a large table, on which lay several copies of Mr Rakshasas's book. "And, of course, you both know the very glamorous Dr Jenny Sachertorte and her son, Dybbuk."

The twins nodded coolly at Dybbuk, who regarded their arrival with his usual mixture of amusement and contempt. At least he did until his mother elbowed him in the ribs.

"Dybbuk has something to say to you both," she said,

smiling sweetly at the twins. "Don't you, dear?"

Dybbuk rolled his eyes and grunted at John and Philippa. "Sorry," he said moodily.

"Your mother explained what happened," said Dr Sachertorte. "How Dybbuk tricked you into helping him do something bad to my ex-husband's wife. He's a good djinn, really. And he has promised that he'll never trick you like that again, haven't you, honey?"

"Yeah," groaned Dybbuk. "Sure. Whatever."

"Otherwise he'll feel the full weight of my power. Won't you, dear?"

"What I always say, Dr Sachertorte," said Mr Rakshasas, "is that the power will come out. Sometimes it has to. It's for his own good that the cat purrs. Isn't that right, Nimrod?"

"Everything is sorted now, that's the main thing," said Nimrod. "The new Mrs Sachertorte has her apartment returned to normal, and Dybbuk here is turning over a new leaf. Aren't you, Dybbuk?"

"Buck," he said, rolling his eyes again – it was a habit Philippa found disconcerting. "Just Buck. OK?"

"John," said Nimrod. "Why don't you and, er, Buck, go and get something to eat while I talk to Philippa about something?"

"All right," said John and the two djinn boys went over to a table where a man was standing behind a large, steaming vat of very hot curry. Once there they amused themselves by trying to see which of them could eat the most hot chili peppers.

"So, tell me," said Nimrod, taking Philippa to one side. "How are the astaragali rolling these days?"

"Well," she said, shrugging, "put it this way. They're in motion. But only just."

"Astaragali", and "Tesserae" are djinn words for dice. The djinn play a variety of astaragali that is particular to themselves, however, and this is called Djinnverso, or more correctly, Djinnversoctoannular. Djinnverso is played with a circular crystalline box with a lid, and a set of seven octagonal astaragali, or dice, which is to say that each astaragali has not six sides but eight. The eight sides of a Djinnverso astaragali feature Spirit, Space, Time, Fire, Earth, Air, Water, and Luck. With the use of djinnpower strictly forbidden during a game of Djinnverso (the crystal box is designed to detect the illegal use of djinnpower) the effects of chance are overcome by the player's ability to bluff his or her opponents.

For one who had been playing Djinnverso for a matter of a few months, Philippa was already quite a proficient player. Mostly she played with her father and one of his friends, a mundane called Bull Huxter, who was one of the few humans aware that Edward Gaunt's twins were djinn. Philippa knew Nimrod was going to ask her if she was entering the forthcoming World Djinnverso Tournament, which took place annually between Christmas and New Year's Eve. But Philippa hadn't yet made up her mind. She was a quiet, retiring sort of djinn and, unlike her brother, not much inclined to showing off, or trying to prove something to herself – or, for that matter, to anyone else.

Nimrod, lighting a large cigar, guessed as much. "Light my lamp," he said. "Surely you're going to compete. Someone with your skills and abilities can't seriously be thinking of not entering the tournament. Bottle me, no. It's unthinkable, Philippa. Completely djinnadmissable." He puffed out a huge cloud of smoke in the shape of a large exclamation mark. "If you don't mind me saying so."

Philippa shrugged and tried to change the subject. "I see you haven't lost your taste for those huge cigars," she said.

"Stop trying to dodge the question. Have you put your name down for the Djinnverso tournament or not?"

"No. And to be honest, I'm not sure that I want to, Uncle."

"It's up to you, I suppose." Nimrod thought for a moment. "Look here, come and meet a djinn of your own age: Lilith de Ghulle. Curious lot, the de Ghulles. They are a family of evil djinn who are trying to persuade everyone they are good. Or at least not as bad as everyone supposes. Which is why Lilith and her mother, Mimi, are here." Nimrod smiled indulgently. "Who knows? Perhaps the leopard really can change its spots."

Mimi de Ghulle wore a fur coat, large earrings, and carried an expensive leather handbag hooked over her arm like a giant padlock. She was talking to Frank Vodyannoy and yawned loudly as if she wasn't having a good time.

Philippa looked at Mimi de Ghulle and shivered. There was something about her she didn't like; only this was something more than what Nimrod had been talking about. When Mimi looked at her, Philippa felt a sense of real hatred that was so strong it made her take a step backward.

"Mimi," Nimrod said pleasantly. "Enjoying the party?"

"Oh, sure," said Mrs de Ghulle. When she spoke it

was from the side of her mouth. "I wouldn't have missed it for the world."

Philippa could see that Mrs de Ghulle didn't mean this at all. She also noticed that Mrs de Ghulle's lips looked as if they'd been inflated with a bicycle pump; not to mention the way that her nose, while perfect in itself and a tribute to the plastic surgeon who had made it, was too small for her face and helped to make her head seem more like a skull.

"And this must be your darling daughter, Lilith," observed Nimrod.

In almost every detail, Lilith de Ghulle resembled Mimi de Ghulle, right down to the fur coat and the choice of handbag. The similarity was not, however, pleasing, and Philippa decided that Lilith looked like her mother in the same way that some dogs look like their owners (and, just as often, the other way around).

"Lilith? I'd like you to meet my niece, Philippa Gaunt."

"Hello," said Philippa.

Lilith smiled an unpleasant, sarcastic sort of fleeting smile in Philippa's direction and carried on chewing gum.

"Lilith is currently the djunior Djinnverso champion," he said.

"That's right," said Mrs de Ghulle. "And this year, she's going to win the tournament again. You watch."

"Lilith," said Nimrod, "perhaps you could persuade Philippa that she should enter. She seems a little reluctant to do so. I'm sure some words of encouragement coming from you might be enough to persuade her."

Lilith, who wasn't much older than Philippa, regarded

Nimrod with amusement. "Are you kidding me? This sappy-looking girl hasn't got a chance. Not while I'm around."

Nimrod chuckled nervously but Philippa felt herself colouring with anger as Lilith proceeded to turn the same look loose on her.

"Take my advice, baby cakes," sneered Lilith. "Stick to your dolls and your playpen. Djinnverso's a game for the grown-ups."

Mrs de Ghulle smiled a smile that was a combination of pride and embarrassment. "Oh, she's just kidding. Aren't you, honey? She's at that awkward age, Nimrod."

"Yes, I can see that," said Nimrod. "Very awkward, indeed."

Nimrod steered Philippa away, toward the table displaying copies of Mr Rakshasas's book.

"That does it," Philippa said firmly. "I'm entering. Just for the chance to beat that awful girl."

"That's why I wanted you to meet her," chuckled Nimrod. "To make sure you understood the urgency of becoming the next djunior champion."

"Do you really think I can win it?"

"If I didn't, I certainly wouldn't have exposed you to Lilith de Ghulle."

"Then you don't think that a leopard can change its spots after all?"

Nimrod smiled. "No. And as a matter of fact I've a good idea what Mimi de Ghulle is up to. She thinks she can make someone believe that she's beyond all the usual Good and Evil stuff that goes on between our side and theirs. Someone in particular."

"You?"

"Light my lamp, no. Mimi doesn't give two hoots what I think about her. No, she's been trying to make an impression on the Blue Djinn of Babylon and, by all accounts, succeeding, more's the pity. It is strongly suspected that Mimi will be the next Blue Djinn, and is only awaiting the word from Ayesha when she attends the Djinnverso tournament as official referee. Ayesha – that's the current Blue Djinn's name – is looking for a successor. Has been for a while, as a matter of fact. Everyone knows that the Djinnverso tournament is where she herself was first identified by the previous Blue Djinn, back in 1928."

"1928?" exclaimed Philippa. "She must be very old."

"Almost two hundred years old," said Nimrod. "But don't forget, Philippa, that we djinn age much more slowly than humankind. To look at her, you would think she was a woman in her late eighties, perhaps."

"But who is the Blue Djinn, and what does she do?" asked Philippa.

"She's the symbolic leader of all the djinn, good or bad. It's a position she is able to command because she is herself neither good nor bad. Ayesha, peace be upon her, is beyond Good and Evil and, for that reason alone, she is able to deal fairly with both sides. As well as caring for the welfare of all djinn, she is also the supreme arbiter of djinn justice, inflicting punishment upon those who are deemed to have broken The Baghdad Rules."

"What kind of punishments? And on who?"

"It was Ayesha who decided that because Iblis murdered poor Hussein Hussaout in Cairo, then the

51

bottle in which you and John and I imprisoned him must be exiled to a place from whence he cannot possibly escape for a period of ten years."

Iblis was the head of the Ifrit, a very wicked tribe of djinn. With the help of his niece and nephew, Nimrod had trapped Iblis in an antique glass perfume bottle that Philippa had believed was safely stored in Nimrod's refrigerator, at his house in Cairo.

"So where's she sending him?" she asked.

Nimrod looked a little sheepish. "She's sending him to Venus on board the European space probe."

"Venus," said Philippa. "How awful."

"I expect it'll be pretty unpleasant on Venus," admitted Nimrod. "But I'm sure Iblis will be all right. In about ten years, a second probe will bring back most of the equipment sent to Venus aboard the first probe, including the pod with the bottle containing Iblis."

Philippa frowned. "I know he killed Hussein Hussaout. And that Hussein Hussaout had a son who now doesn't have a father. But it still seems like a terrible thing to do, to sentence someone to a ten-year exile on Venus. Can't we say something on his behalf?"

"As a matter of fact, I already tried," Nimrod said sadly. "But the Blue Djinn, blessings be upon her, has spoken."

"Then she must be awfully hard-hearted."

"Bottle me, that's rather the point, Philippa. She is. And you say more than you know. The Blue Djinn has the hardest heart in the world. How else could she exist beyond Good and Evil? All of which means that just like human justice, djinn justice can sometimes seem a little harsh." Nimrod picked up a copy of the *Shorter Baghdad Rules* off the table and turned the pages. "You'll find there's quite a lot about her in here, if you're at all interested."

Philippa was very interested in a way she found hard to explain to herself. Which made it seem all the more of a coincidence when, the very next day after the party, she saw the Blue Djinn herself, in person.

Philippa was walking up Fifth Avenue after playing Djinnverso with her father and his friend Bull Huxter in his apartment when, outside the Pierre Hotel, she found the two family pet dogs, Alan and Neil, waiting patiently by the entrance. Mrs Gaunt often had tea with her friends at the Pierre, and Philippa went inside, hoping she might be allowed to have some cake. On this particular occasion, however, her mother was not with her friends but with a very old woman, and, straightaway, Philippa guessed that if her appearance was anything to go by, the old woman just had to be the Blue Djinn.

The old woman wore a sky-blue two-piece suit, a navy blue blouse with a big pussycat bow, and a blue hat on top of a heavily sprayed meringue of blue-rinsed hair. On her fingers were several sapphire rings that matched her earrings, which flashed in the light as she nodded her head, crossly as it happened, for she and Mrs Gaunt appeared to be having an argument. And instead of approaching her mother to say hello, Philippa found herself hiding behind a marble pillar, to eavesdrop.

"No, no, no, no, no," said the old woman in a clear

English accent. The voice, which was very firm and completely lacking in emotion, made Philippa shudder a little. She decided that with her hard, narrowed eyes and small puckered mouth, the old woman looked more like some creepy old dowager Chinese empress than an elderly lady from England. She would have listened longer except that Ayesha lowered her voice almost to a whisper so that she couldn't hear what was being said, and, after a while, Philippa decided to sneak out of the hotel without saying hello. The Blue Djinn, if indeed it was she, looked much too stern to interrupt lightly.

That evening, after dinner, Philippa quizzed her mother about the incident. "I went to play Djinnverso at Bull Huxter's apartment this afternoon," she said.

"Did you, dear? That's nice."

"After our game, I was walking up Fifth Avenue when I saw Alan and Neil outside the Pierre, and I went inside, thinking you might be having afternoon tea with one of your friends. And instead I saw you talking to an old woman dressed in blue. And I wondered if she might be the Blue Djinn of Babylon."

"Yes, dear. She's here for the Djinnverso tournament at the Algonquin Hotel. You should have come and said hello. I know she would like to have met you."

"I would have," admitted Philippa. "Except that she looked kind of scary. Besides, it looked like you and she were having an argument."

Mrs Gaunt shook her head. "No, dear. I think you must be mistaken. We didn't argue. It's just that Ayesha is very old and sure she's always right. Because of her position in the world of djinn, she's used to telling other djinn what to do. That can make her quite difficult sometimes. What's more, it's a very lonely job, being the Blue Djinn. When people don't agree with her, she can get a little impatient, that's all."

"And did you disagree about something?"

"We had a small difference of opinion. But not an argument. No, it wasn't that."

"But don't you have to do what she says? Her being the Blue Djinn 'n' all?"

"That might be true if we had sought her judgment in the djinn court. But not outside, in the mundane world of affairs."

"Is the court in Babylon?

"It used to be. Many centuries ago. But not anymore. Nowadays she receives djinn at her court in Berlin, which is much more convenient for everyone. Only once a year does her role oblige her actually to visit Babylon. It is said, in order that she might harden her heart again, for a whole year."

"How is that possible? I've heard of people having their arteries hardened, but not their hearts."

Mrs Gaunt sighed. "For the moment let's just say that it is. Remember that we djinn are not like humans. We may look like them. Or rather they may look like us, not to mention the angels. But there are profound differences, at an atomic level. And at a subatomic level."

"And is she terribly hard-hearted?

"Yes, terribly." Mrs Gaunt smiled, but Philippa thought it a very sad smile and, even as Mrs Gaunt left the room, she had the idea that her mother had wiped a tear from the corner of her eye. This did little to alter Philippa's impression that something had happened between her mother and the Blue Djinn that she wasn't being told about. Something serious. And she resolved to discuss the matter with John right away.

CHAPTER 5

DJINNVERSO AND THE VICIOUS CIRCLE

Having resisted his first inclination, which was to turn Gordon Warthoff, the boy who was bullying him at school, into a warthog, John had tried to think of a way of dealing with him of which his mother might approve, if she ever found out about it. Animal transformations and elementals were clearly unacceptable and, finally, John decided that the best thing he could do would be to try to increase his own physical strength so that he might stand a chance of defeating the larger boy in a fair fight. The only trouble was that training with even the lightest weights in his father's fitness room for longer than five minutes left John feeling exhausted. So he was delighted to discover that he could pump iron for much longer if he trained in the heat of the sauna where his young djinn body seemed to thrive. And it wasn't very long before he started to build some noticeable muscles – muscles he felt sure would allow him to deal with Warthoff on his own, brutal terms. When Philippa discovered how he was spending his time in the sauna, and listened to John's plan, she was sceptical, however.

"Isn't he the boy whose uncle works for CNN? Tough-looking boy? With zits?"

John nodded and threw some more water on the hot stones to increase the temperature in the sauna. Philippa wrapped a towel around her head, deciding that feeling like a proper djinn again really wasn't worth the hassle of having to wash and dry her hair each time she went in there.

"Surely there's an easier, more subtle way of dealing with him."

"Like what?"

"Like psychology, maybe. Have you asked yourself *why* he's bullying you?"

"Because he's a zit-faced creep, that's why."

"What I mean is, what is it about you that he doesn't like?"

John shrugged. "I don't think he needs much of a reason. He's a bully. That's his job."

"When did he start pushing you around?"

"The beginning of the semester."

Philippa thought for a moment. "Could it be that he bullies you because you're not a zit-faced creep?" Philippa nodded, liking her idea. "In fact, you know, that's it. I'm sure of it."

"I'm not sure I follow," admitted John.

"Do you remember how you used to have a lot of pimples? And then, as soon as you had your wisdom teeth extracted, and your djinn power kicked in, the zits just disappeared?"

"How could I forget? It was one of the greatest days of my life. I could look myself in the mirror without wanting to throw myself under a train."

"So has it occurred to you that he bullies you because

he's jealous of you? Because he still has his zits, and you don't?"

"It's a possibility," admitted John. "But so what? I'm not having the zits back. Not even to get Gordon Warthoff off my case."

"You don't have to. But there's nothing to stop us from making *his* acne disappear."

"You mean with djinn power?"

"I sure wasn't planning to send him a tube of zit cream."

"Even if Mom did agree to me fixing Warthoff's zits, I'm not sure I could ever bring myself to wish him anything other than a broken leg."

"You don't have to," said Philippa. "I'll fix them for you."

John could see that his sister was serious, and since they were in the sauna at the time, he knew she was capable of doing exactly what she said. "Don't you want to ask Mom first?" he asked.

"Right now, I think she's got other things on her mind than the pimples on Gordon Warthoff's face," said Philippa. Lately, Mrs Gaunt had been rather quiet and preoccupied, which seemed to date from her meeting with Blue Djinn.

Philippa gathered her thoughts in preparation for using djinn power. "Besides, I don't see how she could possibly object to my helping him when you consider the possible benefit to you. And this is surely better than you having a fight with him at school."

So she thought of Gordon Warthoff, and she thought of the zits on his face, and then she thought of them being

59

gone the next morning when he awoke, and him becoming a better person as a result. And then she uttered her focus word:

"FABULONGOSHOOMARVELISHLYWONDERPIP ICAL!"

John waited politely for a moment. "Did you do it?"

Philippa nodded. "You'll see. It'll be fine."

John clapped her on the shoulder. "Thanks, Phil." He grinned fondly at his sister. They were not at all similar on the outside; like his mother, John was tall and thin and dark, while Philippa was small like her father, with glasses. But inside they were alike as two sides of the same coin. There wasn't anything John wouldn't have done for Philippa, and he felt he wanted to tell her this. Except, of course, that as soon as he thought it, she knew it already.

"I know," she said. "I know."

Philippa spent the days leading up to Christmas playing Djinnverso with Nimrod, Mr Rakshasas, and either her father or Bull Huxter.

Bull Huxter had been a lawyer, an advertising man, a journalist, and a professional poker player before joining the European Space Program as Head of Marketing and Communications. He was a Canadian from Toronto who claimed to have done everything and met everyone who was anyone. She thought he was a strange sort of man to be involved with something as serious as a space program, even one that was largely European in origin. Every time she mentioned it to him (hoping that she might learn something about Iblis and his terrible fate, for the rocket that would carry him to Venus was to be launched any day now), Huxter changed the subject, and Philippa swiftly formed the conclusion that if she had been in charge of her own father's bank, she wouldn't have lent him five bucks. But he was an excellent Djinnverso player. No human, said Nimrod, could bluff a roll of astaragali better than Bull Huxter and, although he was a bit deaf (from being around too many rocket launches, he said), by playing him regularly, Philippa learned a lot about bluffing.

By contrast with his sister, John wasn't at all interested in Djinnverso. He couldn't see what all the fuss was about and preferred to spend his time reading Rakshasas's *Shorter Baghdad Rules*. In truth, he wasn't much interested in the rules, but he was extremely keen on learning facts about the djinn. Mrs Gaunt called these facts trivia and perhaps they were, but John didn't care; over that particular Christmas holiday, nothing else was as important to him as Mr Rakshasas's doorstopper of a book.

For example, he discovered why it was he disliked the taste of salt and the smell of tar so much. Once, mundane people had actually used these to drive djinn away. According to the book, djinn were also supposed to hate loud noise (which was certainly true in Philippa's case); nor did they care for the touch of iron or steel – which explained why Mrs Gaunt and Nimrod could not abide the touch of any metal, except gold.

Philippa also looked at the book and was especially pleased to discover the information it contained about Lilith's tribe, the Ghuls. The females of the tribe were called *Si'lats* and, traditionally, as hideous to behold as they were malicious. Philippa thought the part in the book about the Ghuls eating human flesh was no less satisfying to read, although she also felt that this seemed hardly likely in this day and age. Not while McDonalds existed, anyway. The book also explained how a Ghul could be killed with a single blow to the face, although strangely it said that a second blow would bring the same Ghul back to life. "If ever I slap Lilith," Philippa told John, "please make sure I don't do it again."

The leather case cover of the SBR – as everyone began to call it – was made of hand-painted camel skin and inlaid with a small oval of silver which, when rubbed with the thumb, summoned a miniature three-dimensional facsimile figure of Mr Rakshasas. Complete in almost every detail, this was like an artificial djinn that, once summoned, would proceed to deliver a useful tip on how to use the book, or a "djinn fact of the day". And John found the artificial Mr Rakshasas especially interesting on the subject of the Blue Djinn of Babylon:

"In the beginning," explained the artificial Mr Rakshasas, whose Irishness seemed no less peculiar than the real one's, "the Blue Djinn's name was Ishtar, blessings be upon her, and she was worshipped as the Queen of Heaven, who succeeded Bellili. Ishtar's symbols were the lion and the colour blue which, to be sure, is also the colour of the Moon and the Night. Now, the Blue Djinn never made the Great Choice between Good and Evil. It is not certain why, but as the centuries passed, the subsequent incarnations of the Blue Djinn became someone and something that all djinn learned to respect; and it became useful to both sides – Good and Evil – to have a powerful djinn who remained above the eternal struggle to control the mundane world's Luck. Eventually, she was even able to lay down the djinn law to all of the six tribes."

"Around the same time, King Nebuchadnezzar the Second built the great Ishtar Gate to his new city of Babylon in honour of Ishtar. He also built himself a magnificent palace, with those famous hanging gardens that were one of the wonders of the ancient world. But Ishtar got angry that Nebuchadnezzar had built his palace and gardens ahead of her own palace. I mean a special gate is very nice, 'n' all, but if the gate leads nowhere in particular, well then it's not much use to anyone. Things got worse when old Nebuchadnezzar set out to conquer the greatest magician of the ancient world, King Solomon, himself. Nebuchadnezzar sacked Jerusalem, stole Solomon's famous grimoire and took all the gold back to Babylon. By this time, it's fair to say King Nebuchadnezzar was aware of the need to make amends to Ishtar and used the gold taken from Jerusalem to build a fabulous palace to her – the so-called Hanging Palace of Babylon, the location of which remains to this day, a closely guarded secret. Ishtar forgave Nebuchadnezzar for the earlier affront but only until, short of money to pay for yet another war, he removed the gold from her palace. This time Ishtar did not forgive him and turned the king into a sheep. He was never seen again."

John listened carefully. He had no idea how important this information about the Blue Djinn of Babylon was soon to become.

"With the decline of Babylon as a major world city,

63

later incarnations of the Blue Djinn began to live in Switzerland, which is a cooler, and historically speaking, politically neutral country. This had symbolic value, for it meant that the Blue Djinn was not interested in using power for herself, but only as a counsellor, or as a judge and lawmaker. Almost all of *The Baghdad Rules* are the result of earlier judgments of the seventy-five incarnations of the Blue Djinn that there have been to date. But following the reconstruction of the famous Ishtar Gate at the Pergamon Museum in Berlin, it was decided by the seventy-fifth incarnation of the Blue Djinn, that her court should move from Geneva, Switzerland, to Berlin, Germany. And, apart from the period from 1940 to 1944, when the Blue Djinn returned to Geneva, she has lived in Berlin ever since, where she remains to this day."

The explanation provided by the artificial Mr Rakshasas left John with a number of unanswered questions. But when he asked his mother about the Blue Djinn, Mrs Gaunt refused even to discuss her. Given what Philippa had already told him about the meeting between their mother and the Blue Djinn that she had observed at the Pierre Hotel, he found this curious, to say the least. And he had to wait until the first day of the Djinnverso Tournament at New York's famous Algonquin Hotel, to quiz the real Mr Rakshasas for yet more information about the Blue Djinn.

"Is the Blue Djinn always a woman?" he asked.

"Always," said Mr Rakshasas. "'Tis said that female djinn are always smarter than the males."

"How is a new djinn appointed?"

"By the old Blue Djinn herself, according to certain

signs that are known only to Ayesha, blessings be upon her."

"And who will be the next one? Do we know yet?"

"There's a strong rumor that it might be Mimi de Ghulle." Mr Rakshasas laughed. "Perhaps it will even be announced at this tournament. But in truth, no one knows, except Ayesha. Ten years she's been looking for a replacement. 'Tis difficult to choose between two blind goats, right enough. I've heard it said that those who might want the post aren't at all suitable, while those who are suitable don't want the post."

"But why wouldn't someone want to be the next Blue Djinn?" asked John.

Mr Rakshasas looked awkward and stroked his long white beard thoughtfully. "Difficult question," he said. "Perhaps only those with a good heart can guess how terrible it might be, to be obliged to have a hard one." He paused and then added, "Which wouldn't be problem for Mimi, to be sure."

John shrugged, not quite sure he understood Mr Rakshasas, which was not unusual. "I expect she'll find someone suitable, in time," he said.

"If she were having the time, she'd sleep more soundly in her bed, I dare say. To be sure there's no need to fear the wind if your haystacks are tied down. But if they're not. . ." Mr Rakshasas shook his head. "And of course, the older she gets, the less time she has, and the harder becomes her heart. In turn this makes her judgments even harsher, which becomes a risk to us all, good and bad. Iblis, poor fellow, found that out to his cost."

"I see," said John.

"No, you don't," said Mr Rakshasas. "Like human beings, we djinn know we're going to die. That's what makes us different from the animals. That and speech. And wearing clothes. And one or two other things, perhaps. But we know we're going to die. We just don't know when. Which is a comfort and a blessing to us all. But the Blue Djinn knows exactly when her term of life will come to an end. It's one of the things that makes her so hard-hearted. At least that is what is generally supposed. There's a great deal about what goes on in her secret palace in Babylon that's a mystery to us all. Even to me."

"How terrible," said John. "I mean to know exactly when you're going to die."

"Sure and when the sky falls, we'll all catch larks."

"Very true," said John, although he had little idea what this really meant.

An earlier attempt to have the Djinnversoctoannular Tournament staged in Chicago had been abandoned when it was recognized that the windy city's winter temperatures, while suitably cold – cold deters the use of djinn powers, and holding the tournament somewhere cold, deters cheating – were much too cold for the everyday comfort of djinn. And, as usual, the tournament was held at the famous Oak Room in the Algonquin Hotel. The competition, which was scheduled to last three days, was open to all of the six tribes, good or evil, with the use of djinn powers strictly forbidden, on pain of disqualification. But in keeping with the hotel's history as the lunching spot for some of New York's cleverest writers and wittiest actors, djinn were allowed – even encouraged – to insult each other with style.

Consequently, when Palis the Footlicker – one of the more notorious members of the evil Ifrit tribe – encountered Nimrod in the doorway of the Oak Room, the first thing he did was to sneer at him and make a disparaging remark. "Ah, there you are, Nimrod," he said. "Man's best friend. Woof, woof, woof." And in no time at all, these two senior djinn were engaged in a verbal jousting match to which John listened with amazement.

"As always, Palis," replied Nimrod, "you look like a shudder waiting to crawl down a rat's spine."

Palis was a tall, thin figure in black who moved around in life as quietly as a few pints of motor oil. His skin was deathly pale, and his eyes looked like water at the bottom of a very deep well. From time to time his enlarged tongue would come out of his mouth like a huge eel, to taste the air in front of it. John knew that Palis was a kind of djinn vampire and that his tongue was looking for human blood. Knowing this didn't make the sight of Palis's tongue any less a source of horrible fascination to John, and aware that the young djinn was staring at him with intense curiosity, Palis looked at him with dead eyes and said, "What are you staring at, you ugly little pup?"

Steeling himself, John answered in kind. "I think I'd rather be an ugly little pup, than an old and rabid dog," he said. "Moreover a dog that's not even house-trained."

Nimrod laughed. "Bravo, John," he said. "Bravo."

"John, is it?" sneered Palis. "You certainly smell like one."

"I'm surprised you can smell anything with that snake

halfway up your nose," said John. He was starting to enjoy himself. Like any twelve-year-old schoolboy, insulting people – mostly other kids in the school yard – was something he'd had a lot of practise doing. "With a tongue like that they should keep you in a post office to lick the stamps."

"Touché," murmured Nimrod.

"Choose your next witticism carefully, boy," hissed Palis. "It may be your last."

Nimrod shook his head. "As always, Palis, you rise to the occasion like damp on a dirty wall. I'm afraid your last remark constitutes a threat, which contravenes the convention of insulting in this tournament: insults only, no threats. I'm afraid you'll have to withdraw that last remark and apologize to the boy, or leave the Algonquin."

Palis was silent for a moment.

"Of course, I could always ask the Blue Djinn herself for an adjudication," said Nimrod.

Palis licked his lips noisily and smiled a crooked sort of smile. "No need for that," he said, making a polite gesture of defeat. "My apologies, young djinn. It's impressive the way you manage to sound like a wit when you come from a tribe that hasn't got any."

But before John could reply in kind, Palis had bowed and withdrawn.

"Bottle me, but that was well done," said Nimrod. "The way you bested him like that. Congratulations."

In Djinnversoctoannular, the seven astaragali, or dice, are rolled and offered to the next player in a closed crystal box with a bid that has to improve on the previous bid. A bid is challenged with the word "mendax", whereupon the lid of the box is lifted and the astaragali inspected; at this point the player who makes the bid or the player who challenges the bid loses one of three "wishes" depending upon whether the bid amounts to less than what is found in the box, or more.

Philippa's first-round match found her pitted against three players, including Marek Qutrub, a poisonous sort of character whose breath smelled of raw meat, and Rudyard Teer, who was the youngest son of Iblis, of the Ifrit.

Having challenged Qutrub successfully, which cost him one of his three wishes, it was Philippa's turn to throw first and, having done so, she found that she had an Ark – four of one kind, plus three of a different kind. She closed the box and, handing it to the next player, who was Rudyard Teer, made her bid. An Ark was an excellent first throw and it was plain that Teer didn't believe her bid. But Teer held Philippa partly responsible for what had happened to his father, and now refused to speak to her. As a result he was obliged to inform Mr Bunyip, the game's umpire, that he was challenging the bid. And, being a true Ifrit, he swore loudly when he opened the box and discovered that Philippa's bid had been true. It was enough to earn him an official warning for bad language.

"Ugh," grimaced the fourth player, Zadie Eloko, who was the game's only other good djinn – a Jann from Jamaica. "It makes my backbone curl when you swear like that."

Rudyard Teer thrust the crystal box at the Jamaican Jann with bad grace. "And what, pray, would you know about backbones?" he said. "If your tribe had one

69

backbone among them they wouldn't have made themselves the servants of mundanes."

It was a remark that cost Teer another wish, for insults were not permitted to players, only to spectators. And Philippa sailed through the first round without dropping a wish, which surprised many who had assumed that Marek Qutrub would provide the main challenge to Lilith de Ghulle.

"Come on," said Nimrod after the game. "*She* wants to meet you."

"Who's *she*?"

"Ayesha, of course. She-Who-Must-Be-Obeyed. The iron lady, that's who."

CHAPTER 6

THE BADROULBADOUR RULE

Ayesha was sitting in a corner of the Oak Room behind a large round table. Beside her sat a small, dusty-looking woman. Seeing Philippa approach with her uncle, Ayesha shooed the woman away and smiled coldly. "Sit down, child," she told Philippa. "Don't be frightened. I won't bite you."

She was a little frightened of Ayesha, but Philippa sat down anyway, and clasped her hands tightly, as if holding on to herself for comfort's sake.

Ayesha looked sharply at Nimrod. "Don't you have something you could be doing, Nimrod?"

"Yes, of course," agreed Nimrod. "I can go and speak to Edwiges the Wandering Djinn. It's nice to see her back in djinn society again."

Ayesha laughed scornfully. "There's no such thing as djinn society," she said. "Look around, Philippa. There is a living tapestry of good djinn and bad djinn and the quantity of luck in the world depends only on how much each of us is prepared to take responsibility for ourselves."

Nimrod smiled politely, as if he didn't quite agree with Ayesha, and then went to look for Edwiges.

"Why is she called 'the Wandering Djinn'?" Philippa asked Ayesha.

"Edwiges? Because she travels around the world in a hopeless quest to help mundanes defeat the gambling casinos that the Ifrit have made for the greater bad luck of humankind."

"Why is it hopeless?"

"Where gambling is concerned, the mundanes do not want to be helped. Logically, good luck only seems like good luck if there exists the alternative possibility of bad luck. That is the thrill of gambling. But I didn't ask you here to discuss the philosophy of gambling. Let me look at you, child."

Philippa said nothing for a moment as the Blue Djinn scrutinized her with the close attention of someone buying a new car.

"You are your mother's daughter, all right."

"Do you know my mother well?"

Ayesha laughed. "Well enough to lament that she has turned her back on her own destiny and chosen to be something that she is not. Or never could be."

"And what's that?"

"Mundane." Ayesha shook her head. "That the best of us should pretend to be an ordinary human is such a waste. Don't you think?"

Philippa didn't answer. "Is that why you and she were arguing at the Pierre Hotel?" And then, before Ayesha could deny this, as Mrs Gaunt had done, Philippa added, "I saw you."

"Oh. You'd better ask your mother about that."

"I did."

"And what did she say?"

"Not much."

"It's her affair, I suppose." Ayesha sniffed loudly, wiped her nose with a handkerchief, and then changed the subject. "And how are you enjoying your first Djinnverso Tournament?"

"Very much," said Philippa. "Only – it's just that the better I do, the more seems to be expected of me. At least, that's the feeling I have. Weird, really. I mean, no one's said anything. But it's there, you know?"

Ayesha nodded. "Yes, I know that feeling, Philippa. In the beginning I did not welcome it. Of course, things are different now. I think I have the strength to do anything that I feel has to be done. Even if what has to be done is sometimes very difficult, and not what we would choose to do. Something for the greater good. You understand?"

"I think so," said Philippa, hardly understanding at all.

"What I mean to say is that it's nothing personal. Try to remember that."

Philippa nodded, although by now she was certain she had no idea what Ayesha was talking about. She thought Ayesha looked about eighty years old, which, given the slower rate of djinn ageing, meant she was probably at least 250 years old. She therefore assumed that being so old, Ayesha might have difficulty in gathering her thoughts coherently. This is a mistake that all young people, not just djinn, commonly make about old people. It hardly occurred to Philippa that Ayesha was making perfect sense; but it wasn't until much later on that Philippa was certain of this.

"Any other questions, child?" Ayesha asked Philippa.

"Yes. Why is the Blue Djinn always a woman?"

"Because on earth there is a universal law that applies

to both djinnkind and humankind. When something needs to be said, you look for a man to say it. But when something needs actually to be done, you look for a woman. Does that answer your question?"

"Yes." Philippa smiled.

"We women have to stick together, Philippa."

"Yes, Ayesha."

"I've enjoyed our little talk, very much. Now off you go and play your next game. And remember what I said."

"Yes, Ayesha."

John watched his sister talking to the Blue Djinn with a mixture of admiration and fear. The idea that this little old woman with a handbag could ruthlessly have ordered Iblis exiled to Venus for ten years was hard to believe. A voice from behind seemed to echo John's thoughts.

"She's losing it, man," said the voice.

John turned to find himself looking at a heavyset boy, perhaps sixteen or seventeen years old. Not a handsome boy so much as one whose features showed a lot of character. He spoke in a softly thunderous, vaguely accented voice that smelled strongly of tobacco.

"She's getting old and forgetful and that makes her dangerous," said the boy. "Not just to herself. But to all of djinnkind. This is why I need to speak to Nimrod, as a matter of urgency."

"And you are?"

"Izaak Balayaga," said the boy, holding out his hand.

John reached to shake it, remembering only at the last moment to fold his middle finger against his palm.

"I work for Ayesha," explained Izaak. "I'm the djinn

guard at the Topkapi Palace in Istanbul."

"That's the capital of Turkey, right?"

"Wrong." Izaak smiled in a superior sort of way. "The capital of Turkey is Ankara. Although I don't know why I would expect an American to know that. Geography's just a word in the dictionary for you people, isn't it?"

John guessed that he was being insulted only because it was the tournament's custom. "Assuming that you're able to remember," he said, "what does a djinn guard do, exactly?"

"Simple."

"I guess it would have to be simple," said John. "Otherwise you'd be looking for another job."

Izaak acknowledged the insult with a polite nod of the head. "Very large gemstones have the capacity to magnify a djinn's power. In the same way that you need a ruby or a garnet to make a solid-state laser. One of the ways djinn power works is because energized atoms release photons, right?"

John nodded vaguely and wondered if the moonstone on Mr Vodyannoy's ring had been used to this effect.

"Well, a gemstone helps pump those atoms to get them into a more excited state. As much as two or three levels above what a djinn might achieve on his own. Nothing to it. Anyway, there's a famous jewelled dagger displayed at the Topkapi Palace that has to be guarded against some djinn trying to steal it. Other djinn guards have similar duties at important royal treasuries all over the world. I assume you've heard stories of how certain large diamonds and rubies can be cursed?"

"Yes, of course," said John, who was already beginning

to grow a little tired of the older boy.

"Well, that's all rubbish. Diamonds don't have curses. It's just that some djinn, not mentioning any names you understand, used to be very vindictive to the human owners of large gemstones. To deter mundanes from owning them. And so they could get their hands on the stones themselves. Gems are the one thing djinn can't make, despite what people might think. This is why most of the really big stones are in museums these days. And guarded by other djinn. D'you see?"

"I see," said John, but at the same time he thought it was a little remiss of Mr Rakshasas not to have made mention of such important information in the SBR.

"It used to be that once a year the Topkapi dagger was removed from its display case," said Izaak. "And, by convention, forty of the Turkish Sultan's men, including a djinn especially appointed by the Blue Djinn herself, had to be present. That djinn was one of my ancestors. Which is how I happen to be doing the job today."

"But Turkey is now a Republic, isn't it?" asked John. "Which means that these days, there's no Sultan."

"Clever boy," smiled Izaak. "You're not as dumb as you look."

"I can always read another book," said John. "But you'll always be ugly."

Izaak grinned. "You're quite good at this insult thing," he said.

"I have a sister," said John. "I get plenty of practice."

"The Sultan may be gone. But a djinn still has to be present when they bring out the dagger. I have to be there with some aloes bark and some words of binding from Solomon's Grimoire to make sure no djinn gets his or her hands on the dagger. That's what I wanted to speak to Nimrod about."

"The Topkapi dagger?"

"No, dork. The grimoire. Solomon's book."

John recalled Nimrod having mentioned it. "That's an important book, right?"

"There are only three known grimoires of any importance to the djinn," said Izaak. "There used to be a fourth: the *Bellili Scrolls*. But those were destroyed when Julius Caesar burned down the great library at Alexandria. So today there are just three. The *Summa Arcanus*, the *Meta Magus*, and the *Book of Solomon*. Of the three, Solomon's Grimoire is by far the most important. Using the invocations that are detailed in that book it is possible for a djinn or a magus to achieve absolute power over many djinn. Because of its great importance, the Solomon Grimoire has been kept by the Blue Djinn for more than two thousand years. She keeps it in a special Heisenberg Electron safe at her court in Berlin."

"A what kind of safe?"

"Heisenberg Electron," said Izaak. "It's the most secure safe in the universe. Any attempt to discover the combination will unavoidably change it. The combination doesn't exist until it has been observed, and the only person who can do that is Ayesha because the safe actually uses some of the electrons from her own atoms." He shook his head impatiently. "Anyway, that's neither here nor there because, of late, she's started forgetting to put Solomon's Grimoire back in the safe after she's used it, and now it's gone missing. The old bat doesn't even know about it. On account of the fact that she's almost completely gaga. I'm the only one who knows what's happened."

"Holy cow," said John. "I can see why you want to speak to Nimrod. It's a matter of life and death that we get this book back to the Blue Djinn's safekeeping, right?"

Izaak shook his head. "Actually it's far more important than that," he said. "Forgive me speaking to you like this, but I don't know Nimrod and it's a convention of the tournament that, if you're a junior djinn like me, you are forbidden to speak to senior djinn unless you've first been introduced or insulted. I saw you speaking to him earlier, and I had hoped that you could introduce me."

"Nothing easier," said John. "Nimrod is my uncle."

"Then you must be the famous John Gaunt. One of the twins who defeated the evil Iblis. I've heard a great deal about you and your sister."

"You have?" John glanced around the room nervously. He was still a little surprised at how many evil djinn were present at the tournament. At least three members of Iblis's immediate family were present, one of whom, Jonathan Teer, was standing only a few steps away.

"Thanks," said John. "But keep it down, OK? Some of the djinn in this room aren't too happy about what happened."

"Yes, of course. How very thoughtless of me."

"Forget about it. Now come and say hello to my uncle Nimrod."

They crossed the thickly carpeted floor of the Oak Room to where Nimrod, easily visible in his usual red suit, was part of a crowd of djinn that was paying very close attention to a Djinnverso game.

"Hey, Uncle Nimrod," said John. "There's a young djinn here who would like to meet you."

Nimrod said nothing, and merely blew a smoke ring above John's head that read ssssh!

"It's kind of urgent," John whispered. "A matter of life and death."

"It's more important than that," insisted Izaak.

Nimrod bent closer to the two younger djinn. "I'm sorry, John, but it will have to wait a while. Can't you see? Your sister is in the djunior final."

Including Philippa, there were three other djinn in the game: Patricia Nixie, from Germany, Yuki Onna from Japan, and Lilith de Ghulle. Lilith had just shouted, "Mendax," challenging Patricia's bid of Aaron's Silver (five of a kind) and, much to her obvious chagrin, she had lost a wish. This left Philippa as the only person in the game with all three wishes intact.

Yuki Onna threw the astaragali and, with a bid of just a Magi (three of a kind), handed Philippa the crystal box.

Philippa glanced coolly at the contents of the box, found three of Fire, and collected the remaining four astaragali in her hand. "Throwing four," she said, obeying the Paribanon Rule stipulating that a player had to be truthful about the number of astaragali being rolled. Glancing over the dice, Philippa could hardly believe her own luck. She'd added four Fire to the three given to her by Patricia, making a Bastion (seven of a kind and, being the highest throw in Djinnverso, quite unbeatable).

Philippa considered the matter for a moment. If she bid Bastion to Patricia, Patricia would have no choice but to challenge her and lose a wish; instead, she decided to gun for Lilith, to whom Patricia would make her own bid. And looking Patricia squarely in the eye, with meaning, Philippa said, "Ruby and Garnet," underbidding what was in the box, in the hope that Patricia would take it and then pass the box to Lilith without throwing any of the astaragali.

This was exactly what happened. And Lilith had no option but to challenge Patricia's bid, with a loud, "Mendax," that turned into an even louder howl of outrage when she saw how Philippa had set her up. Around the table there was a general murmur of appreciation at the subtlety of Philippa's play. This feeling was not shared by Lilith de Ghulle, however.

"So you want to play rough, do you, baby cakes?" Lilith said through the retainers on her yellow teeth.

"I'm just taking you at your word, Lilith," said Philippa. "Djinnverso's a game for grown-ups? That's what you said, isn't it?"

"Funny girl," said Lilith. Since now she had only one wish left, it was her turn to throw first and, having done so, Lilith stared at the seven astaragali angrily for almost a minute, rearranging them obsessively, before closing the box and handing it to Yuki Onna. "Pentad," she said sulkily. (A Pentad is three of a kind, plus two of a kind.)

Yuki took the box, opened it, inspected the astaragali, and announced that she was throwing just one. She made her throw, closed the box, announced that her bid was a Square (four of a kind) and handed the box to Philippa.

Philippa found a Square and a pair and threw just one

astaragali in the hope of making an Ark, but found that she could not improve on the astaragali she had been given. Since Yuki's bid had not included the pair, Philippa only had to add them to the bid. "Square and a pair," she said, handing the box to Patricia.

Patricia deliberated for a moment, accepted Philippa's bid, and opened the astaragali box. Raising an eyebrow, she closed the lid, without throwing any, and handed the box to Lilith. "Ruby and Garnet," she said.

Lilith shook her head. Ruby and Garnet had been what Philippa had bid when a Bastion was actually lying in the box. "No way," she said firmly, adding, "Mendax." And, opening the box, screamed with disbelief as she found yet another Bastion lying there. Lilith was out.

Or so she thought.

"Wait a minute," said Yuki Onna. "That can't be right. My bid to Philippa was a Square. I handed her on a Square and a pair, and she threw one."

"That's right," said Philippa. "And that was what I handed on to Patricia."

"But when I opened the box I found a Bastion," insisted Patricia. "I thought you were doing the same thing as last time. Trying to set up Lilith again. Which is why I didn't throw any and bid her a Ruby and a Garnet – six of a kind."

Yuki Onna bowed politely to Patricia and then to Philippa, as if she could hardly bring herself to utter what she now proceeded to say, "Well, I'm very sorry, but one of you must be lying. There's no way Philippa could have thrown just one astaragali and made Bastion from a Square and a pair."

81

"It would appear," declared Mr Duergar, the match umpire, "that one of you two cheated. One of you must have used djinn power to move the astaragali after the lid was closed."

"Isn't the whole point of the crystal box supposed to be that it can detect cheating?" asked Philippa. "Isn't it supposed to glow if someone tries to use djinn power on it?"

Mr Duergar, who was a very short Englishman, picked up the crystal box and, having examined it, allowed djinn power to leak from his fingers into the box. But instead of turning red, as it ought to have done, the box remained unaffected. "This box is a fake," he said angrily.

There was a gasp around the Oak Room as the many djinn watching the match heard what Mr Duergar had said.

"Come with me, both of you," said Mr Duergar. "I'm afraid the match referee will have to decide."

Everyone watched as Mr Duergar went over to the round table in the corner of the Oak Room – for, of course, the match referee was none other than the Blue Djinn herself – and, accompanied by Philippa and Patricia, he proceeded to make an official report about the incident.

Philippa had a bad feeling about this. She knew very well that she hadn't cheated, but now she could not help but recall Ayesha's strange words to her. They had left her with the strong suspicion that, somehow, she was being framed.

"In all my years," spluttered Mr Duergar, shaking his tiny head. "I've never known such a thing. Really I haven't.

I demand that Your Excellency deals with this most severely."

Ayesha blinked slowly at Mr Duergar liked a bored cat. It was evident that she didn't care for him; but it was equally evident that everyone expected her to do something. Ayesha held up her hand if only to stop Mr Duergar's complaints – as if he himself were the injured party.

"The truth will out," she said gravely. She pointed first at Patricia, who shook her head very firmly. "The power of Ishtar compels you."

As soon as Ayesha uttered these words, Patricia felt herself in the grip of a very strong force that seemed to squeeze that part of her we might call a conscience. It was not an unpleasant feeling, nor was it particularly enjoyable, either. And the enduring sensation was that she had been stripped to the mental equivalent of a swimsuit in front of every djinn in the room.

"I didn't do it," she said, blushing very noticeably. "I didn't do it, I swear."

Ayesha nodded, satisfied that Patricia had only spoken the truth. Then she looked at Philippa who by now was very aware that everyone was looking at her intently, silently awaiting her answer.

"The truth will out," Ayesha repeated, in her flat English accent, and pointed one bony finger at Philippa. "The power of Ishtar compels you."

Philippa told herself that as long as she told the truth she would be fine. This is a useful maxim in life and one that all people, everywhere, even in Crete, should adhere to. However, where the djinn are concerned such matters are not always as simple as first they might seem. She opened her mouth to speak and found that she could not, as if somehow she had been rendered mute. There was no doubt about it. There was another djinn inside her. And even as she realized it, she felt the djinn take charge of her lungs, her voice box, her tongue, and her lips to answer the Blue Djinn's compulsion. Philippa tried to close her mouth, but could not. She tried to put her hand to her mouth, but could not. She even tried to shake her head to deny what she knew the voice was going to say, but could not. Like everyone else in the Oak Room, all she could do was listen to the voice that came from inside her.

"All right," said the voice which, Philippa had to admit, sounded a lot like her own. "I cheated. I switched the crystal box for an imitation one, and used djinn power to turn the astaragali after the lid was closed. It's a stupid game, anyway, and I don't care two pence who knows it. Do you hear, you old bat? I don't care tuppence."

There was a loud gasp around the Oak Room at the ferocity of Philippa's "confession". Bad enough to cheat, but to call the Blue Djinn an "old bat" on top of it, seemed too outrageous. Even to Philippa. But though the voice inside her had now stopped, Philippa herself remained quite unable to speak and contradict what everyone now believed she had said.

"You all heard her," said Ayesha, looking around the room. "She was compelled to speak the truth. She stands condemned by her own words."

Since Ayesha clearly hadn't compelled Philippa to do anything of the sort, Philippa was already asking herself if it had been Ayesha who had made her lie. Except that she was still aware of the other djinn inside her – she could not yet say who this was – controlling Philippa in exactly the same way that she had controlled the squirrel in Central Park.

"I shall ignore the insult to our own person," said Ayesha. "We care nothing for such matters. But using djinn power in the Djinnversoctoannular Tournament is a clear contravention of the Badroulbadour Rule. For which there can be but one punishment. Philippa Gaunt. You are disqualified from this tournament, and all Djinnverso Tournaments, in perpetuity. Do you have anything to say?"

Philippa had a good deal to say, the only trouble was that she could not say it. "Nothing at all," declared the alien voice inside her. "And you can stick your disqualification up—"

"THEN YOU MAY GO!" thundered Ayesha and pointed to the Oak Room door.

It was now that the other djinn chose to leave Philippa's body and, finding herself in control of her own speech centres again, it crossed her mind to speak up in her own defense. This time the only thing that stopped Philippa was the emotion welling up inside her. Philippa wanted to cry, and badly, but would not. She wanted to scream out loud at the injustice of it all, but would not. She wanted to throw herself on the floor and beat the carpet with her fists and declare that she had been framed, but would not. What, she asked herself, would have been the point? Whoever had done this to her – and with so many of the Ifrit present, there was surely no shortage of gloating suspects – was probably hoping she would humiliate herself even further. So she would not

85

give them that satisfaction. Maintaining her composure, her head high, and holding back the tears, Philippa walked to the door of the Oak Room and out into the hotel lobby.

"I don't get it," John told Nimrod. "Phil's never cheated. She's been framed."

"I don't doubt it," murmured Nimrod. "Philippa would never have said 'two pence' or 'tuppence.'"

"You're right," said John. "She'd have said two cents, wouldn't she? Hadn't we better tell someone?"

"Now is not the time. The Blue Djinn has spoken. It wouldn't do to challenge her judgment in front of everyone. We shall have to approach this matter in some other way." He gestured at the door. "Until then, you'd best follow her. See that she gets home all right."

"Yes, sir," said John, and went after his sister.

Nimrod turned to Izaak Balayaga who was staring off into space. "Now then," he said, a little irritably. "What exactly is it you wanted of me?"

"Mmmm?"

"My nephew, John, said there was something important you wanted to speak to me about."

"I'm sorry, sir, for a moment there, I was miles away."

"A matter of life and death, John said," said Nimrod.

"Actually sir, it's more important than that."

CHAPTER 7

THE ROYAL HUNGARIAN EXPRESS

"You do believe me, don't you?" said a very tearful Philippa. She was in the living room at home, sitting as close to the fire as it was possible to sit without actually catching fire herself. With her were John, her mother, Uncle Nimrod, and Mr Rakshasas, who remained in the lamp that was his home, inside Nimrod's pocket.

"Of course we believe you," said John, and repeated what Nimrod had said about how she would never have said "two pence" instead of "two cents."

"Then why didn't you say something at the time?" said Philippa.

"Because it wouldn't have done any good," said Nimrod. "Whoever framed you, Philippa, went to a great deal of trouble to do it properly. For a start, they had a Djinnverso box made that was an exact copy of a tournament crystal box. The real boxes are made of fluorite, because of its thermoluminescent properties. Fluorite glows, when the heat of djinn power is detected. The actual box used however was made of lechatelierite – a cheap, non-crystalline mineral that possesses no fluorescent or thermoluminiscent qualities whatsoever, but still feels like fluorite.

"Moreover, whoever took possession of your body

knew they only had to do it until after the Blue Djinn had given her judgement, after which no one in the room would have dared question her authority."

"But surely," objected John, "if Ayesha really had used the power of Ishtar to compel the truth to come forth, then the djinn possessing Philippa would also have been subject to that power."

"Indeed, so," agreed Nimrod. "And that's what makes whoever did this thing so very clever. You see, John, the djinn inside Philippa – whoever that was – spoke no more than the truth when he or she 'confessed' to having switched the boxes and used djinn power to turn the astaragali. Except, of course, that everyone thought it was Philippa making the confession. It was a very skillful piece of deception."

"This is what happens when you mix with djinn," said Mrs Gaunt. "Some of them are devils. Nasty, disgusting creatures. Which is why, long ago, I decided to have nothing more to do with them and their stupid tricks. Perhaps now you can understand why I have tried so hard to keep you away from djinnkind. I wanted to protect you both from just this kind of thing."

"And if all of us did what you have done, Layla?" Nimrod said gently. "Where would the world be now? Like it or not, we djinn are the keepers of the luck in this universe. With a responsibility to protect the Homoeostasis."

The Homoeostasis is what djinn call the balance that exists between good luck and bad luck; the amount of luck in the world, good or bad is measured by means of a tuchemeter, of which the largest and most accurate, is to be found in Berlin, at the court of the Blue Djinn of Babylon.

"It's up to us to make sure that the bad luck generated by evil djinn does not outweigh the good luck generated by tribes like ours."

Having decided that, perhaps, she had misjudged Ayesha after all, Philippa began to cry again, which drew an exasperated sigh from her mother. "It was so humiliating, Mother," said Philippa. "And in front of everyone, too."

"I know, dear. But Nimrod's right. There's really nothing we can do. Once her mind has been made up, Ayesha is not the kind of woman who goes back on her decision. That lady is not easily turned around."

"I didn't actually say that," said Nimrod. "I said that the Oak Room was the wrong time and place to persuade her to change her mind. There may be a way of getting Ayesha to rescind Philippa's disqualification and thereby restore Philippa's reputation in front of the rest of djinnkind. Indeed, for Ayesha not do so might be to risk her own reputation."

"What are you talking about, Nimrod?" asked Mrs Gaunt.

"Just this. Someone has stolen the Solomon Grimoire."

"But that's impossible." Mrs Gaunt sounded appalled. "How?"

"I'm glad you understand the seriousness of this matter, Layla," said Nimrod. "Can you imagine what might happen if the Ifrit, the Ghul, or the Shaitan ever got their hands on that book?"

"Of course I can," she said. "I may prefer to stay out of

djinn affairs, Nimrod, but that doesn't make me an idiot. The grimoire falling into the wrong hands would be disastrous. No djinn, good or bad, would be safe."

"Not even djinn who wanted to stay out of djinn affairs," said Nimrod.

"Point taken,'" said Mrs Gaunt.

"I remember you telling John and me about Solomon's *Big Book of Moans,*" said Philippa. "Is it the same book?"

"Sadly, no," said Nimrod. "This book is much more important than that. It contains various incantations that give the user limitless power over all djinn. With the use of such an incantation, any one of us would be forever bound to the service of another. It would mean endless slavery. Not to mention a complete collapse of the Homoeostasis. The world, as we know it, would collapse into chaos and anarchy."

"But how on earth did this happen?" asked Mrs Gaunt. "Ayesha is supposed to keep the Solomon Grimoire in conditions of absolute djinnproof security. In a special unbreakable safe designed by a famous German scientist. I remember her telling us about it. And why hasn't she mentioned this to someone? How does she justify taking time out to referee some stupid Djinnverso Tournament when this has happened?"

"Because she doesn't yet know it's missing," said Nimrod. "At least, that's what I've been led to believe."

"By who?"

"Izaak Balayaga."

"I've never heard of him," confessed Mrs Gaunt.

"He's a djinn guard at the Topkapi Palace in Istanbul," John told his mother. "And now I understand. This is the matter of life and death he was going on about."

"Actually, it's more important than that," said Nimrod.

"But how does he know the Solomon Grimoire has been stolen?" asked John. "He works in Istanbul, not Berlin."

"Because Izaak Balayaga was the djinn who stole it," said Nimrod. "Ayesha had taken the book out of the Heisenberg Electron safe to give him the words of an incantation traditionally used to protect the Topkapi dagger from any djinn who might occupy the diamond scabbard. According to Izaak, Ayesha took the book out of the safe and then simply forgot to put it back."

"The idiot boy," said Mrs Gaunt. "What on earth possessed him to go and steal it?"

"The temptation was too much for him," said Nimrod. "Of course, now he regrets it. He took the book on an impulse and now he can't put it back because he can't open the safe. No one can except Ayesha. And he's afraid that if he tells her what he's done she will deal as harshly with him as she dealt with Iblis. Which is why he wants me to intercede with Ayesha on his behalf."

"She's too old to be doing this," said Mrs Gaunt. "It's quite ridiculous that there's no provision for the Blue Djinn to retire. The sooner she nominates her successor, the better. Even if it is Mimi de Ghulle. Has she made the announcement yet?"

Nimrod shook his head. "No, thank goodness."

"But how does any of this help Philippa?" asked John.

"Yes, I'm not sure I understand that myself," admitted Mrs Gaunt.

"Well, for one thing," said Nimrod. "It would

embarrass Ayesha if the theft of the Solomon Grimoire became well-known. Not that I would ever dream of telling anyone other than you three, and Ayesha herself, of course. More important than that, however, Izaak doesn't quite trust me enough to hand the Solomon Grimoire over to me personally. He has said he will only hand the book to John and Philippa. Apparently, he thinks it less likely that you two will try to stop him up inside a lamp or bottle. Possibly, he doesn't think you're powerful enough to do it, either."

"And where and when does he propose that this handover should take place?" asked Mrs Gaunt.

"On a train between Istanbul and Berlin," said Nimrod. "In two days from now."

"It could be a trap," said Mrs Gaunt. "You know that, don't you? At this time of year it will be cold on that train. The twins will have no power and, therefore, no means of protecting themselves. Izaak Balayaga has probably guessed as much."

"I've thought of that," said Nimrod. "And I've thought of a way of protecting the twins."

"A discrimen?" she asked.

Nimrod nodded.

"What's a discrimen?" asked Philippa.

"An emergency wish," said John, and shrugged. "I read about them in the SBR." Very anxious to go to Berlin and Istanbul as he now was, John thought he would wait a few minutes, until Nimrod had finished describing his plan, before telling him about the discrimen that Mr Vodyannoy had given him. Which is how it was that he forgot to mention it at all.

"We simply can't pass up the chance to see the safe return to Berlin of *Solomon's Grimoire*," said Nimrod.

"And then what happens?" asked Mrs Gaunt.

"Philippa wins Ayesha's undying gratitude for her part in the recovery, of course." Nimrod looked at the twins. "That is, if you two are ready and willing to help. I'm sorry, but being the sort of plucky young djinn you are, naturally I assumed you'd both be up for this."

"Of course we're up for it," insisted John. "Aren't we, Phil?"

Philippa nodded firmly. "Yes," she said. "No question about it."

"I've always wanted to go to Istanbul," he added. "And Berlin."

"This will be no sightseeing tour, John," said Nimrod. "It might even be dangerous. As your mother has said, it could very well be a trap."

"If it is a trap," mused Mrs Gaunt, "I'm not sure what kind of trap it could be. If the Ifrit were already in possession of the Solomon Grimoire, then surely they'd have used it against us, by now. And where better than at the Djinnverso Tournament? Where so many djinn were assembled." She frowned thoughtfully. "If the Ifrit, the Shaitan, or the Ghul do have some sort of angle here, then I can't see it."

"Am I to take it," said Nimrod, "that you agree they can go to Istanbul?"

"I'll have to ask their father." She looked at Nimrod's quizzical eye and shrugged. "If you'd ever been married, Nimrod, you'd know that marriage is a partnership. Important decisions have to be made jointly."

"All marriages are happy," observed Mr Rakshasas, from the inside of his lamp. "'Tis having breakfast together that causes all the trouble."

"But provided he agrees," Mrs Gaunt said loudly, for the benefit of Mr Rakshasas, "then, yes, they can go."

But Mr Gaunt did not agree. Not at first, anyway. And it took most of that evening for him to be persuaded. He was a perceptive man, however, and he suspected that Mrs Gaunt would not have persisted in asking him to let the twins accompany their uncle to Istanbul unless she herself had thought their mission was a vital one. "Is it really that important?" he asked her.

"Yes," said Mrs Gaunt. "I'm afraid it is."

"And dangerous?" he asked.

"It might be," admitted Mrs Gaunt. "But I strongly believe that the end justifies the risk."

"If they don't retrieve this book – Solomon's Grim Wire, or whatever it's called – is it possible some harm might come to us?" he asked.

"Yes," said Mrs Gaunt. "And not just us, Edward. Perhaps a great many others – djinn and human alike."

Mr Gaunt was not a tall man – not nearly as tall or as glamorous as his statuesque wife. Short, with longish grey hair and tinted glasses, he looked like a very clever scientist or a university professor. And he never made any important decisions without thinking through all the possible outcomes. These he now proceeded to discuss with Nimrod and Mrs Gaunt at even greater length before, finally, he agreed to let his children travel to Turkey with their uncle. "I have one condition," he announced. "And it is this. That Alan and Neil accompany you. Those dogs are every bit as good as any bodyguards."

"I was going to suggest it myself," said Nimrod.

"And how will you all get there, Nimrod? To Istanbul? I don't want the kids flying there on board some wing-and-a-prayer outfit."

"You can rely on me," said Nimrod. "I'll make sure we choose the safest carrier possible."

"Oh? What airline is that, do you think?"

"A private charter," said Nimrod. "At my own expense, of course."

Mr Gaunt nodded his approval. "Good idea," he said. "Makes it easier with the dogs, I suppose."

"Yes," said Nimrod. "There's that, too."

Naturally, Mr Gaunt assumed that when Nimrod mentioned a private charter, he had been talking about some kind of airplane – a Gulfstream IV, a Falcon or, at the very least, a Learjet. And he might not have looked quite so reassured if Nimrod had admitted that he actually planned to fly himself, the twins, the two dogs, and the lamp containing Mr Rakshasas 4,975 miles to Istanbul on top of an artificial whirlwind.

"There's simply no time to go on a scheduled flight," he told the twins as, very early the next morning, they prepared to leave New York from the rooftop of the famous Guggenheim Museum. "Besides, we've got to pick up Groanin. He'll be back in London now after his holiday in Manchester. There's nothing he hates more than traveling by whirlwind. But that can't be helped."

Groanin was the name of Nimrod's one-armed butler and chauffeur, whose habitually miserable and complaining nature concealed a man of considerable resourcefulness and courage; moreover he was extremely fond of John and Philippa.

Alan and Neil glanced nervously over the edge of the museum rooftop and uttered a series of high-pitched whines as the whirlwind that was going to carry them all across the Atlantic continued spinning its way up the outside of architect Frank Lloyd Wright's famous building. It was clear they shared Groanin's dislike of this unconventional means of air travel. Philippa realized that she was none too happy with the travel arrangements herself, preferring a means of flight that she could actually see.

"Why are we taking off from the Guggenheim?" she asked Nimrod.

"I always come here to make a really big whirlwind when I'm in New York," said Nimrod. "There's something about the inverted spiral shape of the building that makes it easier to whip up a good one. Besides, it renders whirlwind travel much more of an occasion, don't you think?"

"It's certainly that," said Philippa, swallowing uncomfortably. "But, won't it be cold?"

"Naturally, we're using warm air," said Nimrod, placing the lamp containing Mr Rakshasas carefully into his overcoat pocket. "Don't they teach you physics at school? Warm air rises."

"Relax," John told his sister, who felt like he was an old hand at whirlwind travel. "You're going to love it."

"If you say so," she muttered.

Emerging over the edge of the roof, the whirlwind

enveloped them gently with air, and it was several seconds before Philippa realized that they and their luggage had already left the top of the Guggenheim building. Alan and Neil yelped uncertainly as the roof grew smaller beneath their feet and, lying down, covered their eyes with their huge front paws.

"Sit down, sit down," Nimrod told the twins. "Just because you don't see it, doesn't mean you can't sit on it."

John grinned and dropped into what felt like a large invisible armchair; seeing her brother kick off his shoes and put his feet up, Philippa did the same. She found herself gently supported by what felt like a small cumulus cloud that shifted slightly to accommodate her whenever she moved, and breathed a sigh of relief. It was the most comfortable seat she had ever sat on.

As they rose high above Fifth Avenue, John realized that this whirlwind was slightly different from the one Mr Vodyannoy had created to take him home from the Dakota. For one thing, it was bigger and much more powerful, and for another, with this one they were surrounded by the whirlwind, rather than sitting on top.

They floated up and out of Manhattan like a hot-air balloon, heading southeast across New York's East River, Brooklyn, Rockaway Inlet, and Jacob Riis Park, before reaching the Atlantic Ocean. Here the whirlwind started to build up altitude and speed until Nimrod announced that travelling at approximately 750 miles per hour, they were climbing to five thousand feet to pick up the jet stream – a current of fast eastward air – and there achieve their top flight speed of 825 miles per hour.

"Which means we'll be in London in just over four

hours," said Nimrod. "And a couple of hours after that, in Istanbul."

"Four hours?" groaned John as they flew through a cloud, startling a flock of seagulls that were taking the morning air. "What on earth are we going to do for four hours?"

Alan sighed wearily and collapsed onto one side, as if echoing John's concerns.

"Where's your sense of poetry, boy?" demanded Nimrod. "William Wordsworth would have given his right arm to be where you are now."

"William who?" said John.

Nimrod shook his head sadly. He took the brass lamp containing Mr Rakshasas out of his coat pocket and shouted at it. "Do you hear that? The boy's first transatlantic whirlwind flight and he asks what he's going to do for four hours."

"I heard him," said Mr Rakshasas, who was warm and safe inside his lamp. "And sure, you'd think they taught them nothing in those schools of theirs. Just you remember, John: a scholar's ink lasts longer than a martyr's blood."

"Indeed it does," said Nimrod. "Light my lamp, John, this mode of travel is much better than the claustrophobia of a commercial jet." He took a deep and loudly enthusiastic lungful of air. "I mean, just smell that air. It's like being on a mountaintop in Switzerland."

"Oh, don't get me wrong," insisted John. "Really, I'm loving every minute of this. It's just that I wouldn't have minded a movie and an in-flight meal. Or two."

"With a pantry to raid," added Philippa. "Like they do

in business class." She thought for a moment. "And maybe the latest magazines?"

"Don't be angry with them, Nimrod," said Mr Rakshasas, and chuckled. "Aye, it's a bad dog that won't scratch itself, right enough."

Nimrod regarded his young niece and nephew with disappointment. He waved at the semiopaque interior of the whirlwind. "Please feel free to create your own ideal travelling environment," he said coolly.

John nodded. "We would, you know. It's just that well, we're not really warm enough to use djinn power."

"I see," said Nimrod, lighting a cigar. "I suppose you want me to do that for you." He sighed. "Very well. Only I absolutely refuse to watch one of those screens that are no bigger than a packet of cornflakes. If we must watch a movie let us watch one on a big screen."

He blew a smoke ring that flattened out and curved itself around the interior of the whirlwind until they were facing a silver movie screen that was 45 feet tall and seventy feet long. Alan and Neil sat up expectantly. It had been a while since they'd seen a movie on the big screen.

"Awesome," said John.

"Exactly," said Nimrod. "Of course, an awesome screen requires an awesome film. Not some piffling little art-house flick or googly-moogly cartoon. No, this film must be something suitable for djinn. Something about the desert. Something hot. Something inspiring. Something British. Yes, there's only one truly awesome film that fulfills all of those criteria. The greatest film ever made: *Lawrence of Arabia*. Marvellous stuff. These days, it's the only film I ever really watch."

And for the next three hours, they all sat back in the comfort of their warm air seats and watched *Lawrence of Arabia*. Which, incidentally, as Nimrod had correctly stated, is the greatest film ever made.

Arriving in London just after lunch, the whirlwind carried them up the Thames and across Kensington Gardens before depositing them in Nimrod's back garden. It had been a cold, windy day in London, and no one took any notice of the localized wind that waited for several minutes behind number 7, Stanhope Terrace while a stout figure wearing a long undertaker's coat and a black bowler hat, switched on the alarm, locked the back door, and walked quickly up the garden path, carrying a large leather bag with his one arm. For a moment, the figure stood facing the opaque curtain of wind that spun in front of his habitually disgruntled face. He was not happy to be travelling by whirlwind again. Removing his hat, to prevent it flying off, he tried not to feel too self-conscious as the pocket-size tornado treated the thin strip of hair that covered his otherwise bald head like a threadbare windsock.

"It's been a while since I travelled by one of these thermal conveyances, sir," yelled Groanin. "How do I get in, sir? Or do I mean get on?"

Groanin always called Nimrod "sir" when he was feeling particularly disgruntled about something.

"I'm sorry, Groanin," said Nimrod and lifted the skirts of the whirlwind a few feet off the ground so that his butler might step underneath.

Once inside the cone of rapidly twisting air, Groanin regarded the whirlwind with his habitual disapproval. "This is an unnatural way to travel, this. By hurricane.

Especially for a man with my stomach."

"It's not a hurricane," said Nimrod. "It's a whirlwind. There's a difference. And your stomach will be fine, as I think you know."

"If you say so, sir," said Groanin.

"It's nice to see you again, Mr Groanin," said Philippa, who realized how much she had missed Groanin's moaning.

"I've missed you, I say, I've missed you both, and that's a fact. And it's nice, I say, it's nice to see you both again, even if it does mean travelling like a pile of dead leaves."

"As a matter of fact," said John. "The flight over was much more comfortable than a commercial jet. I mean, there's no turbulence and no engine noise. And my ears don't feel like they're full of cotton."

Alan and Neil barked in agreement.

"Well, call me old-fashioned, son, but I like to see a floor beneath my feet and a roof over me head. To say nothing of a toilet with a door and a whiff of bleach. There's something reassuring about the smell of bleach."

"How was your holiday in Manchester?" said John.

"Terrible," said Groanin. He nodded respectfully in Nimrod's direction and changed the subject. "And where, sir, are we gallivanting off to this time, if I might make so bold?"

"Istanbul," said Nimrod. "And then Berlin."

"I hate Istanbul," said Groanin. "I say, I hate Istanbul. The place is full of foreigners, you know."

"What about Berlin, Mr Groanin?" said John, grinning: Groanin didn't seemed to have changed one bit.

"Full of ruddy Germans," he muttered sourly, and

settling back into his invisible armchair, he closed his eyes unhappily.

The sun was setting by the time they reached the Black Sea, so that the Black Sea really did look black. Nimrod's whirlwind took them south, down the River Bosphorous until, at the confluence with another river, the Golden Horn, they saw Istanbul's distinctive skyline of mosques and minarets, cupolas and television antennae. Philippa felt her heart leap as she took in her first view of this ancient city, deciding that it must have looked like the New York of the medieval world. Nimrod steered the whirlwind across the busy Galata Bridge, just to get his bearings, before taking a sharp left along the south bank of the Golden Horn. Finally, just as it was getting dark – which was probably just as well, since the Turks are a superstitious people, and might have regarded their mode of arrival with fear – they landed in the deserted gardens of the famous Topkapi Palace. It was raining and, to the twins' surprise, it felt chilly in Istanbul, even a little wintry, and John was glad he was wearing his fur-lined coat.

"This is where Izaak Balayaga works," said Nimrod pointing up at the palace. "It's about half a mile to Sirkeci Railway Station, from where the old Orient Express used to travel to Vienna, and then Paris. These days, the Royal Hungarian Express, which you'll be catching, is about as near as anyone can get to the old Orient Express experience. Anyway, this is as far as any of the rest of us can come with you both. Izaak was very specific about that. Neither I nor Mr Rakshasas is permitted to come within five hundred yards of the railway station. Alan and Neil will escort you there. I've told them the way."

Alan barked in agreement and then sniffed the ground carefully, making sure that he would be able to find his way back to this exact spot. He had little desire to be left behind in Istanbul.

"After that," said Nimrod, "you'll be on your own until you get to Berlin." He handed Philippa an envelope. "Here are your tickets. The train leaves in exactly one hour. And just so that you know, the train's scheduled to make four stops before it reaches Berlin. In Bulgaria, Transylvania, Budapest, and Prague. Izaak will join you at one of those stops, but only once he has assured himself that I am in Berlin, and you are travelling alone. If all goes well, he will make contact with you aboard the Express, and hand over the grimoire; I will be waiting to greet you at Zoo Station in Berlin. Any questions?"

"Did you say Transylvania?" Philippa asked Nimrod.

"Yes. The train stops at a town called Sighisoara. It's a nice little medieval place on top of a hill. Very picturesque," said Nimrod.

"I don't know about nice," Groanin snorted. "And it's only picturesque if you mean an old horror movie. Sighisoara was Count Dracula's hometown."

"Dracula?" John gulped loudly.

"Yes. You know. The vampire." Groanin chuckled. "If you take my advice, you'll keep your window shut in Sighisoara. And be sure not to cut yourself, neither. Blood, see? They can smell it a mile off."

Nimrod shot his butler a reproachful look, and then smiled reassuringly at John. "There's nothing at all to worry about," he insisted. "The original Count Dracula has been dead for centuries."

"There are some as might dispute that fact," said Groanin.

"Besides," continued Nimrod. "You'll have a nice firstclass compartment all to yourselves. And there's a superb restaurant car, so you can eat as much and often as you want. It's included in the price of your ticket."

"Just make sure that whatever you eat has lots of garlic in it," muttered Groanin. "They don't much like garlic, vampires. Matter of fact, I'm none too fond of it myself."

"And Philippa knows what to do in the event of an emergency, don't you, Philippa?" Nimrod smiled at his niece and tried to prompt her with a nod of his head.

"I do?" Then she remembered the emergency wish that Nimrod had given her for the journey and nodded back at him. "Oh, yes, I know what to do."

Nimrod glanced at his watch. "Right then," he said, rubbing his hands briskly. "You'd better get going. You don't want to miss the train." He hugged them both fondly. "Good luck," he said. "And be careful."

There was a shout from the lamp in Nimrod's coat pocket.

"May you have warm words on a cold evening," said Mr Rakshasas, adding, "*Go n-éirían bóthar leat,*" which is "Have a good journey" in Irish.

"Don't do anything, I say, don't do anything I wouldn't do."

Nimrod glanced sceptically at his butler. "Oh, no. That's not what's wanted at all," he said. "If it was up to you, Groanin, you wouldn't do anything or go anywhere. No, John and Philippa will have to be resourceful and intrepid."

"Better safe than sorry, that's what I always say," shrugged the one-armed butler.

Alan barked loudly and put a paw on John's wristwatch.

"The dog's right, though," admitted Groanin. "You'd best be going."

John and Philippa walked out of the Topkapi Gardens in the direction of Sirkeci Station. At the gate of the gardens, they turned and waved to Nimrod and Groanin and then followed the dogs west, along Ibnike Mal Caddessi, and then right onto Ankara Kaddesi. The dogs walked on either side of the twins, like two motorcycle escorts, scanning the route, ready for almost any kind of mundane trouble.

Istanbul was a very strange city but interesting, and the twins found themselves wishing they could have seen much more of it before boarding their train. It was much colder than they had expected, and both John and Philippa were thoughtful and silent as they realized that on a journey north to Germany, there really was no chance of the temperature becoming warm enough for them to use their powers.

Along the way, citizens of Istanbul regarded the twins and their big, powerful dogs with a mixture of friendly curiosity and caution. Of course, the Turks are a people who believe strongly in the existence of djinn, and there were a few who recognized the twins for what they were, but these hardly dared to speak to them for fear of the two rottweilers. As the twins entered the crowded station, a man offered to sell them a *simit*, a kind of ring-shaped pretzel, from a huge stack he was carrying around the main ticket hall, but swiftly withdrew when Neil growled at him.

It was a beautiful station and, on a handsome redbrick platform, with large stained-glass windows, they found the highly polished wooden train that was the Royal Hungarian Express. At the head of the train, a great red locomotive rumbled like a small electricity-generating station, while well-dressed Russians and Germans boarded the carriages, talking loudly among themselves and ignoring a platform vendor who was trying to sell them bottles of Fruko, a Turkish soft drink. The barrel-shaped stationmaster gripped a furled green flag and eyed the locomotive driver expectantly.

"This is as far as you guys can go," John told the dogs.

The two children knelt down to hug the huge heads of the two dogs who whined companionably, licked their faces, and then bounded off, back to the park where they had left Nimrod and Mr Groanin.

The twins climbed aboard the train, went along a carpeted corridor, and found their compartment. "This is great," said John throwing himself down on one seat and then another. "Look at this. And all to ourselves."

Minutes later, the train began to move, slowly and jerkily at first, as if the driver couldn't quite make up his mind whether to stay or to leave. Picking up some speed, they rounded the Seraglio Point, and then bounced along the coastline, before turning inland and northward, where the train went even faster.

"I wonder where Izaak will get on the train," said John.

"I wouldn't be at all surprised if he's already on the train," observed Philippa. "All that stuff about getting on somewhere between here and Berlin is probably designed to keep us guessing. It might be that he just calls Nimrod from the train. On a cell phone."

"How will he know if Nimrod's in Berlin?" asked John.

"Nimrod said that Izaak will call Nimrod's hotel in Berlin. And if he's there, he'll figure it's safe to make the handover."

"Maybe we should go and look for him now," suggested John.

"What's the point?" said Philippa. "He won't hand over the grimoire until he's ready. And we don't want to spook him into getting off the train."

"No, I suppose not." John stood up. "Then let's go and find the restaurant car. I'm hungry."

CHAPTER 8

TRANS-ELEMENTATION IN TRANSYLVANIA

The Royal Hungarian Express roared on through the night. Philippa fell asleep quite soon after dinner, but John concentrated on keeping awake. Just in case Izaak showed up. This wasn't easy, however, what with the carriage rocking like a cradle, and the hypnotically repetitive sound of the wheels on the railway track. He yawned several times, stretched like a cat, and pressed his face to the cold window, in the hope that he might see something of the moonlit landscape outside. But it was hard to make out anything at all, except his own face, bleary-eyed and pale-looking, reflected in the glass.

John let his eyes close for a moment. The moment became several longer moments as the movement of the train gently carried his thoughts to a quieter, darker place. When would Izaak get on the train? Why couldn't trains have TVs like planes? Why was the train station in Berlin in a zoo? Why were his mother and father on the train? And why were they smiling up at the luggage rack where a large snake with the head of Iblis was staring back down at them? And why had Iblis stopped the train?

John sat up with a start as he realized that the Express was now at a standstill, and glanced nervously up at the luggage rack, even as he realized he had been dreaming. Philippa, now lying across three seats, was still fast asleep, snoring quietly and then, suddenly, not so quietly. A loud clap of thunder followed by a large flash of lightning revealed a deserted station platform and a sign that read SIGHISOARA. They were now in Transylvania. And not just in Transylvania, but in the very place, according to Mr Groanin, that was Dracula's hometown.

John glanced nervously at his watch, saw that it was just after midnight and wished he'd taken Groanin's advice regarding dinner. The Hungarian goulash stew had tasted a bit funny – it was the very kind of food that Mr Groanin, with his delicate stomach, would never have eaten – but he had no idea if that made it any more likely that it had any garlic in it. But for the slow turnover of the locomotive engine, all was quiet inside the train. John turned out the overhead light and, pressing his nose to the window, tried to see something more of the old Transylvanian town. Almost immediately he jumped back in horror as, for a brief second, another flash of lightning lit up a face looking back at him. A face that looked like the easy winner in the Hideous Gargoyle World Championships. With his heart beating like a drum machine, John scrambled down to the opposite end of the couchette, as far away from the window as possible.

"'S'a matter?" Philippa asked sleepily, observing his alarm with one eye open, and quite oblivious to the creature on the opposite side of the window. "You look like you've seen a ghost."

John pointed at the window. "There's something out there," he said uncomfortably.

"Course there is, dummy," yawned Philippa. "It's called Europe."

"No, not that. Something else. Some thing, or someone."

Philippa took a deep breath to help her awaken, sat up, and then looked out of the window as once again a bolt of lightning lit up the station sign; but she could see nothing of any particular interest. The platform was quite deserted.

"Don't tell me, it was Dracula," She shook her head sadly, as if pitying her brother and his juvenile sense of humour. "Funny guy."

"Really, there was someone out there."

"It's a station platform. I guess they have people who stand on station platforms, even in Transylvania. Even in weather like this."

"Someone pretty ugly."

"Ugly doesn't make you a bad person. You should know that."

"There's ugly and there's horror movie," said John, pointing firmly at the window. "Believe me, I know the difference."

"Whatever it was would have to be pretty tall," observed Philippa staring down at the platform. "At least seven or eight feet tall to look in the window of this car."

Ten minutes passed and still the train did not move. Philippa shivered. The possibility that John had not been kidding was now beginning to make an impression on her. Either way, there was something about this station that was beginning to make her feel scared. "I hope the train hasn't broken down," she said anxiously.

John stood up, opened the compartment door and, peering down the train's empty corridor, he listened carefully for a sign that something was happening. But there was nothing and he stepped back into the compartment, closing the door behind him. He didn't want to say anything that would scare his sister any more than she was, perhaps, scared already, but he was certain he'd seen the face at the window before, if only as an illustration in Mr Rakshasas's *Shorter Baghdad Rules*.

Previously, he'd been led to believe that there were only three types of beings in the world: human beings, the djinn, and the angels; however, as the SBR made clear, there was a fourth type of being – fallen angels, also known as demons. Among all the demons he'd read about, Asmodeus was one of the most terrible and the most wicked. This particular demon was supposed to have three heads, including that of a bull and of a ram; but it had been his third head – that of a brutal-looking ogre – that John was sure he had seen, albeit briefly, staring in the window. He wasn't certain, but he thought it quite likely that demons like Asmodeus *were* tall enough to look in the window of a railway car. He certainly didn't think it likely that any self-respecting demon would have bothered to get a box to stand on.

"I'd hate to be stuck here for the night." said Philippa. "After what Groanin said about Sighisoara."

"He was just winding us up," said John.

"Yeah? Well, guess what, bro? Tick-tock, tick-tock."

"Try to look on the bright side," John said, for his sister's benefit. "This is a first-class compartment. If the train has broken down, we've pretty much got everything we could want in here. And, perhaps more to the

111

point, nothing we don't want, either."

Even as he spoke, all the remaining lights in the compartment went out, the locomotive engine stopped and, but for the occasional flash of lightning, everything was plunged into darkness.

"You were saying?" said Philippa.

"Water probably," he said, trying to convince himself as much as Philippa. "In the train's electrical points. All this rain. I bet they'll send a guy now, to try and fix it. He's probably out there already."

John opened the window. Very carefully, he stuck his head out into the cold wet night air, and looked down the length of the train, in the hope that he might see it being repaired. Instead, much farther along the track, standing on the edge of some trees and shrouded in darkness, he could see a huge figure. At first, John hoped that it might be a statue to some Transylvanian hero. But then, a cloud moved away from the full moon, illuminating the track and the platform, and John felt his stomach retreat against his backbone as, horror-struck, he made out the three distinctive heads, the creature's reptilian tail, and then the feet, which were those of a giant black rooster. It was a demon all right, and it seemed to be waiting for someone else to come aboard the Express.

"Can you see anything?" said Philippa.

"No," said John. "Nothing at all." He closed the window and sat down with a big fake smile on his face, as if nothing was wrong. But inside he was wondering if now might be the right time to deploy the discrimen – the emergency wish – that Mr Vodyannoy had given him back at the Dakota building in New York. John had just remembered he still had it; now, if he could only remember the German focus word Mr Vodyannoy had attached to the wish. In fact, he remembered it instantly, as Mr Vodyannoy had intended he should. The only trouble was that while he could indeed remember it – he saw the word DONAUDAMPFSCHIFAH-RTSGESELLSCHAFTKAPITAEN, as if it had been printed on the inside of his eyelids – for the life of him he couldn't think how to pronounce it.

"Don Ow damp schiff. . ."

"Your brain's packed up again, bro," said Philippa. "You're babbling. Making no sense at all."

"Er, yes," said John. His sister's chatter was hardly helping him as he tried to pronounce Frank Vodyannoy's word. "Donut ampfi . . ."

"No, really. In which case we might be here for some time. I mean this is a train, not a car. It might take a while to find a hair dryer big enough to dry out the electrical points." But even as Philippa spoke, the engine started up again and the lights in the compartment came back on. And, for an all too brief moment, John forgot about trying to pronounce the discrimen word that would have wished the demon gone. Now it was his turn to be smart.

"You were saying?" he said, as the train gave a lurch and started to move again.

"Thank goodness for that," said Philippa, and laughed with relief. "I must say I can think of more pleasant places to spend the night."

But the next second they both froze as, in the distance, they heard a loud, bestial roar, like a huge animal of some description.

"What was that?" gulped Philippa.

John decided it was best he didn't provide Philippa with a description of precisely what he had seen. "A cow," he said. "Maybe." There was another roar, louder this time, and John shrugged. "Or maybe a moose."

"They don't have moose in Transylvania," said Philippa. "And unless I'm mistaken, even the largest cows in this country aren't the size of a bus." The creature roared again. "Which is how large that one sounds." She shook her head fearfully. "Besides, you don't roar like that unless you have a lot of teeth and sharp claws to go with it."

A different, galloping noise drew John's attention out of the window just in time to see a small black carriage drawn by two black horses, racing along the station platform past the slowly accelerating train. Both twins pressed their faces close to the window as the black carriage overtook their compartment and then stopped some twenty yards ahead of them. The carriage driver, wearing a thick Ulster coat, and a wide-brimmed hat, threw aside the reins, jumped down from his seat, ran beside the train for several moments, opened one of the doors, and then jumped aboard.

"Do you suppose that's Izaak?" asked Philippa.

"I hope so," said John. "None of the possible alternatives seem at all attractive."

A moment later, they heard the creature roar again, only a little more distantly now, as if the train was already leaving it behind in the Transylvanian darkness. John was almost ready to breathe a sigh of relief.

"What *was* that?" repeated Philippa, as they heard the carriage door bang shut behind the mystery passenger.

It was now that John told her exactly what he'd seen standing farther along the track, and Philippa felt very glad he'd not told her before, thinking she might just have been tempted to use the discrimen that Nimrod had given her for the journey. Her, and not John (who didn't even know she had it) because Nimrod had said that the discrimen was for a real emergency and not John's idea of an emergency, which was feeling bored or hungry, or both at the same time. All the same, she thought there was no doubting her brother's courage. If he had told her before that Asmodeus was on the track then surely she'd have uttered the word SHABRIRI and the wish would have been gone, along with the demon. It was still a long way to Berlin and she felt a lot better about the journey that lay ahead of them, knowing they still had a discrimen at her command. She had absolutely no idea that John was armed with a discrimen of his own.

"Why do you think Asmodeus was watching this train?" she asked, sitting down again.

Footsteps were heard in the corridor of the train and a figure in a wet coat appeared at the glass door of their compartment.

"I really don't know," said John, "but I've a feeling we're about to find out."

The door slid open and the figure stepped into their compartment and collapsed on the seat. He was wearing several scarves, and a hat pulled down low over his ears, and it was another minute before they were certain it was Izaak Balayaga. As he unwound the last of the scarves, he let out a loud sigh of relief and smiled an impish smile at them both.

"Did you see him?" he yelled. "Ashmadai. Did you see him waiting for me, the old scoundrel?"

"Who is Ashmadai?" said John, a little disappointed that he had misidentified the demon he had seen.

"Who is Ashmadai, he asks," chuckled Izaak. "Asmodeus, of course. The creature of judgment, that's who. A raging fiend and a terrible wicked devil, so he is, and best invoked only when you've got your hat off." Izaak threw his own hat onto the floor and, laughing loudly, began to look enormously pleased with himself and, perhaps, his dentistry, too, so wide and white was the grin he flashed Philippa's way. "He also goes by the name of Saturn, Marcolf, and Chammaday." Izaak stood up and shrugged off his Ulster coat. "And lately a few words of my own that I couldn't repeat in front of a lady. Two days that devil's been tracking me now. Two whole days." He laughed bitterly. "Have you any idea what it's like to have a demon of the experience of Ashmadai on your tail for forty-eight hours?"

"No," admitted Philippa.

"It's no picnic, I can tell you. He'd have my heart and liver for his breakfast, without question. Fry them up in goat's blood and have himself a feast. Yes, sir."

"Why was Asmodeus after you?" asked Philippa.

"I should have thought that was obvious, little lady," Izaak said, grinning.

Philippa bit her tongue. She didn't much like being called "little lady," especially by someone only a few years older than she was.

"The beast was after *Solomon's Grimoire*, of course," said Izaak and proceeded to light an enormous cigar, as if somehow he wanted to celebrate his escape. "Asmodeus, as you call him, and Solomon go way back." Izaak was wearing a long black frock coat, with a boot-lace tie, a plain white shirt, and black leather gloves. "You see, when Solomon was king of Israel, Asmodeus got jealous of the fact that the king had a thousand wives and, cunning devil that he was, stole Solomon's ring of power. Slipped it off the King's finger while he was sleeping and wore it himself. Pretended to be Solomon and, because the ring was a magic ring, everyone believed him. Meanwhile, nobody believed that the real Solomon was who *he* said he was, and, for a while, he found himself employed as a cook in the kitchens of his own palace.

"Luckily for Solomon, one of his wives dropped some flour on the floor of the palace and Asmodeus happened to walk through it. And the wife noticed that the tracks in her flour were those of a demon. Guessing what must have happened, she stole the ring back while Asmodeus slept, and the real Solomon was restored to his throne.

"But while Asmodeus was still pretending to be Solomon, who was a great magus, he had access to Solomon's library and discovered the book Solomon had been writing. This contained all his wisdom, and described how power could be had over djinn, angels, mundanes, and demons. So it's fortunate that the next person to have the book was Ishtar herself. A gift from Nebuchadnezzar, it's said. But ever since then, Asmodeus has been trying to get his hands on it." Izaak uttered a rueful laugh. "To tell you the absolute truth, I've sort of only just found this out for myself. It's one of the reasons I'm now so anxious to return the book to

Herself. I've no wish to have Asmodeus on my tail any longer."

"Herself?"

"Ayesha. She-Who-Must-Be-Obeyed-At-All-Times."

"Where is the book now?" asked Philippa.

Izaak picked his coat off the floor and showed her how it contained a cleverly concealed pocket, about the size of a backpack. From inside the pocket, he withdrew a beautifully bound leather book that was embossed with a golden ladder, at the top of which, and also embossed in gold, was the same all-seeing eye – the Eye of Horus – that is to be found on any US one-dollar bill.

"Here it is," said Izaak, and laid the book on the seat beside him.

"But if you have the book," said John, "and the book explains how to have power over demons, couldn't you have used what's in the book to deal with Asmodeus?"

"You'd think so, wouldn't you?" said Izaak. "But it was only after I um . . . borrowed the book, that I discovered it can't actually be opened by just anyone. Only the truly wise and pure in heart can open this book. It's a little fail-safe device that the Blue Djinn left attached to the book, just in case it got itself pinched."

"So you couldn't have used the book, even if you wanted to," said Philippa.

"I'm afraid not. It seems that there are some who can and some who can't. And the very fact of my stealing it meant that by definition, I am one who can't." He shrugged. "So here we all are."

John regarded the book critically. "May I?"

Izaak shrugged. "Be my guest."

Gingerly, John picked up the book and was surprised to discover that it was every bit as heavy as a stone of similar size. "It weighs a ton," he said. "And it smells kind of funny, too. Kind of like flowers, only stronger."

"The book's binding is protected with an unguent of aloes wood," said Izaak. "To stop it from cracking, I suppose."

John laid the book on his lap and tried to open it. "You're right," he said. "The cover won't budge. I can't open it, any more than you can."

"That doesn't makes sense," observed Philippa. "You didn't steal it, John. And you're just a kid, like me. I don't see how you can be anything but pure in heart when you're only twelve years old." She took the book from her brother. "Here, let me try." She, too, noticed the smell of the book and bent her nose close to the cover to sniff it. "Lilies," she said. "That's what it smells like."

"Go ahead and open it," said John, more interested in if she could open the book or not, than what it smelled like – a smell that lingered on his finger's ends. "If you can."

But Philippa also failed to open the book and, feeling somewhat exasperated, she shook her head. Philippa had always prided herself on her inquiring intelligence and her good heart, so it irritated her that a book that was only for the wise and pure in heart should somehow remain closed to her. It didn't make sense at all.

Izaak took back the book, and it was only now that both the twins noticed that he was still wearing his gloves, and that he seemed to be smiling in a peculiar way. It was another minute before John realized that it wasn't Izaak's smile that was peculiar so much as the way he himself was feeling. A strange sensation of numbness was creeping up his fingertips, his hands, and then his forearms in a way that suggested something must have been absorbed through his skin when he had handled the book. This feeling of numbness was quickly followed by one of outrage when he saw Izaak open the book without any apparent difficulty and remove several objects from a hollowed-out section inside it.

"Hey," said John, still not quite grasping the full extent of Izaak's deception. "I thought you said you couldn't open the book."

"I couldn't," he replied. "Not until you both touched it first, or else the binding would have been spoiled."

By now Philippa had also found herself paralyzed from the neck down.

"What's going on?" she said. "I can't move."

"That's just the effect of the unguent on the leather binding," said Izaak. "It contains a skin-absorbed enzyme refined from the venom of a Deathstalker Scorpion. It won't kill you. But it will leave you paralyzed for several minutes. Which is all the time I'll need. And please don't take this personally. I've no real choice in this matter."

John recognized that this time they really were in trouble and, presented with a real emergency, as opposed to a near emergency, he found absolutely no difficulty in giving utterance to the German word unleashing the emergency wish that had eluded him earlier. Exactly as Frank Vodyannoy had intended should happen.

Being John's twin, however, Philippa was already going through the same thought process, with the result that both of them uttered the focus words attached to their respective discrimens . . .

"DONAUDAMPFSCHIFAHRTSGESELLSCHA-TKAPITAEN!"
"SHABRIRI!"

. . . at exactly the same moment.

With the unfortunate result that these two discrimens cancelled each other out, which was another reason why Nimrod had only given the twins one emergency wish between them.

Of course, John and Philippa weren't to know this and assumed, wrongly, that Izaak Balayaga's power was stronger than their respective discrimens. They watched helplessly as, using some aloes wood, some clay, two pieces of animal bone, some silk, and a hair clipping from each of their heads, Izaak proceeded to assemble two little dolls – both of them remarkably accurate and lifelike copies of John and Philippa.

"What are you doing?" asked Philippa.

"This is the djinn binding. You see I can only trans-elementize you one at a time. If I didn't bind you both very firmly first, one of you might trans-elementize me while I was doing the same to the other."

"Trans-elementize?" said Philippa. "Is that like transubstantiation?"

"Didn't that fool Nimrod teach you anything? Transubstantiation," Izaak explained matter-of-factly, "is when you make yourself disappear into a bottle. Trans-elementation is when you do it to someone else.

And against their will." As he spoke, he produced two long thin needles and shoved one of them through John's doll.

John laughed. "That didn't hurt," he said scornfully.

"It's not supposed to," said Izaak. "This isn't some rubbishy voodoo doll, although it is where the witch doctors got the idea from. This is the finished binding. For when the scorpion venom wears off."

John shouted loudly in the hope that the train guard or one of the other passengers might come to their aid.

"Take it easy," Izaak told him. "Everyone's asleep. And you can consider yourself lucky I'm not turning you into a doll yourself. If I'd used a dimunendo and turned you into a doll then you'd be stuck like that until I decided different. In a day or so, you'll be back to your old self. Just you wait and see."

"But why are you doing this?" asked Philippa. "What's this all about? Are you working for Asmodeus?"

Izaak laughed and transfixed Philippa's doll with the second needle. "There is no Asmodeus," he said. "Well, there is. But not in this case. It wasn't the real Asmodeus you saw back there but something I cooked up, to overcome any suspicions you might have of me. A diversion. No, the real Asmodeus would have caught up with this train in seconds and smashed it to matchwood to get his hands on the real book. Which this book isn't, of course. Not for a minute. The real Grimoire of Solomon is much too valuable to bring on a train. The demon you saw was nothing more than my own model, based on the illustration in Mr Rakshasas's new book."

Holding each doll aloft in the air for a moment, Izaak bowed his head, stamped his boot twice on the floor of the compartment, and uttered the following phrase: "I have knocked twice at the great hall doors of the inner earth to bind these two djinn. HADROQUARKLUON!"

Then he threw himself down on the seat and relit his cigar. "There," he said proudly. "That's it. You're bound. I can do what I want now."

"And what's that?" asked Philippa.

"I think I said, didn't I?" said Izaak. "I'm going to put you into two separate containers and then stop you up." And so saying, he produced two containers from his coat pocket and waggled them teasingly.

"You won't get away with this," said John.

"Please," said Philippa. "Don't do this."

Izaak sighed and leaned his face against the carriage window. "I'd like to help you, really I would." He put his finger on the glass and followed a raindrop as it ran down the height of the window. "Only my hands are tied. But don't be so gloomy. It's not that awful."

"I'd like to knock you through that window," said John.

"But you won't, old man." Izaak chuckled. "You can't." He stood up. "I'm sorry. Truly I am. But just try to remember what the fellow said. 'Some of us are good, and some of us are not, but me, I was only obeying orders.'"

He uttered his focus word again, waved his hands theatrically, and one twin disappeared in a cloud of smoke, followed closely by the other.

CHAPTER 9

THE CROUCHER

E ven before the last passenger had left the Royal Hungarian Express in Berlin's Zoo Station, Alan and Neil had started to whine anxiously as they recognized something had gone wrong on the train.

"Now what do we do?" asked Groanin. "I say, now what do we do?"

"We search the train, of course," said Nimrod. "You take Alan and start at the far end, and I'll take Neil and start at the near end. We'll meet up in the middle."

Groanin set off down the platform. "Well, come on then, if you're coming," he called out to Alan, who bounded after him.

Nimrod climbed on the train. By now, he hardly expected to find the twins aboard the Express and was looking for some sort of clue as to what had befallen them. At the very least, he expected the keen noses of the two rottweilers to find something. And indeed the minute Neil entered the compartment where the twins had been sitting, he barked loudly. Nimrod sent him off to fetch Groanin and Alan, and then rubbed the old brass lamp summoning Mr Rakshasas.

"I'm afraid they weren't on the train," said Nimrod, after Mr Rakshasas had achieved transubstantiation.

"Yes, I know, I heard you telling Mr Groanin," said Mr Rakshasas, who proceeded to sniff the air like a dog himself for a short while. "Do you smell that?" he said.

"No," admitted Nimrod. "Nothing in particular. Well, I say nothing in particular, but I do smell a good cigar." He sniffed the air himself. "A Romeo Y Julietta, I should say. A Churchill, probably. The very same kind of cigar I saw Izaak Balayaga smoking at the Algonquin Hotel in New York." Nimrod hesitated. "Was that what you smelled, Mr Rakshasas?"

"No," said Mr Rakshasas, and sniffed the air again. "'Tis a curious thing, but coming out of my lamp, it's a more developed sense of smell I'm having these days, for a short while at least. Right now, I'm picking up a strong smell of aloes wood unguent. As if. . ."

Groanin and the two dogs appeared in the doorway of the railway compartment. Alan had a bone in his mouth, which he dropped at Nimrod's feet. For a brief moment, Nimrod was half-inclined to ignore it, until he realized the possible significance and picked the bone up.

"A sheep's shoulder blade," he said. "That, and the smell you noticed, suggests only one thing."

"Solomon's binding," said Mr Rakshasas, nodding.

"What does that mean?" asked Mr Groanin.

"It means whoever worked his will upon my niece and nephew used a very old and powerful incantation from the very book John and Philippa were supposed to get from Izaak Balayaga."

Neil started to hoover the floor of the compartment with his nose, then the seats, and finally the luggage racks where he barked once again.

"Found something, have you?" said Nimrod. He stood on the seat and glanced over the edge of the luggage rack. Right at the back, almost invisible against the brushed metal of the rack, lay a tube for a Churchill cigar.

"Izaak was here, all right," said Nimrod and, picking up the cigar tube, he unscrewed the cap.

Immediately, smoke started to billow out of the tube as a djinn's transubstantiation got underway. Thirty seconds later, John was standing in the compartment and telling them everything that had happened. Gradually, Nimrod and Mr Rakshasas were able to fathom what it was that had been bothering them: how it was that the discrimen Nimrod had given to Philippa hadn't worked.

"That explains everything," said Mr Rakshasas. "I'm afraid that the wish Mr Vodyannoy gave you and the one Nimrod gave to Philippa cancelled each other out. In the *Complete All Baghdad Rules of the Djinn*, 1940, volume 10, section 62, subsection 49, it states that only one emergency may exist at any one point in time, and that two emergencies require that there shall be two moments in time, and that for the same reason two discrimens cannot exist at the same moment in time, and that by not existing, they shall both be judged to be null and void, and hence inoperative."

"Forget about the stable door for now," said Mr Groanin. "In case you hadn't noticed, the horse has bolted."

"He's right," said John, taking the cigar tube from Nimrod's fingers.

"Izaak had two of those tubes. There must be another

one containing Philippa." He held the tube under Alan's nose for a moment, to let him get the scent. "Go and find it," he told the dog. "Go and find the other tube."

"It's worth a try, I suppose," admitted Nimrod. "But I rather fear he'll search in vain. If Izaak had meant to take you both he'd hardly have gone to the elaborate trouble of trans-elementizing you separately."

"Why would he take Philippa and not me?"

"I don't know. But bottle me if I don't intend to find out."

They waited for Alan to return, which he did after a while, his jaws empty of anything resembling a cigar tube and looking very sad, for he loved Philippa every bit as much as he loved John.

"All right," said Nimrod. "Here's what we'll do. Groanin? You and Mr Rakshasas take Alan and Neil back to the hotel and stay there, in case the kidnapper tries to contact us there with some kind of ransom demand."

"Where are you going?" asked Groanin.

"To the Pergamon Museum," said Nimrod. "I have some questions I need to ask Ayesha."

"Such as?" asked John.

"Such as if the Solomon Grimoire is missing at all. Or if that was just a story Izaak cooked up to lure us into a trap."

The Pergamon Museum, in the east of Berlin, ranks alongside the British Museum and the Smithsonian as one of the world's leading museums of oriental treasures. Fourteen of the Pergamon's rooms are devoted to a collection that includes several world-famous reconstructions of brilliantly coloured

Babylonian monuments, using broken glazed bricks that were excavated by German archaeologists. Not the least of these are the Ishtar Gate – the so-called Blue Gate of Babylon – the Processional Way, and the facade of the throne hall of King Nebuchadnezzar II. But, as Nimrod explained to John, when they arrived at the Pergamon, there is also an entirely secret suite of chambers that the mundane beings who work in, or visit the museum, know absolutely nothing about.

"One of the walls along the Processional Way," he explained, "is a plenum wall, which is to say it serves no other purpose than the purely visual, and conceals a quantum space as opposed to a Cartesian one."

"You mean there's a secret room," said John, reducing Nimrod's words to their simplest meaning.

"Yes," said Nimrod.

"Then why didn't you just say so?" muttered John, following.

Inside the museum, Nimrod led them to the Processional Way where he stopped in front of a wall made of blue glazed brick, with the figure of a life-size lion, raised in relief. "Behind that wall is the court of the Blue Djinn of Babylon," said Nimrod. "It's just a question of going there."

John nodded uncertainly.

"Of freeing one's mind from the normal ideas of time, space, and matter," said Nimrod. "Of going with the flow, so to speak."

Going with the flow sounded just fine to John. He could relate to that. It sounded a lot easier than going against the flow. "So," he said, trying to get a firmer handle on what Nimrod had been saying. "This is a fake wall. We just walk up to it and then walk through it, is that it?"

"Not exactly. You see, you can't walk up to something that isn't actually there. The wall doesn't actually exist. Not for us, anyway. You have to try to think beyond the wall, John."

John frowned as he tried to bend his mind to what Nimrod was suggesting. As far as he could see, the trouble with thinking beyond the wall, was the wall itself. It sort of got in the way. The way a wall was supposed to.

"Come on," said Nimrod. "We'll do it together. Here, take my hand. Ready?"

John nodded. *Go with the flow*, he told himself, as they walked smartly toward the wall. He was doing fine and had convinced himself that there was nothing to it – quite literally – when, at the last possible second, one of the museum's spotlights flickered a little and was reflected on the glazed lion's hindquarters. The next thing he was lying on the floor of the Processional Way, and feeling half knocked-out, in the same way anyone feels when they walk straight into a brick wall at two or three miles an hour. John opened his eyes just in time to see Nimrod's leg disappear through the plenum wall. And rubbing his head painfully, he sat up.

A burly security guard came forward and helped John get to his feet, but since he was speaking in German, John had no idea what he was saying, and so he just smiled, and said he was all right, and apologized for not looking where he was going. He spent the next ten minutes walking up and down the corridor, recovering his senses and pretending to be fascinated with the Processional Way while he waited for Nimrod to return. He might have tried to enter the secret chamber again, except for the security guard who was now watching him very carefully, concerned, perhaps, that John meant somehow to damage the valuable exhibit by walking into it a second time. After a while he was watching John so intently that he hardly noticed Nimrod appear silently through a section of the wall immediately behind his chair. Nor did anyone else, apart from John.

"Hard cheese," said Nimrod, inspecting the lump on John's forehead. "It takes a bit of practice to pull off that kind of quantum leap. I expect you're still feeling a bit affected by that binding Izaak used on you."

"I'm not sure my head could stand trying it again," admitted John. "What did she say?"

"Who?"

"Ayesha, of course."

"She wasn't there," said Nimrod, heading for the *ausgang*, which is German for "exit."

"So where are we going now?"

"Ayesha's house."

"You mean she doesn't live in the museum? Behind that plenum thingy?"

"Good Lord, no," said Nimrod. "Those are her official quarters, where djinn come to seek her advice and her judgement. Out of office hours, she lives in a villa on the outskirts of Berlin. The Villa Fledermaus."

On the street outside the museum, Nimrod hailed a cab and told the driver to take them to number 1, Amon Goeth Strasse. And in the car, John said, "Isn't Fledermaus the German word for 'bat'?"

"That's right. When I was a boy, we used to call the place the 'Bat Mansion'."

"So you've been there before?"

"Oh, light my lamp, yes." Nimrod sighed, a little sadly it seemed to John. "But alas, not for many years."

Bat Mansion was well-named. Surrounded with extra-tall fir trees, the creepy-looking house sat behind a very high iron gate. Nimrod looked cautiously through the gate at the villa and the surrounding gardens, as if he wasn't quite sure of something, which prompted John to wonder if his caution might be connected with a three-word sign on the gate and written in German. John read it aloud:

"Vorsicht, Bissiger Dämon." He shook his head. "I wish I understood German," he added, not really thinking about what he was saying, and forgetting that he was standing next to a powerful djinn. Suddenly, John realized exactly what the sign meant. Feeling a little sorry for his nephew after his experiences on the train and in the museum, Nimrod had simply granted John's wish. And the younger djinn could understand German every bit as well as he could understand English, which made John feel as if his brain had just doubled in size.

"Beware, Vicious Demon," said John.

"Exactly so," murmured Nimrod and opened the gate slowly. "You'd best stay close to me, boy."

"Er, what kind of vicious demon?" said John. "Not Asmodeus, I hope."

"Light my lamp, I hope not," whispered Nimrod. "Whatever put such an idea in your head?"

John wanted to tell him, but Nimrod was still speaking as he marched up the path, the gravel crunching under his stout brogue shoes like the sound of a whole packet of cookies being munched at once.

"No, the demon here is a croucher. An entrance demon, once common in ancient Babylon." Nimrod stopped for a moment, and listened carefully before moving again. "It's a species that tends to lie in wait near the threshold of a house, to protect it against unwelcome visitors." Nimrod glanced above the door as they neared the house. "Or on the roof."

"Are *we* unwelcome visitors?" asked John.

"That is always a possibility," said Nimrod.

It was beginning to get dark, and there were no lights on in the house. The idea that a demon might be crouching close by, ready to pounce on them, was making John feel very uncomfortable. It was a feeling that intensified sharply when Nimrod stepped onto the porch, took hold of a large brass knocker shaped like an anatomically perfect human heart and then seemed to think better of using it on the door. "Ayesha's idea of a joke," explained Nimrod. "She being so famously hard-hearted."

In the full moonlight, they waited at the door for almost a minute.

Bats flitted through the trees and around the darkened turrets and, somewhere in the trees, an owl hooted loudly. But inside the old house, nothing stirred. John bent down and lifting the flap of the mail slot, he peered into the house. In the gloomy hallway he could make out a grandfather clock, an umbrella stand that was fashioned from a woolly mammoth's foot, a huge empty fireplace, a table and, on the floor, a large pile of unopened letters. "No one in," said John.

"I wouldn't do that, if I were you," said Nimrod. "Just in case we disturb something."

"Looks quiet enough," shrugged John.

"I know. That's what concerns me. It's a little too quiet."

Nimrod winced as John let go of the flap of the mail slot, which snapped shut noisily. "Some of the time, anyway," he added.

"Come on," said John, and turned away from the door. "This place gives me the creeps. Let's get out of here."

"John, stop," said Nimrod, but it was too late.

As John's feet touched the gravel path again, out of the corner of his eye he saw something race toward him; something larger than a dog, but moving too fast to see exactly what it was. Instinctively, he knew that this was a croucher, and that he should try to get away from it. But by the time the thought had made its way through his young mind, the croucher was already leaping through the air, its slavering, open jaws reaching for John's neck. Apart from the head, the body was mostly black and shaped like a hyena, with high sturdy shoulders and lower hindquarters. The head itself was massive but recognizably half human, with broad, rounded ears and outsized teeth. These dripped with saliva as, laughing horribly, the croucher lunged into the bite that would have torn John's throat open with one snap.

John screamed, certain his last minute on earth had come and, but for his uncle's presence of mind, he would have been right. Even so, Nimrod had scarcely any time to think, so quick was the croucher (for a split millisecond, John found himself pitying the poor German postman that had to get past such a creature). Nimrod wanted to save his nephew from serious injury, but he hardly wanted to kill the demon, either. It goes without saying that Nimrod disliked killing anything, being an Englishman in whom a sense of fair play was paramount. But he also had some questions that, in the absence of anyone else at the Villa Fledermaus, he thought that only the croucher would be able to answer. And so, partly inspired by what had happened to John with the plenum wall at the Pergamon Museum, Nimrod's shout of "QWERTYUIOP!" resulted in the sudden appearance of a sheet of bulletproof glass (effective against 7.62 mm armour-piercing ammunition) between his nephew and the galloping croucher. The glass Nimrod had chosen was the best on the market, with a clarity level of 91.4 per cent, which meant that John didn't see it. Nor did the croucher. With a loud clanging noise that sounded like a bell being struck, the beast collided with the toughened glass, at almost 31 miles per hour. The croucher bounced several inches off the invisible barrier, collapsed onto the gravel path, and lay still.

John let out a long, unsteady breath and waited for his heart to slow down a bit before, looking carefully through the protective glass, he dared to inspect the thing that had tried to kill him a little more closely. "Is it dead?"

"I sincerely hope not," said Nimrod, kneeling down beside the creature, and pressing his fingers against its neck, in search of a pulse. But even as Nimrod answered, the croucher started to undergo a change. The half human head took on a more completely human aspect, while the four-legged body turned into that of a small man wearing a neat dark suit, a bow tie, and a pair of yellow gloves.

After a while, the little man groaned and rolled onto his back. John had a good idea how the croucher must have felt. He could still feel the lump on his own head from the wall at the Pergamon Museum. And he had been moving at about a tenth of the speed of the croucher.

After a moment, the man sat up, rubbed his own head painfully, took off one of his gloves, touched his mouth, which was bleeding, and then noticed that some of the blood had dripped onto his shirtfront. He frowned irritably.

"Look what you did to my shirt," he said, speaking German in a high-pitched voice. John was pleased to discover he could understand every word.

"Sorry about that," said Nimrod, whose own German was faultless. "But imagine our alarm when we found ourselves attacked by a frightful demon. Namely yourself." Nimrod held out his hand. "Here, let me help you up."

Nimrod assisted the little man to walk over to a stone seat on the porch of the Villa Fledermaus, where he sat down wearily.

"I thank you, sir," the little man said politely. His behavior was so different from that which he had displayed in his demon form that John wondered how they could be the same creature. "Did you not see the sign on the gate?" the man asked Nimrod.

"Yes, Mr –?"

"Damascus. Jonah Damascus." Mr Damascus found a handkerchief and dabbed at the blood on his mouth. "But if you saw the sign" – Mr Damascus was very politely sceptical – "why should you and the boy have risked serious injury by coming through the gate? You're a djinn.

That much is evident. Therefore you know the proper procedure for contacting the Blue Djinn, blessings be upon her. Only at the Pergamon. That's the rule."

"We've already been to the Pergamon," said Nimrod, picking up the flower that had fallen from the buttonhole of Mr Damascus's jacket. "And she wasn't there."

"Then you should have waited. Or made an appointment. In the appointed manner."

"I'm afraid this is an emergency," insisted Nimrod. "Besides, I knew what I was doing. You see, I've been here before."

"You have? How?"

"Never mind that now," said Nimrod. "The fact is, she's not here. And I have some important news for her. About the Solomon Grimoire."

"News? What news?"

"It may have been stolen."

"Impossible," gasped Mr Damascus. "That can't be true."

"Well, if it isn't, someone is using the knowledge it contains. My young nephew here was subject to a powerful djinn binding that could only have come from the grimoire. So, you can see, it's imperative she is informed of this as soon as possible. Do you know where she is, Mr Damascus?"

"Perhaps. But may I first ask you who you both are?"

"My name is Nimrod Plantagenet Godwin. And this is my young nephew, John Gaunt."

Damascus rose from the seat in the porch and bowed. "I have heard of you," he said. "I can tell you only this. She left Berlin yesterday. I drove her to the airport myself.

Apart from Miss Glumjob, who is the Blue Djinn's companion and maid, I do most of what needs to be done around here. Butler, gardener, handyman, security guard, chauffeur."

"Do you know where she was going?"

"Oh, yes. Budapest."

"Now why would she be going there?" said Nimrod.

"I am just her croucher," said Mr Damascus. "I cannot say."

"Uncle Nimrod," said John. "After Transylvania, Budapest was the next scheduled stop for the Royal Hungarian Express."

"Light my lamp, but that's right," said Nimrod.

"Maybe she wanted to get the book back herself," suggested John. "The Solomon Grimoire."

"Maybe," Nimrod said thoughtfully and placed the flower back in Mr Damascus's buttonhole.

"Thank you, sir." Mr Damascus took hold of his lapel, drew the flower toward him, and inhaled it, as if it might help to restore his strength.

"Are you expecting her back here soon?" Nimrod asked him.

"I cannot say," said Mr Damascus. "I am just the croucher. She does not tell me her diary, sir." He smiled, a vain little smile. "However, over the years, I have come to know Ayesha well. Blessed be her name. At this time of year, sir, it would be most unusual for her not to spend at least three or four weeks at her palace in Babylon. Up until and including January thirty-first."

Nimrod frowned. "January thirty-first?"

"The old Feast of Ishtar, sir."

"Of course," said Nimrod. "It was the night when –" Nimrod glanced at John and seemed think better of what he had been about to say. "Thank you, Mr Damascus," he said. "You've been most helpful."

John nodded his own thanks to the nearly recovered Mr Damascus and followed Nimrod down the path of the Villa Fledermaus, where Nimrod was already whipping up another whirlwind. "Couldn't we just hail a cab?" he asked his uncle. "I think I saw one up on the main road."

"We're not going back to the hotel," said Nimrod. "We're going rather farther afield, I'm afraid. Come on, hurry up. We haven't got all day."

"Are we going to Budapest? To speak to Ayesha?"

"No, no. She won't be there now."

"So where *are* we going?" said John, as the whirlwind carried them up into the air.

"To Cairo. To speak to Izaak Balayaga."

CHAPTER 10

THE THREE WISHES OF VIRGIL MACREEBY

"How do you know that Izaak will be in Cairo?" John asked Nimrod, as the whirlwind carried them south, away from Berlin.

"I don't for sure. I'm afraid it's no more than a good guess at this stage. But if I were Izaak and I knew that a much more powerful djinn was looking for me, that's where I'd go."

"Why not Babylon?" asked John. "Isn't it possible he'd have gone there, with Ayesha?"

"Because other djinn, especially male djinn, simply aren't allowed at the Blue Djinn's palace in Babylon," said Nimrod. "If that is indeed where Ayesha has gone, then Izaak couldn't possibly have gone with her. In which case, I think he'll probably panic, and go to Cairo and the House of Kafur."

"I read about the House of Kafur," said John. "In the *Shorter Baghdad Rules*. It's the only officially recognized djinn sanctuary in the world."

"That's right. Once you're there, no djinn or magus can touch you. Section 319, subsection 48, paragraph 900a."

"Djinn sanctuary," said John. "Sounds kind of handy."

"Yes, if you're a scoundrel or a villain. They're the only

sort of djinn who go to a place like the House of Kafur. Most of them are exiles from their own tribes. Or fugitives from more powerful djinn they've offended. Including those who refuse to submit to the judgment of the Blue Djinn."

Wearily, John sat down in the whirlwind. He was not yet wholly recovered from the binding Izaak had used on him. He could still remember the tingling he'd felt on the palms of his hands from the venom of the scorpion. Just the thought of it made him feel sleepy. He closed his eyes and when he opened them again they were already over the green triangle that was the delta of Egypt's River Nile. "Have I been asleep?" he yawned.

"Just a bit." Nimrod smiled. "How do you feel?"

"Much better, thanks. Much better than I've felt in a long time."

This was true. Physically at least, John was feeling much improved. His powers returned the very moment he felt the hot wind of the Egyptian desert on his face. Yet this general sense of physical well-being was spoiled by the worry he was feeling about Philippa. And that was hardly lessened by Nimrod being evasive as to the significance of the Feast of Ishtar, and Ayesha's trip to Babylon – wherever that was. As far as John could remember, Babylon, the capital of ancient Mesopotamia, had been destroyed by the Persians more than two thousand years ago. He had the strong feeling that following Ayesha was not going to be easy.

The House of Kafur was a dilapidated apartment building, overgrown with ivy, which sat on an island in the Nile, in the western quarter of Cairo. It was the kind of place that caused people to quicken their step as they passed its evil-looking entrance, and few would have dared to approach the sinister doorman who, wearing a turban and a long galabiyah, sat outside. Almost toothless, unshaven, and smelling strongly of cats, he cackled with recognition as Nimrod approached the door, followed closely by John.

"Mr Nimrod," he said in a cockney accent. "What a great pleasure, sir. And what brings you 'ere?" The man grinned horribly, for what teeth he had were worn away to yellowing stumps. "As if I didn't know."

"Hello, Ronnie," said Nimrod. "John, say hello to Ronnie Plankton. The keeper of the djinn sanctuary. Ronnie, this is my nephew, John Gaunt."

"Pleased to meet you, sir," said John.

"And you son, and you."

"You're English, aren't you?" observed John.

"S'right. From London. West Ham, to be exact. Been 'ere these past thirty years. On account of a small indiscretion occasioning my sudden removal to a foreign climate."

"Is he here, Ronnie?" Nimrod asked.

"Izaak Balayaga? Arrived yesterday, sir, and in quite a state. He said you might turn up looking for him. Said to tell you he was here, if you did. Fourth floor, number 28. Mind out for the rats, eh? Not the djinn kind, or even the mundane ones, but the ones with tails. They come up from the river to keep us larger rats company." Ronnie laughed. "I expect you know the drill, sir. But perhaps you'd put your young nephew in the picture."

Nimrod bent down to remove his shoes, nodding at

John to do likewise. Then he took out a notebook, wrote his focus word on a piece of paper, and pushed it into the toe of one shoe, before handing both shoes over to Ronnie. John did the same, albeit reluctantly. "But is it safe?" he asked his uncle.

"Ronnie may be a lot of things," said Nimrod. "But he's no thief."

"Thank you for that, sir," said Ronnie. "Much appreciated from a djinn of your breeding." To John he added, "I've been the sentinel at the sanctuary these thirty-odd years, and no one ever yet lost a pair of shoes. Or his focus word. So don't you worry yourself, son."

"Putting your focus word in your shoe like that is a sign of good faith," said Nimrod. "If you were foolish enough to break the rules of sanctuary, Ronnie would be forced to burn your shoe."

"That's right," said Ronnie. "It being your shoe and personal, like, and that being your focus word, your feet would catch eternal fire. Which is not recommended. Not even for you and me what's made of fire already."

John followed Nimrod into a bad-smelling entrance hall covered with graffiti, except that each graffito was an incantation or a binding; some of these were written or painted in English, but most were in Latin, or in Egyptian hieroglyphs, and designed, Nimrod told John, to prevent the exercise of any mind over matter within the building. "It's important you understand that," said Nimrod, as they climbed the steps, each of which was covered with another incantation. "No matter what Izaak tells us, no matter how cross we might be with him, there's no djinn power to be used in here. Besides, with all these incantations around, it would probably go spectacularly wrong."

"But why would anyone choose to stay in such a place?" said John. "Surely, with a bit of djinn power, those needing sanctuary could do a lot better for themselves."

"I'm afraid you don't quite understand," said John. "Djinn power isn't just forbidden to visitors. It's also forbidden to those who stay here in safety. Consequently, you'll find none of the comfort and ostentation that most of us use to furnish the insides of our bottles and lamps."

"Is the alternative really so bad?" asked John. "I mean, would other djinn really do something awful to the ones who have to live here?"

"Ask yourself this: What would you do to Izaak Balayaga if I wasn't here to help you control yourself?"

"I'd turn him into a piece of camel dung," said John.

"I think you have answered your own question," said Nimrod, and knocked at the door of number 28.

As soon as Izaak saw them at his door, he took hold of John's hand, kissed it, and begged his forgiveness.

"Hey, cut it out," said John, snatching his hand away, and pushing them both into his trouser pockets in case Izaak tried to kiss them again.

Bowing worthlessly, Izaak retreated into the dingy apartment. "Come in," he said. "It's not much, but, I didn't know where else to come."

John followed Nimrod through the door and, trying to ignore the strong smell of boiled mutton, glanced around at the threadbare curtains and the damp on the walls. A rat sat in a corner cleaning its whiskers. From the look of the place, John decided that the rat was probably the only creature that ever did any cleaning in Izaak's apartment.

"Tell us what you've done with my sister," John said stiffly. "Tell me or I'll set the worst elemental I can think of onto you."

Nimrod gave John a curious look, as if surprised that he knew about such things. "That's enough. There'll be no more talk of elementals while I'm around. Nasty things. And very hard to get rid of." He looked at Izaak with distaste. "Tell us what happened. And who put you up to this."

"She's got her," Izaak insisted breathlessly. "It was her that made me do it. I hadn't any real choice in the matter. I didn't want to do it. I'm not a bad sort of djinn, really I'm not. But what could I do?"

"Slow down," Nimrod told him. "And start from the beginning."

"Ayesha made me do it. It was her plan, you see? I never stole the Solomon Grimoire. She told me to tell you that. She said you'd never risk the grimoire falling into the hands of the Ifrit and that you'd do whatever was necessary to stop them from getting their hands on it. That business of me only handing the book over to the twins? That was her idea, too."

"I see," said Nimrod. "This explains a great deal."

"But what does Ayesha want with Philippa?" said John.

"Isn't it obvious?" said Izaak. "She wants to make your sister the next Blue Djinn of Babylon."

"What?" yelled John, horrified.

"Ayesha told me that she recognized Philippa's djinntellectual capabilities during the Djinnverso Tournament, as well as certain secret signs that I know nothing about."

"I was afraid it might be something like this," said Nimrod.

"Look, this much I know," Izaak continued. "Ayesha's time grows short. Too short to care about whether or not her successor is a willing volunteer. And so she decided that it would have to be your sister, John. So she made me her accomplice. At first, I refused. And then she told me that if I didn't do exactly what I was told, I would join Iblis in exile on Venus. You know, I suspect that she only sent him there to frighten me and to persuade me to do what I was told. So I agreed. What choice did I have? She gave me the formula of the djinn binding I used on the train, the fake book, everything. After I had imprisoned you and your sister, Ayesha met me at the train in Budapest. That was yesterday. Then she told me to lose myself. I said it wasn't much of a reward for helping her, and she told me that whatever reward she gave me would be worthless because very likely the first thing Philippa would do when she was the new Blue Djinn would be to come after me and punish me. And, what was more, that you might very well do the same. So I came here. It was the only place I could think of."

"I see your dilemma," said Nimrod. "Pity you didn't think of this before."

"Where is she now?" John demanded angrily. "Where is she, you rat?"

"By now, they'll be at Ayesha's secret palace in Babylon," said Izaak. "The Hanging Palace."

John shook his head. "Philippa will never go along with becoming the new Blue Djinn," he insisted. "Ayesha might have succeeded in getting her to Babylon, but she can't force her to be something she doesn't want to be." John glanced at Nimrod's somber face and felt a pang of doubt. "Can she?"

"I'm afraid that force is not required," said Nimrod. "If Philippa stays at Ayesha's palace for any length of time then, like it or not, she will be the next Blue Djinn. Her heart will harden. And what capacity she has for kindness and warmth will dry up. She will take on a new personality, beyond Good and Evil. And the Philippa we know will be lost to us forever."

"I don't understand," said John. "How is that possible?"

"I'm not sure any of us who have not been made privy to the secrets of the initiation can understand," said Nimrod. "All I know for sure is that if Philippa is there for thirty days, at least until the Feast of Ishtar, then something will happen to change her forever. That was how it was with Ayesha. That is how it has always been."

"Then we'll have to rescue her," said John.

"Impossible," said Izaak. "You don't know what you're saying. For one thing, the location of the palace is a secret. Other than that it's in Babylon, and nobody knows where it is. For another, it is extremely well-protected. By things only Ayesha knows about."

John looked hopefully at Nimrod. "There must be a way," he said. "We can't leave her there, Uncle Nimrod."

"I can't tell you how sorry I feel about what's happened," said Izaak. "But there's really nothing that you can do. You're talking about taking on the most powerful djinn there has ever been. Tell him, Nimrod."

"It's true, John," said Nimrod. "Blue Djinn are a bit

like atomic bombs. Each one is more powerful than the last. Ayesha may look and sound like an old bat, but she's irresistible, believe me. Quite omnipotent."

"There must be something we can do," insisted John. "Perhaps Mr Rakshasas will have an idea. He knows a lot about the Blue Djinn. There's a lot more he knows about her than is written in his book, I can tell you that."

"Perhaps he might know something, at that," nodded Nimrod.

"Then there's no time to lose," said John, going to the door.

"What about me?" said Izaak.

"What about you?" John scowled.

"Unless you forgive me, I'll have to stay here for the rest of my life."

John glanced at his uncle, who shrugged. "It's up to you, John," said Nimrod. "As Philippa's twin, you're her nearest relation, without question. If it is your wish to be revenged on Izaak here, then the whole of the Marid tribe would be obliged to seek that revenge on your behalf. It's what we djinn call a *vindicta*. I can tell you the precise form of words to use when we're outside the sanctuary, should you choose to go ahead with such a course of action. A *vindicta* uttered against him would oblige poor Izaak to stay here in the House of Kafur, probably forever. But it's your decision."

"Let me get this straight," said John. "I'm not allowed to use djinn power against him, while we're in the House of Kafur, right?" Nimrod nodded. "But I can utter a *vindicta* against him. When we get outside."

Nimrod nodded again. Izaak stared hopefully at John.

John was still very angry with Izaak. But he couldn't bring himself to wish for a lifelong revenge on the other djinn. On the other hand, he didn't think Izaak deserved to get away with what had happened, entirely. It was quite a dilemma, of the sort that Philippa was usually better at figuring out than he was. And while the djinn half of him considered the matter further, the human half reacted. John punched Izaak hard, and, howling loudly, Izaak sat down on the floor, holding a bloody nose.

"I forgive you, Izaak," said John. "But this had better not happen again. Or I promise you'll get much worse than a punch on the nose."

Izaak began to weep. "It won't," he said. "I promise."

"Come on," John told Nimrod. "Let's get out of here, before I change my mind. Or punch him again."

Back in Berlin, at a well-appointed suite in the famous Hotel Adlon, Mr Rakshasas and Groanin listened patiently as Nimrod and John told them that Ayesha had taken Philippa to her secret palace in Babylon.

"That's torn it," said Groanin. "I say, that's torn it. To kidnap a kid like that? It's inhuman, that's what it is. Inhuman."

"Since neither Ayesha nor Philippa is actually human," Nimrod told the one-armed butler, "then the humanity of the situation, or lack of it, seems hardly relevant."

"You know what I mean," said Groanin. "Sir."

"I'm sorry, Groanin. You're quite right, of course. Inhuman is a very good word for what has happened."

"There's nothing I wouldn't do for that child," insisted

Groanin and, taking out a large handkerchief, wiped a tear from his eye.

In an effort to make John feel better, Alan and Neil licked his hands.

"Where is Babylon, anyway?" he asked, folding their ears.

"Iraq," said Nimrod.

"Blimey," said Groanin. "That's torn it, 'n' all."

John sighed. Iraq was probably one of the most dangerous countries in the world. The very idea of trying to rescue someone from a country with so many human hazards, let alone those that had been created by a powerful djinn, seemed nothing short of foolhardy. But if that was where Philippa was then that was where he would have to go. He could see no alternative. At least Iraq was a hot, desert country, he told himself. At least there, he would be able to use djinn power. How dangerous could Iraq be to someone with his own special powers?

"I guess we'd better go to Iraq then," he said.

Mr Rakshasas shook his head. "Sometimes," he said, stroking his beard, which was always a sign that he was thinking deeply about something, "to get where you really want to go, 'tis necessary to go the opposite way, so it is. Babylon might be southeast of here, but only a fool would go that way before he'd been a long way west. By way of Great Nineveh."

"Please, Mr Rakshasas," said John. "Exactly what do you mean?"

"Just this. That we'll need to find a scabby sheep before we can find our lost lamb." By now Mr Rakshasas was using both hands to stroke his long white beard. "We'll need to speak to Macreeby," he told Nimrod.

"Virgil Macreeby is a rogue and a charlatan," said Nimrod.

"True enough," admitted Mr Rakshasas, smiling gently. "But sometimes even a rogue and a charlatan can show you where to catch the last bus home to Cork. Besides, there's no mundane living who knows more about the esoteric and secret ways of the djinn than Virgil Macreeby."

"Virgil Macreeby is the nearest thing to Solomon there is today," Nimrod told John. "Which makes him very dangerous. For a human being."

"It also makes him someone worth speaking to. Virgil Macreeby's made the study of djinnkind his life's work, right enough. I've heard it said that he's read every forbidden book in the British Museum and the Vatican Library."

"And stolen quite a few, too."

"Which is why his collection of Hermetica and secret books is the best in the world," said Mr Rakshasas. "Even better than my own."

"Yes, that's true enough, I suppose." Nimrod lit a large cigar and puffed out a smoke ring shaped like a dollar sign. "Of course, he won't help us for nothing. And I tell you frankly he's the last person in the world I'd ever want to grant three wishes. He's a wicked, wicked man."

"We might give him a book, for his famous library," said Mr Rakshasas.

"I could give him Solomon's *Querelae*, I suppose. His *Big Book of Moans*. That's a very rare book."

Mr Rakshasas shook his head. "Rare, yes. Interesting, sometimes. Useful, no. Not to a man like Virgil Macreeby. No, there's only one book I think he'd like to own, Nimrod. My own copy of the *Meta Magus*. It so happens I have it with me, in my lamp."

"But it's priceless," objected Nimrod.

"I've made a copy," said Mr Rakshasas, tapping his forehead. "Up here. And now that I've finished the *Shorter Baghdad*, well, I've no more use for it. Besides, you never really own a rare book like the *Meta Magus*. You just look after it for a while. Of course, I'm not saying Macreeby isn't full of tricks. Even giving him a book like the *Meta Magus*, we'd still have to be on our guard. In case he tried to bind us to his own will."

"Three of us together," said Nimrod, shooting a glance John's way. "He wouldn't dare. All right. If you're quite sure that's what you want to do."

Mr Rakshasas nodded silently.

"All the same, I take your point about Macreeby. We'd better all be on our guard. How are you feeling, John? Empowered or torpid?"

John glanced out of the Adlon bedroom window at the cold Berlin night. According to a sign in the hotel lobby, the outside temperature was below freezing. "Torpid," he said. "The desert seems to have left my bones now we're back in Berlin."

"Then I'd better fix you up with a discrimen, just in case," said Nimrod.

"No wait, better to give you three emergency wishes after what happened before. But do be careful, John. These things require very careful handling."

"Yes, sir."

Nimrod puffed his cigar thoughtfully. "Let's see now. I must think of a suitable word you might use."

"How about—"

"No, John, it has to be me who thinks of the word," said Nimrod. "That's how a discrimen works."

"Well, don't make it too complicated," said John. "Mr Vodyannoy gave me a German word that was almost impossible to pronounce."

"How about 'Rimsky-Korsakov'?"

"Rimsky what?"

"Rimsky-Korsakov. A Russian composer whose most famous work, written in 1889, is the symphonic suite, *Scheherazade*. She it was, you'll remember, who sets in motion the cycle of stories that made up the *Arabian Nights*."

John nodded. "Rimsky-Korsakov, huh?" He nodded again. "OK, I can remember that."

"You won't have to," said Nimrod. "In an emergency the discrimen remembers itself for you."

Another whirlwind carried them west to the village of Great Nineveh, in Kent – which is a county in southeastern England – and the Norman-built castle in the middle of a lake that Virgil Macreeby called home.

"There it is," said Nimrod. "Cumbernauld Castle."

John thought Cumbernauld looked like an amazing sort of place to live and, viewed from the air, he would not have been surprised to have seen a lady's arm sticking up from the lake with a sword in her hand, as in the story about King Arthur.

"It seems that we're expected," he added, catching

sight of a rather stout-looking man staring up at the sky from a grass helipad in the centre of the castle island. "That's Virgil Macreeby."

Nimrod steered the whirlwind around the back of the castle, reducing power over the lake, before bringing it slowly down to the heliport. Macreeby was waving now, but looking quite relaxed, as if three djinn arriving by whirlwind was an everyday occurrence at Cumbernauld Castle.

"How could he have known we were coming?" said John.

"With a man like Macreeby," said Mr Rakshasas, who had stayed out of his lamp for the journey, "there's no telling what he knows. Sure, we'd best be careful. Just in case he's laid on a real Dublin Castle welcome."

Having landed them safely, Nimrod dismissed the whirlwind, and Virgil Macreeby walked toward them, grinning affably. He wore a tweed suit, a chin beard that looked like a shoe-brush and had a smooth, well-spoken voice that reminded John of an actor in a play by Shakespeare.

"Wonderful," laughed Macreeby. "You know I never get tired of seeing you people travelling in this way. 'I came in like water, and like the wind I go', eh? And much more friendly to the environment than an aircraft. Yes, I do envy you your whirlwinds, Nimrod. One day you must take me for a ride. It would make a pleasant change from my old broomstick." Macreeby looked at John and winked. "Just joking. I don't really have a broomstick. Although some of the villagers around here think I do. They're a credulous lot in this part of England." Macreeby held out his hand. "You must be young John of

Gaunt. I've heard a great deal about you, young man."

"How do you do, sir," said John, shaking Macreeby's hand with his middle finger folded carefully across his lifeline.

"You've taught him well, Nimrod," said Macreeby. "He knows the djinn handshake."

"His mother taught him that."

"Ah yes, the lovely Layla. How is she? And you, Mr Rakshasas. I'm very much looking forward to reading your book. I do hope you've brought me a copy for my library. It's really quite definitive, I hear. Well, almost. What a great pity you didn't consult me before writing it." He waved them toward his castle. "But come inside, please."

Inside the castle, Macreeby hesitated in front of three heavy doors. "Yes, let's go into the library, I think. There's a fire I'm sure you'll all appreciate. Not to mention some of Mrs Macreeby's famous lemon cake. And we won't be disturbed there."

"It's been a while since I saw the Macreeby collection," said Mr Rakshasas.

Everything about the library was huge: the size of the fire, the number of books, the circumference of the table, the height of the chairs around it, even the slice of lemon cake that Macreeby presented to John as soon as they were all seated. So affable was Macreeby's manner that John was half inclined to believe perhaps, that Nimrod had exaggerated the potential danger posed by the English magus. But then he caught sight of Macreeby's fingernails. They were long and sharpened to points, like tiny swords. And, in the breast pocket of Macreeby's jacket, instead of a silk handkerchief, was a large black spider. All of which prompted John to regard his cake with some suspicion.

"It's all right, boy," Macreeby chuckled, "the cake's not poisoned. Although I can't say the same for this little fellow." Macreeby removed the spider from his pocket and allowed it to sink its fangs into his hand. "It's an *Atrax formidabilis*. A tree-dwelling funnel-web spider. Probably the most venomous spider in the world. I'm training myself to become resistant to its venom by allowing myself to be bitten by a very young one once or twice a day."

John almost choked on a mouthful of cake. "Why would you want to become resistant to its venom?" he asked, as the spider proceeded to bite Macreeby again.

"I believe that in your country, lots of people carry firearms," explained Macreeby. "To protect themselves against attack?" He shrugged. "I carry a spider for the same reason. To protect myself against my many enemies. Of course, handling a spider like *Atrax formidabilis* requires more practice than handling a simple firearm. The venom from an adult male can kill a man in hours. These junior specimens are venomous enough. Lethal even. However, my tolerance of the venom is now such that I can withstand a bite from an adult without any ill effects." Macreeby winced as the baby spider bit him a third time. "Of course, the pain is excruciating. But I do need to keep up my resistance." Macreeby smiled at John. "Would you like to handle him?"

John shook his head.

"He's quite aggressive for such a small fellow, isn't he? No? Well, I can't say I blame you for being cautious. Not after what happened to your poor sister, eh? I think I'll put him back in my pocket for now."

155

"What do you know about that?" John asked Macreeby. "About my sister?"

Macreeby dropped the spider into his breast pocket. "Only what I've heard on the grapevine. But if you really want to know, then let me think. Why yes, I heard it from Mimi de Ghulle, who had it from Izaak Balayaga."

"I didn't know you knew Mimi de Ghulle," said Nimrod.

"We're old friends, Mimi and I." Macreeby waved his hands at the room they were in. "It's thanks to Mimi's original generosity that I can afford to live here." He shook his head. "Frankly, John, I'm amazed you let Izaak off like that. If it had been me, I'd have set a demon on him. I assume that's why you're here. You need my help to mount a rescue mission."

"That's right," said Nimrod, more than a little discomfited by Macreeby having guessed the purpose of their visit. "You and your famous library. We were rather hoping to use it to find some clues as to how we might bring her back from Babylon."

"Well, it won't be easy, I can tell you that straightaway," said Macreeby. He smiled as a thought seemed to enter his head for the first time. "But I must say it is rather ironic, is it not? That you, of all people, Nimrod, should be looking for clues, as you put it, and from me." He chuckled again. "Yes, it must be very embarrassing for you, all things considered."

John was about to ask his uncle exactly what Macreeby meant, when there was a knock at the door and a boy of about John's own age came into the library. He was a studious-looking but sullen boy, with bright green eyes and an impish face. Macreeby regarded him coldly.

"This is my son, Finlay, who's not at all interested in mastering the dark arts and becoming a magus himself. Computers. That's all Finlay's interested in, isn't that so, Finlay?"

"Yes, Father."

"Is there a reason why you've graced us with your presence, Finlay?"

"Grandmother wants to know if our guests will be staying for dinner."

"No, I don't think so," said Macreeby. "I expect they'll want to be on their way as soon as they've picked my brains. They've a long and tiring journey ahead of them. How many miles to Babylon? A little more than three score and ten, eh, Nimrod?"

"Indeed it is," said Nimrod.

Macreeby waved the boy gone from the library like a servant. "Families, eh, Nimrod?" he said. "How they try us both. He's been a great disappointment to me."

"He seemed like a nice young man," offered Mr Rakshasas.

"You see the good in everyone, Mr Rakshasas," said Macreeby. "Even me, no doubt."

"I'd be needing a good pair of spectacles," said Mr Rakshasas.

Macreeby grinned. "Quite so. Anyway, you won't have an appetite for something as mundane as dinner, with so much on your plate. You'll not want to waste time eating that could be better spent reading the *Bellili Scrolls*, for example."

"You're not serious," said Nimrod.

"My apologies, Nimrod. If you really want to stay to dinner, it's really no trouble at all."

"I mean, you're not serious about the *Bellili Scrolls*."

"Perfectly. And, of course, it's just the book you're looking for."

"The *Bellili Scrolls* were destroyed," insisted Mr Rakshasas. "When Julius Caesar burned down the great library at Alexandria."

"That's what I always thought myself," said Macreeby. "But it wasn't true. That's history for you, I suppose. So much of it turns out to be idle rumor. In fact, one basket of rare scrolls was saved – the *Bellili Scrolls*. I found them on a forgotten shelf in the old Vatican Library. I had the very devil of a job stealing them." Macreeby looked at the disbelieving faces of Nimrod and Mr Rakshasas and smiled. "I can assure you, gentlemen, I'm perfectly serious. I've even made a translation of the scrolls, into English. I'd be perfectly willing to sell you a copy."

"You're not serious," repeated Nimrod.

"Of course I'm serious," said Macreeby. "I sold a copy to Mimi de Ghulle, I don't see why I can't sell one to you."

"You did, eh?" said Nimrod. "I wonder what she wanted it for?"

"Would someone mind telling me what these *Bellili Scrolls* are about?" said John.

"Bellili, the White Goddess," explained Mr Rakshasas, "was Ishtar's predecessor. She who was worshipped before Ishtar herself. The scrolls amount to a book written by Bellili's High Priest Eno, and are reputed to contain a detailed description of the secret underground Babylonian world that Ishtar inherited from Bellili: Iravotum."

158

"Not *a* description," insisted Macreeby. "The *only* description."

"Iravotum?" said John.

"Iravotum," said Macreeby. "It's the place where Ayesha has taken your sister, John."

Nimrod and Mr Rakshasas continued to look astonished, which both pleased and exasperated Macreeby in equal measure.

"Look here," he said. "For djinn of your knowledge and learning, ten minutes' examination of the original will reveal that the scrolls are genuine." Macreeby paused so that he might achieve a more dramatic effect. "There's even a map."

"There's a map?" said Nimrod. "Of Iravotum? Incredible."

"Marvellous." Macreeby rubbed his hands excitedly. "Marvellous. I love doing business with people who can appreciate the real rarity of an object. And hence its very obvious value. Yes, there's a map, too. Never go anywhere abroad without a map, John, that's what I always say. Not unless you want to get lost. Which is, of course, what I will tell you all to do if my price is not met. For I tell you quite frankly, gentlemen, I mean to profit handsomely from your lack of knowledge."

"Then let me put my cards of the table," said Nimrod. "Mr Rakshasas is willing to trade you his copy of the *Meta Magus* for a copy of the original and your own translation. Subject to a satisfactory inspection."

"That's very handsome of you, Mr Rakshasas," said Macreeby. "But I hope you still have a card or two up your sleeve, Nimrod, because I'm afraid that doesn't quite match my price. You see, I have a photocopy facsimile of the *Meta Magus*. Everything in that book is now known to me. And I don't mind telling you, I think it has been overrated. Now if you were offering a copy of the Solomon Grimoire that might be a different story. But I don't think you are, are you?" He grinned wolfishly. "We all know who has the only copy of that particular book."

"Name your price, Macreeby," sighed Nimrod.

"Don't be so coy, Nimrod. Let's keep it traditional, shall we? Three wishes. For that you get the original scrolls, my own English translation, and of course, the High Priest Eno's invaluable map."

"Giving you three wishes, Macreeby, would be like giving a child a machine gun. Out of the question."

"Come now. What are three wishes to a djinn like you?"

"Why didn't you ask Mimi de Ghulle?" said Nimrod. "You said she had a copy of the *Bellili Scrolls* from you. I can't imagine she was particularly scrupulous about granting someone like you three wishes."

"The fact is that until she found out I had the *Bellili Scrolls*, I was quite considerably in her debt," said Macreeby. "Uncomfortably in her debt. It so happens I was being squeezed, by the de Ghulle family, quite mercilessly, to fulfill some very rash promises I'd made to them a couple of years ago. For which I had already had three wishes. So it was very fortunate that I did find the *Bellili Scrolls*. Otherwise, I don't know what she'd have done to me, Nimrod, really I don't. You know how vindictive the de Ghulles can be. But when she found out I had found the scrolls, Mimi's attitude toward me changed completely. And I'm happy to say that thanks to my being able to furnish her with a copy of the scrolls, my debt to Mimi is now discharged."

"I wonder why she wanted it," said Nimrod. "Any ideas?"

"I really couldn't say," said Macreeby. "You'd best ask her. But look here, Nimrod, that's my price. Three wishes. Take it or leave it."

Nimrod continued to look sceptically at the English magus. "You're a wicked, wicked man, Virgil Macreeby. There's no telling what havoc you might create if a djinn as powerful as me simply gave you three wishes."

"Wicked? What's wicked about wanting a new roof on this castle? This is an expensive place to run, Nimrod. A new roof wouldn't be too much to ask, surely; I simply can't face having the builders in here for months and months. And then, some money. What's money to someone like you? And perhaps that new model of the Rolls Royce I've been reading about. There's quite a waiting list, I believe. Wicked? I don't think so."

"I wouldn't trust you to limit yourself to those three wishes if I had them written down in your own blood, Macreeby," said Nimrod. "We both know that you're a grand master of saying one thing and thinking another. Even if we were to agree those wishes, at the last possible second, you might wish for something else."

"Surely the *Baghdad Rules* have this situation covered," said Macreeby.

"There's a provision for a djinn and a human agreeing on three Wishes in advance. I know there is."

"Then you also know that the agreement is based on

an oath," said Mr Rakshasas. "By all that you believe in and keep holy. Which in your case, would be a nonsense, since everyone knows you believe in nothing, and are the least holy-minded person ever to draw breath."

"True, true. I'm proud to say that is indeed the case." Macreeby smiled coldly. "Then it seems we have a dilemma, gentlemen," he said. "You want those scrolls. And I want a fair price."

"I won't grant you three wishes, Macreeby," said Nimrod. "Anything might happen. And we both know that Mr Rakshasas is not up to the task of granting wishes anymore."

Macreeby nodded, sensing that Nimrod was about to make a counteroffer. "Go on. I'm listening."

"I think I might have a solution," said Nimrod. "My nephew, John, will, grant you three wishes. As you are no doubt aware his djinn power is not yet fully mature and therefore it may be that there are some wishes that it would be beyond his abilities to grant. In other words, it would therefore be in your interests to keep your wishes within the limits you indicated earlier."

Macreeby thought for a moment. "The boy can do it? He can grant me three wishes? Your word, Nimrod?"

"Yes, provided you're not too greedy."

"What do you say, boy?" Macreeby asked John.

"As my uncle says," said John. "Provided you're not too greedy."

"All right. We have a deal."

"Let's see the scrolls first," said Nimrod. "And the translation you've made of them. Then the three wishes."

Macreeby patted his plump hands together like an

excited child. His cold eyes glistened. But his voice remained complacent, like a cat's purr. "Very well. I'll fetch them for you. And the copy you can take away. It's all quite scholarly, I can assure you. Both of you are aware of my reputation."

He sprang up a tall library ladder as nimbly as a monkey and brought down a book bound in light blue leather and the box containing the scrolls, which he then placed upon the table.

"Scrolls are a little like good cigars," he said. "You have to keep them humidified." Almost reverently he opened the box and then stood back to allow Nimrod and Mr Rakshasas room to examine the original scrolls, and for several minutes the two djinn were silently absorbed with this task.

Macreeby smiled at John. "More cake?" he said.

John shook his head and sat nearer the fire, trying to remember the focus word for the three discrimen wishes with which he had been armed earlier. In persuading Macreeby to have three wishes from John, Nimrod had been clever, he could see that now. There was no way the English magus would have been able to guess that John himself had no power at all, as long as he was affected by a cold climate; and that the wishes John was preparing to grant Macreeby would draw on Nimrod's own considerable powers. He realized that it was a very good way of preventing Macreeby from wishing for something really outrageous. But because this wasn't an emergency the discrimen hadn't remembered itself, which meant John had to do this. Now if he could only think of the name of that Russian guy. *What was it now? Something weird. Like Rumplestiltskin.* Except that wasn't it.

Fifteen more minutes passed and he noticed that the two older djinn were now nodding their approval.

"I'd never have believed it possible," said Mr Rakshasas. "If only I'd had this when I was writing my own book."

"Isn't it always the way?" said Macreeby. "The historian's fate. The biographer's lot."

"Light my lamp," said Nimrod. "There really is a map, too."

"The scrolls are genuine, all right," said Mr Rakshasas. "The quality of the paper. The ink. The language. Incredible."

Nimrod was glancing through the leather-bound volume that was Macreeby's own translation of the scrolls. "This is a fine piece of work, Macreeby," he said. "Very scholarly."

"That's high praise from someone with your djinntellect, Nimrod." But Macreeby was beginning to become impatient. "And now if you don't mind, I've kept my side of the bargain. I think it's time you kept yours."

"Are you ready, John?" said Nimrod.

Rip your corsets off? Surely not that.

"Er, yes, I think so." John stood up, hoping he might yet get a clue as to what the focus word was. *Rum and Sherry Cool you off?*

"If you don't mind," said Macreeby, "I'd rather like Finlay to witness this. Perhaps witnessing a djinn actually granting me three wishes will help to persuade him that his father is not the complete charlatan he thinks he is. Who knows? It might yet persuade the boy to follow in my footsteps."

164

Nimrod glanced inquisitively at John.

"Er, it's fine by me," said John. By now he'd remembered that it was a Russian composer's name he was supposed to have remembered. *Not Tchaikovsky. But something Ovsky, surely. Or Kovich. Like Shostakovich. Another Russian composer. But not him, either. Ovskykovich?*

They went outside to find Finlay, which was Nimrod's opportunity to whisper in John's ear as, by now, it was obvious to him that since this wasn't an emergency, John had forgotten the focus word for the discrimen. "Rimsky-Korsakov," he said. "Rimsky-Korsakov."

They found Macreeby waiting for them in the castle yard, with Finlay. "Watch this," he told his son, rubbing his hands together, excitedly. "Watch and see something that a computer can't do."

"Remember, Macreeby," said Nimrod. "Keep your wishes sensible."

"I mentioned a new roof, didn't I? What could be more modest and sensible than that? Have you any idea how much a new roof costs on a place like this? Yes, I wish this castle had a new roof."

John looked up at the roof. He was using Nimrod's power, but he still had to think hard to put Macreeby's first wish into practice. He didn't know much about architecture, nor for that matter very much about English castles, but it was plain that Macreeby just wanted a roof of the same type as the one he already had; which seemed easy enough. "Rimsky-Korsakov," he muttered. And then, "It's done."

Finlay Macreeby shook his head and laughed out loud.

"What are you laughing about?" demanded his father.

"I can't see anything different about it," said Finlay.

"I didn't think you wanted it to look very different from what you've got now," said John, irritated with Finlay. "That wouldn't do at all. You'll have to go up there and take a closer look to see that it's a new one."

"Yeah," sneered Finlay. "Sure."

"Look," snapped Macreeby, "what's the matter with you, boy? If John says it's a new roof, it's a new roof."

Nimrod glanced at his watch. He was anxious to begin studying Macreeby's translation of the *Bellili Scrolls* as soon as possible. "Second wish," he said, trying to move things along.

"Money," said Macreeby, and shook his head. "Obviously."

"Obviously," chuckled Finlay.

"Let's see now. How much?" Catching Nimrod's eye, he nodded tetchily. "Yes, yes, I know. Not too greedy. A million pounds? How does that sound?" Nimrod nodded. "I wish I had one million pounds, in cash."

"Rimsky-Korsakov," said John and drew Macreeby's attention to a pair of steel suitcases that had appeared in the castle doorway.

With a howl of delight, Macreeby fell on his knees and, opening one of the cases ran his greedy hands over the bundles of pound notes. "You see?" he said, glancing at Finlay.

Finlay gasped. "Wait a minute," he said, grabbing a cellophane-wrapped bundle of fifty-pound notes. "This money is for real."

"Of course it's for real," said Macreeby. "That's what I've been telling you."

"These people really are genies?"

Nimrod winced perceptibly. "We prefer 'djinn,' if you don't mind."

"So this three wishes thing is on the level?"

Macreeby laughed. "Haven't you heard? That's what genies do. Idiot. What do you think I'm doing here? Playing some kind of party game?"

Finlay smiled incredulously as he looked at the money. "And you blew two wishes on a new roof and a lousy million?" He shook his head. "What's wrong with you, Dad? You could have wished for a proper house, instead of this dump of a castle."

"That's enough, thank you, Finlay," said his father.

"No," laughed Finlay, "it's not nearly enough. That's the point. A million is chump change these days. A million doesn't buy anything. Listen, you big dumb bird, you've got one wish left, so this time try not to blow it. Let's see some imagination, you big dumb bird."

"Shut up," said Macreeby. "Shut up and let me think. I wanted a new Rolls Royce. The new one. The Phantom."

"Don't wish for a Rolls Royce," said Finlay. "Wish for all the Rolls Royces in the showroom. Better still wish for the whole company."

"You don't understand," said Macreeby.

"It's you that doesn't understand, you big dumb bird."

"I wish *you* were a bird, Finlay," Macreeby said angrily and, before John could prevent himself – actually, he couldn't prevent himself at all, the wish was out now and it was all he could do just to focus his mind on the best kind of bird he could imagine – he'd uttered "Rimsky-Korsakov" a third time to make Macreeby's wish come true. No sooner had the Russian composer's name left John's lips than poor Finlay had turned into a peregrine falcon.

"Oh, Lord," said Nimrod, "now look what's happened."

"A wish is a dish that's a lot like a fish," said Mr Rakshasas. "Once it's been eaten it's a lot harder to throw back."

The falcon flew up into the sky over the castle yard and wheeled angrily around their heads.

"It's not too late," said Nimrod. "Quick Macreeby, make a fourth wish."

"What?" said Macreeby.

"Baghdad Rule number 18," insisted Nimrod. "A fourth wish uttered without ado, will the previous three undo."

"Lose my new roof and a million pounds in cash? I should think not."

"But what about Finlay?" said John.

Macreeby glanced up at the falcon hovering high above his head. "Maybe this will teach him to respect his father," he said grimly.

"Macreeby, don't be stupid," said Nimrod. "He's your own boy."

"No, he's not." Macreeby laughed cruelly. "Not any more. He's a Bird. And good luck to him."

He picked up the two suitcases full of money and headed into the castle. "Good luck to you, too," he called out over his shoulder. "From what I've read in those *Bellili Scrolls*, you're going to need all the luck you can make." Then he put down the cases in the hallway of his castle, and kicked the door shut behind him.

Sick to his stomach at the terrible thing he had done, John watched the peregrine falcon as it climbed high above the new roof, higher than the gods it seemed, before turning south toward the horizon where, finally, it disappeared.

"I was afraid something like this might happen," said Nimrod.

"What have I done?" moaned John. "What have I done?"

"There was nothing you could do," said Nimrod. "Not once the wish was uttered. You couldn't help yourself."

"He's right, John," said Mr Rakshasas laying a kind hand on John's shoulder. "Well, now you know. 'Tis the risk we always run when we grant mundanes three wishes. That they'll speak first and think later. Sure, I mind well the first time I was obliged to issue the wish as spoken. I was quite cut up about it, so I was." He let out a sigh. "But that's how it is. Experience. You don't learn to swim on the kitchen floor."

Nimrod tucked Macreeby's book under his arm and put his hand on John's other shoulder. "Come on," he said. "Let's get out of here before I turn that man into a sparrow. Then we'd see how he much he liked his son being a falcon."

CHAPTER 11

THE HANGING PALACE
OF BABYLON

Released, after what seemed like an age, from the cigar tube in which she had been imprisoned by Izaak Balayaga, Philippa found herself alone in an enormous, beautifully decorated bedroom that looked as if it had belonged to a queen. Great marble columns rose up to an elaborate ceiling from which hung several huge crystal chandeliers. Windows taller than a bus were framed with heavy yellow silk curtains that matched the bedspread and the upholstery on the gilt armchairs, and everywhere there were white marble statues of children – most of them fat, naked babies wrapped in sheets, or reclining, uncomfortably, on outsized seashells. The room was not to Philippa's taste. Nevertheless there was something about it she liked: a beautiful scent that filled the air, like the freshest, most exotic blossom that had ever filled her nose.

Bright sunlight shone through the windows but when Philippa crossed the thick, pink-patterned carpet to look outside, to her surprise she discovered there was no view – nothing, not even a corner of the building she was in – just more of the same blank white light. This was quite disturbing and, after a while, Philippa decided it was the sort of sight that she might have seen in a dream, and not a very nice dream at that, and so she pinched herself hard a couple of times, the way people did in books when they wanted to make sure that they were awake. Or when they wanted to wake themselves up. But finding herself well and truly awake, the discovery made her wish she wasn't – more so when she went to open the door and found that it was locked.

Philippa's first thought was to scream and shout and hammer on the door until someone came and let her out. But then she remembered who and what she was and, gathering all her strength of mind, she uttered her focus word – "FABULONGOSHOOMARVELISH-LYWONDERPIPICAL!" – and wished herself back home in New York.

Nothing happened, although she was sure it ought to have, for it was hot inside her gilded cage – hot enough to have facilitated djinn power. Which made her think she might be losing her touch since this was the second time in as many days when a focus word had deserted her. First Nimrod's discrimen, and now her own power. There was nothing to do but be patient, something at which, fortunately, Philippa was good. So she lay down on the big, rather soft bed, and waited for something to happen.

And, after a while it did.

Hearing a key in the lock of the door, Philippa sprang off the bed and, crossing the floor with her heart in her mouth, she found herself face-to-face with a small, mousy-looking woman whom she half recognized. The woman was carrying a silver tray on which were some sandwiches, cakes, cookies, and a large jug of fruit juice, all of which made Philippa realize how hungry she was. But she was hungrier still for some answers to some pressing questions, such as where she was, and why she had been brought there.

"Hey," said Philippa. "I know you, don't I?"

The woman nodded and put the tray down on a table. She wore a dress that had been both expensive and fashionable about forty years ago, a pair of lace gloves, and several strings of rather worn pearls. There was dust in her hair, yellow in her teeth, too much powder on her face, and a lot of disappointment in her eyes. "We've met, yes," said the woman. "At the Djinnverso Tournament in New York. I'm Miss Glumjob."

"Yes, I remember now," said Philippa. "You were with Ayesha."

"I'm her lady's maid and travelling companion." Miss Glumjob's accent was from the American deep south.

"Then perhaps you'll tell me why I was abducted and brought here." There was anger in Philippa's voice. "Wherever 'here' is."

"Sure, honey, sure. But before I do, let me tell you this. That your abduction had absolutely nothing to do with me. I am not your enemy. I would ask you to remember that, later on. I will be your friend if you want and I will help you if and when I can, so long as it does not conflict with the wishes of my employer on whom I have been dependent these last forty-five years." Miss Glumjob tried to smile. "Are you thirsty, child? Would you like some apple juice? My momma, from whom I learned the recipe, used to make the finest apple juice in the whole of North Carolina."

"Explanations, first," demanded Philippa.

Miss Glumjob sat down on one of the yellow armchairs, which matched her teeth. "Since you are what you are, then hopefully you won't actually require me to explain how any of this is possible. It is what it is and that's a fact." She looked around the room and nodded. "Well then, this palace is an exact copy, in every detail, of Osborne House, which was the home of Queen Victoria from 1845 until the queen's death in 1901."

"We're in England?"

"Let me finish. Ayesha, who is English herself, of course, always loved that house, ever since she visited the place as a little girl. When, many years later, Ayesha became the Blue Djinn, she decided that if she was going to have to spend any time here in Babylon, which is where we are in reality, then this was how she wanted the interior of her palace to look."

"But Babylon is in Iraq. Are you telling me that we're actually somewhere in Iraq?"

"That's right. We are at the extreme edge of a vast and secret underground cavern called Iravotum." Miss Glumjob paused. "You've heard of the Hanging Gardens of Babylon, of course. Well, this is the Hanging Palace, built by King Nebuchadnezzar for Ishtar, who was one of Ayesha's predecessors in the job. It's called the Hanging Palace on account of the fact that it used to kind of hang on the edge of a precipice. Which is another reason why Ayesha has this place looking like something from Victorian England. She doesn't care for heights at all. Anyway, what the place looks like today is hardly the point. This is the Blue Djinn's spiritual home and she

173

comes here every January to dry out." Miss Glumjob smiled. "That's what we call it, anyway.

"You see, honey, that old lady is famously hard-hearted. Has to be, to keep the peace between all you djinn. But it's being here that does it – that makes her such a tough cookie. I'm not allowed to tell you how but, if she didn't come here once a year, to dry out, then she'd be like anyone's old granny, I guess. Not that I'm blaming her. If I knew what she knows, I'd be much the same, I guess."

"And what exactly has any of this to do with me?"

"Why, I declare! Back in New York, I was led to believe that you were strong in the head department. Surely you must have guessed by now?"

Philippa shook her head.

Miss Glumjob shrugged. "It's true that I myself have no direct knowledge of this whole matter. But it's my understanding that she means to make you the next Blue Djinn of Babylon."

"That's ridiculous," said Philippa. "I'm only twelve years old."

"There have been plenty of kings and queens who succeeded to their thrones before they were out of diapers, honey. Age, or the lack of it, has never been considered much of an obstacle to high office."

"But I don't want the job," insisted Philippa. "I simply won't do it."

"You'll have to tell her, not me. If you like, I can take you to her now, and she'll put your mind right on every-thing that's troubling you, perhaps."

"Yes," Philippa said firmly. "Take me to her. The sooner

I've explained the situation, the better. I can see that it's a great honour. But I'm simply not ready to take on this kind of responsibility."

Miss Glumjob led Philippa out of the bedroom, through several long corridors and down a wide flight of stairs. The house seemed to be empty of anyone else, although Philippa quickly formed the impression that the house was haunted: In one room she saw a vacuum cleaner moving by itself; and at the foot of the stairs, she came across a dust cloth polishing the wooden handrail. Seeing Philippa's obvious alarm, Miss Glumjob explained that Ayesha's servants were, all of them, invisible.

"I am the only visible member of her retinue here in Babylon," she told Philippa. "Invisible servants are best. Somehow one feels an obligation to speak to a servant that one can see. But with an invisible servant, this becomes unnecessary. This is the way the old girl likes it: that they should be heard, sometimes, but never seen."

"But don't they mind being invisible?"

"They're well paid." Miss Glumjob shook her head. "They just do their jobs and when they go home, they become visible again. Really, there's nothing to it."

"I couldn't ever get used to invisible servants," said Philippa with a shudder. "They're people, after all. No, I couldn't ever live here."

"You wouldn't have to," said Miss Glumjob. "When it's yours, you'll be able to do the place up anyway you want: minimalist modern, Gothic, sixties modern, Rococo, anything you like. You could even fix it up the way it used to be, which is kind of ancient. It doesn't have to be like this. I haven't ever been inside a djinn bottle or a lamp –

Ayesha says I wouldn't survive the experience – but I believe the principle is much the same."

Philippa kept on shaking her head. "It could look like the Four Seasons Hotel, and I still wouldn't want to live here."

"Ayesha has her powers, of course. Anything she wishes for, she makes it so. The newest books, the latest movies, the newspapers, the best food and wine. In all other respects she is completely dependent on me. I flatter myself that we've become quite good friends."

They went into an enormous white room that appeared to have been lifted out of the palace not of Queen Victoria but of an Indian maharaja. Miss Glumjob explained: "As well as being the Queen of Great Britain, Victoria was the Empress of India," said Miss Glumjob. "Which is reflected in the design of this room. It's called the Durbar Room, after the Hindustani word for some kind of party. I have never been to India myself. But I have heard it is a fascinating place. And the room, I'm sure you will agree, is magnificent."

"Where exactly are you from, Miss Glumjob?"

"Greenville, North Carolina. One day, I mean to go back there."

"How long is it since you've been home?"

"Not since I started to work for Ayesha, some forty-five years ago."

"It's forty-five years since you went home?"

Miss Glumjob nodded a little wistfully.

"But why don't you take a vacation?"

They sat down in a seat beside a window that afforded a view of nothing at all, just the same opaque light there had been in the bedroom.

"There are no holidays in this job," said Miss Glumjob. "That was part of my agreement with Ayesha when I first entered her service. Another condition was that I could never ask for a pay raise, and so, in the beginning, I was to ask for whatever salary I wanted and that would be my salary for as long as I was in this job. So I asked for 15,000 dollars a year. Let me tell you, back in the fifties, 15,000 dollars a year was a fortune. And I do declare I thought I was set for life. Of course, nowadays, 15,000 dollars isn't so very much. But I don't dare ask her for a pay raise any more than I dare to ask her for a vacation."

"Why don't you try to renegotiate your contract with her?"

Miss Glumjob shook her head. "For one thing, Ayesha is famously hard-hearted. She'd never agree. And for another, she promised me that if I stuck to our original agreement, one day, she would grant me three wishes. Just like in the story books. Three wishes. Imagine it." She smiled, a little sheepishly. "And I have. Imagined it. I mean what I will wish for, when she's ready to grant them to me."

Philippa shook her head, pitying Miss Glumjob a little.

"You can shake your head," said Miss Glumjob, "but back in Greenville, there wasn't much magic around. Just reality. But magic was all I ever wanted." She smiled. "Is there anything wrong with that?"

"Depends on how you look at it. But it seems to me that you've wasted your life, Miss Glumjob. And for what? A dream. Reality is all there is."

"That's easy for you to say," said Miss Glumjob. "You're

a djinn. You can do anything you want."

"She's right, you know."

Philippa looked up and saw that Ayesha was seated in a little minstrel's gallery that reminded her of an organ loft in a church.

"You can alter the world you live in," said Ayesha. "But for her, for any mundane being, reality is just a tree or a rock. Reality's certainly not something to be found in the heart of a human being. That's the part that they wish with. Their hearts. Not their heads, as you'll discover when you learn a little more about this place."

"I don't want to learn about this place," insisted Philippa. "I want to go home. I am honoured by your offer, Ayesha, really I am. But this is not for me.

"This is not an offer you can refuse," said Ayesha, coming down a small flight of stairs. She was wearing a blue silk dress with a high frilly collar and, as always, she had a handbag over her arm and a handkerchief up her sleeve. "I'm afraid you don't have any choice in the matter. For years I've been looking for the right person to fill my shoes when I'm gone. And now I've found her. When I'm gone from this world – which, thank goodness, won't be long now – you will take over. You, Philippa, will be the Blue Djinn of Babylon."

"I'll escape. You can't keep me here. I won't let you."

"To where will you escape?" Ayesha's voice was soft, almost whispered, but there was steel in it, in the set of her jaw, and in her armour-piercing eyes. "You don't even know where you are. If you did, then you'd not be thinking of escape. Iraq is dangerous enough, but it's nothing compared to the hazards that are to be encountered here in Iravotum."

"Where?" Philippa frowned. She had heard of Iraq. And Iran. Who hadn't? But until Miss Glumjob had mentioned the name she had never heard of Iravotum.

Ayesha took Philippa by the arm and led her to one of the Durbar Room's large windows, opaque with white light, but when Ayesha touched it, the glass cleared and Philippa saw how the house faced a dark and impenetrable forest.

"That," she said, "is Iravotum – the place of bad and angry wishes. When humans wish for bad things, this is where those bad things come, in the hope of being corrected. Just this morning, by the gate, I saw a half-skunk, half-human. I happen to know that the poor creature's mother had said out loud, within the earshot of a djinn, 'I wish I had a child, even if that child should turn out to be a bit of a skunk.' And her wish came true. When she gave birth she found that her child was what she had wished for. Half-skunk, half-human." Ayesha smiled coldly. "Be careful what you wish for. Your wish might just come true."

"What kind of a djinn would grant such a wish?" said Philippa.

"Not every practising djinn is as good as your uncle Nimrod. Many of our kind enjoy playing tricks like that on mundane beings. But equally, there are occasions when even a good djinn can grant wishes without knowing it. The dreams of older djinn, for example. Monsters from their sleeping minds. And sometimes, young and inexperienced djinn bring wishes into reality, with calamitous results. Subliminal wish fulfillment, we call it. I think you've had some experience with that, yourself."

Philippa nodded. "Yes," she said, remembering just such an occasion on a plane from New York to London.

"You'll find all of those wishes out there if you are ever foolish enough to leave the palace and look for them." Ayesha touched the windowpane, and the screen of white light returned to cloud their view.

"Why don't you help them?" asked Philippa.

"I didn't make them what they are," said Ayesha. "Besides, they don't last long. Eventually, they're all consumed by a monster called the Optabellower. A powerful monster that crawled from the sleeping mind of Ishtar herself. So, there's no need for my intervention. But I tell you frankly, it's a matter of supreme indifference to me what happens to them."

"That's another good reason why I could never step into your shoes," insisted Philippa. "I'm not at all like you. I'm not the kind of person to stand back and let people suffer without trying to help them."

"No?" The Blue Djinn smiled. "You're much more like me than you think, Philippa. That is why I picked you."

"I don't care how long I stay here, I'll never be as wicked as you."

"Not wicked. Indifferent. There's a difference."

"I think not caring is just as bad as being wicked."

"We shall see what we shall see," said Ayesha. "But fortunately we will not have to stay here for very long before you become as hard-hearted as I am. Then we can go back to my villa in Berlin. You'll like Berlin. And in time – at least, what time I have left – you and I will get along very well."

"Not if you live to be a thousand years old, which is

what you look like, you horrible woman. And especially not after what happened at the Djinnverso Tournament. It *was* you, wasn't it? It was you who moved those dice. And it was you who made me look as though I had confessed to something I hadn't done."

"You're almost right. I did fix the box and the dice. But it was Izaak Balayaga who was temporarily inside your body, answering my questions."

"Yes, but I expect you put him up to it."

"Oh, I didn't put him up to it. I gave him an order. There's a difference. He had no choice, if he knew what was good for him."

"But why? Why did you do that to me?"

"A number of reasons. For one thing I wanted to see how Mimi de Ghulle would react to your humiliation. To see if she really had any of the intellectual qualities to be the next Blue Djinn. Suffice to say that I was not encouraged by her behaviour. But mainly I wanted to test your strength of character. And to see if, despite what had happened, you would take the mission offered to you by Nimrod. If you would try to recover the Solomon Grimoire for the service of djinnkind in general. In other words, if you would put others before yourself." She shrugged. "Which of course, you did, child. After all, you're here, aren't you?"

"Stop calling me 'child,'" said Philippa. "I'm not a child. Please don't patronize me, you old witch."

Ayesha exchanged a look with Miss Glumjob and nodded. "Good," she said. "It has started."

"What has?"

Ayesha sat down on a chair and folded her hands.

"The Garden of Eden used to be not very far from here. Most people who read the story of Adam and Eve remember that there were two trees: the Tree of Knowledge of Good and Evil; and the Tree of Life. In some versions of the story, however, a third variety of tree is mentioned. This was the Tree of Logos, which some call Reason or even Logic. I prefer Logic myself, which exists beyond the knowledge of Good and Evil. Logic needs only to look after itself, Philippa. Everything else is meaningless."

"What does this have to do with me?"

"Everything here is affected by that tree. The air you breathe is full of the scent of the tree's blossom, which, at this time of year, is strong. We also use oil from the blossom in the food that is prepared in our kitchens. Miss Glumjob's apple juice is made with apples picked from the Trees of Logic that grow in the garden. Even our water is affected by the roots of that tree."

Philippa shook her head with disbelief. "I don't believe you," she said.

"Ask yourself this, my dear. Would the nice polite girl I met in New York have called me a stupid old witch? I doubt it."

"Well, I won't be drinking any more apple juice," said Philippa.

"Perhaps. But even djinn have to breathe, Philippa. I certainly wouldn't advise that you stop doing that. Not unless you want to make yourself ill."

"Making myself ill sounds a lot better than making myself like you," Philippa said defiantly and started to walk toward the door.

"You may go anywhere you like in the palace and gardens," said Ayesha. "If you want anything, just pick up a telephone. One of our many invisible servants will bring whatever you need. If you find a door locked, it is not to keep you in, but rather for your own protection against things that you would not like, for you are still young and easily frightened. Remember this above all. You are in Iravotum, not America, no not even properly in Iraq. Despite what your eyes tell you, this place is very old, as old as the pyramids, and here you will find many strange things. Especially in the garden. So, be careful, my child. Always be careful."

CHAPTER 11

THE ROAD TO BAGHDAD

Back in Berlin, at Nimrod's suite in the Hotel Adlon, an exhausted John went to bed while Nimrod and Mr Rakshasas stayed up all night studying Virgil Macreeby's translation of the High Priest Eno's writings. The following morning, he awoke feeling refreshed and, after having something to eat from the enormous breakfast trolley that Nimrod had ordered, John and Groanin, Alan and Neil sat down with the two senior djinn and listened to what they had to say. But it was quickly plain to see that both Nimrod and Mr Rakshasas were reluctant to come to the point.

"From our studies of Eno's writings. . ." Nimrod said slowly.

"He's the author of the scrolls," added Mr Rakshasas. "The priest of Bellili. Who was Ishtar's predecessor."

"The fact is, John, we've formed a number of conclusions. Not all of them agreeable."

"Come on," said John. "What are our chances of rescuing Philippa?"

Mr Rakshasas wobbled his head. "The stag that walks into a hat shop is just asking to draw attention to himself, right enough," he said cryptically.

John groaned with exasperation. He was very fond of

Mr Rakshasas, but there were times – and this was one of them – when he thought that the old djinn would, more usefully, remain silent.

"The boy hits the nail on the head," Mr Rakshasas continued. "To be sure, *our* chances are not good. But *your* chances, John, may be better."

"What he's trying to say is that I'm not coming with you," said Nimrod.

"If I came within a hundred miles of Iravotum and the Hanging Palace of Babylon, Ayesha would detect it, and deploy certain countermeasures."

"What sort of countermeasures?" asked Groanin.

"I'm not sure," said Nimrod. "Eno's not very clear about that. On the other hand, you John, have two very definite advantages. One is that being Philippa's twin makes you almost impossible to detect in the same way. Ayesha would ascribe her sensing that you were close, John, to Philippa herself." Nimrod paused.

"And the second definite advantage?"

"Is a double-edged sword, right enough," said Mr Rakshasas. "Being less powerful than Nimrod makes you hard to detect, but not impossible."

"He means that you would only remain concealed from Ayesha's senses so long as you refrained from using djinn power yourself."

John smiled thinly. "Let me get this straight," he said. "You expect me to travel alone, in one of the most dangerous countries in the world, without any djinn power to protect me?"

Nimrod nodded. "That's about the size of it, yes."

"Without so much as a discrimen?"

"Without so much as a discrimen," said Nimrod. "You are under no obligation whatsoever to do this, John. You're up against some very difficult odds, make no mistake about that. Perhaps you should even reconsider. No one, least of all me, will think any the worse of you for not going."

"I'm going," John said quietly.

"If you do, then Mr Rakshasas will accompany you, in an advisory capacity, since he can remain undetected providing he stays in his lamp. And, of course, Alan and Neil will also come with you."

Both dogs barked simultaneously. And Mr Groanin cleared his throat loudly.

"With all due respect to you, sir," said Mr Groanin, "but aren't you forgetting something?"

Nimrod frowned. "No, I don't think so, Groanin."

"You're forgetting me, sir. I'll accompany the lad. I may have just the one arm, but I can look after myself. I say, I can look after myself. And, like I said before, there's nothing I wouldn't do for these two young people."

"Thank you, Mr Groanin," said John, who was very touched at this display of affection from Nimrod's butler.

"Yes," said Nimrod. "It's very noble of you, Groanin."

Groanin shook his head. "Noble, no sir, not noble. Just human. Yes, I think that's what I'd call it. Human. Sometimes you djinn forget what we humans are capable of."

Alan barked loudly, as if remembering what he himself had been capable of when he had been a human.

"But where is Iravotum?" asked John. "And how do we get there?"

"Now there we do have some good news," announced Nimrod. "The High Priest Eno provided detailed instructions on how to get there, how to effect an entry, as well as a few of the hazards you are likely to face on an underground journey through the secret kingdom of Iravotum. There's even a map he drew that shows you the most favourable route to take."

"You did say underground, didn't you?" said John, wondering how he'd cope with the claustrophobia on such a journey. Taking a charcoal pill to cope with a few hours aboard an aeroplane was one thing, but travelling underground might be something else.

"The Hanging Palace and Iravotum, which is the place of bad and angry wishes that surrounds the palace, are several miles below the surface of the earth," said Nimrod. "As befits a secret, Hermetic place. The actual location is below the ruins of ancient Babylon, which is itself about fifty-five miles south of Baghdad. Eno doesn't actually say how Ishtar and her descendants gain entry to the palace. But he does describe in detail the existence of a second secret entrance, underneath the site of the ancient Tower of Babel."

"That's a real place?" said John. "I thought that was just a story about how lots of people suddenly found themselves speaking hundreds of different languages, and couldn't understand what anyone else was saying."

"Babel was a real place, all right," said Nimrod. "The site lies a hundred or so miles to the north of Babylon, at a place called Samarra, where a tower of sorts continues in existence to this day. Eno tells us how to get in the secret entrance underneath that tower, and how to travel to Iravotum. According to the scrolls, there's an underground sea, and a boatman who will row you across."

"Blimey," said Groanin. This was his excuse to recite a verse from a poem, something he was fond of doing:

> "Crossing alone the knighted ferry
> With the one coin for fee,
> Whom, on the wharf of Lethe waiting,
> Count you to find?
> Not me."

He chuckled grimly. "I say, not me."

John nodded. "Groanin's right," he said. "Isn't this just a bit, like, Gothic?" He was beginning to wonder a little about being a djinn. Lately things had been just a bit too hair-raising and creepy for comfort, and half of him wished he was back in New York doing something normal, like getting bullied by Gordon Warthoff. Which prompted him to wonder for a moment if Philippa really had made the other boy's pimples disappear, and if that had made him a better person yet. No doubt he would find out if he ever survived the ordeal that now lay before him, and managed to return to school for the next term. Of one thing John was quite certain, however. He badly missed his sister's wisdom and counsel. With her gone from his side it was like a part of him was missing.

"Gothic, you say," said Nimrod. "It is what it is, John. If mundane beings have used Iravotum as the basis of silly myths and legends, that's hardly a matter of much importance to us." He glanced at his wristwatch. "It's time we were on our way. I shall convey you all by whirlwind, to Amman, in Jordan, which is as far as I can come with you."

"Jordan is the country bordering Iraq, right?" said John.

"Yes. From there we will have to find a more mundane means of transporting the four of you across the Iraqi desert."

Several hours later found them checked into the best hotel in the capital city of the Hashemite Kingdom of Jordan. Leaving Groanin and John in one of the hotel's many restaurants, Nimrod and Mr Rakshasas went to look for some transport. The hotel was popular with British and American businessmen and journalists, several of whom were also intending to travel across the border into Iraq. But from the stories John overheard while eating a delicious hamburger, Iraq sounded even more dangerous than he had first supposed.

"I hate this place," said Groanin, dipping a teaspoon into a jar of baby food. Distrusting most food that had not been cooked in England, Groanin had brought along a large backpack laden with dozens of jars of the sterilized baby food that he regarded as the only safe thing to eat in a hot country. Safe the baby food might have been, John thought it was pretty disgusting for a grown man to eat a sort of brown-coloured goo that was called Shepherd's Pie with Carrots. And John would certainly risk having an upset stomach rather than eat Leek and Cauliflower with Cheddar Cheese: just the smell of that

189

one was enough to make him feel quite sick.

"You don't know what you're missing," said John, stuffing as much of the hamburger into his mouth as his jaws could accommodate. "This is excellent."

"If you want to risk eating it, that's your affair," said Groanin. "Besides, it has been my experience, while looking after your uncle all these years, that you djinn can eat pretty much anything. I won't say more than that. I don't want to sicken myself. But if you consult that book, the one that Mr Rakshasas wrote, then you'll see exactly what I'm talking about."

Meanwhile, Nimrod had found a driver who was willing to take John, Groanin, and the two dogs (not to mention the lamp containing Mr Rakshasas) across the desert to Samarra. And, very early the next morning, at four a.m., when it was still dark, the driver was waiting outside the hotel with the car – a large, diesel-powered Mercedes sedan.

"By heck," complained Groanin, as the driver, Darius al Baghdadi, introduced himself. "It's a boy, for Pete's sake. How old are you, sonny?"

Darius grinned proudly. "Sir, I am twelve years old," he said.

"And what does your dad have to say about driving a car?"

"My father is dead," said Darius. "I support my family now. I am very good driver. You'll see, mister."

"Everyone I've spoken to says that Darius is one of the best drivers in Iraq," explained Nimrod. "He's from Baghdad and knows the road across the desert like the back of his hand."

"What about the bodyguard?" said Groanin. "You said you were going to hire one. Where is he?"

Darius was shaking his head. "No bodyguard," he said. "Bodyguards attract attention. Make people think we are worth robbing. Best not to have bodyguard."

Groanin, whose duties included driving Nimrod's Rolls Royce when they were in London, groaned unhappily. "I hate this place," he said.

"You will like Iraq," said Darius. "Iraq is a very nice country. Very nice people."

"I doubt that very much," said Groanin.

John shook the Iraqi boy's hand. "Nice car," he said, envying any twelve-year-old boy who was allowed to drive.

"Mercedes Benz is very strong, very reliable," said Darius. "But the servicing and dealerships are no good. It was my father's car. I prefer Ferrari."

"Me too," agreed John.

"I want to be a racing driver when I get older," said Darius. "Grand Prix. Like Michael Schumacher. Schumacher is my hero."

"I like him, too," agreed John, although he preferred Indy cars to Grand Prix.

Darius had a big smile and an even bigger head of thick black hair that fell into his eyes and which John thought made him look like one of the Beatles. He wore jeans, a fake gold Rolex, and a T-shirt that said HASTA LA VISTA, BABY. Darius said the T-shirt had been a present from a British soldier. Around his waist he sported an empty holster containing not a gun, but his money, and an empty silver scabbard that contained not a knife, but a pair of sunglasses. Darius seemed to like Alan and Neil very much and said that no one would think the dogs were Americans. But he insisted on taking John and Mr Groanin to an Arab men's clothing store near the hotel, so that they could each buy a thobe – the long white shirt that Arab men wear down to their ankles – and a bisht, which is the loose robe worn over it.

"Best to look like Arabs when travelling," explained Darius. "That way any bandits who see us will think you are not worth the trouble to rob."

"And what about you?" Groanin asked Darius, feeling silly in his long robes. "You don't dress like an Arab."

Darius laughed. "Yes, but I *am* an Arab. If there is any trouble I will speak Arabic and they will not try to rob me. But if anyone suspects you are English or American, then maybe they will try to rob you."

Groanin swallowed uncomfortably. "You've got a point, I suppose."

"I wish I spoke Arabic," said John. It was going to be a hot day. The previous evening the temperature had been in the nineties, and the desert had warmed John's bones, returning his djinn power. So that he no sooner had wished to speak Arabic, and uttered his focus word, than he could.

"You'd better watch out for that kind of thing," said Nimrod when, later on, he heard John speaking Arabic, and guessed what had happened. "Making wishes. Remember. Once you're over the Iraqi border there must be absolutely no use of djinn power. Just in case Ayesha picks it up on her djinn radar." He handed John a cell phone. "Call me here, in Amman, when you get back up to the surface of the earth. I don't expect you'll get a signal before then, anyway."

Alan and Neil each barked loudly, once, and then bounded into the car's backseat.

"Good-bye, sir," said Groanin, shaking Nimrod stiffly by the hand.

"Good-bye Groanin, and thank you."

The English butler climbed into the backseat, alongside the two rottweilers and settled down to read his *Daily Telegraph*.

"What are you going to do?" John asked Nimrod. "While we're in Iraq?"

"Be assured, I shall be very busy, " said Nimrod. "If we are to stop Ayesha from making your sister the next Blue Djinn of Babylon, then it is also our duty to find Ayesha a replacement, and as quickly as possible."

"But I thought nobody wanted the job."

"That's not entirely true," said Nimrod. "Part of the problem has been that Ayesha, being as hard-hearted as she is, has lost her people skills. She's old. She rubs a lot of djinn the wrong way. But I'm much more persuasive and diplomatic. As a result it's quite possible I might easily succeed where she has totally failed."

"So where will you look?"

"I rather thought I'd try Monte Carlo," said Nimrod. "It's the European capital of bad luck, and there's someone there who just might fit the bill."

Nimrod hugged John and then rubbed his hands with a fake show of enthusiasm, trying to conceal the concern he felt at his nephew setting out on such a dangerous quest. "Well, then. Good-bye John, and good luck."

"Good-bye Uncle," said John and quickly jumped into

the front seat of the Mercedes, before Nimrod could see his own fear. He looked at Darius and then at Groanin. "Have we got everything, Mr Groanin?" he asked.

Like any good butler, Groanin had a list. "Cell phone, charger, first aid kit, water, teabags, flashlights, umbrella, wet wipes, Mutt 'n' Pooch dog food – fifty six cans – toilet paper, baby food – fifty six jars, Kendall Mint Cake, Arab sandwiches . . . that's all of it, I think."

"An umbrella?" said John. "What on earth's that for?"

"In case it rains, of course."

"It doesn't rain in the desert," laughed John.

"I think you've been misinformed," said Mr Groanin. "It rains everywhere. And best be prepared, that's what I always say."

"Aren't you forgetting something?" said Nimrod and, through the open window of the Mercedes, he handed John Virgil Macreeby's leather-bound translation of the *Bellili Scrolls.* "Eno's book."

"Yes." John smiled. "We'll need that."

They set off through the suburbs of Amman and, almost immediately, John spotted a sign for Samarra that said it was 500 kilometers away, which is just over 300 miles. A journey of six or seven hours lay ahead of them. Or perhaps less given the speed at which Darius drove the car. John thought the Iraqi boy drove with great skill, especially when he considered that Darius was seated on top of several volumes of the Baghdad telephone directory so that he could see over the dashboard. There were other modifications made to the Mercedes to help him drive it. The business end of a golf club had been taped to the gearshift, and the height of the foot pedals had been increased by a skilled metalworker using a selection of empty coffee cans. By the time dawn broke they were on the desert road, driving through a treeless, almost Martian landscape; it was here that Darius really put his foot down.

"Does he have to drive so fast?" Groanin complained.

"I am a very good driver," laughed Darius, and touched a picture of Michael Schumacher that was hanging from his rearview mirror for luck, before increasing his speed. "See? Very fast. Just like Schumacher, yes?"

Groanin groaned loudly and, leaning backing his seat, started to eat a jar of Roast Pork with Apple Sauce, for comfort.

"When did you get your license?" John asked Darius.

The Iraqi laughed back at him. "What license? I no have license. I have family to support. Mother and four sisters. No license needed."

Groanin groaned loudly again and, settling down behind his two-day-old newspaper, tried to ignore what was happening in the front seat.

Theirs was not the only car travelling to Baghdad. Ever since leaving Amman, there had been three white Range Rovers on their tail, containing several Western journalists, photographers, and their well-armed bodyguards. Darius nodded at them in his rearview mirror. "They're trying to keep up with us," he said happily. "You want maybe I should lose them?"

"Lord, no," said Groanin. "There's safety in numbers, surely."

"Not here in the desert," said Darius. "Safety in

numbers in England or America, maybe. But numbers here, equals target. Best to travel alone. I think."

"And I don't think," protested Groanin. "In fact, pull over a moment and see if they'll stop. They might have a more recent newspaper than this one."

"Ok," said Darius. "You're the boss. But it's best we wait until Safawi, I think, and pull over there."

Safawi was a Jordanian truck-stop town where the drivers of huge rigs would grab a cold drink and a kebab, or some flat bread from one of the many storefront bakeries. Darius swerved off the road and pulled up in front of a makeshift gas station. The three Range Rovers followed suit, and a posse of men and women stepped down. One of them, a beautiful but severe-looking woman, approached John while the drivers refueled the vehicles, and Groanin begged them for a newspaper.

The woman wore a black shirt, black riding breeches, black riding boots, a black flak jacket, black shades, and she was wearing several cameras around her neck the way rap artists wear medallions. "You British?" she asked.

"American," said John.

"What are you doing out here?" she asked. "This isn't a theme park ride. This place is dangerous. Is that guy with one arm your father, or what?"

"No," said John. "He's not my father. Look, thanks, but don't worry about me. I'm dressed like an Arab. I speak fluent Arabic. And I'm in a car with Iraqi license plates. Unlike yours. I'm probably a lot safer than you are."

"You've got a point." The woman smiled. She held out her hand and John took it, carefully, as he told her his name.

"I'm Montana Retch," she said. "From the Beretta Press Agency? Maybe you're familiar with my work."

"Not really, no," said John.

"No matter. Hey, kid, do you mind if I take your picture?" Miss Retch was already pulling the lens cap off one of her cameras. "You don't see many American kids out here. Certainly not dressed the way you're dressed. Kind of like Lawrence of Arabia."

John smiled a little vainly. Like Lawrence of Arabia sounded just fine with him. "Go ahead," he said. "Take your picture."

"Where are you headed?" she asked, looking through the lens.

"Samarra."

"Is there a story there?"

"Not since the seventh century," said John. "That was when the Persians conquered the Moors. At least that's what the Iraqi guidebook says."

"Oh," said Miss Retch, looking vaguely disappointed. "Well, you can't blame a girl for asking."

John turned around as Groanin uttered an ear-piercing whistle in his direction and waved a newspaper in the air. Over by the gas station, Darius had finished refilling the car.

"I've got to go," said John.

"Well, it was nice speaking to you, John," she said.

"You too, Miss Retch. And good luck with your journey."

"Thanks," she said. "I'll hold you to that."

CHAPTER 13

DAY OF THE LOCUST

They reached the Iraqi border just before midday where, at no fewer than six checkpoints, they were obliged to show their passports, first to Jordanian, and then Iraqi officials. John's American passport and his obvious youth attracted some attention, but he and Mr Groanin stuck to the story that Nimrod had cooked up for them – that Groanin was taking John to meet the grandmother he had never met – and, after several hours of explanation and waiting, they were finally permitted to continue on their journey.

On the Iraqi side of the border, the highway was as good as any John had seen back in the United States. Guardrails ran the length of the road and every sixty miles, there were even concrete picnic tables with metal umbrellas. At a rest area next to a field of maize, they stopped for lunch, which was when Groanin discovered that the backpack containing his baby food had been stolen – presumably at one of the checkpoints. A further search of the car revealed that the cooler containing the falafel sandwiches for John and Darius were gone, too, as were all the cans of Mutt 'n' Pooch dog food.

"That's torn it," complained Mr Groanin. "Now what are we going to do? I say, now what are we going to do?"

"Who'd steal fifty-six cans of dog food?" John asked Darius.

"Some people in Iraq, very poor," said Darius. "Probably eat the dog food themselves. We can get some food near Fallujah. I know a good place. Plenty falafel. Plenty everything."

"No, thanks," said Groanin. "We'll probably end up being served our own dog food."

John pointed at the field of maize. "Maybe we could find some food in that field."

"The maize is too small to eat yet," said Darius.

"I wasn't thinking of eating vegetables," he said. He hated corn almost as much as he hated broccoli. "No, I was thinking of something else."

According to the SBR, desert-dwelling djinn sometimes ate locusts and their larvae (which was even considered a great delicacy among more sophisticated djinn), called *jarad*. Reading about the subject back in the hotel in Amman, *jarad* had been an item of horrible fascination for John. Then, he had thought it unlikely that he could ever have eaten *jarad*. But now that he was in the desert, hot and hungry, too, the idea of trying some proper djinn tucker did not seem quite so revolting, and so, armed with a tote bag, he went into the field to see if he could find some insects or their larvae that were large enough to eat.

Locust plagues were a serious problem for local farmers and the first locust John picked up was a good eight inches long. To John's hungry djinn eyes, the locust looked like a square meal in itself, and in less than ten minutes he had filled his bag and brought it back to the picnic table where Darius had already made a small fire to boil some water for tea and coffee.

Groanin was horrified. "You're not going to," he said.

"According to the SBR, they're delicious," he told Mr Groanin. "Did you know that they ate locusts in the Bible? Locusts and wild honey."

"They ate a lot of things in the Bible that you wouldn't want to eat yourself," said Mr Groanin, who felt sick at the very idea of eating locusts. "Me, I like my food to stay still on the plate when I'm eating it."

Securing the bag so that none of his wriggling catch would escape, John went to back to the car to fetch the lamp containing Mr Rakshasas for advice on how to best to prepare *jarad*. And the old djinn told him he should first find something on which he might skewer them, like a kebab stick. Looking on the floor of Darius's car, John saw something suitable.

"How about a piece of broken car antenna?" he asked.

"Fine, fine," said Mr Rakshasas. "Skewer them, toast them on the fire, then pluck off the legs and break away the head and thorax, the same way you'd eat a crustacean. The insect body that remains will be good meat. I'd love to be eating *jarad* with you, and that's a fact. It's been years since I tasted it." Mr Rakshasas sighed. "However, it's best I stay in my lamp. Just in case Ayesha picks me up on her radar."

Having cooked six or seven locusts on his makeshift skewer, John now prepared to eat one, sliding it off the antenna, and removing the legs and head. Darius and

Groanin looked on with horror as John placed the insect body inside his mouth and started to chew, slowly at first, and then more quickly as he began to enjoy the taste.

"You know what?" he said. "They're delicious. Kind of like a cross between a boiled egg and jumbo shrimp."

Groanin turned away, holding his ample stomach in revulsion. "I think I'm going to be sick," he said weakly.

Alan and Neil were watching, too, but unlike Groanin and Darius, they envied John his improvised meal. Shifting impatiently on their haunches, they licked their chops and whined with hunger as John swallowed one locust and started another.

"You guys want some?"

The two dogs barked loudly.

John fed some hot insect bodies to Alan and Neil and cooked some more. "Are you sure you won't try one?" he asked his human companions, with locust juice running down his chin. "They're better than they look."

Groanin swallowed queasily and shook his head. "No, thank you very much," he said grimly. "I'd rather starve. I say, I'd rather starve."

"Well, if you're sure," said John, chewing another. "It's your funeral."

"More like yours," snorted Groanin.

But Darius was nodding. "Perhaps I will try one after all," he said, and pulled a locust off the now blackened car antenna.

"That's the spirit," said John, speaking fluent Arabic to him for the first time, and helping peel the legs off the other boy's djinn snack.

Darius nibbled the edge of the locust body, swallowed,

grinned at John, nodded, and then ate the rest. "It's good," he said to John. "But how is it that you speak such excellent Arabic? And how do you do that trick with the voice in the lamp? Are you a ventriloquist?" He ate another locust. "If I didn't know better I'd say that the voice was a djinn. And that perhaps this djinn was your slave."

"Actually," said John. "I'm a djinn myself."

"No fooling?"

"No fooling."

"That's great," said Darius. "If some bandits come and try to rob us, you'll be able to turn them all into locusts and then we can eat our enemies."

"I'm afraid I'm not allowed to use my powers," John told Darius. "You see, my sister, Philippa, has been kidnapped by a very powerful djinn and I've come to rescue her. If I use my power, this djinn will know that I'm here, and take her away somewhere else. Or use her power against us."

"I understand," said Darius speaking English again for Groanin's benefit. "Then we will have to be hoping that bandits do not come. But, more important, perhaps, we will have to hope that Utug and Gigim do not come. I have never seen them myself, but everyone in these parts knows of them. They are two desert-dwelling demons whose territory we will have to pass through. Since the war, they mostly leave people alone." He shrugged. "But a young djinn like yourself? Who knows what they will do if they know you are here, John? They may demand some sort of tribute from you. It's how they are, I'm told."

"Have we got some kind of a tribute?" asked Groanin.

John shrugged and asked Mr Rakshasas for his advice.

"Demon tributes are traditionally in the shape of a great feast or some beautiful flowers," he said. "Or a fabulous gem, perhaps."

"That's good," said Groanin. "We've got buckets of gems." He shook his head grimly. "Come on. We'd best be on our way before I change my mind about eating one of them creepy-crawlies."

An hour down the road, they passed a large bomb crater, right in the middle of the highway, and then an abandoned armoured personnel carrier. Two helicopters zoomed overhead and, in the distance, they saw a plume of black smoke from a burning oil trench. Minutes later, Darius was forced to swerve to avoid a speeding car heading directly toward them on their side of the road. And John yelled out as he saw a man in the other car pointing a gun at them.

Darius spun the steering wheel in the opposite direction and then hit the gas. Behind them they heard several shots being fired, and something metallic hit the car, but the Iraqi boy kept his nerve and his foot hard to the floor – or at least as near to the floor as he could manage. It was several miles before he lifted his foot off the gas again, and steered the car to a small group of palm trees about a hundred yards off the road.

"We've lost them," he shouted, looking visibly relieved.

"So why are we stopping?" asked Groanin.

"Because, sir, we must change the wheel," said Darius. "We have flat tire. I think a bullet must have hit it."

"Better it than us, I suppose," said Groanin.

Darius stopped the car behind a large sand dune, so

that they would not be seen from the road. "Please not to make very much noise," he said, getting out of the car. "This is edge of demon country. Bandits, too. Very bad place to make stop."

A quick inspection confirmed Darius's suspicion. They would have to change the wheel. "Can I help?" said John.

"Yes, please," said Darius.

Mr Groanin helped, too, or at least as much as he was able to help with just one arm. Meanwhile, Alan and Neil went off to do what dogs do, but minutes later they were barking loudly and chasing a fox, which is also something dogs do. John called them both angrily to heel.

"Didn't you hear what Darius just said?" he said. "Keep the noise down." Alan hung his head, licked John's hand penitently and then went off to look at the front page of Groanin's newspaper while Neil jumped into the car, switched on the radio and, pressing his ear close to one of the speakers, listened to Radio Baghdad with the volume down low.

"Those are very clever dogs," observed Darius.

"That's because they're not really dogs," explained John. "They're my uncles." And he explained how his mother had turned the two men into Rottweilers following their attempt to kill his father.

"The man who killed my father," said Darius, speaking Arabic. "I should like to turn him into a dog." Fetching the car jack from the trunk, he grinned at John. "Perhaps you could do it for me."

"I don't do that sort of thing," he said, remembering how terribly guilty he had felt when obliged to turn Finlay

Macreeby into a falcon; it was something that would haunt him for the rest of his days. "Not to anyone."

"Pity," said Darius, and started to undo the wheel nuts. "But to be quite frank with you, I can't really see the point of being a djinn at all if you don't turn some people into animals. Especially people that you dislike."

By now the sun was starting to go down and all the time he was working to change the wheel, Darius kept on glancing over his shoulder and reciting an Arabic incantation against the two desert demons he had mentioned earlier.

"Utug and Gigim are most impervious to pity and benevolence," he explained to Groanin. He pointed to the side mirrors on the car. "If you see them, we shall have to use these mirrors to deflect them, for they will see their own images and be terrified. At least, that is what my father told me."

Darius and John had just removed the old wheel and were threading the replacement onto the axle when the boy driver stood up abruptly, as if he had seen something very frightening. Silently, Darius pointed toward the brow of a hill where two figures stood against the setting sun. And even as John followed the line of Darius's arm, Alan and Neil appeared at his side, growling as if they sensed danger to their young master and his friends.

"Sumatt wrong, is there?" asked Groanin.

"Utug," whispered Darius, "and Gigim. The desert demons. Aiee! Their shapes are those of giant locusts." He gulped loudly and shook his head. "I fear they are already angry with us, young master."

It was true. The two figures on the nearby hilltop, both

as tall as a tall man, had the legs and arms of a human being, but the heads and wings of enormous locusts. Realizing that they had been seen, the two creatures took off into the air with a horrible buzzing noise and headed straight for the car.

John grabbed the lamp containing Mr Rakshasas from the front seat. "There are two desert demons coming our way," he yelled at it. "Utug and Gigim, Darius calls them. I couldn't say for sure if those are their names. But they're both shaped like horrible giant locusts."

"After your feast of *jarad*, that's unfortunate, so it is," said Mr Rakshasas, from inside the lamp. "They won't take kindly to your having eaten their friends. Desert demons are hot-tempered, which is why they live in the desert. Pure fiery evil, so they are, without a reasonable bone in their bodies. They'll be positively incandescent with you, John, make no mistake."

"If you've got any good ideas," said John, as the demons grew closer, "now would be a good time to think of them."

But it was too late. The desert demons landed in front of John, Darius, and Mr Groanin. Alan and Neil growled at these hideous creatures but John held the dogs by their collars, sensing that if they attacked they would be immediately destroyed. Darius had certainly been right. Utug and Gigim both looked utterly impervious to pity and benevolence. Moreover, they seemed physically to radiate the heat of their anger. The temperature was above 120 degrees Fahrenheit, but near the two demons, it felt as if someone had left an oven door open. John decided that if this extra heat was due to the anger of the demons, then they really were in trouble. Meanwhile, Groanin's attempts to turn the car's side mirrors so that these might reflect the horrible images of the demons against them, had come to nothing.

"I do believe he is trying to scare us with our own reflections," said the taller of the two, who was Utug. His voice was deep and dry, but it was his laugh that John thought was really frightening. It started like a wheezy cough and then continued for several seconds, without a trace of moisture.

"Pathetic," said Gigim, whose voice sounded no less parched than Utug's. Like the other demon's, his locust face, which contained some human features, such as a mouth and two large eyes, was a permanent grimace. "Look, he's only got one arm," he added, pointing at Groanin, while his antennae wriggled horribly on top of his dark brown and entirely hairless head.

"Perhaps the small djinn broke it off and ate it," Utug said with a sarcasm directed at John. "Just like he did to our flying friends. I'm sure I can smell their bodies on his breath, and hear them wriggling around inside his stomach. We'll see how *you* like it, being skewered, roasted alive on some hot coals, and then eaten."

"Haven't you heard of animal rights?" demanded Gigim. "There are laws against cruelty like yours, even in Iraq."

"I didn't know that those locusts were your friends," John said bravely. "If I'd known that, I never would have eaten them. I'm really very sorry."

"That makes it all right, does it?" sneered Utug, from whose small, vestigial ears smoke was emerging, as if his

207

anger was becoming hotter by the second. "Let me tell you, little djinn: a locust has feelings, too."

"Not just feelings," insisted Gigim. "Rights. As much right to live as any djinn or human."

Utug took a large step toward Groanin. "I'm looking forward to eating this fat one," he said. "But it's a pity he's only got one arm. It's the arms I like eating best of all. Especially the fingers."

"The skin on the fingers is tasty. But me, I like crunching the heads the best. Especially when they've got lots of hair, like the small human."

Small whirlwinds played around Gigim's toes sending hot dust up into the air, searing John's eyes and burning the inside of his nose. He sneezed straight at Gigim and the sneeze sizzled on the desert demon's leathery brown chest like a raw egg landing on a hot frying pan.

"Oh, that's charming, isn't it?" grimaced Gigim.

"Tear him to pieces for his bad manners," said Utug. "Tear him apart for his rudeness."

Alan and Neil barked loudly.

"Chew his dogs for their ugly faces."

"Do something," Groanin yelled at John. "Or we're flipping toast."

"I can't," said John. "If I use my power, Ayesha will feel it and then we won't stand a chance of rescuing Philippa."

"We won't stand any chance at all if we're all dead," protested Groanin, and let out a roar of pain as Utug touched him with a long bony finger. "Blimey, the creature's on fire. His finger's like a red-hot poker."

"Truly," Darius said to Groanin, "his fieryness is

terrific." And so saying, he ran off into the desert.

"Good," Gigim laughed wheezily. "We can hunt him down when we've eaten this lot. I like it when they run. It's more fun." He poked John with a red-hot finger. "Why don't you run away? Better still, why don't you try to save yourself with your powers? Go ahead." He laughed in way that made John think that even if he'd wanted to use his djinn power, it might not have been enough to have prevailed against these two demons. "Try."

"He's too wet and soppy, to try," said Utug. "Har, har, har."

"That's right." Gigim chuckled horribly. "He's too wet. Har, har."

It was the mention of the word "wet" that did it. John glanced up at the sky in the vague hope that a cloud might appear above the two desert demons and cool them off with a squall of rain. But no sooner had the thought entered his head that this might happen than it *did* happen. A large cloud suddenly appeared in the sky immediately above the two demons and, a moment or two later, it began to rain. This was no ordinary rain, either, but a pocket-sized monsoon that left all of them soaked to the skin in seconds, and quickly had the two demons squealing with alarm and discomfort.

"Call it off," yelled Gigim. "Call it off."

John was too astonished at this strange turn of events to say anything for a moment. "Call what off?" he said finally.

"Your water elemental, of course," spluttered Utug. There was steam coming off his body which was already turning from brown to green. "Call it off, please. Water hasn't touched me for years. I can't stand the pain. Really, I can't." And before John could say another word, both demons had fled, closely pursued by the large rain cloud and the monsoon it continued to pour on top of them both.

John laughed and hoped that the water elemental would follow them for at least a day or two, which it did.

"I never thought I'd actually see a cloud that had a silver lining," remarked Groanin. "But that was it all right. Where the heck did it come from? Something you conjured up, was it?"

Mr Rakshasas, speaking from the inside of his lamp, was no less surprised than Groanin, but he was also concerned that Ayesha would now know that John was in Iraq.

"I didn't do anything," insisted John. "I certainly didn't utter my focus word. And I didn't feel any power come out of me when it started to rain."

"Whatever happened," said Groanin. "I told you I might need the umbrella."

But by now John guessed what had happened. He told Mr Rakshasas about Dybbuk and the water elemental he had tricked John and Philippa into helping him to create back in New York. "It must have been with me all along."

"In which case," said Mr Rakshasas, "we are fortunate that nobody thought to have that elemental revoked. Which is always the proper thing to do with an elemental. And you're quite right, John. It would not have required any use of your own djinn power to set the water elemental on those two. Your merely thinking of it raining on those demons would have been enough for that to have happened. Since the elemental already existed independently of you, sure, Ayesha will pay it no regard."

John peeled off his wet clothes to wring them out. Groanin did the same and then looked in the direction in which Darius had run off. "Right then," he said. "Let's go and find Michael Schumacher so we can be on our way again. And don't, for Pete's sake, eat any more of those locusts. We don't want to bug anyone else."

CHAPTER 14

PHILLIPA GAUNT'S JOURNAL

D AY ONE: I have decided to write this journal as a way of keeping myself company while I am a prisoner in Ayesha's strange underground palace. . .

I say underground, but that's a little hard for me to believe, given the sheer size of this place. While the sky outside has a strange quality, it's almost impossible to imagine such a place as this could ever exist below the surface of the earth.

. . . Anyway, I hope this journal will help me to keep an eye on my time in this place and serve as a way of finding out if I am becoming as logically minded and heard-hearted as Ayesha; that's what she's told me will happen if I stay here long enough. But even though I can refuse to drink Miss Glumjob's apple juice, which is made from the fruit of the Tree of Logic, I can hardly stop myself from breathing the air contaminated by its blossom. What would John do, I wonder? Not necessarily the right thing. But something decisive, I expect. I have the feeling that he's not so very far away, and it would be just like him to try to rescue me. I hope I'm not wrong.

After I met Ayesha in the Durbar Room I was angry, and a sort of wild feeling came over me. I ran up and down the stairs, kicking the walls, and shouting at the top of my voice, but, after a while, feeling helpless, I returned to my room and sat down to decide on my next move. It goes without saying that my djinn power seems to have deserted me. But if ever my power returns and I should see that little jerk Izaak Balayaga again, I'm going to turn him a duck-billed platypus, one the most primitive mammals that has ever existed. Being both venomous – it has a poisonous spur on its hind legs that can kill a dog apparently – and somehow stupid-looking, this will suit him very well.

Incidentally, it really freaked me out when having kicked the wall, and left quite a mark, later on I saw a wet sponge and bucket of soapy water working, apparently on their own, to remove the mark. Invisible servants take quite a bit of getting used to.

My first decision was to try to find out all that I could about Ayesha and this Hanging Palace of hers (I've yet to see just how and where it hangs) as this may help me to outwit her. With this in mind, I went to the large library that's on the ground floor of the palace. Here, I was pleased to find a vast number of books in English – whole shelves full of them – as well as the very latest US magazines, and all the English newspapers. The books were on a variety of subjects and included several about the real Osborne House. There were also quite a few books about the original Hanging Palace, and I decided to study these carefully. While I was selecting these particular books to read in my room later on, the door opened and Ayesha entered the library. She greeted me warmly – or at least as warmly as she is able, which is not saying very much.

"I'm glad you've found your way here," she said politely. "I'm sure there's a lot in here to interest you, and help you pass the time."

Thinking it better to conceal from Ayesha's curiosity the books about the palace I was planning to read, I did so, and smiled back at her to deflect attention. I must be careful not to awake her suspicion that I am gathering information in order to plan my escape. "Oh, well," I said. "I often go to the library at school." And, with several books and magazines under my arm, I left Ayesha to read her newspaper.

Alone in my room, I flicked through the magazines, and then started to look more closely at the books I had chosen. One in particular looked as if it was going to be very useful: a guide to the Hanging Palace and Iravotum that had been written by Eno, a former high priest of Ishtar, or Bellili as Ishtar was previously called. Eno describes quite a lot of useful facts, as it happens. For instance, there is something here called the *Bocca Veritas* – which means the mouth of truth. According to Eno this is nothing less than an oracle that will answer with absolute truth all questions put to it. The only problem is that he doesn't say where this is, so I'm going to have to search the palace for it. If such a thing really does exist, then, with the right questions, I might obtain some answers that will help me to get out of here.

DAY TWO: MIDNIGHT: I'd spent most of the day searching the palace for the BV, while at the same time trying to avoid Miss Glumjob, who follows me around like a dog and continually tries to have a conversation with me. I think she's lonely. But I can't afford to let myself trust her. Not if I'm going to escape.

Early one morning I had gone into the garden, which is very different from the one that Queen Victoria must have walked in, and I'm pretty sure that this must be the one that surrounded the original palace for, on one side at least, it exists on as many as a hundred different levels that descend down a high cliff face. One garden is built overhanging the other, and is perhaps, what those original Hanging Gardens of Babylon must have looked like.

On the other side of the house, there is an English-looking lawn, with a gate, and beyond the gate lies Iravotum proper, which seems to be mostly impenetrable forest. The gate is locked and too high to climb, and doesn't encourage further exploration, for there appears to be some large and probably horrible creature lurking invisibly just behind the tree line. I couldn't see it, but I heard it quite distinctly and it sounded as big as a bull elephant and twice as fierce.

Anyway, I was on the other side of the house, walking around one of the hanging gardens, enjoying the strong scent of jasmine and lavender when I came across a small wooden door about the size of a fireplace, in a brick wall. And thinking that this might conceal the BV, I tried to open it. It was locked, but the sound of the handle turning seemed to awaken something inside, for I could hear a voice calling out very faintly from behind the door. Looking around, I tried to see something with which I might break the door open, for the handle was old and after a few good blows with a rock, I soon had the little

215

door open. Behind it was a tiny cell, to the damp wall of which was chained a curious-looking bottle made of copper, with a long, crooked neck. Curious because the bottle looked more like a porcupine, with spines and sharp needles all over it so that it was almost impossible to pick up. Almost, but not impossible, and having picked it up quite gingerly, I heard a voice speaking to me from inside it.

"Let me out," said the voice.

"Are you the *Bocca Veritas* – the voice of truth?"

"I might be," said the voice.

"That hardly sounds like a truthful answer," I said.

"All right, no, I'm not. I'm a prisoner in here, like yourself."

"Not quite like myself. After all, I'm walking around this lovely garden while you are stuck inside a prickly-looking bottle which, until a few moments ago, was locked in a tiny cell."

"But you are a prisoner, nonetheless," said the voice, which was a Frenchman's.

"Why do you say so?" I asked.

"Because you said you weren't *quite* like myself when I suggested that you were a prisoner like me. If you weren't a prisoner you'd have said so."

"True."

"If you let me out of here, I will help you to escape."

"I don't see how you can help me when you don't seem able to help yourself."

"True. However, the fact that I'm in here at all would seem to indicate that an extra level of security is required to guarantee my confinement. That I might escape if I was not inside this bottle and inside the cell."

"That might be true," I said, "if the only reason for keeping you in that bottle was to prevent your escape. Another reason for keeping you in there instead of merely imprisoning you out here might be to punish you more severely."

"Sadly, you speak only the truth," said the voice. "Only it is much worse than you could ever imagine. Ayesha has also inflicted upon me an extra level of punishment in that I am obliged to wear an iron mask forever."

"Can't you take it off?"

"It's more like a helmet, really, attached to a metal collar around my neck and is padlocked, to which Ayesha has the only key."

"How horrible," I said, and began to try to shift the stopper from the neck of the bottle. Given the spines that covered its body, this was not easy. "I'll certainly let you out, if I can. Any enemy of Ayesha's is a friend of mine. What's your name?"

"Ravioli Poussin," said the French djinn.

By now I'd worked out how to open the bottle and, hardly afraid of a djinn with a name like Ravioli Poussin, I pulled the stopper from the neck. A few seconds later, when a foul-smelling green smoke had cleared (which I believe is not uncommon after a long period of confinement in a djinn bottle) and Ravioli Poussin's transubstantiation was complete, a rather creepy-looking man stood in front of me. He was wearing a long, black leather frock coat with sleeves that seemed too long for his arms, a white shirt with a high wing collar that seemed to make his head too big, a black cowboy belt that made his legs seem too short, and a black cravat. And straightaway I noticed that he was not wearing an iron mask at all. His hair was white and long and collected in a large ponytail and he wore a pair of oversize dark glasses.

"Where's your iron mask?" I asked him stupidly, for by now I had guessed that he had tricked me.

With a grim smile, which revealed his rather sharp-looking teeth, and released some of his rank-smelling breath, Mr Poussin said, "I don't wear an iron mask. I only wear black. To match my heart."

"I see," I said, nodding carefully, hoping to make my excuses now and leave, as quickly as possible.

"No, I don't think that you see at all," he said, pressing one hand to his cheek, and arching his back like a cat. "When Ayesha puts you inside a bottle she takes away your powers to make it comfortable. She gave me a bed, a chair, and one book from her library. One book for all the years I've been stuck in that stinking bottle. And do you know what that book was?"

I shrugged. "A long one, I hope," I said.

"*The Man in the Iron Mask,* by Alexander Dumas." He stamped the Cuban heel of his small boot upon the ground like a petulant child. "I must have read that lousy book more than a hundred times. So many times, I am now able to recite the entire book by heart." He clasped his heavily ringed hands in front of him and, for a moment, he almost looked like a priest. "For the first five years I promised myself that no matter who released me, I would be their slave forever. For the next five years I told myself that I would destroy anyone who released me from my bottle."

Mr Poussin smiled again and, this time, his breath was so bad, I almost fainted. It was obvious that Ayesha had also neglected to give Mr Poussin a toothbrush and some toothpaste.

"Guess where you came in. That's right. At the end of the second five years." He bit his thumbnail excitedly. "You know I'm glad you're a female djinn because I hate female djinn. You can blame Ayesha for that."

Mr Poussin laughed in a way that sent a chill down my spine and his eyes lit up like coals as he caught hold of my arm before I could run away.

"First of all, I'm going to turn you into a mouse. Then I'm going to turn myself into a cat so that I can enjoy playing with you before I kill you."

I decided there was nothing to do but to meet Ravioli Poussin head-on. To bluff him, as if he and I were in a game of Djinnverso. "It seems to me that you're the stupidest djinn I've ever met," I said, with my heart in my mouth. "Because if I was someone who'd spent the last ten years with nothing to read but *The Man in the Iron Mask*, then the first thing I'd want would be to hear a new story. In fact, I think I'd want someone to tell me a new story so badly that I'd make that my top priority, ahead of shaving my ears, cleaning my teeth, having my hair cut, and turning someone very insignificant into a mouse." I shrugged as nonchalantly as I could manage given that I was in fear for my life. "But then, I don't know, maybe you just prefer *The Man in the Iron Mask*. And why not? It's a great book."

"It's a terrible book!" roared Ravioli Poussin. "I think I'd die if ever I had to read that book again." He held me closer

219

for a moment – so close I could smell his breath turning to green cheese inside his mouth. "Do you know any good stories?"

"I'm a kid," I said. "Of course I do. My whole life has been taken up with stories. Being read to by my mom and dad, listening to books on tape, reading books from our local bookshop, from our local library. Me, I'm the Story Princess of Madison Avenue. And Madison Avenue, in case you didn't know is the storytelling centre of the world's storytelling capital city. New York *is* all the stories."

"All right, then," said Mr Poussin, taking up my implied challenge. "Tell me a story. And if it's a good one, I won't kill you. How's that?"

"Fair enough," I said. "Are you sitting comfortably?"

The horrible djinn whom I had been stupid enough to release and who wasn't sitting at all, immediately sat down on a stone bench between two lavender bushes and folded his arms expectantly.

"Then I'll begin," I told him. "Once upon a time," I began, racking my brain for a story that might have to last for several hours; after all, there still existed the strong possibility, as soon as I had said "and they all lived happy ever after," that Ravioli Poussin would use this as an excuse to kill me. It appeared as if it would be in my interest to keep the story going for as long as possible, since I hardly thought he would dare kill me before the story had ended. The only trouble was that I've never been much good at creative writing. At school they aren't terribly interested in that kind of thing so much as the ability to marshal lots of facts, as if facts, rather than storytelling are what really matter, when in fact anyone knows that the opposite is true. Therefore my story wasn't exactly an original one and it was fortunate I am quite well-read. It started out as a sort of cross between *Oliver Twist* and *Great Expectations* (both, novels by Charles Dickens), but with some special additions made to satisfy my listener, specifically sword fights of the kind I suppose happen quite regularly in *The Man in the Iron Mask*, otherwise he would yawn and look bored. I had hoped that after a while Ravioli Poussin would fall asleep, or inform me that he needed to take a five-minute break, which might have enabled me to get away. But no such luck came my way and, after a marathon six hours of continuous storytelling, I felt obliged to stop for a moment.

"I hope that's not the end of the story," said Mr Poussin, pulling irritably on several long hairs growing in the palm of one of his small hands.

"I need something to drink that's all. My throat is getting rather dry."

"Better a dry throat than one that's been cut," said Mr Poussin, adjusting his sunglasses.

"Oh, quite, yes. But really the story's hardly begun."

"There's a water tap on the wall that the gardener uses," said Mr Poussin, who had an unnerving habit of using a switchblade to clean his long fingernails and the insides of his ears. He gouged a piece of wax as big as a lump of sugar from his left ear, flicked it into the bushes and pointed behind me. "You can drink from that if you must."

So I got up and went over to the wall where I could now see a brass tap and, having taken a drink of water, I also caught sight of an almost invisible stairwell that descended to the level below, or so I presumed.

"Hurry up," he roared and, seeing me glance down the stairwell, added, "If you must know what's down there, it's the *Bocca Veritas* that you asked about. If you were standing in front of it now it would tell you that if the story doesn't start again in ten seconds, your future looks nonexistent."

"Try to have some patience," I said, sitting down in front of Mr Poussin once more.

"Patience?" he screamed. "Don't talk to me about patience. After ten years in that bottle, I've had enough of patience – forever."

I resumed telling him my story.

Another eight hours passed, and Mr Poussin showed no sign of sleepiness or fatigue. By now I was quite exhausted and started to throw sword fights into my improvised narrative just to keep myself awake. John is so much better at this kind of thing than I am.

Then, just as I thought that I really couldn't go on, Ayesha appeared in the garden, followed closely by Miss Glumjob. It seemed that the invisible gardener had seen my distress and informed Ayesha that Ravioli Poussin was out of his bottle. She looked very angry – with me and with Mr Poussin, who was already begging for mercy. But after I explained what had happened, that I had spent all day telling Mr Poussin a story for fear that he would kill me, Ayesha laughed out loud.

"Perhaps that will teach you not to go around releasing strange djinn that have been bottled up for the protection of others. Not that this Ifrit could have done anything to you. I'm the only djinn that can have power in this place. He's quite powerless now. And he knows it."

"But he said he was going to kill me," I said. "He said he was going to turn me into a mouse and himself into a cat and that he was going to hunt me and play with me before killing me."

Ayesha laughed again. "He could no more turn you into a mouse than Miss Glumjob could."

"Well, really," I said, and stared angrily at Ravioli Poussin, who was now on his knees in front of Ayesha, begging for mercy. "Please, Ayesha," he said, whipping off his sunglasses. "Please don't punish me."

"I'm not going to punish you," said Ayesha, and then pointed at me. "She is."

I shook my head for a moment as I tried to think of a punishment for Poussin. Normally, I'm quite a forgiving sort of person and, in most circumstances I'd have told her to forget it. But something hardened inside me when I considered the distress I'd suffered at the French djinn's hands. Perhaps it was because I also felt like an idiot – the way he'd tricked me into believing he might kill me – that I found myself suggesting something.

"I think you should make him read *The Man in the Iron Mask*," I told her. "Out loud. *In English*."

"So shall it be," said Ayesha.

That was OK. It was the part that followed I found really troubling.

"And when you have finished reading it aloud," she added. "You shall begin it again. And so on. Until the end of your life."

Ravioli Poussin's howl of despair was cut short as he found himself chained to a large chair, one of his hands held inside an iron gauntlet to which a large copy of the book had been bolted, and powerless to prevent himself from reading aloud:

> *"Whilst everyone at court was busily engaged upon his own affairs, a man mysteriously entered a house situated behind the Place de Grève. The principal entrance of this house was in the Place Baudoyer; it was tolerably large, surrounded by gardens enclosed in the Rue Saint-Jean by the shops of tool makers, which protected it from prying looks, and was walled in by a triple rampart of stone, noise, and verdure, like an embalmed mummy in its triple coffin."*

Ayesha was already walking away, followed closely by Miss Glumjob.

"That seems a little harsh, don't you think?" I said, hurrying after her.

Ayesha ignored me.

"OK," I said, "but when I become the Blue Djinn I'll just reverse the punishment. Let him go. And I mean the very minute you're dead." She continued to ignore me and, feeling irritated with her, I added, spitefully, "Which ought to be quite soon, from the look of you." Again, that wasn't like me at all. My mother would have been horrified to have heard me say that to a woman of Ayesha's age.

This time Ayesha stopped and fixed me with a curious look. "How soon do you think that might be, my child? When I die, I mean."

I shrugged. "I dunno. But soon enough, I guess, if you've brought me here in these circumstances."

She smiled coldly. "Come with me. There's something you need to see."

We went into the house and up into the clock tower. I found myself led inside an intricate labyrinth of staircases which, except for Ayesha, I was certain I could never have found my way in or out of. At the centre of the labyrinth, Ayesha showed me a metallic fireplace about the height of a giraffe, at the centre of which grew a bush about two feet tall, bearing flowers varying in colour from pale purple to white. The bush gave off a strong odour like lemon peel, but what was even more curious about this bush was that the atmosphere around it was burning with a gentle blue flame, without any apparent injury to the plant. The tall metallic fireplace was marked with regular measurements, like a ruler and, on closer examination, it was plain that the blue flame, which surrounded the plant like a halo, had once reached all the way up to the top.

"Among all living creatures," said Ayesha, "it is given only to the Blue Djinn of Babylon to know precisely when she will die. This bush of fire is nothing less than my own soul, child. The djinn fire that burns within you, for me burns here on the outside, and is a measurement of my power. Or more precisely, my dwindling power. Once, the flame reached all the way up to the top, and life seemed almost without end. Now, as you may see for yourself, it hardly burns at all. Every year I come and look at this little flower and know, to the very minute when the day of my death will come. So do not talk of my death idly, child. If you want to know when that will happen, you need only come in here and take a look for yourself." Ayesha pushed me forward a little. "Go on. Look."

Horrified, I stared more closely at the measurement and saw that the height of the blue flame showed only a few months more of life for Ayesha. And while I looked, Ayesha held her hand steadily in the flame, like someone dipping their hand in a pond of water on a hot summer's day.

"Doesn't it hurt?" I asked.

"No, child. Not to us. Not to the children of the lamp."

Ayesha led me to the bottom of a golden spiral staircase. "The fire of your own djinn soul lies up there, Philippa. Whenever you are ready, you may climb the staircase and discover precisely how long you have to live."

"What a horrible idea," I said. "I can't think of anything worse than knowing the time of my own death. I can't see how you could possibly live a happy life if you knew exactly when you were going to die. Not knowing helps make life enjoyable and carefree."

Ayesha smiled. "Those are your emotions talking, Philippa. When you have been here longer and enjoyed more of the scent and fruit of the Tree of Logic, things will look very different. You will come to perceive that there are actually many advantages to knowing precisely how long you will live."

Afraid, I ran back to my room where, after a while, I

sat down and wrote more in this journal.

I'm beginning to see that being a djinn is not without its downside. Even so, despite what happened earlier, I'm still going back to the garden. Now that I know where the mouth of truth is to be found, I am determined to find out something that will help get me out of here.

CHAPTER 15

THE TOWER OF BABEL

As soon as John and Mr Groanin had found Darius and told him that the two desert demons had fled, they finished changing the tire on the car and then continued on their way.

"You must be a great djinn to have defeated those demons," said Darius, as they drove slowly now, because it was dark. "I was sure we would all be killed."

"That makes two of us," said Mr Groanin.

Alan and Neil barked their agreement, as if to say, "Actually, that makes four of us."

"The truth is," said John, "I'm not a great djinn at all. Most of the time I haven't got a clue what I'm doing. My sister's the clever one. The one with the talent. She knows much more about this djinn thing of ours than I do."

Darius shook his head and replied in Arabic. "I hear what you say, John. But only a great djinn would speak so modestly about himself. Truly, only a great and courageous djinn would come to a place as dangerous as Iraq without his power, to fetch his sister home."

It was past eight o'clock when they reached the outskirts of Samarra, which wasn't much more than a few palm trees and some poor-looking, mud-coloured buildings, most of them bomb damaged.

"Samarra was once a capital city for the Caliphs," said Darius as they drove into town. "But it was abandoned more than a thousand years ago. Now only soldiers and archaeologists come here."

Finally, they arrived at the place they had been looking for: the spiral-shaped tower of Samarra which, Darius assured them, with all the confidence of an experienced tour guide, was built on the site of the original Tower of Babel, and to much the same design. "The foundations are the same," he insisted. "At least, that is what my father always told me."

This was also the place where, according to Bellili's High Priest Eno, they were to look for a secret entrance to the underground land of Iravotum. As soon as they saw the tower, they were faced with a more immediate problem, however: the spiral tower was surrounded by a small American Army military base that looked as if it would be harder to get into than any secret entrance. The base lay behind several rows of barbed-wire fence, and a couple hundred thousand sandbags.

"That's torn it," said Groanin. "Now what do we do?"

"Find a way in through the wire, I suppose," shrugged John.

"That's not a bunch of Boy Scouts camped there," said Groanin. "And they're not looking to have visitors. Especially visitors dressed like us."

Darius stopped the car at a safe distance and they took a long hard look at the camp and tried to think of a plan.

"The Arab clothes are no problem," said John, shrugging off his bisht and pulling his thobe over his head. Underneath he was wearing his normal, Western-style clothes. "Besides, I have an American passport. Maybe we should just go over there and kind of throw ourselves on their mercy."

"I don't have an American passport," said Darius.

"No," said John. "But I was kind of assuming you'd want to stay with the car. To make sure that no one steals it."

"True," said Darius. "I will stay with the car."

"I don't have an American passport, either," said Groanin.

"No, but you have a British passport. And Americans and British are allies."

"So we've always been led to believe," said Groanin, although his tone made it quite clear he didn't put much faith in this alliance. "But how are we going to explain what a one-armed English butler and a twelve-year-old Yank are doing in one of the most dangerous countries in the world?"

"We'll say that you're my guardian," said John "Which means you'll do most of the talking, Mr Groanin. We'll tell them that my grandmother lives in Baghdad and that she's sick. In fact she's not expected to live. And that she's never seen me. So there's an urgency to my being here. We'll say our driver was supposed to take us to Baghdad but lost his nerve and abandoned us."

"Sounds plausible enough." Groanin nodded. "But suppose we do manage to bluff our way into the camp. Then what?"

John thought for a moment. "This might work," he said. "When Darius first heard me speaking to Mr Rakshasas inside his lamp, he asked if I was a ventriloquist. So we'll say you're a professional ventriloquist. You work with a lamp in which you pretend to have a djinn. That will be Mr Rakshasas, of course. What's more, Mr Rakshasas can use the library in his lamp to look up any question in the world. So, as well as the ventriloquist stuff, you can be doing a Mr Memory act at the same time."

"But how does that help?" asked Groanin.

"You can do a show to entertain the troops," said John. "While they're distracted, I'll take a look around the camp with Eno's map. See if I can't find that secret entrance."

"That sounds just daft enough to work," said Groanin.

"Of course it will work," insisted John. "With Mr Rakshasas to help us, you'll look like the best ventriloquist in the world."

"An excellent idea," said Mr Rakshasas, who had been listening carefully from within his lamp.

They said good-bye to Darius who wished them luck and told them he'd wait for them at the Kebabylon Restaurant just outside town, an establishment that was run by his mother's second cousin. "It's on the road to Baghdad," he said. "You can't miss it. All the furniture is purple and on the wall is a big picture of Michael Schumacher. My mother's second cousin, Mrs Lamoor, is liking Michael even more than I am."

The Samarra Tower lay in the middle of a large, flat, arid open space. Beyond the barbed wire and the sandbags, several dozen tanks, and some armoured personnel carriers, were about twenty US military Quonset huts grouped around the tower itself. In the wire was a gate with two checkpoints, both of them floodlit and overlooked by a machine-gun post.

John, Groanin, and the two dogs approached the gate where Groanin, who turned out to be quite an actor, told their unlikely sounding story to a couple of fresh-faced sentries. The two sentries listened in polite but vigilant silence until Mr Rakshasas, pretending to be Groanin's own voice coming from within the lamp that Groanin held in his hand, challenged both of the soldiers to test his memory.

"All right," said one of the sentries. "I'm from New Mexico," he said. "Maybe you could tell me the state capital."

"Too easy," said Groanin, gaining a little time for Mr Rakshasas to find the information in his set of *Encyclopedia Britannica*. "You should have asked me something difficult." He held up the lamp. "But let the genie of the lamp tell you the answer."

"The capital of New Mexico is Santa Fe," said Mr Rakshasas. "Which is the longest continuously occupied capital city in the United States. With a population of seventy thousand, it's also seven thousand feet above sea level."

"Heck, even I didn't know that much," admitted the soldier.

"If we could just stay here tonight," said Groanin. "We really don't have anywhere else. Even if you don't take me, then surely you could take the boy. After all, he is an American citizen."

"I'll call the Lieutenant," said the first soldier. "See what she says."

Inside the largest of the Quonset huts, Lieutenant Kelly Sanchez listened to Mr Groanin's story. She was thin and pale with short red hair and dark circles under her green eyes, which she used to look at Groanin with strong disapproval. "Don't you think it was kind of foolhardy?" she said stiffly. "Bringing a child to a place like this?"

"I can see why you'd think that," said Groanin. "But the boy does speak fluent Arabic. On account of the fact that his mother, my half-sister, is Arab-American herself."

"All right," sighed the Lieutenant. "You can stay one night. But one night only. In the morning I'll have someone arrange for your transportation to Baghdad, if that's really where you want to go."

"Thank you," said Groanin. He looked at John and smiled. John smiled back. "Isn't that good news, John?"

"Yes," said John. "Thank you very much, Lieutenant."

"As I mentioned, I'm a professional ventriloquist," said Groanin, "I'd be very happy to put on my act for you and your men, as a way of showing our thanks. I've done cabaret all over Europe and America. Go ahead, Lieutenant. Ask the genie of the lamp anything you like."

"How about three wishes?" said the Lieutenant.

"The impossible I can perform," said Mr Rakshasas. "Feats of magic take longer. But I'd be happy for you to test the limits of my knowledge."

"Ok," said Lieutenant Sanchez. "In college I studied math before joining the army. So can you tell me what the folium of Descartes is?"

"The folium of Descartes," repeated Groanin. "Did you hear that, O genie of the lamp?"

"René Descartes, born La Touraine in France, March 31, 1596," said Mr Rakshasas. "Died Stockholm February 11, 1650. French mathematician and philosopher. The folium of

233

Descartes is the curve defined by the Cartesian equation x3 + y3 = 3axy."

"That is amazing," admitted Lieutenant Sanchez and, for the first time since John and Groanin had sat down in her office, she smiled. "Maybe you're right. This might be good for the men. What do you think, Sergeant?"

"Sir, yes, sir," said the sergeant standing immediately behind John.

"Say in a hour's time?" said Sanchez.

"I can see no reason why not," said Mr Rakshasas.

"Very good," smiled Sanchez. "Very good."

A soldier showed John, Groanin, and the two dogs to a smaller Quonset hut where they were to be quartered, but then stood guard outside their door. This was something they hadn't bargained on.

"It's not going to be easy getting in and out of here with him standing outside," said John.

Groanin nodded at the map John had been studying carefully. "Have you any idea by now where the secret entrance might be?" he asked him.

"It seems to be in the north side of the tower, immediately behind what looks like the shower tent," said John.

Groanin let out a long sigh. "Then there's only one thing to be done," he said. "You'd best go on to Iravotum without us."

"You mean, go on my own?"

"Take Alan and Neil, of course," said Groanin. "But don't wait for me and Mr Rakshasas. With that guard outside, you may only get one chance to get in that secret entrance. You'd best take it when you can."

"Mr Groanin is right, John," said Mr Rakshasas. "This might be your one and only chance, to be sure."

"Besides, I expect a man with one arm would only slow you down," Groanin said bravely, for he hated the idea of abandoning John. "I say, a man with one arm would only slow you down, lad. Not that you'll need my help. From what I've seen so far, you've got more courage than most people twice your age and size. If anyone can rescue your sister, it's you, John."

Mr Groanin folded John to his stomach and then wiped a tear from his eye. "Good luck, son," he said. "And hurry back. We'll be waiting for you with Darius at the Kebabylon Restaurant. Won't we, Mr Rakshasas?"

"Indeed, we will," said the old djinn.

"But what will you tell Lieutenant Sanchez when she finds I've disappeared off the base?"

"I'll just tell her that you've been acting a bit doolally, on account of the heat probably, and that you've legged it somewhere, but that I'm going to stick around in the general area until you show up again. I'm sure we'll be all right with Mrs Lamoor at the Kebabylon Restaurant.

"Come on, Mr Rakshasas," he said, picking up the lamp containing the old djinn. "We'd better get on with the show. It doesn't do to keep the military waiting."

The soldier led them to the R & R tent, where the performance was to take place, but about halfway there, the two dogs and John – wearing a small backpack containing Eno's book, a trowel, a flashlight, a bottle of water, and several Hershey bars given to him by Lieutenant Sanchez – gave them the slip, unnoticed.

"Looks like it's just the three of us now," said John, as they went along to the shower tent.

The shower tent backed onto a huge pedestal on which the Samarra Tower rested. There were several communal latrines, communal showers, a row of sinks, and several dozen baskets that were full of dirty laundry. The floor was composed of a lattice of duckboards on which the soldiers could walk without getting their wet feet covered in sand. It all looked very basic, but quite functional.

John pushed his head and shoulders through a flap in the tent behind some laundry baskets and shone a flashlight along the base of the tower. A small lion's head carved into the wall marked the spot, exactly as Eno had described. "This is it," he told the dogs. "We're right above the secret entrance to Iravotum."

He moved one of the laundry baskets and then lifted one of the duckboards to find a floor of hardened sand. They were going to have to dig, and immediately it was clear that the small trowel John had brought would hardly do the job. It was fortunate that a soldier had left a pack hanging on a peg, to which was attached a folding entrenching tool. John took the tool and prepared to dig. He could already hear Groanin "warming up" his audience with some terrible jokes which, to John's surprise, seemed to go down surprisingly well. But John had barely scratched the surface of the sand when, hearing someone come into the tent, he and the dogs were obliged to hide inside one of the laundry baskets.

John listened as half a dozen soldiers came into the shower room, removed their body armour and their uniforms, and then whooped with pleasure as they stepped under the hot water. John could have used a shower himself. His shirt was sticking to his body with sweat and he wished he'd thought of having one before setting out on the next stage of his rescue mission.

Finally, the last of the soldiers left the shower tent, and John breathed easily again. "Come on," he told the dogs, flinging open the basket. "Let's find the way in."

Taking up the entrenching tool, John started to dig, although it was still a little hard to believe what Eno had written: that the sand concealed a lion-shaped handle that he needed only to grasp before uttering the secret word that would open a door underneath. If what Eno had written was true, this would just be the beginning of his problems. The high priest had written of "seven guardians," to six of whom John would have to "submit without question." Most alarming of all was Eno's sternly worded instruction that "the interloper must kill the seventh guardian without demur or face the total confoundment of his esoteric ambitions" – by which, presumably, Eno meant he would fail to get into Iravotum.

John stopped for a moment to rest and to listen for a moment as Groanin continued his "act." The soldiers seemed to like him and applauded enthusiastically as, apparently, he performed yet another feat of ventriloquism, which was to recite a poem while drinking a bottle of beer.

Once again, he started to dig even though he was beginning to lack confidence in the whole enterprise. The secret words of entry sounded as if they belonged in some creaky old fairy tale. Or as if Macreeby had made them up. Even as this thought crossed John's mind, the entrenching tool hit something metallic and, shoving his hand into the sand, John pulled up a heavy brass ring that was shaped like the head of a lion. The handle was attached to a chain that descended into the sand below him.

"Well, here goes, I suppose," he said and uttered the secret words, "Open, Simsim!" although with no great expectation that they would work.

Nothing much happened, except that the rest of the sand collapsed into the hole, and disappeared into the darkness. Uncertain if this was the result of the secret words or not, John shone his flashlight down the hole and seeing a round trapdoor beneath him, dropped down on top of it.

"There's a door all right," he said to Alan and Neil who remained at the top of the shaft, looking down at him. John placed his feet either side of the door, took hold of the lion handle and pulled at the chain. The trapdoor, old and rusted, lifted a few inches but it was another five or ten minutes before he had managed to lift it all the way open.

Resting the trapdoor against the wall of the shaft, John picked up his flashlight and shone it along an ancient-looking stone tunnel, although he hardly needed it now for, as he looked, somehow the tunnel lit up, as if this was the result of the door being opened. "I expect the oxygen from the outside must have done that," he said.

Returning up the shaft, he urged the two dogs to jump in and then hauled the duckboard down behind them to cover the hole, just in case the soldiers found the shaft and decided to explore it themselves. The last thing John wanted was a group of soldiers on his tail. Then he grabbed his backpack and stepped through the trapdoor. Gritting his teeth, for he was already feeling claustrophobic, John took a charcoal pill and the three of them started down a gently sloping spiral path. This, he quickly concluded, was of the same design as the Samarra Tower above the ground, and gradually he saw that the part belowground was much bigger than the part above, rather like an iceberg. He wondered if there might even have been a time when the whole of the tower had been aboveground. In which case it seemed quite possible that the tower would have been as big as many a New York skyscraper. Mounted on the walls of the tunnel were a series of torches that burned with a steady but curious, violet-coloured flame.

"I wonder who keeps these lit," he said aloud.

Almost immediately he was aware of the strangest sensation: he was now speaking a language that he didn't recognize. He knew what he was saying, it was just that by the time the words came out of his mouth they were alien to him. And not just to him. Neither Alan nor Neil could understand what he was saying – something he knew for sure when Neil traced a question mark with his paw in the dirt on the path, and Alan whined an uncomprehending sort of whine.

"That's very strange," said John, but out loud, the words sounded completely different. And it was a moment or two before he guessed that he was experiencing what Eno had described as the "Babel effect," after the story in the Book of Genesis when men had suddenly stopped understanding one another's speech, and had started speaking different languages.

"Don't worry," he tried to tell the dogs. "In the *Bellili Scrolls,* Eno says this might happen. It's something to do with this being the site of the original Tower of Babel." Except that neither Neil nor Alan had a clue what he was saying. And several minutes passed before it dawned on John that he was actually speaking the language of the Lakota Indians of North America, better known as the Sioux. He knew this because he had recently watched a television program that showed an old Lakota woman teaching some movie actors to speak her language. The sensation was not unpleasant and John reminded himself that, according to Eno, the Babel effect was only temporary.

But a little way farther along the spiral path, he and the dogs came across something rather less agreeable. It was a large man, bare-chested, wearing silk trousers and carrying a sword. Even with Alan and Neil to protect him, it was plain to see that there could be no getting by the man without at least one of them being killed or seriously injured.

"Look here," said John. "A mistake has been made. I am a friend. Honestly. My name is John. Who are you?" Except that in Lakota Sioux this sounded something like "*Hoka hey. Wonunicun. Miyelo ca kola. Zunta. Micaje John. Nituwe he?*"

The man with the sword grinned back at John – rather horribly it seemed to him – although it was plain to see that he did not understand a word of what had been spoken to him. Quickly, John consulted the High Priest

Eno's book for advice on what to do next, in case he had missed something. But Macreeby's translation was quite clear: "Life teaches us that only he who is truly resolute will succeed. To seek, you must first make yourself humble. Therefore, you must submit to six of the seven guardians, without question, or your quest will be forever confounded. Six times you must yield to whatever is encountered, no matter how terrifying or lethal these things may seem."

Eno had hardly exaggerated. The man with the sword looked as lethal as he was terrifying. Even if John had wanted to resist him, he did not see how. "All right," he said. "Let's go." Which came out as *"Hin, hoppo."* John bowed and then walked slowly toward the man with the sword, bowing several times more for good measure and repeating *"colapi,"* which is the Lakota word for "friends."

As he neared the man, John felt a heavy hand fall on his shoulder, forcing him to kneel, and gulped as the silent man took a step backward and then raised his sword. The blade glittered in the strange underground light, and John felt it gently touch the nape of his neck as the swordsman readied himself to strike. How could he yield to this? All his instincts told him that if remained on his knees he would surely be beheaded. How could it possibly be to his advantage to submit to this ordeal, if submission ended in his death? What if Macreeby's translation had simply gotten it wrong? Suppose Eno had actually said that he should *not* submit to this guardian, and Macreeby had left out this crucial word?

Alan and Neil growled as the man's well-muscled arm carried the sword behind his shoulder. John told them to stay and closed his eyes. "Look out teeth, look out gums," he muttered in Lakota, as the man swung his sword toward John's head. "Look out neck, 'cause here it comes!"

CHAPTER 16

BEYOND GOOD AND EVIL

N ow as any djinn will tell you, nothing is a matter of pure chance. When the universe was created, man was given dominion over the earth, the angels dominion over the heavens, and the djinn dominion over Luck, which is the interaction of the two. Many of the games of chance beloved of mundanes the world over were invented by evil djinn, such as the Ifrit, for the general torment of humankind, and to save themselves the trouble of exercising their powers, for the Ifrit are a very lazy tribe of djinn. But there were more than a few good djinn who had devoted their lives to combating the bad luck generated through gambling. One of these good djinn, Edwiges the Wandering Djinn, had sought to ruin the casinos by devising gambling systems to defeat the odds and win games, again and again. The only trouble was that since good djinn are forbidden to make money from gambling themselves, Edwiges was obliged to give away her systems for free. And since there were very few humans prepared to risk money using a system they had acquired for nothing, there were few of them who ever won as much as they might have done.

Nimrod found Edwiges standing on the steps of Monte Carlo's beautiful Belle Epoque casino. She was an eccentric-looking woman of late middle-age and kindly disposition, like someone's favourite aunt and, indeed, because of her many kindnesses to him, Nimrod had grown up always calling her Aunt Edwiges, although in fact she was no relation of his at all. She was wearing a vaguely shaped floral dress and, as usual, gave off an air of general forgetfulness, which did little to enhance mundane confidence in any of her gambling systems. But underneath her maiden-aunt exterior and eccentric forgetfulness was a prodigious mathematical brain. She couldn't have told a policeman her correct address or her telephone number, but if someone had asked her to solve Fermat's Last Theorem, she could have done it while baking a sponge cake.

"Nimrod," she said, pleasantly surprised.

"Hello, Aunt," he said, hugging her fondly. He looked over her shoulder at the handful of booklets she was holding. "May I?" She handed him a booklet that he opened and then read aloud the title page,

> *"Foolproof system for the beating of the odds in the pernicious game of roulette, the correct employment of which will result in the immediate enrichment of the conscientious user. Note: Requires a small knowledge of probability theory, Newtonian mechanics, and air-conditioning."*

"I call it my Three-Minute System," said Edwiges. "Using

it, a mundane might turn five hundred dollars into twenty-three million dollars with just three spins of the roulette wheel."

"Won't it just encourage the mundanes to gamble more?" asked Nimrod.

"Only in the short term. If enough mundanes take up my system, the casinos will start to lose their edge. And eventually go out of business. I've calculated I only need six people to use the system and win, for it to become statistically significant." She sighed. "Sadly, a foolproof method is not an easy thing to give away. Mundanes just won't put their trust in something they get for for nothing."

They went across to the nearby Café de Paris where Nimrod ordered them some coffee and dessert.

"So what brings you to Monte Carlo?" asked Edwiges. "Holiday?"

"I'm afraid not," he said. "No, I'm here on djinn business. You see, Ayesha has kidnapped my niece, Philippa, it seems with the intent of making her the next Blue Djinn of Babylon."

"Philippa?" said Edwiges. "Yes, I can see why Ayesha would want her. She's charming, bright, good at Djinnverso. She seemed to have a very thorough grasp of the mathematical principles underlying a game using seven octagonal astaragali. But Philippa's still a child and much too young to become the next Blue Djinn. She deserves to see something of life before such responsibility should be thrust upon her. No, it should have been someone who has seen something of life. Someone like the awful de Ghulle woman. I believe she's quite desperate to be the next Blue Djinn. By all accounts she's been telling everyone for ages that she's got the job."

"Oh, I agree," said Nimrod. "But I rather think Ayesha chose Philippa in something of a panic, simply to thwart Mimi de Ghulle's chances of having the job."

"Mimi's an awful woman, it's true. But, when you think about it, what harm could there be in her doing it? Once Mimi's put herself beyond Good and Evil there's an end of it, and it won't matter what tribe she's from."

"It ought not to matter whether the next Blue Djinn is chosen from a good tribe or an evil one. In this situation, however, it does. Very much."

"How?"

"Recently I came into possession of a copy of the *Bellili Scrolls*."

"I thought that book was only a legend."

"So did I. But I bought a copy from Virgil Macreeby."

"That rascal. Is it genuine?"

"Oh yes. And I learned something interesting. Interesting and disturbing. As well as containing information on how to enter Iravotum, Bellili's High Priest Eno describes how an unscrupulous djinn might undermine the normal processes by which a djinn advances to a state beyond Good or Evil. It seems that indifference to Good or Evil is brought about by exposure to the Tree of Logic. To the fruit and to the scent of the blossom."

"I always did wonder how that worked," said Edwiges.

"However, according to Eno, if the juice of the fruit is refined and then fermented to make alcohol, it becomes many times more powerful, and an indifference to evil is blocked. In other words we could be talking about a djinn as powerful as Ayesha who is only indifferent to good."

"And what makes you think that's a possibility, Nimrod?"

"When Macreeby sold me a copy of his translation he told me that one other djinn owns a copy. Mimi de Ghulle. At the time I didn't attach much importance to this. But since then, I've read the book for myself and I'm now convinced that's why Mimi wanted it. So that if she becomes the next Blue Djinn she could pervert the Blue Djinn rites and use the position for her own advantage. If that happened, the balance of power would be destroyed and chaos would reign again."

"This is shocking," said Edwiges. "We can only shudder at what might happen if Mimi did somehow manage to become the Blue Djinn. She would get her hands on *Solomon's Grimoire*, and any sense of there being a balance of power would disappear out of the window. Mimi's new ability to bind other djinn to her will would make her a virtual dictator. Or to be more accurate, a virtual dictatrix." Edwiges shook her head grimly. "Mimi always did have an ambitious streak. And she wouldn't stop there. She'd probably try to make sure that her daughter – what's her name –?"

"Lilith."

"Yes, Lilith. Nasty child. She'd probably try to make sure that she succeeded her as Blue Djinn. So we could even be looking at a dynasty of de Ghulles in Babylon."

"I never thought of that," admitted Nimrod. "But you're right, of course. What are we going to do?"

"We must stop her, Nimrod. That's what we must do.

I mean, we can't let Ayesha make Philippa into the next Blue Djinn, any more than we can permit Mimi de Ghulle to have the job. Mimi would be a very bad alternative. Especially if, as you say, she's worked out a way to pervert the Blue Djinn rites to her own wicked ends. The only question is, if it's not going to be Philippa and it's not going to be Mimi de Ghulle, then who will it be? You know what? You need to find someone else who'd be suitable. It would have to be someone female, of course. And someone you can trust not to use the position for her own ends."

"Yes, I quite agree," said Nimrod. "Which is the real reason I'm here in Monte Carlo. I was thinking that you might do the job."

"Me? Whatever gave you that idea? I'm not at all suitable."

"Nonsense," said Nimrod, putting his arm about Edwiges's shoulder. "As a matter of fact, you'd be perfect. You're single, intellectually advanced, more than a hundred years old, with a lifetime of public service behind you, and above all, you're a good person. Indeed, I can't think of anyone better suited to the job."

Edwiges smiled. "Do you really think so?" Edwiges kept on smiling for a moment; then abruptly, the smile vanished and she was shaking her head. "But I couldn't possibly do it. It's one thing to put yourself beyond Evil. But it's something else again to put oneself beyond Good. I wouldn't like that at all. Then, there's my work to consider. I'm far too busy. I'd like to help you, Nimrod, really I would. I've always been fond of you. Ever since you were a young djinn yourself. But there are a hundred different reasons why I can't do it. And just because I can't think of any more than two right now, doesn't mean they aren't important reasons."

Nimrod nodded patiently. It was going to require some very careful handling if he was ever going to persuade Edwiges to become the next Blue Djinn of Babylon. But looking at the little booklet in his hands, he suddenly had an idea.

CHAPTER 17

OEDIPUS SCHMOEDIPUS

After several long moments, John opened one eye and then the other, put his hands around his neck, swallowed experimentally and, relieved that his head still appeared to be attached to his shoulders, looked around slowly. The man with the sword was gone. Although John had felt something touch his neck, clearly it hadn't been a sword. Or had it? Brushing the back of his neck, where the blade had momentarily rested, his forefinger came away with a spot of blood. He gulped loudly and cleared his throat – as if he wanted to check that everything was working properly in the neck department – before actually shaking his head and speaking to Alan and Neil, who remained lying on the ground, their paws covering their eyes.

"Hey, guys." He was pleased to discover that he was speaking English again. "It's OK. The swordsman's gone. And I still have my head."

The two dogs jumped up and ran to lick his face and hands.

"I guess that looked a lot worse than it felt," he said, folding their ears and nuzzling them back. "Although it felt real enough, I can tell you. It's weird but I can still remember the sensation of the sword on the back of my neck." He shivered and grinned. "Just like a trip to the barber's shop."

Alan barked and ran over to inspect something that was lying on the ground. It was the sword.

Picking it up and brushing the blade against his thumb, John had no doubt that the sword was real; it was sharp, too. He hefted it in the air several times, uncertain if what he had experienced had been an illusion or not. Would the six other guardians that lay ahead of him still be any more real than this? He decided to take the sword with him, just in case.

They proceeded down the spiral path, but they hadn't been walking for more than five or ten minutes when they came upon a mounted Arab lancer, clad entirely in black, his face covered with his matching headdress. The horse, also black, paced nervously under its rider as he extended the lance toward John who touched the point and discovered that, like the sword, it felt quite substantial.

"Bare your chest," the rider said in Arabic which, fortunately, was now a language that John could understand. Even so, he was no less nervous about submitting to the swordsman's spear point than to the executioner's sword. Not that he thought he could have made much of a fight of it; a boy with a sword seemed no match for a horseman with a lance.

John did as he had been ordered, praying that the thrust of the spear would be no more lethal than the sword had been. Unbuttoning his shirt, he exposed his chest and watched as the horseman galloped a few yards down the path, and then wheeled his horse around. The next second, the rider levelled his lance at John and then charged.

"Stay where you are, guys," shouted John and, muttering a silent prayer, closed his eyes.

This time he even felt the ground vibrate under his feet and detected a strong smell of horse in his nostrils before, opening his eyes a crack, he found himself wreathed in a cloud of dust sent up by the black stallion's hooves, but still very much alive and the horseman nowhere to be seen.

Alan let out a loud sigh of relief and coughed as the dust caught in his throat. Neil shook his head and then lay down wearily as he watched his young master inspect his own chest and then button up his shirt.

"According to Eno," said John, trembling with fear, "there are still four more guardians to whom I have to submit before killing the fifth. I just hope it's the idiot who thought up these stupid ordeals. I'm a nervous wreck." He pulled Alan's head close to his chest. "Listen to my heart," he said, uttering a nervous laugh. "It feels like a small bird trying to get out of a cage. I guess by the end of today we'll know if my heart's in good shape or not. Then again, maybe that's sort of the point."

Bravely, John advanced down the spiral path and, in fairly quick succession, was obliged to submit to an archer who fired an arrow that didn't actually hit him, and then a huge wrestler who picked him up and crushed him without actually crushing him. By the fifth ordeal – which required John to place his head in a lion's mouth – he was becoming almost blasé about these subterranean guardians.

"I think after three, you get the idea," he said, walking through the fire breathed by a fire-breathing dragon. "That nothing much is going to happen. I mean, three would have been enough."

But with six of his seven ordeals now complete, John was emotionally exhausted and hardly equal to the task of killing a locust, let alone whatever was waiting around the next bend on the path. And, feeling the strain of what had been required of him, he tried to talk up his own courage to face the last of the seven guardians. "I expect the thing is that I'll not actually be killing anything," he told Alan and Neil. "No more than I've been killed myself. What do you think?"

The two dogs barked their encouragement, but quietly hoped that if John did have to kill something, it might be a real cow, in which case they'd each get to eat some fresh meat. For, being dogs, neither of them had their human master's scruples about killing another living creature – at least one that wasn't an insect.

But nothing could ever have prepared John for what he met around the next bend on the spiral path. For there, all five feet one inches of him, wearing his favorite Badoglio pin-striped suit, and his best Cascio Ferro shoes – he was even wearing the shirt John and Philippa had bought him for Christmas – was John's own father.

"Hello, John," said his father. "It's good to see you."

"Dad," said John. "What on earth are you doing here?"

"No, what are *you* doing here?"

Alan and Neil ran toward their brother but, just as they were about to jump up and lick his face, in the way they usually did at home, and which often obliged Mr Gaunt to remove his glasses and dry them – for on their hind legs, both dogs were as tall as Mr Gaunt – they stopped suddenly, and then backed away from the figure on the path, growling nervously, as if they sensed that something was wrong. Alan and Neil looked at John and barked several times, and John didn't need to ask the dogs to know that the man on the path was not – could not be – his father. And yet. . .

"How did you get here, Dad?

"That's a good question. I'm not exactly sure myself."

This was a good answer, as far as it went. But given the previous six guardians, John was not much inclined to believe the evidence of his own eyes, that his father was actually here. Unless of course, all of the previous ordeals had been cleverly designed to mislead him about the reality of this last guardian. John went over to his father and laid a hand on his shoulder. The material of the suit was cashmere, and that certainly felt right. And wasn't that his father's favorite cologne? Even the Beezer mint on the tip of Edward Gaunt's tongue looked right: Mr Gaunt always sucked two or three Beezers after smoking a cigar. If this was a figment of John's imagination or some kind of illusion, then it was as accurate as the gold watch on his father's wrist. All of which were very good reasons why John now realized that he couldn't strike this man with the sword and kill him, without making absolutely 100 per cent certain that he was dealing with an imposter, or something that wasn't even there.

"Dad," he said carefully.

"Yes, John."

"You know that little gold statue of liberty that sits on the desk in your study? Well, I broke the hand holding the torch. It was an accident. I've been meaning to tell you about it for a while. I superglued the hand back on, only I didn't do a very good job. I'm really sorry about it."

It had been a situation he'd been planning to rectify until Nimrod had turned up asking the twins to help him recover the Solomon Grimoire. There was no excuse for his having damaged the statuette. He couldn't say how he'd done it, just that he'd been handling it carelessly, pretending that he'd been given an Academy Award, and the hand with the torch had just broken off. The stupid thing had cost $25,000, for Pete's sake and, to John, it seemed highly unlikely that his father would be cool about it. Any more than he thought his father would be happy about him coming to Iraq. After all, he'd only agreed that John and Philippa could go with Nimrod to Istanbul and Germany.

"I really don't know how it happened," he said. "Only that it did happen. The way these things do. Sometimes." John shrugged. "Sorry."

"That's all right, son. I understand. It can't be helped. Besides, it's just an ornament, right?" And Edward Gaunt smiled his nicest, most indulgent smile. He didn't swear or threaten to ground John, and he didn't cut off his allowance for six months. Which was not at all like the real Mr Gaunt. At least, the Mr Gaunt that existed in wintertime. Philippa was fond of accusing her parents of caring more about their furniture and their works of art than they did about their children, and while John knew this wasn't actually true, he remained quite certain his real father would have given him the lecture to end all lectures. Even here, in Iraq, he was sure his dad would have been furious about it.

"Dad? I just want you to know. This is nothing personal, OK?"

Even as he spoke, John struck his father with the sword, mindful of Eno's sternly worded instruction: "The interloper must kill the seventh guardian without demur, or face the total confoundment of his esoteric ambitions". John wasn't quite sure what "esoteric" meant, but he was sure that not obeying Eno's instructions to the letter might have resulted in him never seeing his sister again – at least the sister he knew and loved.

But if John had expected his sword to pass through thin air, he was wrong. Through the handle of the sword, the blow he delivered felt horribly solid. What was even worse, John's father screamed out loud, as if he really had been killed. Nor did he disappear, as the other guardians had done. Instead, he just fell, face-first, onto the ground and then lay still in a pool of blood. Blood which looked all too wet and real and red.

John screamed.

"What have I done?" he wailed.

John threw aside the sword and quickly knelt beside his victim, feeling sick to his stomach and now terribly worried that he had done something dreadful. He was haunted by the idea that Eno had got it wrong or, as before, that Virgil Macreeby's translation of Eno's book, had been mistaken. In death, this man still looked exactly like John's father.

"No, no, no, please, no, this can't be happening."

With trembling hands, he took off the dead man's glasses and tucked them in the breast pocket of his suit where he discovered a cigar holder containing a Manyana Grand Cru, which was his father's favorite cigar. Why would an illusory Edward Gaunt have had a cigar at all?

"Dad, please, wake up," he said. "I didn't mean it." But it was plain from the amount of blood on the ground and the colour of his face that the man on the ground was past all help. John closed his eyes tight, as tears started to spill out of them and onto the dead man's pale face.

"I'm sorry," he said, now almost helpless with grief and, in spite of all previous evidence to the contrary, quite certain that he really had killed his own father. "Dad, I'm so, so sorry."

Unable to reassure John that this was certainly not his own father, Alan and Neil tried and failed to pull him away from the corpse. And for several minutes John remained, kneeling beside the body with his eyes closed.

Then Neil barked loudly and, opening his eyes again, John saw that the corpse, only too real a moment ago, had now disappeared.

John shook his head and let out an unsteady breath. He smiled weakly at Neil, recognizing that it had been an illusion after all. Even so, he knew he wouldn't feel at all comfortable about what had happened until he put his arms around his real father again and hugged him tightly.

Alan, who had run on down the path to scout the way ahead, now came bounding back. He barked several times and, taking hold of John's shirt sleeve, tugged at it in an effort to get him to his feet.

"OK, OK," said John. "I'm coming."

Following the dogs down the path and around the next bend in the spiral tunnel that wound its way around the underground part of the Samarra Tower, it was suddenly easy to understand the dog's excitement, for the path had ended, and they were faced by a low door in a wall. About as tall as a table, the door was made of ancient-looking wood, studded with black nails and furnished with a great black iron handle that had been fashioned in the shape of a human head. The head was that of a man, his beard braided and his hair hanging in great curls around his face. But what was more remarkable about this handle was that the man's iron tongue had been drawn out of its mouth and nailed to the door. It was, thought John, a very striking, not to say meaningful design – as if someone, Eno perhaps, had wanted to warn anyone thinking of turning the handle, never to talk about the secret of what lay on the other side of the door.

Eno had provided only a little information about what John might now expect. And after his ordeals, John was understandably nervous about turning the handle. Iravotum lay on the other side of this door, but he would hardly have been surprised to learn that a seven-headed tiger was waiting for him. Or something worse that, at present, he was unable to imagine.

"What do you think, guys?" he asked Alan and Neil, who proceeded to sniff at the door for several seconds. "Hey, I just had a thought. Suppose it's locked."

Indeed, so it proved and it took John several minutes to determine that the nail could be removed from the metal head's protruding tongue which, thus liberated, could be lifted, and the door, which was on a simple latch, opened.

"Cool," said John, and drawing the door toward him,

bent down and walked through.

Unlike the torch-lit, winding spiral path that had led them around the buried part of the Samarra Tower, several hundred feet down into the earth – perhaps more – here, on the other side of the door, it was almost impossible to believe that they were underground at all and, for a moment, John and the two dogs stood still in amazement.

A sea stretched out in front of them and gently lapped at a shoreline made of fine, golden sand. A light wind stirred John's hair and carried a refreshing and salty spray into his face. But what really amazed him was not the size of the sea, nor even the wind that rippled its empty surface, but the fact that he could see across it, thanks to a special light of clear, almost lunar whiteness that gave off no heat and seemed to suggest something of electrical origin. And examining the air above his head, John was reminded of documentaries he had seen on TV about the aurora borealis, the so-called northern lights. The overall effect was of a world within a world.

He tried to imagine what kind of geological event could have explained the existence of this underground place. Once, with his parents years before, he'd visited a cave of giant proportions in Kentucky. But that had been a rabbit hole in the ground compared to what John was seeing now. Even the world's largest caves didn't come with their own climates and strange lights.

After his seven exhausting ordeals, the general sense of amazement John was now feeling seemed to restore him to full energy. Perhaps it was the clean, bracing air which smelled and tasted very different from the gasoline-tainted atmosphere he had become used to breathing on the earth's surface. Alan sniffed loudly at the edge of the water and then looked at John, almost as if to say, "Well, what happens now?"

"Eno mentioned something about there being a boat," said John, tossing a couple of quarters in his hand. According to the high priest, it was necessary to give the boatman two coins and, although he didn't make it clear what currency was in use, Nimrod had said it probably wouldn't matter. "Not that there's any sign of a boat."

Even as John spoke, Neil, whose eyes were keener than those of his brother and his young master, and who had been studying the uncertain horizon – for it was impossible to say exactly where the earth above them actually rested on the earth below them, no more than it was possible to say for sure where the sea ended and the luminous, electrical sky began – barked as something appeared in the distance on the water's surface.

"What is it, Neil?" asked John, following the line of the big dog's eyesight. "Do you see something?"

Neil barked again and advanced into the water, only to yelp loudly and run out of it again for, as John now discovered, the ocean lake was quite hot. "That explains the clouds down here," he said. "They're steam clouds." He licked the finger he had dipped into the water. "Other than that, it's quite drinkable. Too bad we didn't bring some instant coffee. Really, it's almost hot enough."

It wasn't much longer before John had identified the object on the water as a human figure, standing erect in the stern of the boat and rowing toward them with a long single oar, like a Venetian gondolier. But it was only when the boat finally touched the shore that he realized it was only the image of a human being, for the boatman was an automaton, a sort of robot made of brass.

"Hello," John said nervously. "I was wondering if you might take us across the water, to the palace of the Blue Djinn of Babylon?" He handed over the two quarters he had brought, which hardly seemed adequate. Silently, the boatman took the coins in his brass hand, and then pointed at some seats in the bow of the boat. Quickly, they all climbed aboard.

With a superhuman strength, the tall brass oarsman pushed the boat away from the shore and, within a matter of minutes, they were moving through the hot water at a speed that would have seemed impossible had it not been for the strange metal man working the oar. And it wasn't very long before the shore had disappeared behind them.

John knocked experimentally at the oak timbers of the boat. "I hope this thing is all right," he said. "I'd hate to have to swim for it. Five minutes in this water and I'd look like a Maine lobster." He was worried more for the dogs than himself; as a djinn he didn't think the hot water would have affected him much; but he wasn't so sure about the dogs.

An hour passed, and then another and, after a while, John fell asleep and dreamed about something pleasant. This was forgotten immediately he opened his eyes again, and saw that they were at last in sight of a distant shore with trees. Alan and Neil shifted impatiently in the boat for they were anxious to do what dogs do when, following a journey, they find a nice tree.

John looked at the boatman and, nodding affably, said,

261

"This is very kind of you. I really don't know how we'd have managed, otherwise."

The boatman said nothing.

"If it's not a rude question," said John, persisting in his attempt to engage the brass boatman in conversation. "And I've got nothing at all against the idea. I mean, it takes all kinds to make a world, doesn't it? But why are you made of brass, exactly?"

The boatman could not talk. That much was certain. But just as it could row, it could also point, and so it did. The boatman stopped rowing for a moment and, in answer to John's question, pointed one long, brassy finger at the sky above them, before rowing again. John nodded politely and it was several seconds before he understood just what significance was attached to the brass oarsman's gesture. For only an oarsman made of brass could ever have survived what happened next.

CHAPTER 18

PHILIPPA GAUNT'S JOURNAL (cont'd)

NATURALLY, I've hidden this diary, just in case Miss Glumjob, Ayesha, or one of her invisible servants finds it, for I guess they would take it and destroy it, if only because, as well as providing me with a means of figuring out how long I've been here, it also enables me to reflect on some of the things I've said and done, and be aware of any changes in myself. Changes of the kind described by Ayesha and brought about by breathing the air here and drinking the water – although I have not drunk any of Miss Glumjob's apple juice. Changes caused by being around the Tree of Logic.

I have seen the tree, which doesn't look like much. It grows in a special room here in the palace, and looks more like an ancient oak tree than one with apples, although there are apples on it. But there can be no doubt that it's having some sort of an effect on me. How else can I explain what I said to Miss Glumjob at breakfast?

She was looking misty-eyed and sounding all gooey about what she was going to wish for before going back to Greenville, North Carolina, (presumably after Ayesha has gone to the great lamp in the sky). It was all very predictable stuff. Anyway, I listened to all this and then fixed her with my most evil-looking eye and then told her that "when the old bat" was dead, I was going to come after Miss Glumjob and set an elemental on her.

"A fire elemental," I told her spitefully. "A really hateful and deceitful one that will attach itself to you permanently."

There was more, much more. But I'm ashamed to write down the really horrid things I said to poor Miss Glumjob, which sent her away from the breakfast table in tears. Ayesha herself seemed quite indifferent to what I had said to her servant and companion, which is, I suppose, all that one expects of someone who is above Good and Evil. But this prompted me to tell her that it seemed to me that it wasn't a logical person I was becoming so much as a thoroughly nasty one.

"That is entirely normal in the beginning," she said. "Logic can be a demanding master, Philippa. Until you learn how to accommodate it, your mind will push the logic of a fact to its ultimate conclusion in an unmitigated act. Sometimes that can be very unpleasant. You see Miss Glumjob as one of the obstacles in the way of your being away from here, therefore you would like that obstacle removed."

Whatever the truth of what Ayesha said, I have no doubt that I've started to become the same hard-hearted sort of person that she is. And this fills me with horror. But what can I do?

DAY THREE. Actually I'm not at all sure how long I have been here since daylight seems to last a very long time indeed, and the darkness hardly any time at all. It may be that time itself is slowed here in the same way that happens when you work a transubstantiation and put yourself inside a bottle or a lamp. Perhaps, in a similar way, the Hanging Palace and Iravotum exist outside of normal three-dimensional time and space. There's nothing about this in Eno's book, but he was writing several thousand years ago; I don't suppose an ancient High Priest of Bellili would have known about such things as relativity and astrophysics.

Anyway, the bottom line is that on two occasions I've gone to bed when it was light outside, and awoken to find it was still light. I asked Miss Glumjob about this but, after what I said to her yesterday, she's no longer speaking to me. Of course, I couldn't let this be without saying something else that was hurtful to the poor woman. And, weirdly, this time I actually felt something harden inside me – as if my heart, or whatever it is inside a person that causes them to care about another person's feelings, had made itself into a little fist. A very strange feeling indeed. And yet. . .

Well, this isn't all bad. There are some benefits that come from the introduction of a little more logic in one's life. For example, I am beginning to understand something quite important: that how things are in the world is a matter of complete indifference for what is higher. Sometimes things just are, and there's no sense in judging them right or wrong.

I do wish that John would come, however. I sense him more strongly now, which makes me think that the feeling I first had, when starting this little journal – that he is coming to rescue me – was, and is, correct. It may be that he is nearer than I think. Which is, of course, another reason why I am hiding this diary in my room. I believe that Ayesha doesn't feel his presence at all. Or if she does, that my being John's twin, makes her confuse his presence with my own.

THE SAME EVENING. On two occasions I have been back to the garden to visit the stairwell that, according to Mr Poussin, leads down to the *Bocca Veritas* – the mouth of truth. But both times I found Miss Glumjob there, tending the roses. Today, however, Miss Glumjob was nowhere to be seen and there was only poor Mr Poussin, chained to his chair and still reading out loud from *The Man in the Iron Mask*. Before running down the stairwell, I paused and apologized to him, which was very nice of me, I think, after what he put me through.

"For what it's worth, Mr Poussin, you won't be here forever," I told him. "When I am the Blue Djinn, I will release you from this punishment."

> "D'Artagnan, still confused and oppressed by the conversation he had just had with the King,"

said Mr Poussin still reading, for it seemed that no other kind of speech was now permitted to him. He smiled weakly, but did not stop reading.

> "...asked himself if he were really in
> possession of his sense; if the scene had
> occurred at Vaux; if he, d'Artagnan, were
> really the captain of the Musketeers and
> Fouquet the owner of the chateau in which
> Louis XIV was that moment partaking of his
> hospitality."

Leaving the poor man to his unfortunate fate, I ran down the stairwell to where I hoped I would find the BV.

I found myself in a dimly lit grotto. The light was a little stronger at the end of the grotto, so I went toward it where a horrific encounter now awaited me. For there, set in a niche in a brick wall, like a vase of flowers, was a human head whose eyes flickered open at my presence and stared at me, bright and unblinking, like tiny lights. Since all of the hair was gone and what flesh that remained on the head had turned to the colour and texture of leather, it's impossible to describe this gross-looking creature beyond the fact that the head had once been a man's.

"Ask your question," said the head, although the lips – what there were of these – moved so little that I almost looked around to see if someone was playing a trick on me. The voice sounded quite in keeping with the head, however – like something coming up from a deep, dark pit. I was so moved by the head's plight I hardly felt it polite to ask about my own situation.

"Who are you?" I asked the head "And how did you get here?"

"Once I had a name. The name was Charles Gordon. Some men called me Chinese Gordon, although I was born in London. I was once a general in the British Army, captured by my enemies more than a hundred years ago, and handed over to some sorcerers and demon worshippers. They put me up to my neck in a barrel of sesame oil and kept me there for forty weeks. During this time certain, unspeakably wicked rituals were performed. And the flesh fell from my bones. Finally, my head was removed from my body and I was carried around in a great silver box for many years, exhibited at bazaars and giving out prophecies. Then, Ayesha rescued me and placed me here where, since then, I have enjoyed a measure of peace in the cool of this grotto. For I can never be buried, since I cannot ever die. That is who I am. That is how I got here. Your question has been answered truthfully."

"What an awful story," I said. "Isn't there anything anyone can do? No hope at all?"

"All hope is fallen," said Gordon. "And the hope I dreamed of was but a dream. Hope is no more than a memory long forgotten. Your question has been answered truthfully."

"Is there nothing *I* can do for you?"

Chinese Gordon's head was silent for a moment. "I should like to have a cigar again," he said. "Your question has been answered truthfully."

"Then I'll get you one," I said.

It seemed the least I could do. I ran back to the house to take a cigar from the large humidor on the library table. Ayesha likes to smoke one after dinner, with her coffee.

Back in the grotto, I placed the cigar between

Gordon's stretched lips, lit it, and watched his obvious satisfaction.

"It's been years since I had a cigar," said Gordon.

"My uncle Nimrod says that smoking is bad for humans," I said. "That only the djinn should smoke." I smiled and considered this carefully. "But, under the circumstances, I don't suppose it will do you any harm." I smiled. "How long have you been here?"

"One hundred and twenty years to be precise. Your question has been answered truthfully. But, do you know, Philippa, in all that time, you're the first person who ever asked me that question?"

"What question was that?"

"You asked me, 'Is there nothing I can do for you?' Your question has been answered truthfully."

"How do you know my name?"

"The same way I know everything else. I am the mouth of truth. That is my purpose. To speak the truth of that which is. That is why you are here, is it not? Your question has been answered truthfully."

"If you know me, then you know my twin brother, John."

"That is not a question."

"Is my twin brother, John, coming to rescue me?"

"Yes. Your question—"

"Where is he now?"

"Close. Quite close. But he is in danger. Your question has been—"

"What kind of danger?"

"The Rukhkh. Your question. . ."

"Who or what is a Rukhkh?"

269

"The Rukhkh is a huge, carnivorous bird. Dangerous to anyone but the old and vain, for it is certain that the hair of anyone who eats the Rukhkh's chick will never turn gray. Your question has been answered truthfully."

"Will my brother survive? Please, Mr Gordon, tell me what's going to happen to him."

"I cannot foretell because here in Iravotum there is no future and there is no past. That is for everyone except the Blue Djinn herself. Here there is only the present. Your question has been—"

"Why must you speak in riddles?" I asked angrily.

"Because the present is as much of a riddle as the future. And because the solution of the riddle of life in time and space lies outside time and space. Your question has been answered truthfully."

It worried me a lot to hear that John was in danger. But what could I do? I was powerless to help him any more than I had the power to help myself. Or was I? It occurred to me that I only had to ask Chinese Gordon to find this out for sure.

"Can I help him?"

"One twin can always help the other, be they djinn or human. The wishes of twins are always fulfilled, especially over the weather. That is why twins are sometimes called 'children of the sky'. Because of this secret power. Your question has been answered—"

"Will you please tell me how this helps me to deal with the Rukhkh?"

"The Rukhkh is a bird. A bird flies in the air. Now, the atmosphere of Iravotum is very sensitive. Over several thousand years, it has become quite unpredictable, unlike the atmosphere on the earth's surface. Being a twin, you may affect that atmosphere by the breath in your body and the motion of your hands. In short, you will make a wind. Birds, even large ones, don't much like wind. Therefore, you must go to the highest place in the garden and blow at the horizon. That will deal with the Rukhkh. But be quick. Your question has been answered truthfully."

"Thank you, Chinese Gordon," I said. "You've been very helpful." And I turned to leave the grotto.

"But you have one more question, do you not?"

"Yes. How did you know?"

"I am the mouth of truth. That is my purpose. To say what is. Your question has been answered truthfully."

"Why did Ayesha choose me? That's what I'd really like to know."

"Because you are Ayesha's granddaughter, of course. Your question has been answered truthfully."

At this, I heard myself yell out loud, but there was no time to hear anymore. Each second I delayed was another second when John might be killed by the Rukhkh. I ran up to the highest level in the hanging gardens, where I took a deep breath and blew toward the horizon, with all my strength, even waving air in the same direction with my hands. I did this for a full twenty minutes, until I was almost blue in the face, before I returned to this room, to write all this down, and to reflect upon what Chinese Gordon had told me about Ayesha.

CHAPTER 19

THE LUNATIC IS ON THE GRASS

The attack had come from nowhere. One minute the brass oarsman was propelling the boat through the steaming water, and the next John and the dogs were cowering in the bow as a bird the size of a prehistoric Quetzalcoatlus (the largest pterodactyloid) swooped over them, snapping at their heads with a huge beak that looked as if it could have torn open the side of a Boeing 747. Only the brass oarsman remained erect in the stern of the boat, beating at the giant bird with his oar, so that one of its feathers fell on John's head.

As the bird soared away only to wheel around and attack again, John saw that the feather was as big as a chicken's wing. This bird could have picked up an elephant as easily as an owl would have taken a field mouse. Growling like an alligator, the giant bird swooped again and the boatman landed a blow on it with his oar. John understood why the boatman was made of brass. No human oarsman could have withstood the creature's fierce beak and claws. But with every swing of the boatman's oar the deck wobbled uncertainly beneath his feet, and John saw it wouldn't take much for them to be toppled into the water. This worried him most of all. Even if *he* had been able to endure the volcanic temperature of the water –

and he wasn't exactly sure of that – there was no way the dogs could survive it.

On the third attack the giant bird fastened its claws on the boat and, might even have lifted it out of the water but for Alan and Neil, who jumped up and fixed their jaws in the creature's scaly ankles. The giant bird screamed loudly and, releasing its hold on the boat, flapped its huge wings and rose up into the air, with Alan and Neil still attached to its ankles.

"Let go!" John yelled at the two dogs. "Let go or you'll both be killed!"

They might have let go, too, except that the very next moment an enormous gust of wind from the landward side caught the terrible bird and pushed it violently away from the air above the boat. And it was suddenly clear that if Alan and Neil did release their grip on the bird's ankles they would certainly perish in the hot volcanic sea.

"Hold on!" John shouted to them, contradicting his previous command. "Don't let go or you'll both be killed!"

Despite its obvious pain, the huge bird attacked the boat a fourth time but, once again, the wind buffeted it away. And finally conceding defeat, the creature flapped its wings and then headed for the distant shore, along with Alan and Neil, their jaws still fixed determinedly to the bird's ankles.

"After them," John told the boatman who returned his oar to its rowlock and then propelled the boat forward again. Kneeling in the bow, John kept his eyes fixed on the bird as it grew smaller on the horizon. Then, just as it reached the shore, he thought he saw the two dogs let go and fall onto the sandy beach.

"Hurry," he said. "Please hurry." And, to John's surprise the boatman obeyed, rowing faster than before, so that they covered the half mile that separated them from the shore in only a few minutes.

By now, John's heart was in his mouth. Sick to his stomach, he told himself that the sand would have cushioned the impact of their fall but, as they grew nearer and he saw the two motionless bodies, John began to think that it would have been a miracle for them to have survived.

With ten yards to go before the boat reached the shore, John leaped into the water and ran up the beach to where Alan and Neil were lying. A few feet separated their bodies and he saw they were both still breathing, but only just and, as soon as he touched them, he recognized the worst, that neither dog was going to get up again. Tears welled up in his eyes.

Alan stopped breathing first, then Neil, and John lay down between them feeling lonelier than he ever had been in his life. Whatever wrong his two faithful companions had done as human beings had been made up for, and more, by their steadfast loyalty and courage. No one could have had two better friends than these.

The oarsman watched John all the time but did not move from the boat. Finally, John said, "They're dead," and lay down beside the bodies of the two dogs. After what he had imagined happening to his father, this seemed too much for him to deal with. And wanting to be dead himself he pushed his face hard into the sand, trying to scour away the tears that were already running down his face, and thinking that if ostriches really did bury their heads in the sand, he had a pretty good idea why. Sometimes the world just seemed too unbearable to face. Finally, when there were no more tears left in him, he sat up and stared sadly at the two bodies lying beside him, hoping that their deaths might also be an illusion, like that of his father. But the bodies of the two dogs remained.

After a while he wondered if he should try to bury them, only he had nothing to dig with, having left the army entrenching tool back on the surface. So he got some palm fronds and used them to cover the bodies, thinking that perhaps, Philippa would know what to do with them when he found her. The chances were that they would have to come back this way, anyway. Eno hadn't thought to provide an indication of an alternative way out of Iravotum.

According to the high priest's map, there was very little distance now. The palace was only a few miles away and all he had to do was walk along a path that led through the apparently impenetrable forest, and he would arrive at the palace gates. Of course, this wasn't going to be a walk in the park. Eno hinted at other dangers that still lay ahead of him and had suggested that any traveller thinking of taking the path should beware of snakes. So, taking out his Swiss Army knife, John cut himself a long staff, said good-bye to his two dogs, wept some more, and then stepped onto the path.

Almost immediately, he caught sight of a beautiful bird perched on a branch of a nearby tree. It was a peregrine falcon and, instinctively, John knew that this falcon was none other than Virgil Macreeby's son, Finlay, for whose current avian shape John was himself largely responsible. Perhaps, he thought, there might yet be a way of returning the boy to his original body. John took off his backpack, cut a large piece of the padded material away, wrapped this around his wrist and, holding up his arm, called to the bird.

"Finlay," he said. "Come here."

The bird hardly hesitated and, taking wing, came gliding smoothly through the air to settle on John's arm.

"Listen," said John, stroking the bird's small head. "If you help me, I'll help you. As soon as I've found my sister, I'll try to return you to your original shape, supposing that I can. All right?"

The falcon screeched once and dipped its head.

"I'll take one screech as a yes, and two screeches as a no," said John. "You can be my eyes. Like Horus. You can fly above these trees and see any dangers ahead. Just as important, you can be my friend if you like, since all my friends are dead now or left behind."

The falcon let out one shriek and hopped onto the shoulder strap of John's backpack so that he might have the use of his arm as he walked.

About a mile farther on, the path widened, and John was presented with a broad avenue lined with two neat rows of large earthenware jars. Each was as tall as a door, shaped liked an inverted bell, and stood on a small pyramid of sand. He wondered what was in the jars, if anything, and suggested to Finlay that he might fly up and take a look, since he himself was not nearly tall enough to see inside them. Finlay flew into the air and hovered over one of the jars and then another. These appeared to be filled with oil and, satisfied that they posed no apparent danger, he returned to John's shoulder.

"Did you see anything? I mean, anything dangerous?"

Finlay screeched twice, which meant "no", and somewhat reassured, John went on his way. But mindful of what Eno had said about snakes, he kept on tapping the path ahead of him, like a blind man. In this way he swiftly discovered that Eno had hardly exaggerated the danger, for the path was booby-trapped. Each jar contained only a thin layer of oil that covered a lid, underneath which lurked a hidden serpent. The vibration of John's footsteps, or perhaps the stick, caused the pyramid of sand supporting the first jar to collapse, tipping it forward in front of him so that it cracked open like an egg, hatching out a snake that was almost fifty feet long. If John had possessed any doubts as to whether or not the snake was dangerous, these were swiftly answered. Grabbing his staff in its saddle-sized jaws, the snake wrapped the stick in its coils and crushed it like a matchstick before hissing loudly and fixing its eyes on John himself.

Seeing the snake's eyes, Finlay hardly hesitated and flew at them, his claws fully extended, attacking the snake's head with all the screaming ferocity that had characterized the Rukhkh's attack on the boat. This was John's chance to make a run for it and, while the giant snake tried to prevent the plucky little falcon from tearing out its eyes, he set off at a lick, reaching the end of the avenue, which was a good half mile, without mishap. There he sat down and, leaning against a tree, rested until, several minutes later, and minus several tail feathers, Finlay caught up. There was blood on his talons.

John drank some water, closed his eyes and, in the silence of the forest, gradually became aware of something large moving in the forest ahead of him. At first he thought it might be another huge snake, or even the Rukhkh and, sending Finlay up into the branch of a tree for safety – for, from the air, the forest was so thick that Finlay could not see below the tree canopy – he decided to creep up on whatever it might be, Indian-style, to find out what it was.

At the edge of a clearing, John dropped onto his belly and waited, certain that whatever the thing was, this was where it had been standing just a few moments before. It seemed impossible that a creature so large could have moved so quickly. But then something moved in front of him, something that was almost invisible, and yet not quite, for the air around the thing seemed to vibrate, giving whatever it was an indefinable shape. And, gradually, John saw that it was a kind of ghost – a huge ghost, the ghost of a giant perhaps, for it was as tall as a tree and as wide as a house. From time to time the ghost groaned a little and crackled with a greenish electrical current, so that the vaguely human shape grew momentarily more defined.

Slowly, John took out Eno's book and found that while the high priest himself was a little vague about what this creature might be, Virgil Macreeby had supplied a footnote to his own translation that seemed to hint at a more specific explanation for what John was almost looking at:

278

*It is not only rash, angry, evil, and idle wishes
that gravitate to Iravotum. In an appendix to
his book, of which only a fragment now
exists, the high priest suggests that just as
the results of these wishes go to Iravotum so,
too, do all the human wishes that remain
unrealized – the wishes that never did, and
never could come true. Eno comments
that the energy of these unrealized wishes
collects as a larger, supernatural force that he
calls the Optabellower, or Optabelua. This
translates, roughly, as "wish monster." It is
said that this being, if it can be described as
a being, first emerged from the sleeping mind
of Ishtar, when she herself wished that
Nebuchadnezzar would build her a temple.
This may also be the explanation of a saying
common among the djinn, "to be careful
what you wish for".*

Looking at this greenish, nearly invisible creature, and
listening to the low moaning sound that emanated from
within its shapeless, nebulous centre, John wondered
what else it could be, and decided that a simple
experiment might help him to be sure. Putting his focus
word out of his mind for a moment – just in case Ayesha
felt his power – John wished as hard as he dared that Alan
and Neil were alive again.

His experimental wish had an immediate effect. A
crackle of electrical current seemed to ripple through the

creature, and John could have sworn that it grew a little in size. There could be no doubt about it, he thought; this was the wish monster, all right. And while he didn't know exactly how, he sensed that it was dangerous. But as he turned around to creep away, John came face-to-face with a peculiar-looking man who, like him, was on all fours. There the similarity ended, however, for the man was naked and wet with dew from the grass through which he had been crawling, not to mention eating. Hair grew on his body like a bird's feathers and the nails on his fingers and toes were like a bird's claws. John might have yelled with fright except that the grass-eating man placed a strong and rather smelly hand over John's mouth and shook his head silently, until John acknowledged, with a nod that he would not cry out. After a moment, the man removed his hand and crawled quietly away on his hands and knees, with John following.

When they had gone what seemed like a safe distance, the man stopped and sat down in front of John, plaiting his long beard and occasionally plucking up a handful of grass that he placed in his green mouth and chewed like a cow. He showed no immediate inclination to speak.

"Who are you?" John finally asked.

"I am the king. Peace be multiplied unto you."

"King who?"

The man shrugged and ate another handful of grass. "Just the king," he said, offering some to John.

"No, thanks," said John. "It gives me gas." He smiled in his usual affable way, as if greeting a new boy at school. Minutes later, Finlay swooped down onto John's shoulder, to the delight of the grass-eating king.

In the silence, John fell to wondering if the man really was a king. Eating grass, not cutting your hair and your toenails, and crawling around on all fours was hardly the behavior John associated with being a king, but then, anything seemed possible in Iravotum. And, after all, even kings went crazy sometimes. This one looked a little crazy, but not dangerously so.

"That thing back there," he said. "Was that the wish monster?"

The King grinned. "Yes," he said. "Wish monster."

"Is it dangerous?"

"Very dangerous. All things that come to Iravotum have one wish. But it is a very strong wish. The wish to be made right, somehow. Or the wish to be undone. Or the wish to come true, perhaps. But the wish monster feeds on them, consumes them and, more important, the wish that drives them." The king banged at his own chest meaningfully with one hairy fist. "This makes him very powerful. Very strong." Then he pointed at Finlay and shrugged sadly. "He will be consumed if he stays here long enough. And so will you. It is only a matter of time. That, or not wishing for anything at all. But, I ask you, who can do that? Who can make himself truly content?"

The king stuffed a large handful of grass into his mouth and began to munch it loudly. Then he broke wind, very loudly, for almost thirty seconds, which seemed to make him happy.

John guffawed with admiration. "That was awesome," he said. And then, "What about you, Your Majesty? I mean, are you content?"

"Yes, I am content," said the king. "I wish for nothing.

My punishment was just. That is why I have survived. Because I haven't a wish in the world. All that I need is here. Plenty of juicy grass to eat." He burped happily. "Plenty of water to drink. What more could a king want?"

"Search me," said John politely. "If that's what floats your boat, then good for you, sir. How long have you been here, anyway?"

"A long time." The king thought for a moment. "Let's see now. There's a tree around here I've been making notches on, just in case anyone ever asked me that question. Although you are the first, as it happens."

He crawled off into the undergrowth, with John and Finlay following. A little way farther on, the king stopped in a small clearing and pointed proudly to a tree on which several hundred notches had been carved. "Here it is," he said. "There are exactly 250 notches in this tree. Each notch, represents a year, I think." But finding a delicious-looking clump of grass, the king ripped it up and started to eat again.

It was then that John noticed there were in fact several other trees, similarly scarred with notches. He counted them up and found that there were a total of ten trees with 250 notches, and one with just 65. He felt his jaw drop as he made the calculation. "Are you telling me you've been here for 2,565 years?" And suddenly John had a shrewd idea he knew who the king was.

"A long time," said the king. "A very long time to someone like you, from the outside. But not here. Not in Iravotum."

"But didn't you ever try to escape?" asked John.

The king shook his head. "Where would I go? I have

all I need right here. Plenty of juicy grass to eat." He broke wind again.

"Yes, I can see and hear how much you enjoy that," said John.

The king smiled his green smile and stared dreamily at the treetops.

"The Hanging Palace of Babylon," said John. "Is it near here?"

"You mean the Palace of Ishtar?"

John nodded.

"Yes," said the king. "Quite near."

"I need to go there," said John.

"Everyone who comes here wants to go to the Palace of Ishtar. They won't help you there."

"You don't understand. I don't want them to help. My sister is a prisoner there. I need to get in there, bring her back here and then go home to New York. That's a city. A great city. Bigger than Babylon."

The king's eyes lit up at this mention of Babylon. "Bigger than the great city of Babylon? Truly?"

"Truly."

"Are the buildings very tall?"

"Taller than some mountains."

"I should like to see this great city of yours."

"I'll make a deal with you, Your Highness," said John. "Get me into Ishtar's Palace, and I'll take you to New York."

The king nodded. "There is a way in. No one knows this way except me. I will take you there. And then you will take me to New York. Yes?"

John thought about this for a moment. There were all

283

kinds of people roughing it in New York. Who would notice one guy eating grass in Central Park? Even one with toenails as long as the king's. There were Texas oil billionaires whose behavior was more eccentric. Besides, with a manicure, a good haircut, a shopping expedition on Madison Avenue, a decent dietician – in short, a bit of djinn power – the king might scrub up quite nicely.

"Come on," said John. "Let's go, before that thing comes looking for us."

CHAPTER 20

JOHN BOY

Philippa had stopped keeping her journal. There no longer seemed to be much point in writing it. Her previous thoughts and reflections appeared trivial to her, even a bit embarrassing. Even so, she couldn't quite bring herself to destroy it. In a way it amused her, like something she'd had when she was a baby. Instead of writing in her bedroom, Philippa now spent most of her time in the library, reading books by philosophers such as Aristotle, Plato, Kant, and Wittgenstein, or playing Djinnverso with Miss Glumjob and Ayesha.

By now, it made perfect sense to Philippa that Ayesha should be her grandmother. It explained Ayesha's interest in Philippa. It surely explained the argument Philippa had seen Ayesha having with Mrs Gaunt at the Pierre Hotel in New York, and why her mother had been so evasive about it later. It probably explained why neither her mother, nor Nimrod had ever mentioned her grandmother – Philippa had always assumed she was dead. And it certainly explained a certain similarity she now perceived between her mother and Ayesha: the well-groomed glamour and a sort of steeliness. The only surprise was that she hadn't noticed it before. Or that someone else hadn't thought to mention it to her. There was no doubt about it, Layla was

Ayesha's daughter, all right. And cleverer than Uncle Nimrod, the way Philippa herself was cleverer than her brother, John.

Poor boy. Whatever would he do without her to keep him out of trouble? Not that she cared. Relatives were a bit of a nuisance really. A nuisance and an embarrassment. Not that she could really remember very much about John now except that he was a grotesque caricature of herself. His face she found almost impossible to fix in front of her mind's eye. She'd quite forgotten the colour of his eyes, for instance. Did he even have red hair like her? Or was he dark? And it occurred to her how often she'd had to bear in mind her brother's good points just to find his presence at all tolerable.

Her father, Edward, she didn't think of at all. That was most embarrassing of all. A mundane human being for her father. Really! What on earth could her poor mother have been thinking? He wasn't even good-looking. Indeed, even for a mundane, he seemed quite mundane.

All of these thoughts, however, she kept to herself. There seemed nothing to be gained in talking about her family with Ayesha. What would have been the point of it? It wouldn't, couldn't have changed anything. Not now. Nor did she feel at all inclined to discuss these things with Miss Glumjob. What would have been the point of that? Indeed what, wondered Philippa, was the point of Miss Glumjob at all? It hardly made sense that someone as intelligent, as well-educated, and as logical as Ayesha should have kept on an insect like Miss Glumjob as her maid and companion. Philippa herself would employ someone cleverer to be her own companion when she became the Blue Djinn, which she couldn't see happening soon enough, given Ayesha's failing mental powers. How else could you explain the fiasco that had been the supposed exile of Iblis to Venus?

Philippa had learned that Ayesha had paid $10 million to Bull Huxter to place a canister with the bottle containing the Ifrit aboard the *Wolfhound Space Probe* to Venus. According to the newspapers, however, the rocket carrying the *Wolfhound Probe* had yet to take off from the French Space Centre in Guiana. Delayed by technical problems. Or so it was reported in the newspapers. But what was more worrying was that Bull Huxter had completely disappeared with the canister containing Iblis and Ayesha's money. What was worse, the tuchemeter in Iravotum – measuring the luck in the world, good or bad – was showing a period of severe bad luck ahead. The Homoeostasis, which is the fine balance that exists between good and bad luck, was no more, at least for the time being. This, declared Ayesha, was consistent with Iblis being at large once again, and intent on revenge.

"And whose fault is that?" said Philippa. "You should never have entrusted such an important djinn task to a mundane like Bull Huxter. He must have discovered what was in that canister. And thought that he could make some sort of a deal with Iblis. Let him out of the bottle in return for three wishes, that kind of thing. Why didn't you just leave him here, in one of the rooms in this old house? We might as well be on Venus for all that ever happens here. Plus, you could have saved yourself ten million dollars."

"You're taking this very personally, Philippa," said Ayesha.

"Of course I'm taking this personally. Obviously, you've forgotten that it was me who helped Nimrod to imprison Iblis. From my mercifully short acquaintance with him, he struck me as a very nasty djinn, just the kind to utter a *vindicta* against Nimrod, my brother John, and more important, myself. So, naturally, I'm concerned that he's disappeared, yes."

"You're exaggerating, child," said Ayesha.

"During the Djinnverso Tournament I had to play a match against Iblis's youngest son, Rudyard. He couldn't even bring himself to speak to me, Ayesha. He had to make bids directed to me through Mr Bunyip, the umpire. Believe me, if looks could kill I'd be dead already." Philippa shook her head. "This means trouble, you mark my words. A lot of trouble."

"I think I'll be the judge of that, child, not you."

"Right," laughed Philippa. "And we'll see where that gets us. I didn't ask to understudy you, Ayesha, but it seems to me that if I'm going to do this, you might try to make it look as though you know what you're doing."

Ayesha bit her lip for a second. But it was when Philippa began to swear under her breath at her that she became really annoyed for, old though she was, Ayesha enjoyed excellent hearing. This kind of disrespect – she couldn't think what else to call it – was intolerable to a djinn like Ayesha, who hated bad manners almost as much as she hated a show of emotion.

"Philippa, go to your room, please. And stay there until your manners have improved."

Philippa leaped up off the sofa with alacrity. "Love to," she said and walked to the door where she stopped for a moment, adding insolently, "but if I am bad mannered, it's you who've made me like this, with your stupid Tree of Logic, and your ugly boring palace." By now, Philippa was laughing and found that she couldn't resist throwing an insult Miss Glumjob's way, just for good measure. "Not to mention your dried-up old prune of a companion there. Miss Glow-worm, or whatever her stupid name is."

"Leave the room, please," Ayesha said firmly.

"With pleasure."

Philippa slammed the door loudly behind her, just for good measure and started back along the corridor to her room, with pleasure indeed.

At first she hadn't liked her room and thought it much too big and too palatial. But now she found she liked it just fine. All the silks and the gilt and the marble. She liked the invisible way things got done. You couldn't fault Ayesha's logic on the subject of servants. There Philippa had to hand it to the Blue Djinn. Servants were, after all, a necessary nuisance for most people in Ayesha's position, but a nuisance they were – at least they were so long as they were visible. Now that she had grown used to seeing – almost seeing, anyway – her room being dusted and vacuumed, the bed made, and the flowers replaced by invisible servants, she couldn't imagine living any other way. The pity was Miss Glumjob wasn't invisible as well.

Turning a corner in the corridor, Philippa found herself confronted by a very dishevelled, dirty-looking boy whom she eyed severely, especially his coarse hands and dirty boots. At first she thought he might be one of the servants become, momentarily visible. The boot boy, perhaps.

Except that no servant would have dared to speak to her. She was sure of that.

"Hullo," said the boy, trying to smile but hardly finding himself equal to the task, so cool was Philippa's stare.

"Did you wish to see Ayesha?" she asked him.

"No," returned the boy, crossly. "Of course not."

"Well then, boy, state your business and begone, for that rug you're standing on and muddying with your dirty boots is an expensive one."

"I couldn't care less," said the boy. "What's the matter with you?"

"Nothing at all's the matter with me," she said. "I'm not the one who looks like he's been dragged through a hedge."

"As a matter of fact I *have* been dragged through a hedge," declared John. "In a manner of speaking. And that's because I've had a terrible journey getting here. Philippa, it's me, John. Don't you recognize me? I've come to take you away from this dreadful house."

At this, John tried to take his sister's hands but she snatched them away as if she feared some awful disease. "As a matter of fact," she said, "this dreadful house, as you call it, is a palace. Which is probably why you look so out of place in it, boy, with your filthy fingernails and the grass in your hair. A palace, do you hear? Queen Victoria died in this house."

"I'm not in the least bit surprised," said John, frowning irritably. He hadn't counted on this at all. She looked like his sister all right, dressed like her, too, even sounded like her a bit, but she hardly acted like her. This awful girl behaved like she didn't know him from Adam. "And stop calling me 'boy,'" he said. "I'm your brother, John, you little witch."

"My," laughed Philippa. "Doesn't that sound brotherly?"

"And I'm here to take you home," he said, trying to ignore her.

"You already said that, boy." Philippa laughed contemptuously and pushed John away. "Maybe you should clean out your ears after you've gouged the dirt from under those atrocious fingernails. This is a palace. This is my home now. This and some other palaces that Ayesha owns. Look at it. Magnificent, isn't it? My bedroom is the size of a tennis court. I sleep on silk sheets and dine off gold plates, so what makes you think I'd want to go back to that box in New York you call a home?" She pushed him again. "Answer me that, boy, if you can."

John glanced up at the magnificent staircase and the huge chandelier. He took in all the beautiful antique furniture and the fine paintings. His father had some nice stuff, but nothing like this. And suddenly he felt humiliated, like a dog in disgrace, as if her scorn was justified. He'd never really thought about it before but home did seem kind of small now that he'd seen this house. He was starting to feel like something vulgar, as if home wasn't quite good enough for Philippa anymore. As if she'd already left him behind. Was he too late? Had she already changed forever?

"Go ahead and cry," she said. "You look like you want to."

"No, I don't," said John.

"Yes, you do," she said triumphantly, pushing him a third time.

"No, I don't," insisted John. "And stop pushing me, or you'll be sorry."

Philippa laughed. "What could you possibly do to me?"

291

She pushed him a fourth time. "Boy."

John turned away, thinking that otherwise he would have hit her. Like most brothers and sisters they'd exchanged their fair share of blows. Once, she'd even kicked his butt. But somehow it felt wrong to have come all this way just to kick hers. Which was exactly what he felt like doing. And he caught hold of the table in the middle of the hall just to stop his hand from turning into a fist and giving her one in the kisser like she richly deserved.

"Why, you rotten little witch," John muttered, reflecting on the many hardships he had endured to find his sister again. Not just him, either. Alan and Neil had sacrificed their lives for her, and this was all the thanks they got.

Philippa turned and put her foot on the staircase, still laughing at him. "Stupid boy." She said a lot of other nasty things as well that made John feel a lot more ignorant and ignoble than he thought he would have felt upon completion of his near-impossible mission. Not that Philippa cared how he felt. She was all dried up inside, from drinking the juice of the fruit of the Tree of Logic and inhaling the scent of its intoxicating blossoms. Dried up and hard, like a piece of ground in a severe drought.

John decided that it was time to soften that ground. He removed the flowers from a large vase that stood on the table and threw them on the carpet. Then he picked up the vase, heavy with water and, before Philippa realized what was happening, followed her a few steps up the staircase and, furious with his sister, tipped the contents onto her head.

"There," he said. "There's what I think of you."

Philippa let out a scream as almost a gallon of water cascaded over her. And, for a moment, she just stood where she was, in a state of absolute shock at the sudden realization of where she was and what she had almost become. Finally, she seemed to recognize him properly for the first time. But John was still too angry with her to notice.

"And there's what I think of your stupid carpet and your stupid vase," he said, throwing the vase onto the floor, where it broke into several pieces.

"John," Philippa said joyfully. "You're here. You came." She looked about around her and added. "How did I get here?"

"Phil?" John took her by the shoulders and smiled. "You do recognize me, after all."

"Of course, I recognize you, you idiot." And then she clung to her brother and laughed and wept for joy. She coughed and spluttered a little too, because some water from the vase had gone up her nose and down her throat, and so John gave her a drink from the water bottle in his backpack, just enough to dilute and counteract the effect of the Tree of Logic. The next moment a black, poisonous-looking substance welled up in her mouth and spilled down her chin and neck.

Guessing the water he had brought had worked some restorative effect on her, Philippa took the bottle from his hands, and drank all of it. More of the black stuff came out of her mouth and with each small eruption of logos – for that was what it was – more of the old Philippa was restored until she took him by the hand and said, "Is there a way out of here?"

"Of course."

"Then let's go."

John led her down into the basement to a series of corridors she had already explored, several times. "Where are we going?" she said. "There's nothing down here. I already looked."

Ignoring her, John took her along a more ancient-looking passageway that seemed to lead to a dead end; upon reaching the far wall, he took out his Maglite and shone it on some lettering in the plasterwork near the ceiling.

"Hold the flashlight," he said and, standing on a chair he had placed there earlier for this precise purpose, he drew his finger over the lettering. As he did so, the letters seemed to turn to gold and then to glow, and Philippa saw that there were possibly four words, although the lettering and the language was not one she recognized. As soon as John's finger had finished tracing the last of these ancient letters, the wall turned into a door.

"'*The moving finger writes,*'" said John, stepping down from the chair. "'*And having writ, moves on.*' Or at least we do, if we're sensible."

"I don't know what's more weird," said Philippa. "That hidden door, or the fact that my brother just quoted some poetry."

"That's a poem?"

"Sure. From the *Rubaiyat of Omar Khayyam.*"

"Well, whaddya know? I thought it was just some junk I read in a magazine somewhere."

Philippa grinned. "It's good to see you again, bro."

John led them through the door. "So far, so good," he said. "Let's hope the king's still here to lead us back through the labyrinth."

"King? What king?"

"I'm not exactly sure what he's called," said John. "Not exactly. Just try not to be scared when you see him. He looks and acts kind of gross, but actually he's a pretty nice guy. And we're taking him back with us, just so you know. He wants to see New York."

Having met the grass-eating king and learned how old he probably was, Philippa told John she thought the king might be Nebuchadnezzar.

"That's what I thought," said John. "Nebuchadnezzar the Second. The ancient king of Babylon."

The king got very excited at the sound of this name, which seemed to clinch it. "King Nebuchadnezzar the Second, yes," he said, swallowing the cud he'd been chewing for several minutes. "The king of Babylon, yes. That's what I've been trying to remember, all of these years." He offered Philippa a handful of grass.

"No thanks, Your Majesty," she said politely.

"This way," said the king. "And no wandering off. The labyrinth is very complicated. There are several miles of paths."

The labyrinth ahead of them was a maze made from hornbeam hedging, and two or three feet taller than the king, although it was a little hard to tell, since the king only seemed to go anywhere on all fours, which meant that their progress was quite slow. Especially as the king seemed always to keep one hand on the wall when coming to a junction, and would make a turning so that his hand never came off the hedge; and in this way Philippa was able to understand how he knew his way through the labyrinth.

While they walked, the king asked the twins more about New York and what it would be like. "Do they have hanging gardens?"

"Yes," said John, thinking of the garden on the roof of the apartment building opposite. "In a way."

"And lots of grass to eat?"

"Sure," said John. He tried to picture Central Park and remembered that when they'd left New York, the park had been covered with several inches of snow. "Actually, there's maybe not a lot to eat right now. We'd just had some snow when we left. But in the spring, the summer, and the fall there's plenty of grass for everyone."

King Nebuchadnezzar was already looking less enthusiastic about the idea of leaving Iravotum, however, and seeing this John added, "But we can fix that. We're djinn, my sister and I. We can fix it for you to have as much grass as you want. Or, and this is just a suggestion, Your Majesty, if you're fed up with being a vegetarian, then you couldn't pick a better city to live in than New York. Man, you've not lived until you've tasted hot pastrami. Or a dry-aged porterhouse steak. Take my word for it, sir, you'll have a blast."

At which point the king broke wind again.

"In a manner of speaking," added Philippa.

Emerging from the maze, the king tore up a few handfuls of grass and ate them silently, as he looked suspiciously around him. Finlay flew down from one of the trees and perched on John's shoulder, and he was in the process of introducing the peregrine falcon to his sister when the king signalled them all to be silent.

John looked around the forest. The trees remained still and there was nothing to indicate that anything other than them was alive, let alone that they were being hunted. "What is it?" he whispered to the king. "What's hunting us?"

"Optabellower," said the king. "The wish monster."

CHAPTER 21

MONSTERS OF THE MIND

Deep in the forest, something stirred. There was an audible crackle of static electricity followed by a loud moaning sound and then the ground shook as somewhere in the trees, a large creature moved. John told Philippa about the wish monster. "Try not to wish for it to go away," he said. "That will just help it to find us. In fact, try not to wish for anything at all."

"Easier said that done," whispered Philippa. "Fifty per cent of thinking seems to have a wish at the bottom of it."

"Perhaps you two should split up," suggested the king. "To separate your wishes. That way the Optabellower will find it hard to track you."

John shook his head. "No way," he said. "We've only just got back together. We'll take our chances."

The trees shook again.

"Then you'd better *not* think of something very quickly," said the king. "It's getting nearer."

"I've got it," said Philippa. "We have to think about mathematics. A proposition of mathematics does not express any kind of a thought or a wish. It's transcendental. The wish monster can't lock onto us if we're doing mental arithmetic."

Although it was hard for John to bend his mind to

doing maths without wishing he was doing something else, he figured this was as good a solution to their dilemma as any. Better, probably, if he knew his twin sister. So, while Philippa applied herself to a solving a few quadratic equations in her head, John went through the 13, 14, 15, 16, 17, and 18 multiplication tables. And, for a time, the forest was silent, which seemed to indicate that the wish monster was finding it hard to get a fix on them.

"Nineteen times seventeen is . . . three hundred and twenty-three," John muttered quietly to himself, after a great deal of effort. He realized he wasn't going to be able to keep this up for much longer. The wish monster might have gone quiet but King Nebuchadnezzar's demeanor strongly indicated that it was still somewhere close by. He had to think of a better plan or they would be stuck there for ages. Suddenly, he had an idea, and moving Finlay down his arm, he looked the little falcon directly in the eye.

"Listen Horus," he said, "whose right eye was the sun and whose left eye was the moon. I need your help."

Finlay flapped his wings expectantly, eager to perform a useful service for the young djinn that would help earn him his freedom.

"But it's dangerous," added John.

Finlay lifted his beak in the air and screeched silently, as if to reassure John that he was equal to the task, no matter how dangerous it might be.

"I need you to distract the wish monster. I need you to hover over him, just out of reach and wish hard to be a boy again. While you're doing that, my sister and I will make a

299

run for it, to the beach, which is where we'll wait for you. Have you got that?"

Finlay uttered a short screech and, as soon as John had lifted his arm above his head, took off on his mission, already wishing hard that he could be a boy again. As soon as he was back in his normal body he was going to have such revenges on his father – he would do such things to him. What these were he didn't yet know, but they would be the terrors of the earth.

Catching sight of the only just-visible creature, Finlay stooped down toward it, wishing with all his might. And, feeling the falcon's earnest wish, the wish monster stood up, and with a terrible, unearthly roar, tried to grab him with its strangely shapeless hand. Finlay had miscalculated the size of the creature and its reach and only just managed to keep out of its obviously lethal grasp. He had no doubt that the electricity running through the wish monster's shifting body would have sucked all of the energy from him. Finlay flew a little higher and wished again with all his might.

As soon as Finlay had taken to the air, the king led John and Philippa back through Iravotum's thick forest. For obvious reasons, he avoided the path but, following a trail that only the king could have recognized, they were soon on the golden beach at the edge of the ocean lake.

There a shock awaited them. By now John had told Philippa of the deaths of Alan and Neil and he had planned to show her the two bodies and have her help him bury the dogs before getting into the boat. But there was no sign of the oarsman, nor of the bodies of Alan and Neil.

The dogs had disappeared from under the palm fronds with which he had covered them.

"Are you sure they were dead?" asked Philippa.

"Quite sure," said John.

"Maybe the boatman took them," she suggested. "Or someone else."

John thought this seemed like the most obvious explanation. He didn't like to mention either the giant snake or the Rukhkh to Philippa, but it now occurred to him that the bodies of his two loyal friends might have been eaten. He simply hadn't done a good enough job of hiding their bodies.

Reproaching himself for this carelessness, John walked down to the water lapping gently on the sand, just like before, and looked anxiously for the boatman to appear again on the horizon.

"He'll be here," said a man's voice. Thinking the accent too New York to be the king's, John turned around and saw two men walking toward him. Both of them were wearing business suits and neither was very tall. One of them had glasses and looked just a little like John's father.

"Don't you recognize us?" said the man wearing glasses.

"Why, for Pete's sake, would they recognize us?" said the other man. "They've never seen us before. Not looking like this, anyway."

"I guess you're right." The first man grinned.

"Sure, I'm right." The one without the glasses, who looked quite like the other man, pointed at the horizon. "I'd say that's our ride coming now."

"I see your eyesight's just as good as it always was,

Neil," said the man with glasses.

John's jaw dropped onto his sneakers.

"Uncle Neil?" he exclaimed. "Are you my uncle Neil?"

"I sure am, kiddo," said Neil, and embraced his nephew, even as Alan hugged his young niece.

"Uncle Alan?" she said. "Is it really you?"

"It's me," confirmed Alan. "Although I don't mind telling you, it feels great to be walking on two legs again. I won't miss having four legs at all. "

"I thought you guys were dead," said John, with tears streaming down his grimy face.

"So did we," said Alan. "That was a heck of a fall we took."

"Don't remind me," said Neil. "My behind still feels sore."

"What happened?" said John, laughing with joy. "How is it you're human again?"

"Search me." Neil shrugged. "Frankly, I don't remember very much about what happened after that bird took off with my jaws around its ankle. A few hours ago I woke up under a pile of leaves and, apart from realizing that neither of us was a dog anymore, that's about it."

"I expect Layla could tell you," said Alan. "If she was here. After all, she's the one who turned us into dogs in the first place. It was her binding or wish, or whatever she calls it." He shook his head. "Not that we didn't deserve what happened. Given what we did, or tried to do to your father."

John glanced back at the horizon where the unmistakable figure of the oarsman, standing in the stern of the boat, could now be easily seen.

302

"There hasn't been a day since then that I haven't wished we'd never done that," said Neil. "With all my heart, I wish that we'd never done it."

"It's my most earnest wish now," said Alan, "that your dad can forgive us when he sees us again. I do wish that most of all—"

"No," said the king. "Don't say that. Don't wish for anything!"

But it was too late. About a hundred yards up the beach, behind the tree line, a loud crash followed by a roar and a crackle of static electricity told John and Philippa that the wish monster was on their trail again. A moment or two later, Finlay swooped down and, minus a couple more tail feathers after his near brush with the Optabellower, landed a little awkwardly, on John's arm. He screeched loudly and flapped his wings in a way he hoped would communicate a need for urgency. But John was already shouting at the boatman to get a move on. And, much to everyone's surprise the boatman seemed to obey, rowing faster than before, so that he covered the last hundred yards between himself and the shore in less than a minute. But not before the wish monster had emerged from the trees and begun to make its way, slowly but surely, toward the little group of people standing by the water's edge. The monster was less than fifty yards away as, finally, the boat hit the beach and everyone jumped into the bow – everyone except the king, that is, who put his powerful, hairy shoulder against the prow of the boat and helped the brass oarsman push off from the sand.

"Quick," John yelled out to the King as the boat floated free. "Jump in."

But the great Nebuchadnezzar was already backing away on all fours, like a nervous horse, and, catching John's eye, he smiled and lifted a hairy hand to wave good-bye. John yelled again, pointing to the wish monster that was almost upon the king.

"It's all right," shouted the king. "He won't harm me. It's like I told you already, John. I wish for nothing. And I suspect the grass is greener here than on the other side of the sea."

The king said some more but this was lost as, roaring furiously, the wish monster lurched down to the edge of the water. With John, Philippa, Alan, Neil, and Finlay all desperately wishing to be away from the beach, the creature was quite maddened by the prospect of their escape. But the temperature of the water seemed to deter it from wading in after them, and soon the boatman's quick work with the oar had left the beast from the subconscious mind of Ishtar far behind, still roaring impotently on the shore.

"Phew," said Philippa. "That was much too close for comfort."

"We're not out of the woods yet," said John, staring nervously at the sky. "On the journey here we were attacked by a giant bird."

"Oh, yes," said Philippa. "That must have been the Rukhkh. I heard about that." And she told John about Chinese Gordon and his mouth of truth, and how she'd created a wind to help drive the creature away.

John didn't have the heart to tell her that it had been this wind that had carried not just the bird away, but Alan and Neil, too.

The Rukhkh did not reappear, however, prompting Alan and Neil to remark that they were hardly surprised, considering the mauling they'd given the huge bird's feet. "I think it'll be a while before that thing can stand without thinking of us," Alan said proudly. "Funny thing about that bird's feet. They tasted of cheese. Toasted cheese. I can still taste them now." He pulled a face and spat out of the boat. "Horrible."

After a couple of hours, the boat reached the other shore and, having said good-bye to the brass oarsman (unfortunately, they neglected to thank the boat itself, the oak prow of which had the power of speech, and who thought them all very rude) they went through the low door in the wall and started back along the spiral path that led up and around the underground part of the Samarra Tower. And gradually, as they neared ground level, and it grew warmer, Philippa started to feel just a thin bat squeak amount of her djinn power returning.

"Has anyone given any thought," Alan said to no one in particular, "to how we're going to explain our sudden arrival back in that army camp?" He looked at John. "John, you're the only one of us that woman, Lieutenant Sanchez, has seen before. I don't think she's going to take too kindly to finding three complete strangers and a peregrine falcon turn up in what's supposed to be a secure zone."

"I've been thinking about that," said John.

"Well, think fast, Nephew," said Neil. "I don't much care for the idea of being locked up in an Iraqi jail while they figure out what to do with us."

"I think maybe it's time," suggested his brother Alan,

"that you kids rustled us up a magic carpet, or something."

John shook his head. "No djinn power until we're back in Jordan," he said. "Nimrod was really strict about that. Besides, I'm really tired. The way I feel now I couldn't make a magic beer mat, let alone a magic carpet."

"I'm the same way," yawned Philippa. "I don't know what was in that air back there, but I'm exhausted."

"Prison, here we come," muttered Neil.

"Wait a minute," said John. "Maybe *we* can't use djinn power. But there's nothing to stop Nimrod from doing something."

They were now just below the shaft that led up into the shower area.

John took out his cell phone, checked that he was receiving a signal, and waved it at his two uncles. "I just had a great idea."

It hadn't been easy, persuading Edwiges to be the next Blue Djinn, but Nimrod was quite sure he'd managed it. Reasoning that Edwiges was more likely to abandon her mission to bankrupt the casino at Monte Carlo if some mundanes were actually persuaded to employ her system, Nimrod had found her a group of people who were perfectly willing to risk some money using it. In the Café de Paris, opposite the famous old casino, Nimrod and Edwiges had happened upon a group of eight old ladies from England who were on a church-organized bus tour of the Cote d'Azur. They had been very taken with Edwiges and, thanks to Nimrod's skillful diplomacy and salesmanship, they were soon equally enthusiastic about trying out her roulette system.

The eight Cheltenham ladies each put fifty Euros in the pot to buy about $500 worth of chips in the old sporting club, and then went up to the tables where, as instructed, they proceeded to count ten spins in a row without making a stake, recording the results carefully, and then placed their bets according to what Edwiges had recommended in her little booklet. The first bet won them $18,000. The second, $648,000. And the third bet brought them a staggering $23,328,000. They would have bet a fourth time, since by now they had rightly decided that Edwiges's system couldn't fail, but at this point the management closed down the casino for the rest of the day. This was perhaps just as well for the house, as a fourth win would have returned the old ladies a staggering $839 million, which would almost certainly have bankrupted the casino. Perhaps the whole of Monte Carlo. Nevertheless, Edwiges declared herself entirely satisfied with the result and, soon afterward, was persuaded to become the next Blue Djinn, whereupon she joined Nimrod aboard his own private whirlwind to fly to Amman, in Jordan. From where he proposed to make contact with Ayesha the minute he heard from John that Philippa was rescued.

Nimrod and Edwiges were in the lobby of the hotel when he got John's call on his cell phone. After congratulating John and expressing his enormous relief that he and Philippa were all right, Nimrod admitted he was a little puzzled.

"If Alan and Neil have become human again then Ayesha will have felt Layla's power. For only it could have restored them to their former selves. In which case it hardly matters if you use djinn power or not. What's more, Ayesha will certainly be aware by now that Philippa has escaped. Bottle me, if I'm not just a little surprised that she hasn't tried to stop you from leaving Iravotum already. You'd better be on your guard, just in case she's planning something else."

"I hear what you say about how it's OK to use djinn power again," said John, "but I'm tired. I haven't slept in ages. If I wanted to make a hamburger disappear it would be all I could do just to eat it, that's how tired I am. And I think Phil's feeling the after effects of whatever it was that made her such a piece of work. I do have an idea, however. Only I'm going to need your help, Uncle Nimrod."

Lieutenant Sanchez was polishing her boots when a female corporal marched into her hut to tell her that she was needed urgently in the shower room. She arrived to find two men in dark business suits accompanied by two children, and a bird of prey.

"What in heck's going on here?" she asked the sergeant who was guarding the unauthorized quintet. "Who are these people?"

"I found them coming up from a hole in the ground behind the dirty laundry baskets," said the sergeant. "These two gentlemen claim they're CIA."

"That's right, Lieutenant," said Neil. "And we're on a top secret mission here."

Lieutenant Sanchez could hardly contain her sense of outrage. After all, soldiers or not, this was still a ladies' shower room. "What possible reason could the CIA have for being in a hole in the ground underneath my girls' shower?" she said to Alan. "And who are these two children?"

"I'm afraid that's classified top secret," said Alan.

"The heck you say," said Sanchez. "Wait a minute," she added, recognizing John. "I know you, don't I? You were the kid who was here with the ventriloquist. The guy with one arm."

"Lieutenant," said Neil. "Do you have a computer here?"

"Sure."

Still under guard, Alan, Neil, John, and Philippa followed the lieutenant to her office where Alan asked her to log on to the CIA's website.

"Now what?" said Sanchez, when the CIA's website appeared on her laptop.

"Bottom of the page," said Neil. "The *Contact Us* section. Choose the e-mail form. And in the message section, type in the names Alan and Neil Gaunt. The site should recognize our names and generate a reply verifying who we are and what we've told you about the nature of our mission."

Sanchez disliked spies, even the spies who were on her own side, but she shrugged and did what she was told. Being in the Army it was easier that way.

Thousands of miles away, in the CIA's own mainframe computer in Washington, the lieutenant's e-mail was quickly processed and, thanks to Nimrod's quick work – in return for Nimrod's having granted him three wishes, an old friend in the Agency had typed in some operational records where none had existed before – a reply was swiftly generated.

"Alan and Neil Gaunt are field agents currently operating in the Iraq theatre, searching for two children, code names John and Philippa, who were believed to have been involved in a secret weapons program. You are requested to give Agent Gaunt and Agent Gaunt any help they desire to facilitate the completion of their mission. By order of the Deputy Director of Real Intelligence."

When she had finished reading the CIA message, Lieutenant Sanchez stared at John and Philippa with disbelief. "I must say, Agent Gaunt, they look kind of young to have been involved in this kind of thing. I mean, they look like ordinary children." She thought for a moment. "Apart from the falcon on the boy's shoulder. That is a little unusual."

Neil smiled. "They might look like ordinary children," he agreed. "But believe me, these two kids are anything but ordinary." He looked at John. "Go ahead, kid. Show her some of the juice."

John nodded. "Watch that coffee cup," he said, and pointing his forefinger at the mug on the lieutenant's desk, he muttered, "ABECEDARIAN." With his near-depleted power, he had only intended to make the cup disappear. But John was tired, very tired, and instead he caused the mug to shatter into several pieces. The cup was full of coffee, which added to the general effect, and immediately convinced the lieutenant that she should cooperate fully with Alan and Neil.

"Wow," said the lieutenant. "If I hadn't seen it with my own eyes, I'd never have believed it possible. These two kids. They're like something out of a comic book."

"Like I said," said Alan. "This is classified top secret.

What you just saw, didn't happen. These children were never here. You never heard of us. Got that?" He looked at the sergeant, who nodded back.

"Yes, sir," said Lieutenant Sanchez. "Anything you say. Just tell me what to do."

"All right," said Neil. "Here's what you can do to help. We want a jeep to take us to the Kebabylon Restaurant, here in Samarra."

"I took the guy with one arm there," said the Lieutenant. "He said his name was Groanin. He turned up here with the kid a day or two ago."

"Professor Groanin? He's one of them, too."

"That would certainly explain the way he could throw his voice like that," said Lieutenant Sanchez.

"You'd be astonished what he can do, ma'am," said Alan. "But you can leave him to us. We'll take care of Professor Groanin."

CHAPTER 22

MAGNUM OPUS

At the Kebabylon Restaurant, nobody seemed to mind that Groanin didn't eat the kebabs prepared by Darius's mother's cousin, Mrs Lamoor. Darius had told Mrs Lamoor that for religious and dietary reasons, Groanin was obliged to eat the MREs given to him by the army.

"Me, I'd rather eat locusts than eat that rubbish," said Mrs Lamoor.

Darius smiled quietly at the memory of the *Jarad* he had eaten with John. "Me, too," he said, thinking that the MREs Groanin ate looked OK as long as you enjoyed the taste of plastic.

An MRE is a Meal, Ready-to-Eat, and is a self-contained operational ration consisting of a full meal packed in a flexible bag that is as sterile as a jar of baby food and can last for up to three years. On leaving the army camp at Samarra, Groanin, whose memory-man ventriloquist act had gone down very well, had been presented with a case of twelve MREs, for which, in the absence of his usual baby food, he was very grateful. He was busy using the flameless, ration-heating device to cook his entrée when someone he half-recognized looked around the door of the restaurant. It was one of the journalists they'd met on the road from Amman; and it wasn't so much her face he recognized, as the black leather trousers and jacket she was wearing.

"Hey there," she said, smiling warmly. "Mind if I join you?"

"Be my guest." Groanin pointed at the purple plastic seat opposite.

She sat down and sniffed the air. "Smells good," she said. "What is it?"

"It's what the military johnnies call an MRE," said Groanin. "It provides an average of twelve hundred and fifty calories, not to mention one-third of the recommended daily allowance of vitamins and minerals deemed essential by the Surgeon General of the United States. All very tasty and as sterile as a politician's argument. I have a delicate stomach you see, which is why I can't be eating any of that foreign muck. Would you like one? A menu? I have several left."

"No, thanks," said the woman.

"Go on, treat yourself," said Groanin. "Why don't you have my fudge brownie. They're delicious."

"All right, then. I will."

"That's the spirit. I say, that's the spirit. You could do with a square meal, by the look of you, lass. You're wasting away."

Groanin rummaged in the box of MREs – which was where he was also keeping the lamp containing Mr Rakshasas – before coming up with the fudge brownie. "There you go, love," he said. "Tuck in."

The leather-clad journalist unwrapped the fudge brownie and took a bite. "You're absolutely right," she said.

"It's delicious." She eyed the people sitting on the other side of the restaurant, underneath a large poster of a grinning Michael Schumacher. "Don't they mind? I mean, this is a kebab restaurant. If you're eating MREs, you're not buying kebabs."

"They don't mind." He shook his head. "As a matter of fact, these are very nice folk. Very hospitable. Very kind. That Mrs Lamoor is a real treasure. Nothing's too much trouble for her. And if it wasn't for my delicate stomach, I'd certainly eat here. No question about it. Besides, I'm paying them for my accommodation while I'm waiting for my young friend to show up. You know. The lad I'm travelling with?"

"Oh? Where's he gone?"

"To look at some of the ruins, that's all," said Groanin, who saw no reason to tell her the truth. "He's interested in archaeology, is John."

"Is that safe? I mean, he's just a kid, isn't he?"

"He can look after himself, that lad. Take my word for it Miss –?"

"Montana Retch. I'm a photographer."

"Groanin," he said, shaking Miss Retch's outstretched hand. "Harry Groanin."

"Maybe you're familiar with my work?"

"Not really, no," said Groanin. "Not unless your pictures are ever in *The Daily Telegraph*, that is."

"So, any luck finding his sister yet?" asked Miss Retch.

"How's that?" Groanin frowned.

"John said she'd gone walkabout, or something."

"He did, did he?" Groanin shrugged. "I expect she'll turn up."

"What are you, their uncle or something?"

"I am employed by the children's uncle. In point of fact, I am that gentleman's butler. In London."

"Gee, I never met a real butler before." Miss Retch laughed nervously. "May I take your picture, sir?"

"If you wish, madam, if you wish. Although I can't imagine why you'd want to photograph a poor, one-armed creature like myself."

"You're too modest, Mr Groanin," said Miss Retch. "You're really a very distinguished-looking man. And that English accent of yours is so lovely." She picked up her camera bag and, selecting a camera, began to take pictures.

"What a waste of film," protested Groanin. "All those pictures of me. What a waste, I say." But he was smiling and feeling very flattered.

"It's not at all wasted," said Miss Retch, who only spoke the truth, for there was no film in her camera.

Montana Retch had no more interest in taking Groanin's picture than she had in photography and, if he had been a little less pleased with the fact that she thought him "distinguished" (in life, a man should always be on his guard when a woman describes him as "distinguished") Groanin might even have noticed that Miss Retch had not thought to remove the lens cap from her camera. Because Miss Retch was not a photographer. She was a professional djinnfinder, contracted by Mimi de Ghulle to find Philippa Gaunt.

But it was even worse than that, since finding a djinn – which is a skilled job for a mundane, requiring enormous ingenuity and demonstrable courage – was only half of what Mimi required the djinnfinder to do. For Mimi was a true Ghul and every bit as black-hearted as Nimrod had suspected she was, and despite her attempts to win the favor of Ayesha, Mimi had always known that her best hope of becoming the Blue Djinn would require much more drastic action. With the result that two wishes of Montana Retch's three-wish fee were to be earned by killing the person Mimi perceived to be the main obstacle to her becoming the next Blue Djinn of Babylon. And Mimi had contracted Montana Retch to kill Philippa Gaunt as soon as she'd heard from Izaak Balayaga that Ayesha planned to anoint Philippa as her successor – a decision of which Mimi's daughter, Lilith, had heartily approved. "I hate that girl," said Lilith. "I just wish I was there to see Philippa Gaunt get what's coming to her."

But finding and binding a djinn was a difficult, dangerous job; and killing one – even a young one like Philippa – even more so. For Montana Retch, however, the job was worth the risk. The first of her three-wish fee was now waiting for her in a safe deposit box at the Suchard and Lindt Bank in Zurich, Switzerland. Cash. Tons of it. More cash than the Swiss banker who had taken charge of the money had ever seen. Enough cash to buy a small African country; or certainly an estate on one. Montana Retch was looking forward to spending her money, when, eventually the job was done. She was a patient woman. She had to be. And she had decided that the easiest way of finding Philippa would be to follow her twin brother, John. Which was how she had turned up in Samarra, asking questions, and finally tracking Groanin down to the Kebabylon Restaurant on the Baghdad road.

She stopped taking pictures of Groanin and placed the camera back in her bag, on top of the very large Magnum Opus revolver with which she planned to shoot her victim. Experience had taught Miss Retch that the best way of killing a djinn was to shoot one with the fastest bullet available. With smaller handguns, she'd pulled the trigger only to discover that the djinn had transubstantiated before the bullet had travelled more than a couple of feet out of the barrel. This wasn't possible with the Magnum Opus, however. The bullets came out of that at more than 3,000 feet per second. The one disadvantage of using this weapon was the weight; you didn't pick up a Magnum Opus, you had to lift it. At five pounds, it was as heavy as a dumbbell. Most people used the Magnum Opus against grizzly bears; for Montana Retch, it was her weapon of choice. She called the gun her djinnvigilator.

"You're really very photogenic," she told Groanin.

The butler smiled happily. It had been a while since a female had paid him such a compliment.

Miss Retch was still sitting in front of him when, half an hour later, John came through the door of the restaurant, followed closely by his sister, a peregrine falcon, and two men Groanin didn't recognize. To record their loud and obviously very happy reunion, Miss Retch chose another camera and held it up to her eye, pretending to take yet more pictures. This was a camera Miss Retch *did* know how to use, however. It was a thermal camera, used to detect the heat given off an object or a body, for it is a simple fact of nature that djinn bodies emit twice as much heat as mundane ones.

"Philippa," said Groanin, hugging the girl to his ample stomach.

"Mr Groanin," said John. "I'd like you to meet Alan and Neil."

"You don't mean?"

"I do mean."

"This is a great pleasure, gentlemen. I say, this is a very great pleasure, indeed." Groanin shook the hands of Alan and Neil, whose bodies showed up yellow, exactly like his under the scrutiny of Miss Retch's thermal camera.

Miss Retch smiled pleasantly as John acknowledged her presence with a nod of his head. This, like his sister's head, was uniformly red in the camera's viewfinder, and therefore hot. He was a nice kid, she thought, and it was a shame she'd have to kill him as well. Killing the djinn sister and leaving the djinn brother alive would be just asking for trouble.

Darius came up and embraced John warmly. "Good to see you again," he said.

Miss Retch put the thermal camera back in her bag and her hand on the rubberized grip of the nickel-plated revolver. While Groanin hugged John, and Philippa introduced herself to Darius, Miss Retch thumbed the cylinder open and checked that each of the five charge holes contained its long bullet. Satisfied that everything was ready, she closed it again, pushed off the safety catch and held the gun by her black leather side. She thought that if John moved a few feet to the left, so that he was standing right in front of Philippa, she could probably nail both twins with one shot.

* * *

Miss Montana Retch was focused on her work now, and didn't even notice the tall, rather glamorous woman who had appeared behind her in the shadows. If Miss Retch had looked at this other woman through the viewfinder of the thermal camera, her body would have looked quite red. As red as the twin bodies of the woman's two children. For this djinn was none other than Layla Gaunt, whose unexpected and, so far unnoticed arrival in the Kebabylon Restaurant was the result of her having sensed what had happened to Alan and Neil.

No djinn can fail to detect when someone, which he or she has turned into an animal, has been killed. And it was Alan and Neil's very good fortune that, more than a decade before, when Mrs Gaunt had first turned them into dogs, she had thought to make their punishment last for only the lifetimes of the animals they had become. In this way she had always intended that when the dogs' lifetimes ended, Alan and Neil would be able to resume their human ones. She was just that kind of djinn.

Of course, Mrs Gaunt was also aware that if Alan and Neil both died simultaneously, then this could only mean that the twins were in very serious trouble. Since by now, even she – who had little or no contact with the world of the djinn – had heard on the grapevine that Philippa had been kidnapped by Ayesha, Mrs Gaunt had broken her vow never again to use djinn power, and had come at once from New York on a powerful whirlwind for an emergency meeting with Ayesha.

Mrs Gaunt didn't see the gun in Miss Retch's hand. Not immediately, anyway. She was too busy looking at the twins and feeling enormously relieved that they were all right. Another reason Mrs Gaunt didn't notice the gun in Miss Retch's hand was that there was a tear in her eye. A tear of regret, for only Mrs Gaunt knew precisely why it was that Ayesha had not pursued Philippa. It was because Mrs Gaunt herself had agreed to take her daughter's place.

She herself would be the next Blue Djinn, when Ayesha died.

Mrs Gaunt now knew only too well that this had always been Ayesha's intention, ever since their meeting at the Pierre Hotel in New York, when Ayesha had told Mrs Gaunt that she wanted her to become the next Blue Djinn. Then, Mrs Gaunt had refused as, perhaps, Ayesha had always known she would. But Mrs Gaunt had never for a moment considered the possibility that Ayesha would be so hard-hearted as to kidnap Philippa as a means of forcing Mrs Gaunt to do as she asked. Mrs Gaunt had underestimated Ayesha – it was only too painfully obvious. And that her own mother could do such a thing was, of course, very upsetting. But this couldn't be helped now. And, for the moment at least, the agreement she had made with Ayesha would remain a secret.

"Nobody move," said Miss Retch and leveled the fifteen-inch barrel of the Magnum Opus at Philippa's head.

They were the last two words that Montana Retch ever spoke for, no sooner had she uttered them, there was a bight blue flash and a loud bang so that, for a moment, anyway, all of the humans in the room were quite convinced that Miss Retch had pulled the trigger. Only John and Philippa knew better, for the angry use of djinn power is often accompanied by a strong smell of sulfur, which is a mineral present in djinn bodies.

There was a loud clatter as the revolver, all five pounds of it, bounced off the purple plastic table and onto the floor of the restaurant. And it was now noticed first, that Miss Retch had completely disappeared; second, that a gray cat was occupying the space where she had been standing; and, third, that Mrs Gaunt had arrived, apparently from nowhere.

"Mother," said Philippa and ran to Mrs Gaunt a split second ahead of her infinitely more weary brother.

"Hello, darlings," she said, embracing the twins very fondly.

Groanin picked up the revolver and hefted it in his only hand.

"Miss Retch," he said. "Don't tell me she was–"

"I'm afraid so, Mr Groanin." Mrs Gaunt kicked open Miss Retch's bag and, seeing the telltale thermal camera, nodded. "By the look of things she was a professional djinnfinder. And assassin."

"But she seemed so friendly. So nice," said Groanin. He glanced again at the Magnum Opus in his hand and realized just how serious Miss Retch had been. "But who put her up to it? Ayesha?"

"No, not her," Mrs Gaunt said with absolute certainty. "Someone else."

"Who then?" said Philippa.

"I have my suspicions," said Mrs Gaunt, although she knew she wouldn't actually know for sure who had been behind what happened, unless she bothered to reverse the binding and bring Miss Retch back to human shape. And this seemed like far too much trouble. Besides, perhaps it was best that she didn't know, for the moment at least.

"Is that why you came?" asked Philippa. "Because you knew we might be in danger?"

"Yes," agreed her mother. "I guessed something was badly wrong when I felt what had happened to Alan and Neil. It was just our good fortune that I got here in time to stop that woman."

"Well, whatever she was, and whatever she planned to do," said Philippa, picking up the cat and stroking its head, "she's now a very sweet-looking cat. Can we keep her? Mother? Please? Especially now we don't have any dogs. You know I always wanted a little cat."

"Yes dear," said Mrs Gaunt. "If you like." She glanced at Alan and Neil and smiled warmly. "It has always been my experience that domestic animals that were once humans make excellent family pets."

"I probably wouldn't be here now if it wasn't for these two guys," said John.

"I know, John." Mrs Gaunt walked over to Alan and Neil and shook both their hands. "Thank you, both," she said. "And no hard feelings, I hope."

"No hard feelings, Layla," said Alan. "As a matter of fact, it's been a lot of fun. Being a dog." He looked at Mr Groanin and shrugged. "Really. It had its moments."

"Except when John tried to rename us Winston and Elvis," said Neil.

"I know Edward will be delighted to see you both again," said Mrs Gaunt. "Almost as much as I am. He's missed you a lot."

"Look, Layla, we deserved everything we got," insisted

Neil. "And we've certainly learned our lesson."

Alan was looking at the cat in Philippa's arms like he badly wanted to chase it. "I must say I'm glad you turned us into dogs and not cats," he said. "I don't think I could have stood being a cat. I hate cats."

"That's the dog in you talking, Alan," said Neil. And he was right. For ever after, there would a small part of the two brothers that was a real dog.

John tickled the cat under the chin. "What are we going to call her?" he asked. "The cat. We can't call it Miss Retch."

"The woman's first name was Montana," said Groanin. "You can't call it that, either. Montana's no name for a silver-spotted British shorthair." He thought for a moment. "Something in keeping with the cat's previous name, perhaps. And yet something feline. And above all, something appropriately British, as befits this breed. I know. Why don't you call it Monty? After the famous British general."

"Monty, it is." John said nodding. "By the way, does this mean that you're back in the family business?"

Mrs Gaunt smiled. There was no point in spoiling the happiness of this moment with the exact truth about why she had come to Iraq. "Yes, it does, dear. Like it or not. You see, according to *The Baghdad Rules*, a djinn's renunciation of his or her power must be respected by other djinn and thereafter left alone. *However*. If the djinn goes back on that renunciation, if she breaks her oath no longer to use her powers, then she cannot expect the renunciation ever to be respected by other djinn again. No more can she make a second oath. The plain fact of the matter is that now it would be simply too dangerous not to use my powers. And while I might respect my oath, other djinn, enemies of our tribe, would not. Need not."

"Dad's not going to be happy about this, is he?" said Philippa.

"No, dear, he's not. But there it is. That can't be helped now. But I'm sure he'll understand, after I've explained everything that has happened. He always does understand. That's one of the reasons I married him."

"Which reminds me," said John, who was still haunted by the illusion of killing his own father. "How is Dad?"

"He's fine," said Mrs Gaunt.

"Really? He's quite well?"

"Really. I saw him yesterday. He sent you his love, dear."

John let out a quiet sigh of relief. "Hey, I'd better call Nimrod. Tell him we're OK."

"Yes," said Mrs Gaunt. "And it's high time we were leaving. Your father will be worried as well."

"I can't imagine how we're going to fit in that car," moaned Groanin. "There are seven of us now. Eight if you count Finlay."

Mrs Gaunt shook her head. "We won't have to go by car. I left a whirlwind waiting somewhere in the desert."

"Oh, good," said John. "Because I just can't do that yet. I mean whip up a whirlwind."

"I'm too exhausted to even try," admitted Philippa.

"Ayesha put a djinnhibitor on you, I expect," Mrs Gaunt told Philippa. "A binding to stop you using your powers against her, dear. It'll take a while for it to wear off completely."

"Even so," said John, putting a hand on the young Iraqi boy's shoulder. "I'd like to do something for Darius and his family, Mother. He's had a tough life, having to drive a taxi to support his family. I mean he's only twelve."

"All right," said Mrs Gaunt. "I'll make sure his family are well provided for. That way, Darius will be able to go back to school."

"School?" Darius pulled a face.

"There's only one kind of school Darius wants to go to," laughed John. "And that's the kind where you learn to be a Formula 1 racing driver." He pointed at the poster on the wall. "Just like Schumacher."

"Very well," agreed Mrs Gaunt. "When he's old enough I'll fix it so that he is able to attend a racing driver's school as well. But until then he has to go to a proper school. OK, Darius?"

Darius was delighted. Even at the prospect of going back to school. "But are you sure you couldn't do me one more favour?" he asked John. "The man who killed my father? Could you please turn him into a cat perhaps? Or a dog. Dog, cat, it's all the same to me. But I should very much like for him to become some sort of animal."

"No," laughed John. "Absolutely not." But Darius's request had reminded John of the promise he had made to Finlay, the falcon. And holding his mother's hand, to draw on her power, he uttered his focus word, and the little peregrine turned back into a boy. Which was just as well, as the falcon and the cat had been eyeing each other in a rather unpleasant way.

"Thanks very much," said Finlay, and then spat the remains of a half-eaten sparrow – his last meal as a falcon – onto the restaurant floor.

"Need a lift?" said John. "We can drop you in London, if you like. Mr Groanin lives there with my Uncle Nimrod. Right now he's waiting for us in Amman. That's where we're going next. Have you ridden on a whirlwind before, Finlay? It's fun."

CHAPTER 23

EPILOGUIANA

The moment Nimrod heard from his sister, Layla, that Ayesha had found someone other than Philippa to be the next Blue Djinn, he guessed what must have happened: that Mrs Gaunt, had volunteered herself for the job, in order to spare Philippa. It was, he thought, quite typical that she should have behaved in such a selfless manner. And he felt very proud of her. But, for the sake of the twins, whom he was very happy to see again, and out of respect for his sister, he decided to say nothing. Even when the twins brought the subject up over a late lunch in the hotel in Amman.

"I wonder who the next Blue Djinn will be now," said Philippa.

"Oh, I expect Ayesha will find someone," Nimrod said innocently, trying to avoid his sister's eye.

"In a way I feel sorry for her," continued Philippa. For the moment she, too, was trying to avoid mentioning her discovery that Ayesha was her grandmother and, Layla and Nimrod's mother. So far she hadn't even mentioned it to John. "For Ayesha, I mean. It must be terribly lonely, being the Blue Djinn of Babylon."

John, who was unaware that Edwiges had come to Amman at Nimrod's instigation, with the aim of volunteering herself for the position, said, "It's not something you'd want to take on, Edwiges?"

Edwiges, who had also guessed that Mrs Gaunt had got there before her, smiled uncomfortably and shook her head. "Oh, no, John, not me. I'm much too busy with my work. As a matter of fact, I'm on my way to Cairo now. To take on the casinos there."

"I ought to come with you, perhaps," said Nimrod. "A little earlier on today, I had a telephone call from Creemy. As most of you know, he looks after my house in Cairo, and watches the tuchemeter I keep there. He tells me that the tuchemeter is showing a very definite swing toward bad luck. I'd like to check it myself before trying to find out why."

"I think I might be able to help you there," said Philippa.

"You, Philippa?" said Mrs Gaunt. "How?"

"When I was with Ayesha, she learned that Bull Huxter had disappeared with the canister containing Iblis," she explained. "You know, the one that was supposed to be put on that European rocket going to Venus."

"Disappeared?" exclaimed Nimrod. "What do you mean, disappeared?"

"We both formed the conclusion that Bull Huxter had tricked Ayesha," said Philippa. "That he had taken off with her money. To say nothing of his probable intent to use Iblis for himself. You know. To get three wishes out of him in return for releasing him from the bottle."

"Light my lamp, child," said Nimrod. "You mean to tell me that all this time we've been sitting here having a long and leisurely lunch, a *vindicta*-minded Iblis might be on the loose?"

328

Philippa nodded quietly.

"Why didn't you tell me this straightaway?"

"I'm telling you now, aren't I?" she said and, feeling more than a little aggrieved, added, "You know I think it's a bit much that you should be angry with me, after all I've been through *at the hands of my own grandmother.*"

But if she had thought she might have dropped a bombshell on the table, she was mistaken.

"Oh, never mind that now," said Nimrod, standing up from the table. "This is much more serious. We have to find Bull Huxter, and fast."

"I think I might know where he is," said Mrs Gaunt. "Edward spoke to him on the telephone the day before yesterday. He was in French Guiana. At a place called Kourou."

"We can go there on the way to New York," said Nimrod. He glanced ruefully at Finlay. "I'm sorry, Finlay," he added politely. "But I'm afraid our return flight to England will have to wait a while longer. It's imperative that we go straight to French Guiana. You see, there's a very dangerous djinn called Iblis –"

"That's all right," said Finlay. "I don't want to go back to England."

"Look here," Nimrod said kindly. "I'm sure I can help straighten things out between you and your father. When what happened, happened, he was angry. I'm sure he's had time to reflect upon that and regret what he said."

"It's true, I was beastly to him," admitted Finlay. "I wasn't a very good son. But that's only because he was such a lousy dad. Besides, I've spoken to Edwiges and she's agreed that I can go with her to Cairo. With her help,

I'm going to try to make enough money to finish my schooling. I'm going to get a job for a short while, and then we're going to use my wages to make some real money."

"Yes, that's right," said Edwiges. "Finlay and I will get along very well, I think. Provided he sticks to my system."

"I'm not sure that I approve," said Nimrod. "Gambling is a vice."

"Oh, it's not gambling," insisted Finlay. "Not with the system. Edwiges has told me all about it. Gambling implies chance, which implies that you might actually lose your money. But with this system, it's not gambling. It's a sure thing."

In view of what had happened in Monte Carlo, Nimrod could hardly argue with the boy's logic. Besides, he didn't have the time to disagree.

"Good luck," John told Finlay. "I'm sorry about what happened."

"Forget it. Being a falcon was a lot of fun."

"Isn't it?" agreed John. "Isn't it just a blast?"

Galibi Magãna was a French Guianan boy, aged about ten he thought, although he wasn't exactly sure, who made his living as a scavenger at a large waste dump near the capital city of Cayenne. Galibi was just one of almost a hundred children who stayed at the dump, sometimes working for six or even eight hours without a break, finding stuff people had thrown away that he could sell for a few cents. He worked with bare hands and feet, and no mask, although the dump was hazardous. Sometimes, he even slept in the rubbish. Mostly he looked for cow bones, soft-drink cans, polythene, paper and plastic water bottles, but one day he found a smooth metal canister that looked very different from the sort of stuff he usually found at the dump. He thought it was made of aluminium and quite valuable. The beauty of the canister however, was as nothing compared to the beauty of what was inside it – a crystal bottle, which wasn't at all the usual kind of thing people threw away.

When Galibi found the canister and the little crystal bottle he didn't tell anyone about his two finds. There were reasons for this: One was that he was worried someone might steal them from him. The canister and the crystal bottle were so beautiful – especially the bottle. When he held this up to sun, the light caught the long cylindrical neck so that it resembled one of the space rockets which, from time to time, took off from the nearby space centre at Kourou. Any one of Galibi's friends would have envied him such a bottle. But another, more important reason why he didn't tell anyone was that there was a voice inside the crystal bottle – a voice that spoke to him – and Galibi worried that his friends would tell him he was crazy and maybe he would have to stop work. How else was he to explain the voice in the crystal bottle?

French Guiana is in South America, and Galibi, who couldn't read and hadn't ever been to school, had never heard of genies or djinn, nor of the tradition whereby a djinn might grant three wishes to someone that released it from a lamp or a bottle. So he was more inclined to think he was going crazy than to believe that the little voice belonged to something that could, as it promised, do him a very good turn. Or even three very good turns.

Galibi thought that if he really wasn't losing his mind,

then maybe it was a *Kayeri*. A *Kayeri* was a dangerous demon that was often present where there were many ants, which of course there were at the dump – millions of them.

This was the problem that presented itself to Iblis, the Ifrit, for he was the djinn trapped inside the bottle: how to persuade someone with no knowledge of the *Arabian Nights*, or Aladdin, or any of those rubbishy old Middle-Eastern stories, that he could do him a favour. Or even three favours.

"Surely you know the story of the genie of the lamp," said Iblis, hating himself for using the word "genie", which was a word that ignorant mundanes seemed to use in preference to the more correct djinni. No djinn would ever have used it. "Surely you must have seen it at the movies, or on TV."

Iblis almost bit off his own tongue when mentioning TV. He hated television more than anything. He'd like to have destroyed every TV set on the planet. As it was he had to make do with spoiling television signals and interfering with the reception of programs that were of inexplicable importance to mundanes. If there was one thing that made Iblis believe that mundanes were well-named, it was their fondness for television.

"I don't have a TV," Galibi told Iblis. "And I haven't heard of Aladdin or this genie of the lamp you talk about."

Iblis bit his tongue again. It was just his luck to be picked up by an illiterate boy who'd never even heard of the djinn. Even so, that was still, probably, an improvement on the last mundane who had possessed the bottle that now imprisoned him. Some cretin called Bull Huxter, to whom Ayesha had paid $10 million to place him aboard the *Wolfhound Space Express* to Venus. Iblis had assumed he was in luck when Huxter had taken Ayesha's money and, instead of putting the canister aboard the rocket, had kept it in the trunk of his car. Iblis had assumed that Huxter was doing this because he had discovered that the canister contained a powerful djinn, and was after the usual three wishes. But, as things had turned out, Huxter, who had sold three times as much payload space aboard the rocket as was actually available, had no idea that the canister contained a djinn, and had shown no inclination at all to open it. Moreover he was as deaf as a post, having been around too many rocket launches, and had been unable to hear a word Iblis had shouted at him. Even with the canister in his hands, Bull Huxter hadn't heard a single word Iblis had said. At least this small child could hear him, even if he didn't yet trust him.

But Iblis was clever. Very clever.

"I am not a demon, Galibi," he said smoothly, trying to overcome what he felt were the boy's quite sensible fears about demons. "I am a scientist who was conducting an experiment that went wrong. Not a demon. But a man who had an accident and got shrunk. Nevertheless, I can quite understand your concerns that I might be a demon. In which case there's no need for you to open the bottle. All you have to do is deliver this bottle to someone who will give you a very handsome reward for its safe return. All you have to do is make a telephone call to the United States. Do you know what a collect call is, Galibi?"

"No."

"I give you the number and, when you call it, the person at the other end pays. I'll tell you what to say. The person you're calling will come here and give you lots of money. A well-deserved reward, just like I said. Simple as that."

"Suppose that person is also a demon like you."

"Galibi," said Iblis. "How many times do I have to tell you? I'm not a bad spirit. I'm a good one." But Iblis was already thinking of the miserable and cruel fate he would inflict on this boy when, at last, he was freed. Bull Huxter, too, when he caught up with him, just for being deaf. Of course the real malice of Iblis would be reserved for Nimrod and the two meddling djinn kids who'd put him in the bottle in the first place.

"You could be a *Kayeri*," said Galibi.

"What is a *Kayeri*? Do tell."

"You have to be careful of them in the rainy season and be alert to their presence whenever ants are conspicuous."

Iblis sighed. "Look here, Galibi, I'm not a *Kayeri*. I hate the rain. And I'm not much fond of ants, except to eat, of course."

For a moment Iblis thought he'd made a mistake, and it would have been with most mundane kids: the idea of eating ants would have been more than enough to put them on their guard, and make them suspect that there was something fishy about the voice in the bottle. But Galibi was poor. Very poor. And sometimes, a handful of ants were a useful source of extra protein.

"You like eating ants, too?"

"Of course," said Iblis, noting the fascination in the boy's voice. "Especially –" And this was a typically Ifrit stroke of evil genius. "Especially ants that are covered in chocolate."

"Chocolate?" said Galibi, almost breathless with awe. "Really?"

"Really," said Iblis. "They're delicious. Quite the most delicious thing I think I've ever eaten."

"I should like to eat some of those," confessed the boy.

"Galibi, dear boy, if you call my son, Rudyard, like I asked, I can promise you all the chocolate ants you can eat."

To the north was the Atlantic Ocean, full of deadly sharks. To the south was rain forest where Nimrod's whirlwind had landed them after a ten-hour flight. Emerging from the trees, John and Philippa, Nimrod and Mrs Gaunt, Alan and Neil, Mr Groanin and Monty, and the lamp containing Mr Rakshasas found themselves facing an electric fence that ringed the Centrel Spatial Guyanais – the French Guiana Space Centre. Just a few miles from Devil's Island, where France had once sent its convicts on their holidays, and guarded by the French Foreign Legion – that part of the French Army that is renowned the world over for its fairness and courtesy – the CSG Spaceport looked impregnable. To everyone but five djinn and their three mundane associates.

"I don't think they're going to like seven foreigners and a cat just turning up inside their space centre," observed Alan. "This is supposed to be a high-security area. I mean, we gotta be careful here. We could wind up getting shot or something. Or maybe guillotined."

But muttering "QWERTYUIOP," Nimrod had already cut the power to the electrified fence and installed a mini-version of the Arc de Triomphe in the wire for them all to pass through safely, and in a way that was also pleasing to the eye.

"They're not going to like that either," observed Alan. "It

looks kind of disrespectful. Like you're making fun of them."

"Nonsense," said Nimrod. "How could they not like the Arc de Triomphe? It was commissioned by Napoleon shortly after his victory at Austerlitz. And that's a perfect copy, one-tenth the size of the real thing. However, I do take your point about us not being French. You're right. Perhaps I had better go on by myself. I speak perfect French, so I don't suppose anyone will pay too much attention to me."

"In that suit?" scoffed John.

Nimrod glanced down at himself. A stoplight couldn't have looked more red than he was. Red suit, red shirt, red tie, red shoes, red handkerchief, and red socks. "Yes, you're right," he said. "Perhaps this would be better. QWERTYUIOP."

In the blink of an eye Nimrod stood in front of them wearing the uniform of a General in the French Foreign Legion. With his white kepi, white gloves, and bright red epaulettes, he looked really quite distinguished.

"What do you think?" he asked.

"Very *Beau Geste*," said Mrs Gaunt.

"Wish me luck," he said. Then he saluted smartly and marched through the Arc, to find the space centre headquarters.

Everyone else sat down and waited for him to come back.

"Is the Blue Djinn really our grandmother?" John asked his mother, after a while.

"Yes, dear."

"Why didn't you tell us before?"

"I didn't like to talk about it," she said. "It upset me

that she chose to be the Blue Djinn in preference to looking after your uncle and me. That's what I thought at the time, anyway."

"Were you very young?" asked Philippa. "When she went away?"

"We were a little older than you, perhaps," she said. "Not much older." She paused for a moment. "I think it was probably one of the reasons why I decided to renounce being a djinn in the first place."

"Why did she do it?" asked John. "Why did she leave you?"

"I think she just felt that it was something she had to do."

"The same reason she kidnapped me, probably," said Philippa.

"Yes, that might be right."

"Ayesha isn't bad, exactly," continued Philippa. "But then you couldn't say she was good, either. She's just. . ." Philippa shrugged. "Life isn't always about doing what is logical. Sometimes, doing the wrong thing is just as important as doing the right thing. That's what makes life fun. It seems to me that to live your life in any other way, is to deny life itself."

Mrs Gaunt remained silent for a moment, and she was glad to see Nimrod returning so that she wouldn't have to answer. He was driving an armoured personnel carrier that he'd borrowed from a junior French officer.

"*Allons y,*" he shouted in French. "I mean, come on, everyone. Jump in."

"Where are we going now?" asked Philippa as she climbed inside the APC.

"The Hotel des Roaches," said Nimrod. "In Kourou, just a mile or two from here. It seems that Bull Huxter is there under house arrest. The French fired him when it turned out that he'd been running a little scam selling the payload space on their rocket several times over. They're pretty mad about it. But at the same time, they've been trying to keep it quiet, *naturellement*."

"So how did you find out about it?" said John.

"That's the funny thing about being a French army general," said Nimrod. "Soldiers tell you what you want to know. They even give up their armoured personnel carriers when you tell them to."

Bull Huxter was in a pretty sorry state when they found him at the well-named Hotel des Roaches. He was running a fever but after a cup of strong black coffee and a cold shower, he told them what they wanted to know: where he'd dumped the canister that Ayesha had given to him. And this was where they went next. To the huge rubbish dump near Cayenne.

They smelled the place long before they saw it and were predictably disgusted. But their disgust was nothing beside the shock they felt when they discovered that as many as a hundred children made their living off the site, in apparent competition with the dozens of seabirds who used the place as a fast-food outlet.

"What a terrible way to spend your childhood," said John.

"Most children in poor countries can't afford a proper childhood," observed Mrs Gaunt. "They don't go to school. Instead they have to go to work as soon as possible, to help support their families." She shook her head sadly. "The minute I get back to New York I'm going to do something to help these children."

Meanwhile, Nimrod summoned all the little scavengers and, speaking French, offered them fifty American dollars for information leading to the recovery of a silver canister, which he then proceeded to describe in some detail.

The children looked at each other – fearfully, it seemed to John and Philippa – but, eventually one boy, whose name was Herbin, plucked up courage and took them to the canister they were looking for. Nimrod opened it immediately but, as he had expected, the little scent bottle it had contained was gone.

Nimrod told Herbin that the canister had contained a very valuable glass bottle, made in Egypt, and that he would pay another fifty American dollars for its safe return. At first, Herbin was reluctant to say any more than he had already told them. But finally he confessed that he'd seen his friend Galibi hiding just such a bottle, the day before. The mention of Galibi's name prompted some alarm among the rest of the children. A few even started to cry. Nimrod knew that this was not a good sign.

"Where is Galibi?" Nimrod asked the dirty-looking boy. "I have to speak with him very urgently."

Herbin looked pained. "Galibi has disappeared," he said.

"Is that why some of the others were crying?"

"Yes. They think he has become a victim of voodoo."

"Voodoo? What on earth do you mean?"

"I am not one of these people who believes in such things myself," said Herbin. "But it cannot be denied that

Galibi is gone. Nor can it be denied that only his doll now remains."

"I'd like to see this doll, if I may," said Nimrod.

Herbin led Nimrod and the others to a small shrine on the edge of the dump where various objects had been laid in front of a rudimentary cross; among these was an astonishingly lifelike statue of a boy, about two feet in length. The boy appeared to be about eleven years old, was barefoot and wearing a ragged pair of jeans and a dirty T-shirt.

"I do not know what it is made of," said Herbin. "But it is quite heavy, monsieur. And a perfect likeness. Especially the eyes. You see? They seem to follow you. Which is why everyone is scared of it."

Nimrod produced a tiny flashlight on a key chain and shone a small beam of light into the statue's eyes. "Most lifelike, indeed," he said grimly, as he noticed the pupils of the figure's eyes contracting against the flashlight. He turned to Mrs Gaunt, speaking English so as not to upset Herbin. "It's him, all right," he said.

"You mean that's a real boy?" said John.

"No doubt about it." Absently, Nimrod picked something off the figure's mouth. At first he thought it was a bit of dirt, but in his fingers he realized that it was actually an insect, apparently covered in chocolate.

"What is it?" said Philippa.

Nimrod sniffed the insect suspiciously. "It appears to be a chocolate-covered ant," he said. "Very likely it contains a diminuendo. A djinn binding you eat that causes you to get smaller and turns you into a doll like this one."

"The poor boy," said Philippa. "Nimrod. Mother, we have to help him."

"What can we do?" said Mrs Gaunt. "This is Iblis's doing. His power, his binding. It's not something that can be unravelled by anyone else but him. That's the way these things just are, Philippa."

Philippa looked imploringly at her uncle, who shook his head wearily. "Your mother's right. It's just the kind of nasty, rotten thing he would do to someone who released him from a lamp or a djinn bottle. Not give him three wishes. But instead to reduce him, literally, to this living doll."

"Living?" exclaimed Mr Groanin. "I say, you don't mean you think he can hear and see us?"

"I'm afraid that's exactly what I mean," said Nimrod.

"There must be something we can do for him," said John.

"Not without having Iblis in our power," said Nimrod. "You see John, it's the same as when you turned poor Finlay into a falcon. Only you could reverse the power that made him a falcon."

Hearing a shout, they all looked around as several of the other scavenger children came running over. One of them was carrying the little antique glass bottle that Nimrod had used to imprison Iblis back in Cairo. The stopper was missing, and a piece of paper had been inserted into the bottle's neck. It was a note, addressed to Nimrod.

"*My dear Nimrod*," he said, reading the note aloud. "*By the time you read this I will be long gone. But don't worry. You and those horrible twins will be seeing me again. Sooner than you think, perhaps. They say that children like dolls. So I'm leaving John and Philippa with something special to play*

341

with. Just to remind of them what to expect when we all meet again. Call it a very late Christmas present from their uncle Iblis."

"We're taking this child back to New York with us," said Mrs Gaunt.

"I thought you said we couldn't help him," said Philippa.

"That was before I knew Iblis was planning to visit us in New York," said Mrs Gaunt. "If he does show up, we'll be ready. And when we've got him where we want him, stopped up in a bottle of household bleach, we'll see if we can't persuade him to do something about poor Galibi here." Mrs Gaunt bit her lip angrily. "If it's the last thing I do before I −" She stopped herself from finishing her sentence. Catching Nimrod's eye, she added. "I'm going to make Iblis regret he ever threatened my children."

After French Guiana, Jordan, and Iraq, New York felt very cold. Even the mundanes were complaining about how cold January was. The day after John and Philippa got back home the temperature was minus 16° F, which the TV newscasters said was the coldest temperature ever recorded in Central Park. It certainly felt that way to John and Philippa who, on the few occasions when they ventured outdoors, carried the hot salamander stones Dr Sachertorte had given them in backpacks, to help them maintain their core heat. And there was always the sauna in the basement at home when they needed to feel like proper djinn again.

Just about the first thing John did on his return was to hug his dad and check that he really was alive, for he was still haunted by the memory of killing the seventh guardian underneath the Samarra Tower.

"What's the matter with you?" asked Mr Gaunt as John squeezed him all over.

"Nothing," grinned John. "Nothing at all. It's good to see you again, Dad." He kept on grinning with pleasure when, having confessed to breaking the gold statue of liberty, Mr Gaunt stopped his allowance for four weeks.

"It's not funny, John," said Mr Gaunt. "You might look a little more sorry about it."

"Yes, sir," said John, and continued grinning.

"Well, just for that, it's two months. Two months without allowance."

John shook his head and tried to stifle the grin. "Yes, sir," he said. "I'm sorry. Very sorry." And then he hugged his father again, for good measure.

Monty took to life with the Gaunts rather well and confined her homicidal tendencies to killing the odd mouse or sparrow. She wasn't much for watching TV, like Alan and Neil had been, but enjoyed lying in the glovebox in the hall closet, or close by the stove in the kitchen, listening to the radio with Mrs Trump, who appreciated her most of all. Sometimes she even went home with Mrs Trump, to the apartment in the Dakota building, for there was nothing Monty liked more than the music of John Lennon, of which Mrs Trump had become very fond. Occasionally, Monty went to the movie theatre on East 86th Street when there was something playing there that she really wanted to see. Anything involving an assassin. Or a cat.

Edward Gaunt was, of course, delighted to be

reunited with his brothers, Alan and Neil. This helped to take his mind off the discovery that his wife had now resumed the use of her djinn powers, and very generously he took them into his investment finance business as full partners. Not long afterward Alan and Neil masterminded the takeover of Mutt 'n' Pooch's – America's largest pet food company, a deal that made the three brothers even more rich. The shareholders of the company were most impressed by the faith demonstrated in the company and its products by the Gaunt brothers, two of whom ate several cans of Mutt 'n' Pooch's Beef without Grief, and Slam Dunk Lamb, at the company's annual general meeting.

Meanwhile, Mrs Gaunt persuaded Ayesha to speak to the Djinnversoctoannular Club committee and set aside Philippa's disqualification. Mrs Gaunt also sent a djinn message to Mimi de Ghulle – a parcel containing Montana Retch's Magnum Opus gun, her leather gloves, and three packets of dried cat food.

Two weeks after his return home, John received a postcard from Cairo. It was from Finlay who had some good news. Using Edwiges's system, he had broken the bank at the Groppi Casino and was now barred by the Ifrit from ever again entering one of their casinos. But tens of millions of dollars better off, this hardly mattered, and the postcard was swiftly followed by a parcel for John. Weighing as much as one of his father's dumbbells, the parcel contained the statue of a black bird – a falcon, about fifteen inches high. There was a note from Finlay attached to the bird, which read: I'M SENDING YOU THIS *rara avis* AS A LITTLE MEMENTO. DON'T LET IT FLY AWAY.

John placed the black bird on the mantelpiece in his bedroom where his father saw it and admired it. Picking the object up he weighed it in his hands. "Heavy," he said. "What is it?"

John smiled wryly. "The stuff that dreams are made of."

APPENDIX

The Official Rules of Djinnversoctoannular, being an ancient game of dice, or astaragali.

Djinnversoctoannular is a game for any number of djinn players using a set of seven eight-sided elemental dice or astaragali. Each astaragali is marked with Spirit, Space, Time, Fire, Earth, Air, Water, and Luck. Luck, Spirit, Time and Space, Wood, Air, Water, Fire, and Earth; the faces, as listed here, are in order of value with Luck being the best.

The astaragali are rolled and offered to the next player along with a claimed poker style bid better than the previous bid. When a bid is challenged the offerer or recipient loses a "wish" depending upon whether the bid was genuine or a lie. Each player has three "wishes." A player exits the game when all three wishes are lost.

Play

Any number of djinn players sits around a convenient table so that a set of djinnverso astaragali can be passed clockwise from player to player without disturbing the rolls. The game is best played with four to eight players, and in a tournament shall be played with four players only. The use of djinn power is strictly forbidden during a game of djinnverso, and the astaragali shall be rolled inside a special crystal box that is designed both to conceal a player's throw and to detect the illegal use of djinnpower;

thus, the effects of chance or djinnpower are overcome by the player's ability to bluff his or her opponents.

Any player found to be using djinnpower shall be immediately expelled from a game.

The starting player is determined by highest astaragali roll. Matching highest players re-roll to tie-break.

In turn, each player rolls all/some/none of the astaragali at his or her discretion, usually hiding them from the other players' view. The starting player must roll all seven astaragali. A player must state accurately how many astaragali he or she is rolling. *This convention was queried when these rules were last discussed. The conclusion of the Ultimate Arbiter was that the rule stands. And is now referred to as the Badroulbadour Rule.*

He or she then offers the hidden astaragali to the player on his or her left, stating that they are some bid (excluding runs). This bid must be better than the offer made when he or she accepted the astaragali. (The starting player may name any bid.)

The next player may either accept the astaragali and have his turn, or he may challenge. A challenge is signified by the use of the word "mendax." If challenging, the astaragali are exposed. If the hand equals or betters the stated bid, the recipient loses a wish and the dice pass to the player on the recipient's left who starts again. If the hand is worse than the bid, then the offerer loses a "wish" and the recipient becomes the starting player.

The above procedure is often done in a confusing manner in order to make other players play harder.

Each bid need not be fully specified, in which case it is deemed to be the weakest possible bid meeting constraints stated. **Better** is a valid bid, as is **Much better** meaning *Better than better*, etc.

Should a player make an undercall, it is treated as **Better**. The undercall can be pointed out by any player at any point in the future of this hand, up to and including the exposure of a challenged set of astaragali.

When the bid reaches Seven Luck (L,L,L,L,L,L,L), the player who needs to improve the bid must roll all and then may roll all/some/none of the astaragali twice more to achieve another seven Luck. If he achieves this, then no one loses a wish and the next player starts a new hand, otherwise he loses a "wish." When a player only has one wish left after losing his or her second wish, he or she rolls the astaragali again rather than the next player.

Each player has three wishes and is out of the game when he or she has lost them all. The winner is the final player with a wish.

If a player is absent when his or her turn comes, the player is deemed to have accepted the bid and to be passing the dice, unrolled, as **Better**. This is the Cairo rule.

Bids

There are no runs in astaragali. Getting progressively stronger, the types of bids are:

- Singleton
- A pair
- Two pairs
- Magi: three of a kind

- Three pairs
- Pentad: three of a kind plus two of a kind, the three being more valuable
- Barracks: two triples
- Square: four of a kind
- Four of a kind plus a pair
- Ark: four of a kind plus three of a kind
- Aaron's Silver: five of a kind
- Five of a kind plus a pair
- Ruby and Garnet: six of a kind
- Bastion: seven of a kind
- Djinnverso: seven of Luck

A bid is often just **Better.** You have to pay attention since after three or four **Betters** in a row, it is easy to lose track of what level the bid has reached.

There is no obligation for a player to repeat his or her bid to clarify a situation for any player once the astaragali have been accepted by the recipient.

You must be truthful about the number of astaragali that you roll. This is the Paribanon Rule. You do not have to be truthful about which astaragali you are rolling. This is the Solomon Rule.

Techniques

You do not have to look at the astaragali on your turn, though it is usually wise to do so.

It is necessary to remember what the most recent bid is – even if this is determined by analyzing **Betters**. It is advisable to remember exactly what astaragali you passed to your left and how many astaragali each player has thrown since you saw them.

Cooperation with the players to your left and right is a good strategy, ganging up on the players on the far side of the table.

Conduct

Swearing, bad language, and the insulting of players are not permitted. These are only permitted to spectators. Spectators may not threaten one another. A threat from one spectator to another shall be deemed to constitute an offense punishable by exclusion from the tournament.

T he beginning of the horror occurred, as horror often does, in the dead of night, when most people were asleep. The house where this terrifying event took place was a government building in London. A deceptively large, brick Palladian house in Whitehall with the oldest and most celebrated address in the world. Outside the famous black front door stood a policeman, and on the opposite side of the street were more government buildings all the way up to Westminster and the Houses of Parliament, and beyond, the muddy river Thames.

Long after midnight on a cold April morning in the last years of the last millennium, Number 10 Downing Street was quiet. An eleven-year-old girl was alone in her room, but she was not sleeping; she was lying under the quilt with a torch, reading a book. Her father, the prime minister of Great Britain and Northern Ireland, and mother were fast asleep down the hall, and on duty downstairs in an office behind the Cabinet Room were the prime minister's detective, and his press secretary. At approximately 12.40 a.m., the girl glanced up from her novel with a frown of puzzlement. She thought she heard the sound of laughter. Odd, female laughter. The giggling of someone mischievous and juvenile.

Funny.

She poked her head out from under the tent of her quilt and listened carefully for a moment, then dismissed it.

I'm hearing things.

But as the girlish laughter returned, she sat up and, no longer able to concentrate, tossed her paperback aside.

That giggling. It gives me the creeps.

She got up to investigate. Pulling on a dressing gown she opened her door and looked down the hallway. The giggling seemed to be coming from her parents' bedroom.

What's going on? That's not my mother who's laughing. She doesn't laugh like that. Since moving in to Downing Street, she doesn't laugh at all.

The girl padded down the hall and the giggling suddenly grew louder, more mischievous, even a little bit nasty, but as she pushed open the prime minister's bedroom door and stepped into the room, the giggling abruptly ceased – if only for a moment.

What the heck is going on?

Her mother was huddled in the corner of the room looking round-eyed and plainly terrified. Her father was sitting bolt upright in bed but with both eyes closed, and breathing heavily through his flared nostrils as if he had been running. He didn't look himself at all. His face was pale, his pyjamas were soaked with sweat, and his hair lay matted on his head like damp straw. Then his eyes flickered open, rolled up into the top of his head like a couple of marbles, and closed again.

Then she noticed the heat. The room. It felt like an oven. She padded over to the window. Opened it. She touched the radiator. Cold.

That's very odd.

"What's wrong with you, Mum?" she said softly.

"There's nothing wrong with *me*," her mother whispered. "It's your father."

The girl went over to her father's bedside and leaned closer to him, brushing aside his teddy bear, Archibald, with the back of her hand. "Dad? Are you OK?"

More heavy breathing. Then his green eyes opened and focused on her in a peculiar way that caused a shiver to run down her spine.

"Stop it, Dad. This isn't funny. You're scaring Mum."

This was when he started to laugh. Except that it wasn't him laughing at all. It was the laugh of a young girl that came out of his mouth, almost as if there were someone else inside him, someone alien and unwelcome and possibly unwholesome, too. Someone or some*thing*.

Cold, expressionless eyes that were quite at odds with the giggling held her inquisitive stare for several more seconds before the voice of a girl – who sounded not much older then she was herself – spoke at last.

"Get me the home secretary," said the voice. "And the metropolitan police commissioner. And the director of public prosecutions. And the attorney general. I want someone arrested and thrown into the Tower. Immediately. Tonight. There's no time to lose."

"You can't throw someone into the Tower," the girl said. "Not any more. Not just like that. There are proper procedures to be observed. Laws."

"Then get me the Queen on the telephone," said the voice. "I want to make a new law. Right now. A law that will permit me to arrest and execute someone. Tonight."

She felt her jaw drop on to her chest.

"Well, what are you waiting for, you stupid girl? Get on with it. Don't you know who I am? I'm the prime minister. And while you're at it, close your mouth. You look like a goldfish. Not a very intelligent goldfish, either. I've seen cleverer faces than yours on a broken clock."

Badly scared, the prime minister's daughter backed away from him, trying to flatten down the hair on her head that was now standing on end.

"And fishface? Make sure everyone knows I'm serious about this. Otherwise a vulgar display of power will be forthcoming. Got that, fishface?"

The prime minister giggled girlishly, which was the cue for his young daughter to start screaming.

Out now!

THE AKHENATEN ADVENTURE

Meet the Djinn twins for the first time
and follow them as they journey to the
terrifying lost tombs of Egypt…

An extract…

J ohn and Philippa found themselves in a huge dusty
yard filled with larger stone Egyptian artefacts, many of
which looked, to their eyes at least, like the real thing. In
one corner stood another open door with a rather smelly
lavatory that several flies seemed to find very attractive; and
in another, a third door through which could be seen a
rickety old staircase leading to the floor above.

"In here, I think," said John, heading for the staircase.
"Nimrod said there was a special room upstairs where all
the good stuff was kept."

After the bright sunshine in the yard the staircase was
very dark and gloomy and, Philippa thought, a little bit scary
– especially the way it creaked underfoot as they climbed
up, like in a horror film. With so many ancient Egyptian
objects around she half expected to find an unwrapped
mummy waiting for them at the top of the stairs.

"I don't like this," she admitted as they reached the
landing and turned the corner into a dark and dusty
corridor that was lined with framed photographs of old
excavations and explorers.

"Take it easy," said John. "We'll just give the place the once over and then go downstairs again."

It was then that they heard a low moaning sound coming from an open doorway at the end of the corridor. Philippa felt her blood turn to ice. "What was that?" she hissed and grabbed her brother's arm.

"Stay here if you like," he whispered.

"On my own?" said Philippa, glancing around at the long, dim corridor. She was feeling so scared she had to keep her focus word at the front of her mind in order that she might find the courage to put one foot in front of the other. "No thanks. I'm coming with you."

But for a long moment she turned her face to the wall, pressing it against the cool, slightly damp plaster.

"Are you all right?" Taking her hand, John squeezed it affectionately. "Come on. We ought to take a look. Or Nimrod will be disappointed in us."

"I think," gulped Philippa, "he'll be more disappointed if we're torn apart by some monster."

Even as she spoke another moan emanated from the room at the end of the corridor, a low, inhuman moan that could have come from a tomb, or an open sarcophagus. By now they were close enough to hear not just the moans but also a rasping, breathing noise that sounded like some vicious animal or a person experiencing great pain; or great fear.

Philippa thought that the sound was not as loud as the beating of her heart and, filled with a sense of dread, and wondering from where John got his courage, she hardly dared to follow him as he stepped through the open doorway and into the room from where the moans were coming.

If you would like to write to P.B. Kerr, please visit
www.pbkerr.com